GEPT 初試1次過

初級 全民英檢聽力測驗

全音檔下載導向頁面

https://www.booknews.com.tw/mp3/9789864543670.htm

iOS系統請升級至 iOS13以上再行下載

下載前請先安裝ZIP解壓縮程式或APP，此為大型檔案，建議使用Wi-Fi連線下載，以免占用流量，並確認連線狀況，以利下載順暢。

PRELUDE

準備初級英檢聽力，為什麼每天只要花 10 分鐘就可以了？

相信多數參加過各種英文檢定考試的考生都可以認同，考前「大量刷題」是一件必須做的事情 — 因為訓練考試的手感很重要！在真正考試時，由於時間緊迫，很多都是瞬間反應，當手感熟悉後選對題目幾乎成為反射動作，但如果每天都寫完整的考題，加上檢討得花費大量時間，對於忙碌的現代生活來說，最後往往中途而廢，或敗在力不從心了。因此，本書將所有初級聽力常考的題型，設計成 1 天 14 題，每天不但都可以練習到每一個 PART，且能熟悉作題的感覺又不必花費太多時間。每日短時練習注重的是效率，不僅減輕學習壓力，也確保你在短時間內集中精神學習，學習效果最佳。

透過每天 10 分鐘的學習，能夠讓你養成良好的學習習慣，而日積月累的實力將可發揮滴水穿石的效果。這種細緻的積累比耗費金錢與通勤時間，更具持久效果且不容易倦怠。最後，這樣的學習方式不僅讓你應對考試不害怕，還能夠持續提高語言水平。這種持續進步的學習方式，使你在更高級的英語學習中也能夠輕鬆應對挑戰。

這套訓練計畫的架構不僅緊密貼合新制初級英檢聽力的考試內容，更注重每一位學習者的日常時間管理。每日各 PART 的練習題都經過精心挑選，旨在循序漸進地提升學習者的詞彙辨識、情境理解力以及上下文分析能力。透過這 28 天的有計畫學習，包含 2 回完整測驗，以及每一道題目的中文翻譯、答題詳解以及提升能力的補充學習內容，這樣的豐富資源確保讀者不僅能應對考試挑戰，還能深入理解每道題目，強化英聽技能，學習者也能夠在短時間內感受到明顯的進步，不僅為英檢初級聽力考試做好準備，更在英語學習的長遠道路上建立起穩固的基石。系統性的學習結構讓讀者能夠有效安排學習時間，輕鬆培養英語耳的習慣，迎接下一個等級的挑戰。

國際語言中心委員會

本書特色與使用說明

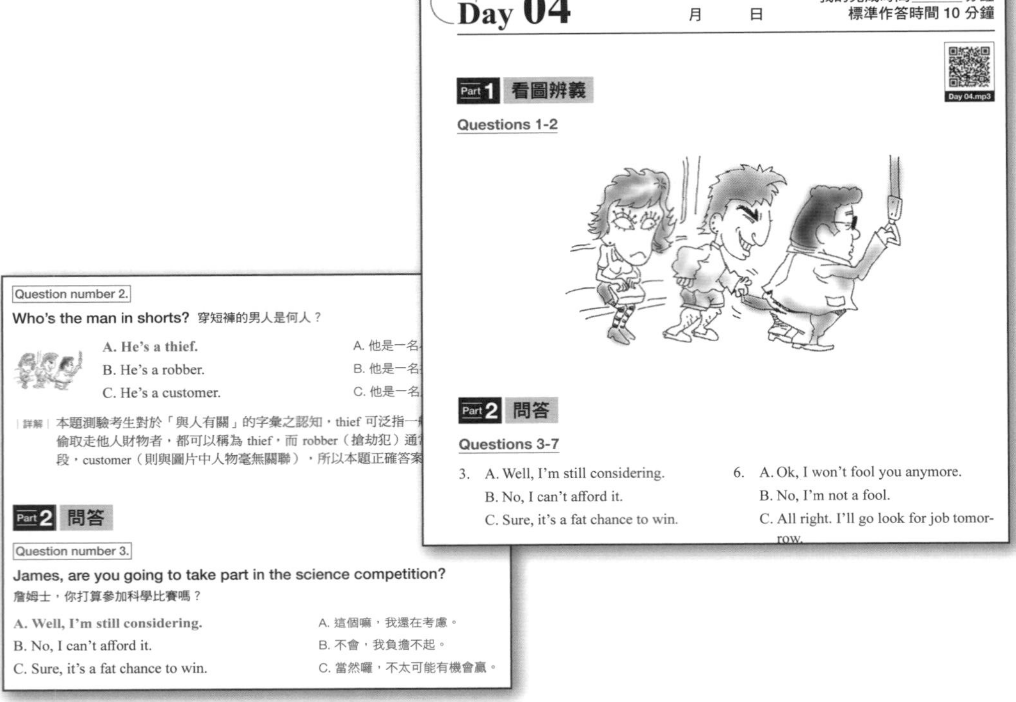

Day 04　月　日　我的完成時間______分鐘
標準作答時間 10 分鐘

Day 04.mp3

Part 1 看圖辨義

Questions 1-2

Part 2 問答

Questions 3-7

3. A. Well, I'm still considering.
B. No, I can't afford it.
C. Sure, it's a fat chance to win.

6. A. Ok, I won't fool you anymore.
B. No, I'm not a fool.
C. All right. I'll go look for job tomor-row.

Question number 2.

Who's the man in shorts? 穿短褲的男人是何人？

A. He's a thief.　A. 他是一名
B. He's a robber.　B. 他是一名
C. He's a customer.　C. 他是一名

詳解｜本題測驗考生對於「與人有關」的字彙之認知，thief 可泛指一
偷取走他人財物者，都可以稱為 thief，而 robber（搶劫犯）通
段，customer（則與圖片中人物毫無關聯），所以本題正確答案

Part 2 問答

Question number 3.

James, are you going to take part in the science competition?
詹姆士，你打算參加科學比賽嗎？

A. Well, I'm still considering.　A. 這個嘛，我還在考慮。
B. No, I can't afford it.　B. 不會，我負擔不起。
C. Sure, it's a fat chance to win.　C. 當然囉，不太可能有機會贏。

1

請在每一個 Day 的最上方填入當天的自我測驗日期，除 Day 14 與 Day 28 為完整的聽力測驗之外，測驗時間皆為 10 分鐘。（音檔長度約為 7 分鐘，剩下 3 分鐘請養成檢查答案的習慣。）

每一個 Day 首頁右上方 QR 碼線上音檔，隨時隨地開始每天 10 分鐘的自我訓練！

Part 1 看圖辨義，加強你的觀察力、理解力和快速判斷能力。

每天只需解答 2 個看圖練習題，根據所看到的圖片，對於口語句型的敏感度，更有效地理解表達用語，並且在考試中能夠迅速反應，選出正確的答案。

Part 3 簡短對話

Questions 8-12

8. A. The man is not telling the truth.
   B. The man's computer is better than hers.
   C. The man is happy with his computer.

9. A. She's going to move to Africa.
   B. Her husband is a Japanese.
   C. She's going to get married.

10. A. He forgot to bring his crown to the party.
    B. He was not allowed to the party.
    C. He missed his final exam.

11. A. Husband and wife
    B. Employer and employee
    C. Hotel staff and check-in guest

12. A. In a meeting room
    B. At an airport
    C. In a bank

Part 3 簡短對話

Question number 8.

M: My second-hand PC is much better than a new one. 男：我的二手電腦比

W: Come on, Peter! Your computer always shuts down for no reason. 女：拜託，彼得！你 機耶。

M: At least it much cheaper than a new one. 男：至少它比新機便

Question. What could the woman mean? 女人的意思可能為何

A. The man is not telling the truth. A. 男人並沒有說實話

B. The man's computer is better than hers. B. 男人的電腦比她的

C. The man is happy with his computer. C. 男人很滿意他的電腦。

詳解 題目要聽清楚，本題問的是「女子的觀點」，從她的回應可堆支，她並不認為男子的二手電腦有多好，即使男子真的認為很好且很滿意，所以她可能認為男子沒有說實話，正確答案為選項 A。

2

Part 2 問答，訓練你聽取句子的辨析能力、口語表達以及即時思考的回答能力。每天解答 5 小題，培養即時回答問題的技巧，並且鍛煉口語表達的流暢度和準確性，進而能夠在考試中有效地回答問題，展現英語溝通能力。

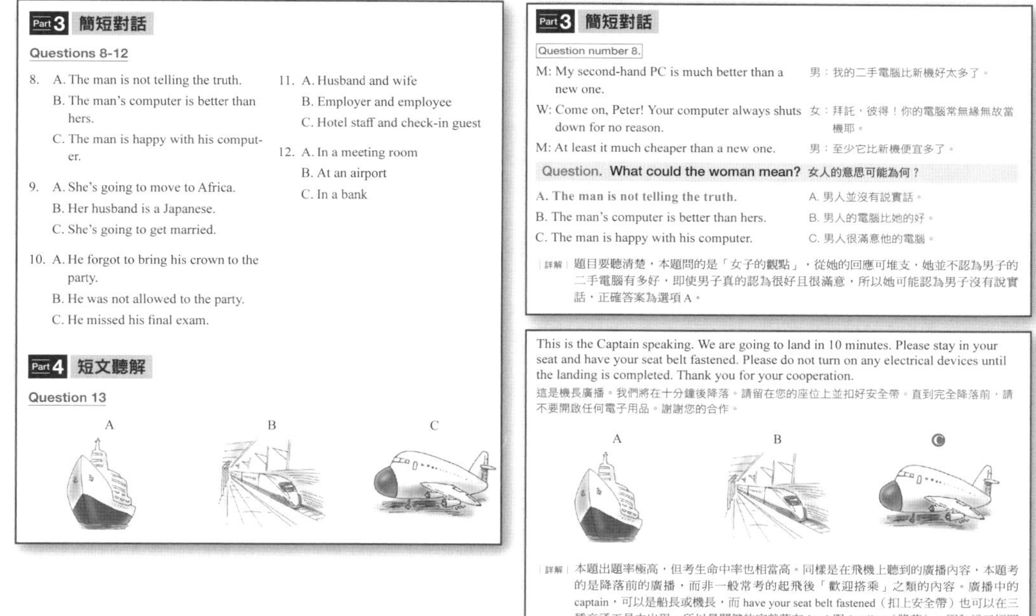
Part 3 簡短對話

Questions 8-12

8. A. The man is not telling the truth. B. The man's computer is better than hers. C. The man is happy with his computer.

9. A. She's going to move to Africa. B. Her husband is a Japanese. C. She's going to get married.

10. A. He forgot to bring his crown to the party. B. He was not allowed to the party. C. He missed his final exam.

11. A. Husband and wife B. Employer and employee C. Hotel staff and check-in guest

12. A. In a meeting room B. At an airport C. In a bank

Part 4 短文聽解

Question 13

A B C

Part 3 簡短對話

Question number 8.

M: My second-hand PC is much better than a new one. 男：我的二手電腦比新機好太多了。

W: Come on, Peter! Your computer always shuts down for no reason. 女：拜託，彼得！你的電腦常無緣無故當機耶。

M: At least it much cheaper than a new one. 男：至少它比新機便宜多了。

Question. What could the woman mean? 女人的意思可能為何？

A. The man is not telling the truth. A. 男人並沒有說實話。

B. The man's computer is better than hers. B. 男人的電腦比她的好。

C. The man is happy with his computer. C. 男人很滿意他的電腦。

詳解 題目要聽清楚，本題問的是「女子的觀點」，從她的回應可堆支，她並不認為男子的二手電腦有多好，即使男子真的認為很好且很滿意，所以她可能認為男子沒有說實話，正確答案為選項 A。

This is the Captain speaking. We are going to land in 10 minutes. Please stay in your seat and have your seat belt fastened. Please do not turn on any electrical devices until the landing is completed. Thank you for your cooperation.

這是機長廣播。我們將在十分鐘後降落。請留在您的座位上並扣好安全帶。直到完全降落前，請不要開啟任何電子用品。謝謝您的合作。

A B C

詳解 本題出題率極高，但考生命中率也相當高。同樣是在飛機上聽到的廣播內容，本題考的是降落前的廣播，而非一般常考的起飛後「歡迎搭乘」之類的內容。廣播中的 captain，可以是船長或機長，而 have your seat belt fastened（扣上安全帶）也可以在三種交通工具中出現。所以最關鍵的字就落在 land 跟 landing（降落），因為這三幅圖中只有飛機能「降落」，所以答案為 C。

3

Part 3 簡短對話，訓練你對於一段對話的理解力，以及快速判斷和回答問題的能力。每天解答 5 個題組，提高對於真實對話內容的敏感度及理解能力。Part 4 短文聽解，每天解答 2 個題組，從觀察 3 張圖片的共同點及共同關係，在「刷」過眾多題目之後，都可以猜到短文會講什麼、題目會問什麼！

Day 14　月　日

我的完成時間______分鐘
標準作答時間 20 分鐘

Day 14.mp3

Part 1 看圖辨義

Questions 1-5

1.　2.　3.　4.　5.

4

結束 13 天的練習之後，可以在第 14 天訓練一回完整的測驗，驗證自己的能力提升。

上頁簡答
解答與詳解

1. (C) 2. (B) 3. (C) 4. (A) 5. (C) 6. (A) 7. (A) 8. (B) 9. (B)
10. (C) 11. (A) 12. (C) 13. (B) 14. (C) 15. (A) 16. (C)
17. (B) 18. (A) 19. (C) 20. (A) 21. (B) 22. (A) 23. (C)
24. (B) 25. (B) 26. (B) 27. (B) 28. (A) 29. (B) 30. (B)

Part 1 看圖辨義

For questions number 1-5, please look at the following pictures.

Question number 1.

What is true about the picture? 關於這張圖，何者為真？

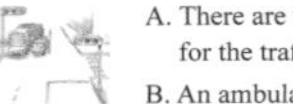

A. There are two light trucks waiting for the traffic light.　A. 有兩部小貨車在停等紅燈。

B. An ambulance is running through the red light.　B. 一輛救護車正闖過紅燈。

C. We can't see any passengers on the sidewalk.　C. 人行道上看不到任何行人。

5

本書最後面提供「答對題數與分數對照表」，讓你在每天進步的過程中，激發動力，不僅增強信心，還讓學習變得更有趣。

聽力測驗答對題數與分數對照表

答對題數	分數	答對題數	分數	答對題數	分數
30	120	20	80	10	40
29	116	19	76	9	36
28	112	18	72	8	32
27	108	17	68	7	28
26	104	16	64	6	24
25	100	15	60	5	20
24	96	14	56	4	16
23	92	13	52	3	12
22	88	12	48	2	8
21	84	11	44	1	4

CONTENTS

目錄

GEPT 全民英檢初級聽力測驗初試 1 次過

Prelude 2
本書特色與使用說明 4

Day 01 英檢初級聽力 10 分鐘測驗
題目 10
詳解 12

Day 02 英檢初級聽力 10 分鐘測驗
題目 19
詳解 21

Day 03 英檢初級聽力 10 分鐘測驗
題目 28
詳解 30

Day 04 英檢初級聽力 10 分鐘測驗
題目 38
詳解 40

Day 05 英檢初級聽力 10 分鐘測驗
題目 46
詳解 48

Day 06 英檢初級聽力 10 分鐘測驗
題目 55
詳解 57

Day 07 英檢初級聽力 10 分鐘測驗
題目 64
詳解 66

Day 08 英檢初級聽力 10 分鐘測驗
題目 74
詳解 76

Day 09 英檢初級聽力 10 分鐘測驗
題目 84
詳解 86

Day 10 英檢初級聽力 10 分鐘測驗
題目 94
詳解 96

Day 11 英檢初級聽力 10 分鐘測驗
題目 104
詳解 106

Day 12 英檢初級聽力 10 分鐘測驗
題目 113
詳解 115

Day 13 英檢初級聽力 10 分鐘測驗
題目 122
詳解 124

★ **Day 14** 英檢初級聽力完整 1 回模擬測驗
題目 132
詳解 136

Day 15 英檢初級聽力 10 分鐘測驗
題目 152
詳解 154

Day 16 英檢初級聽力 10 分鐘測驗
題目 162
詳解 164

Day 17 英檢初級聽力 10 分鐘測驗
題目 172
詳解 174

Day 18 英檢初級聽力 10 分鐘測驗
題目 182
詳解 184

Day 19 英檢初級聽力 10 分鐘測驗
題目 192
詳解 194

Day 20 英檢初級聽力 10 分鐘測驗
題目 202
詳解 204
Day 21 英檢初級聽力 10 分鐘測驗
題目 211
詳解 213
Day 22 英檢初級聽力 10 分鐘測驗
題目 220
詳解 222
Day 23 英檢初級聽力 10 分鐘測驗
題目 229
詳解 231
Day 24 英檢初級聽力 10 分鐘測驗
題目 238
詳解 240
Day 25 英檢初級聽力 10 分鐘測驗
題目 247
詳解 249
Day 26 英檢初級聽力 10 分鐘測驗
題目 256
詳解 258
Day 27 英檢初級聽力 10 分鐘測驗
題目 266
詳解 268
★ **Day 28** 英檢初級聽力完整 1 回模擬測驗
題目 276
詳解 280

答對題數與分數對照表......295

Day 01

月　　日

我的完成時間＿＿＿分鐘
標準作答時間 10 分鐘

Day_01.mp3

Part 1 看圖辨義

Questions 1-2

Part 2 問答

Questions 3-7

3. A. Sure, please.
   B. Yes, I am.
   C. No, I would.

4. A. Nothing special. What about you?
   B. I'm moving this month.
   C. I can't go with you.

5. A. Not long, just a couple of minutes.
   B. I work as a secretary in this company.
   C. Since 2004, almost twenty years.

6. A. I have good news for you.
   B. I don't feel like talking about it now.
   C. The view up there is fantastic.

7. A. What about a picnic in the countryside?
   B. I don't mind working on Saturday.
   C. No, I'm fine.

Part 3 簡短對話

Questions 8-12

8. A. Three people will go.
   B. He goes by himself.
   C. Two people

9. A. She was away for days.
   B. She had a headache.
   C. She is worried about her exam.

10. A. Go to a musical with him
    B. Listen to some old songs
    C. Enjoy some music of a new album

11. A. At a hospital
    B. At a drugstore
    C. At a shopping mall

12. A. Hang up on her client.
    B. Ask her client to wait for her on the phone.
    C. Ask her mother to wait for her on the phone.

Part 4 短文聽解

Questions 13-14

13.

A

B

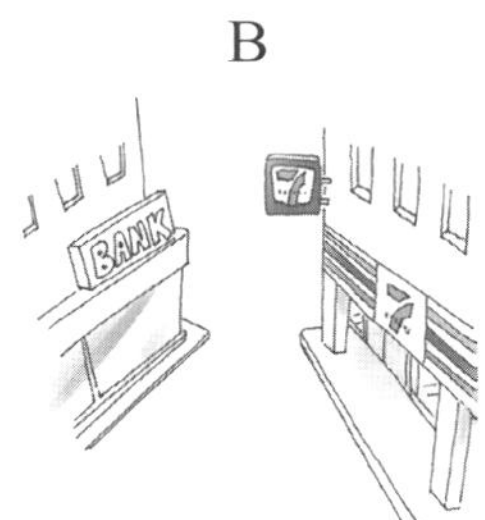

C

14.

A

B

C

上頁簡答

解答與詳解

1. (B) 2. (A) 3. (A) 4. (A) 5. (A) 6. (B) 7. (A)
8. (C) 9. (C) 10. (C) 11. (A) 12. (B) 13. (B) 14. (C)

Part 1 看圖辨義

For questions number 1-2, please look at the following picture.

Question number 1.

What's the man doing? 這個男人正在做什麼？

A. He is welcoming the woman. A. 他正在迎接這位女子。

B. He is talking on the cellphone. B. 他正在講手機。

C. He is drinking a glass of water. C. 他正在喝一杯水。

| 詳解 | 圖中的男子坐在辦公桌前講電話，所以正確答案為 B。

| 補充 | 中文常說的「講電話」，英文就是「talk on the phone」，注意介系詞 on 的使用。另外，phone 也可以替換成「mobile phone / smartphone / cellphone」等。如果要表達「用 LINE 講電話」，可以說「Talk on LINE」，這裡就不能再加冠詞 the 了。

Question number 2.

What does the woman do? 女子是做什麼的？

A. She is a secretary. A. 她是一位祕書。

B. She is a waitress. B. 她是一名女服務生。

C. She is the manager of this company. C. 她是這家公司的經理。

| 詳解 | 「What does... do?」就是在問「職業」，本題問的是女子是做什麼的，圖中她拿著一杯水給經理（manager），因此最適當的答案當然就是 secretary（祕書）了，所以正確答案是選項 A。

Part 2 問答

Question number 3.

Would you like to have a drink? 你想喝點飲料嗎？

A. Sure, please. A. 當然，麻煩了。

B. Yes, I am. B. 是的，我是。

C. No, I would. C. 不，我會的。

| 詳解 | drink 可以當動詞，也可以當名詞。從本題中「have a drink」來看，是名詞的用法，「飲料」的意思。題目用「Would you...?」來問，不可能回答用「I am.」，所以選項 B 錯誤。選項 C 應該說成「No, I wouldn't.」或「Yes, I would.」。所以正確答案是選項 A。

Question number 4.

What's your plan this weekend? 這個週末你有什麼計畫嗎？

A. Nothing special. What about you? A. 沒有什麼特別安排，你呢？

B. I'm moving this month. B. 我這個月要搬家。

C. I can't go with you. C. 我不能跟你一起去。

| 詳解 | 這題聽到 what 這個疑問詞，答案可以先預測跟事情、活動有關。所以選項 C 不用考慮。題目是問 this weekend，但選項 B 卻說 this month，所以也刪除，故本題正確答案為選項 A。

Question number 5.

How long have you been waiting here? 你在這裡等多久了？

A. Not long, just a couple of minutes. A. 沒多久，才幾分鐘而已。

B. I work as a secretary in this company. B. 我在這公司擔任祕書。

C. Since 2004, almost twenty years. C. 從 2004 年到現在，差不多二十年了。

| 詳解 | 「how long」是指「多長」或「多久」，所以答案絕對跟時間或長度有關。再聽到題目句的 waiting 時，就可以更確定答案一定跟時間有關係，那麼選項 B 可以剔除，剩下選項 A 跟 C。題目問「在這裡等了多久」，選項 C 的回答完全不合邏輯，所以正確答案為選項 A。

Question number 6.

What's your view on the news? 你對這則新聞有什麼看法？

A. I have good news for you. A. 我有好消息要告訴你。

B. I don't feel like talking about it now. B. 我現在不想談論它。

C. The view up there is fantastic. C. 上面的風景很漂亮。

| 詳解 | 首先，我們要知道 view 這個字除了「風景，景色」外，也有「看法，意見」的意思，這是本題的關鍵字。因為考題只播放一次，所以有一點難度。本題是問對於這則新聞（the news）詢問意見，評估三個選項，選項 B 是正確答案。回頭來看選項 A，顯然是要混淆考生，如果沒有聽清楚 view 這個字，就容易選 A 為答案。若聽清楚了 view，但不知道 view 的另一個意思，則容易選 C 為答案。

| 補充 | 本題的 view 是影響答案的要角，它既是動詞也是名詞，例如：The sea view is awesome.（海景真美。）view 在此為名詞，指「景色」。I have similar views.（我有類似

的看法。）view 在此為名詞，指「看法」。We were viewed as the winner.（我們被視為勝利者。）view 在此為動詞，指「視作，看待」，常與介系詞 as 搭配。另外，選項 B 的「feel like」相當於 want、would like，但不同的是，它後面接 Ving 作為其受詞，而 want、would like 則接不定詞（to-V）。

Question number 7.

Tomorrow is Saturday. Anything in mind? 明天是星期六，你有打算做什麼嗎？

A. What about a picnic in the countryside? A. 到郊外野餐如何？

B. I don't mind working on Saturday. B. 我不介意星期六工作。

C. No, I'm fine. C. 不，我很好。

| 詳解 | 題目的第二句是重點，mind 在此是「想法」的意思，「Anything in mind?」字面意思就是「有沒有什麼想法或打算」，加上前面這句提到「明天是星期六」，所以可以朝「休閒活動」的方向來選擇，故正確答案為選項 A。

| 補充 | 題目的 mind 和選項 B 的 mind 雖然是意思完全不同的兩個字，但那是因為詞性不同的關係，其實兩者源自於同一個核心概念，那就是「心」！當名詞時，表示源自於「心底」的想法，當動詞時，表示「心裡介意」的事。不過要特別注意的是「mind + Ving」的用法。

Part 3 簡短對話

Question number 8.

M: I'm out for dinner. See you later. 男：我出去吃飯囉，待會見。

W: Who are you going with? 女：你跟誰出去呢？

M: Oh, Emily, and maybe Kevin, too. 男：哦，艾蜜莉，凱文也可能去。

Question. How many people are probably going to dinner with the man?
有多少人可能與男子一起吃晚餐？

A. Three people will go. A. 三個人會去。

B. He goes by himself. B. 他自己去。

C. Two people. C. 兩個人

| 詳解 | 從選項中可以推斷問題應該跟人數有關，所以要注意聽名字或數字的部分。在對話中男人表示 Emily 與 Kevin 可能跟他一起去，所以答案應該為 C。雖然總數是三個人，但題目是 with the man，所以自己不能算在內，故不能選 A。

| 補充 | 選項 B 中的 himself 是反身代名詞，其他還有 myself（我自己）、ourselves（我們自己）、yourself（你自己）、yourselves（你們自己）、himself（他自己），herself（她自己）、itself（它自己）、themselves（他們自己）…等。反身代名詞可當副詞，放在

主詞之後，例如：She herself did the laundry.（她自己洗衣服。）或放在句尾如：She did the laundry (by) herself.。但切記反身代名詞不可以當主詞用，例如：Herself did the laundry.（×）。

Question number 9.

M: Lisa, what's the matter with you? 男：麗莎，妳怎麼了？

W: I couldn't sleep well for days. 女：我好幾天都睡不好。

M: How come? 男：怎麼會這樣？

W: Final exam is just a few days ahead. 女：過幾天就要期末考了。

Question. Why can't the woman sleep well? 為什麼女人睡不好？

A. She was away for days. A. 她有幾天不在家。

B. She had a headache. B. 她頭痛。

C. She is worried about her exam. C. 她擔心她的考試。

｜詳解｜選項全都是關於女性說話者，所以要注意女子的對話內容。從選項內容可以推斷這是某狀況的原因，而從女子回答的「Final exam is just a few days ahead.」可知，正確答案為選項 C。

｜補充｜「What's the matter with you?」是相當普遍的「你怎麼了？」的用法，也可以說「What's wrong with you? 」、「What happened to you?」。ahead 有「在前，事前」的意思，例如 the trees ahead（前面的那些樹）或 You'd better plan ahead.（你最好事先計畫。）答案 C 中的 worried 是「（感到）擔憂的，憂慮的」，而動詞 worry 後面可接 about 或 over。例如：My mother worried about my studies.（我媽媽擔心我的學業。）或 He worried over his father's health.（他擔心他父親的健康。）

Question number 10.

W: Hey, Thomas. What are you listening to? 女：嗨，湯瑪斯。你在聽什麼？

M: It's Coldplay's latest album. Interested? 男：這是 Coldplay 的最新專輯，有興趣嗎？

W: No, not really. I'm not a rock fan. 女：不，沒興趣，我不是個搖滾迷。

M: Maybe you should give this a try. 男：也許妳該聽聽看這張專輯。

Question. What did the man suggest the woman do? 男子建議女子做什麼？

A. Go to a musical with him A. 跟他一起去音樂會

B. Listen to some old songs B. 聽些老歌

C. Enjoy some music of a new album C. 享受一下一張新專輯的音樂

｜詳解｜選項都跟聽音樂有關，所以可以推測對話應該是關於音樂的話題。整個對話都沒提到男子要和女子約會，所以選項 A 不對。對話中提到「It's Coldplay's latest album.」所以不是老歌，選項 B 也錯誤；接著男子建議女子聽聽看這張專輯（Maybe you should give this a try.），this 就是指「Coldplay's latest album」，所以正確答案為選項 C。

Question number 11.

M: Have a seat, Lisa. What's the matter with you?	男：麗莎請坐，妳哪裡不舒服？
W: I haven't slept well for days and I've been running to the bathroom several times a day.	女：我好幾天睡不好而且一天跑好幾次廁所。
M: Um, I see. Do you feel like throwing up?	男：嗯，明白。妳會想吐嗎？
W: No, because I haven't eaten anything since yesterday.	女：沒有，因為從昨天到現在我什麼也沒吃。
M: Don't worry. Let's do a check-up.	男：別擔心，我們來做檢查。

Question. Where does the conversation take place? 這段對話在哪裡進行？

A. At a hospital	A. 在醫院
B. At a drugstore	B. 在藥局
C. At a shopping mall	C. 在購物中心

| 詳解 | 從三個選項中可推知問題跟場所、地點有關。對話中「can't sleep well」（睡不好）、「run for bathroom」（跑廁所）、「throwing up」（吐）都在提示，最後男人建議女人做 check-up（檢查）就更確定答案是在醫院或診所，所以正確答案為選項 A。

| 補充 | 一般常見人們會到診所或醫院看診的疾病原因有：fever（發燒）、flu（流行性感冒）、soar throat（喉嚨痛）、runny nose（流鼻水）、headache（頭痛）、cold（感冒）、cough（咳嗽）、toothache（牙痛）、diarrhea（腹瀉）、stomachache（胃痛）、allergy（過敏）、dizziness（頭暈）、sunstroke（中暑）…等。

Question number 12.

M: Julia, there's a call for you. Are you available now?	男：茱莉亞，妳的電話，妳現在方便接嗎？
W: Sorry, I'm with a client on the line.	女：抱歉，我正在跟客戶講電話。
M: I think it's your mother. Should I tell her to call back?	男：我想是妳媽媽。我要請她待會再撥嗎？
W: No, please put her through.	女：不用，麻煩你幫我接進來。

Question. What will Julia do next? 茱莉亞接著會做什麼？

A. Hang up on her client	A. 掛斷客戶的電話
B. Ask her client to wait for her on the phone	B. 請客戶在電話中等候
C. Ask her mother to wait for her on the phone	C. 請她的母親在線上等

| 詳解 | 由選項可得知對話是電話上的對談，考生也應注意到當中包含兩位人物：client（客戶）跟 mother（媽媽）。對話的結尾 put her through 是關鍵，因為女子請男子把她媽媽的電話接進來，也就是「插播」的意思，並非把原來正在講電話的另一方掛掉，所以選項 A 不對，正確答案為選項 B。

| 補充 | client 是指「客戶」，一般指有生意上往來的客戶。customer 是「顧客」，一般指來消費、享受服務的客人。consumer 則可翻譯成「消費者」。「put somebody through」如果是跟電話有關，就是指把某人轉接給他要找的人。另外，「put somebody through」也有使某人接受考驗的意思，例如：The policeman put the suspect through a severe examination.（警察對嫌犯嚴加訊問。）

Part 4 短文聽解

Question number 13.

Please look at the following three pictures. Listen to the following message for Susan. Which convenience store should Susan meet her friend at?

請看以下三張圖片。聆聽以下給蘇姍的訊息。蘇姍應該在哪個便利商店跟她朋友碰面？

Morning! Susan. Don't forget to meet me at the convenience store around the corner across from the bank. See you there at 11.

蘇姍早哦！別忘了在街角銀行對面那一家便利商店跟我碰面，十一點見。

| 詳解 | 本題要注意的是位置與方向，雖然乍聽之下有很多指示（convenience store, around the corner, across from the bank），但其實只要抓到 across from the bank（在銀行對面），答案就呼之欲出了。這裡很明顯的答案就是 B。

Question number 14.

Please look at the following three pictures. Listen to the following announcement. Where would you probably hear it?

請看以下三張圖片。聆聽以下的廣播。你大概會在哪裡聽到這個廣播？

Good evening. This is Easy Mall information Center. We have a lost child here. His name is Kevin, a 7-year-old boy wearing a blue jacket and black jeans. He's waiting for his parents at the counter on the 1st floor. Thank you for your attention. Easy Mall wishes you a wonderful shopping day.

晚安，這是易購購物中心服務台。我們有一位走失的小朋友。他的名字是凱文，七歲，男孩，穿藍色夾克跟黑色牛仔褲。他在一樓服務櫃台等他的父母親。感謝您的留意，易購購物中心祝您購物愉快。

|詳解| 本題測試的是地點，廣播中的關鍵字 mall（購物中心）出現在最前跟最後，考生絕對可以確認自己的答案。另外，1st floor（一樓）跟 shopping（購物）都是很清楚的線索，仔細聽就可以選出正確答案 C。

Day 02

月　　日

我的完成時間______分鐘
標準作答時間 10 分鐘

Part 1 看圖辨義

Questions 1-2

Part 2 問答

Questions 3-7

3. A. Please don't be mad at me.
   B. I've bought that for months.
   C. I can't believe it either.

4. A. Sure, bring me a pack of cookies, please.
   B. Yes, you can place an order now.
   C. No, thanks. Water would be good enough.

5. A. I'm afraid I don't have the time.
   B. Of course! You've got my ear.
   C. That sounds interesting.

6. A. I don't see Donna as a party killer.
   B. Nice, count me in!
   C. I think the killer will be arrested soon.

7. A. Tell me what happened.
   B. It's no big deal.
   C. That's what I'm thinking about.

Part 3 簡短對話

Questions 8-12

8. A. She sent a present to Joe.
   B. She's going to wear black high-heels.
   C. She doesn't like the man's idea.

9. A. At the cleaner's
   B. At Frank's house
   C. At a restaurant

10. A. She usually gets up late.
    B. She does it totally different from the man.
    C. She thinks what the man does is stupid.

11. A. He is just looking around in the shop.
    B. He is asking for help.
    C. He's going to buying a window.

12. A. To confirm the time of a meeting
    B. To call off a meeting
    C. To change the time of a meeting

Part 4 短文聽解

Questions 13-14

13.

A

B

C

14.

A

B

C

上頁簡答

解答與詳解

1. (C) 2. (A) 3. (C) 4. (C) 5. (B) 6. (B) 7. (C) 8. (B) 9. (C) 10. (B) 11. (A) 12. (B) 13. (B) 14. (B)

Part 1 看圖辨義

For questions number 1-2, please look at the following picture.

Question number 1.

Where are the two girls? 那兩個女生在哪裡？

A. They're in a restaurant. A. 她們在餐廳裡。

B. They're cute. B. 她們很可愛。

C. They're in a pet shop. C. 她們在寵物店裡。

| 詳解 | 以這張圖片來說，考試的方向很有可能是「女孩們在看什麼」，或「女孩們在哪裡」。英檢初級聽力經常出現 what（什麼）、where（哪裡）、when（何時）的疑問句，只要熟記這些疑問詞的意思，答題就能十拿九穩。本題一聽到 where 的問句，就能判斷答案一定跟地方有關係，故選項 B 不對，剩下 A、C 可選。而圖片裡面有寵物，故選 C。

Question number 2.

What is true about this picture? 關於這張圖，何者為真？

A. There're at least two kinds of animal on sale. A. 至少有兩種動物販售中。

B. You can only buy animals here. B. 你在這裡只能買到動物。

C. The girls have a bit of fear of these animals. C. 女孩們對於這些動物有點恐懼。

| 詳解 | 本題考的是對於圖片的整體觀察，所以應仔細聽清楚每一個選項的敘述。圖片中可以看得清楚的動物，至少有狗和貓，所以正確答案就是選項 A。圖片中除了有動物之外，還有寵物食物在販售，所以 B 是錯的；圖片中兩個女生表情看起來是開心的，所以 C 也是錯誤的。

| 補充 | fear 可以當動詞，也可以當名詞。如果要用 fear 來表達「害怕什麼東西」，可以說「(to) fear + 害怕的人事物」，或是「have a fear of...」。另外，fear 當不及物動詞時，通常表示「擔憂」，例如：I fear for her safety.（我擔心她的安危。）

Part 2 問答

Question number 3.

Wow! You score 90 in the math exam! 哇！你數學考了 90 分耶！

A. Please don't be mad at me. A. 請不要對我生氣。

B. I've bought that for months. B. 我買了好幾個月了。

C. I can't believe it either. C. 我自己也不相信呢。

｜詳解｜ 題目一開頭就來個「Wow!」表達對於什麼事情感到讚嘆，不用聽後面的也可以先剔除選項 A。接著題目說「你數學考了 90 分耶！」，那麼選項 B 當然就可以確定是錯誤的了，故正確答案是選項 C。

｜補充｜ 選項 A 的 be mad at = be angry at，是指「對…生氣」，但 be mad about somebody = fall in love with somebody，是指「對某人著迷」。這種令人煩惱的用法經常出現，別搞錯了哦！

Question number 4.

Would you like to order any drinks first? 你們要先點飲料嗎？

A. Sure, bring me a pack of cookies, please. A. 當然好，麻煩給我一包餅乾。

B. Yes, you can place an order now. B. 好的，您現在可以下單了。

C. No, thanks. Water would be good enough. C. 不用，謝謝。開水就可以了。

｜詳解｜ 聽到 order，就知道題目跟點餐有關係。從題目的 drinks 可以推測答案跟喝的相關。選項 A 說的是餅乾，所以不符。選項 B 刻意以相同字彙 order 來混淆，但「place an order」是「下訂單」的意思，沒有針對問題回答。故正確答案為選項 C。

Question number 5.

Can I talk to you for a second? 我能跟你談一下嗎？

A. I'm afraid I don't have the time. A. 我恐怕不知道現在幾點。

B. Of course! You've got my ear. B. 沒問題！我洗耳恭聽。

C. That sounds interesting. C. 聽起來很有趣嘛。

｜詳解｜ 本題考生只要聽懂「Can I talk to you」，就可以選出正確答案，當然選項中仍有陷阱，千萬不可大意。選項 A 中的「the time」就是讓你跳進去的洞。「don't have the time」是「不知道現在幾點」，而非沒有時間。選項 C 完全不符，正確答案為選項 B。

｜補充｜ 選項 B 中的「You've got my ear.」也可以說成「I am all ears.」，是口語中常用的一種表達，很好記也很好用，把它學起來吧！

Question number 6.

Mike's going to hold a party at Donna's home. 麥克打算在唐娜家開派對。

A. I don't see Donna as a party killer. A. 我不覺得唐娜是個掃興鬼。

B. Nice, count me in! B. 不錯啊，算我一份！

C. I think the killer will be arrested soon. C. 我想兇手很快就會被逮捕。

| 詳解 | 對於「某人將在另一人家裡開派對」的消息，選項 C 顯然是完全不相關的回應，可以先剔除掉。既然是要在 Donna 加辦派對，卻冒出一句說「我不覺得 Donna 是個掃興鬼」，顯然是顛三倒四的回答，故選項 A 錯誤，本題正確答案是選項 B。

| 補充 | 「count (someone) in」是「算（某人）一份」的意思，它的相反是「count (someone) out」，而要簡單表達「我加入」、「我參加」，也可以說 I'm in.。

Question number 7.

I'm so tired! Can we take a break? 我好累啊！我們可以休息一下嗎？

A. Tell me what happened. A. 告訴我發生了什麼事。

B. It's no big deal. B. 這沒什麼大不了。

C. That's what I'm thinking about. C. 我也這麼想。

| 詳解 | 題目很容易理解，說話者表示很累想休息一下，如果回應是「發生了什麼事」，顯然不符，選項 A 錯誤；如果選項 B 可以再加些敘述，可能會符合題意，例如： It's no big deal. Why are you so tired?（這沒啥大不了的。你怎麼搞得那麼累？）但在英檢考試裡面，會把比較直接、正面的說法視為正確答案，而比較間接、負面、取笑的說法視為不正確。所以正確答案是選項 C。

Part 3 簡短對話

Question number 8.

M: Jean, You look great in that dress. 男：珍，妳穿那件洋裝看來美呆了。

W: Thanks. It was a present from Joe. Does it go perfectly with a pair of white high-heels? 女：謝謝，那是喬送我的禮物。你覺得很配一雙白色高跟鞋嗎？

M: Uh ah, or a pair of black ones. 男：嗯，或是一雙黑色的。

W: Thanks. I'll take your advice. 女：謝謝，就聽你的。

Question. What is true about Jean? 關於 Jean，哪個選項是正確的？

A. She sent a present to Joe. A. 她送了一件禮物給喬。

B. She's going to wear black high-heels. B. 她將穿黑色高跟鞋。

C. She doesn't like the man's idea. C. 她不喜歡男子的建議。

| 詳解 | 選項都是 She 開頭，其實已提示考生必須仔細聽女子說話的內容。根據對話，洋裝是 Joe 送給 Jean 的禮物，所以選項 A 不對。女子最後選擇採取男子的建議（I'll take your advice.），所以選項 C 不對。故正確答案為選項 B。

| 詳解 | 介系詞 in 和 on 都可以用來表示「穿戴衣物」，但注意主詞的不同。以「You look nice in yellow.」以及「Yellow is nice on you.」這兩句來看，都表示「你穿黃色很好看。」前者主詞是「人」，後者主詞是「衣物」。又例如：She ran in high heels.（她穿著高跟鞋跑。）、Did you see the wedding ring on her finger?（你有沒有看到她手指上戴的婚戒？）

Question number 9.

W: It's chilly outside. I need a sweater.	女：外面很冷，我需要一件毛衣。
M: Good idea. I'm going to find one for myself too.	男：好主意，我也幫自己找一件好了。
W: Oh, no! I did the laundry yesterday and now it's gone!	女：噢，不會吧！我昨天才洗好的，現在不見了！
M: I saw you put it in your bag when you went out for dinner with Frank last night.	男：妳昨天跟法蘭克出去吃飯的時候，我看到妳把毛衣放在包包裡。
W: You're right. My bag is at the cafeteria.	女：你說得對，我的包包在自助餐廳裡。

Question. Where is the woman's sweater? 女子的毛衣在哪裡？

A. At the cleaner's	A. 在洗衣店
B. At Frank's house	B. 在法蘭克家裡
C. At a restaurant	C. 在餐廳裡

| 詳解 | 三個選項都是地點，而且看似完全不相關的場所，考生可推測對話中將逐一出現。本題無法用個別單字或片語甚至邏輯來推敲，考生必須理解整段對話才能找出答案。女人最後說她的包包放在餐廳，所以正確答案為 C。

| 補充 | laundry 除了是「洗衣店」，也指「所洗的衣物」或「待洗的衣物」，所以「do the laundry」就是「洗衣服」。另外「the cleaner's」就是外面的乾洗店，適合在外面租房子，剛好房子又沒有洗衣機的單身男女。而 cafeteria 就是台灣人買便當的自助餐廳。

Question number 10.

M: I prefer staying up late to study rather than getting up early the next morning.	男：我寧願熬夜讀書也不要早起唸書。
W: I don't think that's a good idea.	女：我不認為那是好的想法。
M: I find I'm more focused at night.	男：我發現我在夜晚比較能夠專注。
W: I understand, but I'm in higher spirits in the morning and can be ready to deal with tasks.	女：我了解，但我早上精神會比較好且能夠準備處理任務。

Question. What does the woman mean? 女子的意思是什麼？

A. She usually gets up late. A. 她通常晚起。

B. She does it totally different from the man. B. 她的做法完全不同於男子。

C. She thinks what the man does is stupid. C. 她覺得男子的作法很笨。

｜詳解｜ 選項皆以 She 為主詞，所以考生可以專心在女子的對話內容上，比較可以找出正確答案。女子說「I don't think that's a good idea.」，意思就是她不認為「熬夜讀書是好的」，所以正確答案為選項 B。當然，從她的發言中也看不到她認為男子的做法很笨，所以 C 是錯誤的。

｜補充｜ prefer A to/rather than B（寧願要 A 而不要 B）的句型幾乎是必考的題型，請記下來！另外一種相同的說法是「would rather A than B」，也是指比較喜歡 A 勝過於 B。stay up late = burn the midnight oil，即為「熬夜」的意思。

Question number 11.

W: How may I help you? 女：我能為你服務嗎？

M: No, thanks. I'm just window-shopping. 男：謝謝。我逛逛就好。

W: All right. Call me if you need some help. 女：好的。如果需要幫忙的話請叫我一聲。

Question. What is the man doing? 男子正在做什麼？

A. He is just looking around in the shop. A. 他正在這店裡四處看看。

B. He is asking for help. B. 他正尋求幫助。

C. He's going to buying a window. C. 他將要買一扇窗戶。

｜詳解｜ 三個選項都是表示「男人正在做…」，因此可以推測問題應該是「正在做什麼事情」。男子說的 window-shopping 是「四處逛逛」的意思，相當於「looking around」，所以正確答案是選項 A。對話中是女人主動詢問男人是否需要服務，而不是男人主動尋求幫助，所以選項 B 不對。選項 C 則是利用 window-shopping 的中文直譯來製造陷阱。

｜補充｜ window-shopping 按照字面意思是「流覽商店櫥窗」，通常只是看看，沒有很大的購買意願。此外， 中級的 browse 這個動詞，也有「逛逛，瀏覽」的意思。例如「(to) browse store windows」就是「瀏覽商店櫥窗」，也就是四處逛逛看看。

Question number 12.

W: Good morning. I'm calling to cancel my meeting with Mr. Wang.
女：早安，我打來是要取消下午與王先生的會面。

M: Yes, Miss. May I have your name, please?
男：是的，小姐。請問您的大名？

W: I'm Mary Jane.
女：我是瑪莉珍。

M: Thank you, Miss Jane. Your meeting with Mr. Wang is cancelled. Would you like to set up a new time to meet with him?
男：謝謝你，珍小姐。您與王先生的會面已取消。您要再安排一個新的時間與他會面嗎？

Question. Why is the woman calling? 女子為什麼打了這通電話？

A. To confirm the time of a meeting
A. 為了確認會面的時間

B. To call off a meeting
B. 為了取消一場會面

C. To change the time of a meeting
C. 為了更改會面的時間

| 詳解 | 從選項中可以知道對話內容是關於會面（meeting）的約定，同時要特別注意各個搭配 meeting 的動詞（片語）。confirm 是「確認」，call off 是「取消」（= cancel）。由於女子第一句話就說「I'm calling to cancel my meeting with Mr. Wang.」，後面的對話就不重要了，故正確答案是選項 B。

| 補充 | 通常與某人的會面也可以用中級的 appointment 這個字，也可以表示正式的「會議」，或是醫院、診所的「預約看診」，例如：I have an appointment with Dr. Chen next Monday.（我下星期一跟陳醫生約了看診。）

Part 4 短文聽解

Question number 13.

Please look at the following three pictures. Listen to the following short talk. Who is the man talking?
請看以下三張圖片。聆聽以下簡短談話。在說話的男士是哪位？

Welcome back to FM101, City Radio. This is your Sunday host, Josh Lin. We have just listened to a great song from the city's most popular boy band. And in a second, they will be here in the studio singing on air. Stay tuned.
歡迎回到 FM101 城市電台。我是你的周日主持人 Josh Lin。剛才我們聽到的是來自本市最受歡迎男孩團體的歌曲。而待會兒，他們將來到電台在空中為你演唱。別轉台哦。

A

B

C

| 詳解 | 平常收聽英文電台的考生，本題絕對能輕鬆過關，說話者一開始就給了非常明確的線索 FM101 和 radio（FM 是「調頻」，radio 是「廣播」）。他在電台上班，是 Sunday host（星期天的節目主持人），所以即使沒有收聽電台習慣的考生聽到 radio 也可以推測出正確答案是 B。而最後一句 Stay tuned.（tune 是指「符合電台的頻率」），字面意思是「保持現在的調頻狀況」，也就是請聽眾不要轉到別的電台，更足以確認答案。

| 補充 | tune 雖然是個英檢中級的單字，但相信大家都知道 iTune 這個東西，是跟歌曲、曲調有關的，而 tune 當動詞時就是指「調音，調整... 的音頻」，這裡用它的過去分詞 tuned 當形容詞，用「stay tuned」來表示「不要調換到別的頻道去」。另外，tune 也有「協調一致」的意思，例如：The colors are perfectly tuned to each other.（這些顏色很協調。）

Question number 14.

Please look at the following three pictures. Listen to the following short talk. Which picture is true for the short talk?

請看以下三張圖片。聆聽以下簡短談話。對於此短對話，哪張照片是對的？

Every day, Diane gets off work at 6 and has dinner at round 7. Before having her meal, she likes to spend some time with Max. Playing with him is her happiest time after a tiring day.

戴安每天六點下班，大概七點吃晚餐。在吃飯前，她喜歡花點時間陪馬克斯。跟馬克斯一起玩是戴安一天辛勞後最快樂的時光。

| 詳解 | 本題考的是時間以及事情的先後順序。考生首先從圖中整理出女人會做的幾件事情：下班、在家吃飯、跟狗玩耍或跟男友講話，如此就能對敘述的內容有初步概念。接著圖中都有標示時間，代表有先後順序的要求。選項 A 的問題出在吃飯的時間，敘述裡的第一句就說明女人每天都在約七點時吃晚餐，所以選項 A 不符。選項 C 的問題也是發生在時間上，七點應該用餐而非跟男友講話，故正確答案為 B。本題的陷阱是 Max 也有可能是狗的名字。

Day 03

月　　日

我的完成時間＿＿＿分鐘
標準作答時間 10 分鐘

Part 1 看圖辨義

Questions 1-2

Part 2 問答

Questions 3-7

3. A. I don't know Frank is going with us.
   B. We should have left earlier.
   C. Let's break these into four.

4. A. I'm glad you enjoyed it.
   B. Exactly. I know you'll agree.
   C. You should not talk about this soon.

5. A. Where is the nearest pub?
   B. Billy's sure to be excited.
   C. No way! How is he now?

6. A. It's not up to you.
   B. I want to order delivery.
   C. Go and get it yourself.

7. A. Don't worry. It's just a bug.
   B. Please keep your eyes closed.
   C. John is saying "Good-bye" to you.

Part 3 簡短對話

Questions 8-12

8. A. He doesn't understand why the woman is so sad.
   B. He doesn't consider it strange to take a shower with a dog.
   C. He's going to die with his pet.

9. A. They're to decide the prize.
   B. They're to take part in the Lantern Parade.
   C. They're going to have a lantern making contest.

10. A. He chose to live with his sister.
    B. He didn't accept a good job that is far from his home.
    C. He is moving to the United States.

11. A. He didn't have enough sleep.
    B. He needs a better pillow to sleep well.
    C. He doesn't like to sleep on the pillow.

12. A. Teacher and studen
    B. Dentist and patient
    C. Father and daughter

Part 4 短文聽解

Questions 13-14

13.

A

B

C

14.

A

B

C

上頁簡答

解答與詳解

1. (A) 2. (A) 3. (B) 4. (A) 5. (C) 6. (B) 7. (A) 8. (B) 9. (C) 10. (B) 11. (C) 12. (C) 13. (A) 14. (B)

Part 1 看圖辨義

For questions number 1-2, please look at the following picture.

Question number 1.

What is true about the picture? 關於圖片，哪一項陳述是真的？

A. The fax machine is a thousand and fifty dollars. A. 傳真機是 $1,050。

B. The laptop is ninety-nine thousand dollars. B. 筆記型電腦是 $99,000。

C. The digital camera is the cheapest. C. 數位相機最便宜。

詳解 本題主要考的是金額數字的表達。數位相機 2,500 元可以說成 two thousand（$2,000）and five hundred dollars（$500）或 twenty five hundred dollars（25 個 100 元）。筆電 9,900 元，可以說成 ninety-nine hundred dollars 或 nine thousand and nine hundred dollars。選項 B 的 ninety-nine thousand dollars（$99,000）與實際標價不符，選項 C 的 cheapest 為便宜（cheap）的最高級，也就是「最便宜的」，但傳真機 $1,050 才最便宜。故正確答案為 A。

Question number 2.

If you want to buy a fax machine and a camera, how much should you pay?
如果你想買一台傳真機跟一台相機，你要付多少錢？

A. Three thousand five hundred and fifty A. 3550

B. Three thousand five hundred and fifteen B. 3515

C. Three thousand five hundred and five C. 3505

詳解 本題主要考的是相似數字英文聽力，其次是用英文考買賣交易的理解力。首先考生要聽懂是要買一台傳真機及一台相機，然後把兩個價格相加得到所要付的金額 3550，其次要能分辨 50（fifty）跟 15（fifteen）的重音差別，才不會選到陷阱的 B。正確答案為 A。

Part 2 問答

Question number 3.

Frankly, we can't arrive there by four. 坦白說，我們無法在四點前抵達那裡。

A. I don't know Frank is going with us.　　A. 我不知道法蘭克要跟我們去。

B. We should have left earlier.　　B. 我們應該早點出門。

C. Let's break these into four.　　C. 讓我們把這些分成四份吧。

| 詳解 | frankly 並不是男生的名字，它是副詞，「坦白地，老實說」的意思，跟 Frank（法蘭克）沒有關係，所以選項 A 不符。選項 C 的 break into 是指「拆成」、「分成」，當中的 four 是指四份，跟時間沒有關係。所以正確答案為 B。

| 補充 | 有些人說話很含蓄，真心話都留在心裡，可能覺得這樣比較「客氣」，要他們坦白說出真心話的時候，他們可能會用「坦白說」、「老實說…」作 開頭，這裡的「Frankly, ...」也可以說成「Frankly speaking, ...」、「To tell (you) the truth」、「Honestly, ...」、「Honestly speaking, ...」、「To be honest, ...」等。

Question number 4.

Thank you for taking me here. The show's really excellent.
謝謝你帶我來這裡。表演珍的很精彩。

A. I'm glad you enjoyed it.　　A. 我很開心你喜歡它。

B. Exactly. I know you'll agree.　　B. 沒錯，我就知道你會同意。

C. You should not talk about this soon.　　C. 你不應該這麼快就談到這件事。

| 詳解 | 本題關鍵字句在 show... excellent（表演很精彩），題目沒有詢問意見或是否同意，所以選項 B 不符。選項 C 的回應也許會引起誤會，因為如果別人跟我們說 thank you，我們可以回答 you are welcome 或 don't mention that（不客氣），而選項 C 可不是什麼「快別這麼說」，那是一種警告甚至責備的話語，並非此意。所以三個選項中最符合的為選項 A。

Question number 5.

Billy was beaten up in a pub last night. 比利昨晚在酒吧裡被海扁了一頓。

A. Where is the nearest pub?　　A. 最近的酒吧在哪裡？

B. Billy's sure to be excited.　　B. 比利一定很興奮。

C. No way! How is he now?　　C. 不會吧！他現在還好嗎？

| 詳解 | 題目中說「Billy was beaten up」，意思是「他被揍」，所以選項 B 說他一定很 excited（興奮的）絕對不是正確答案。選項 A 的詢問更是莫名奇妙，所以正確答案為 C。

| 補充 | 「No way.」除了用來表達你對某件事情感到非常驚訝，就是我們常說的「真的假

的？」也可以用來強烈地表達「不要」、「門兒都沒有」。例如：A: Are you inviting your supervisor to your birthday party?（你要邀請你主管來你的生日派對嗎？）B: No way!（才不要咧！）

Question number 6.

What's for dinner tonight, Mom? 媽，今天晚餐吃什麼？

A. It's not up to you. A. 由不得你。

B. I want to order delivery. B. 我想叫外送。

C. Go and get it yourself. C. 自己去拿吧。

| 詳解 | 選項 A 的「up to you」就是「看你，由你自己決定」，否定用法就是「由不得你」，問吃什麼晚餐卻回答「由不得你」完全不合邏輯，而選項 C 則要小孩「自己去拿」，也是不知所云的回答。因此，媽媽回答「叫外送」才是最恰當的答案，所以正確答案為選項 B。

| 補充 | delivery 雖然是中級的單字，但它衍生自初級的 deliver，應該很容易理解是「（信件或貨物的）遞送」之意，現在日常對話中很常被用來表示「外送」。所以餐點的外送服務，我們會說 delivery service。

Question number 7.

Honey, what's that strange sound outside? 親愛的，外面奇怪的聲音是什麼？

A. Don't worry. It's just a bug. A. 別擔心。只是蟲子罷了。

B. Please keep your eyes closed. B. 請閉上你的眼睛。

C. John is saying "Good-bye" to you. C. 約翰在跟妳說「再見」。

| 詳解 | 本題關鍵是「strange sound」（怪聲音），選項 B 要你把眼睛閉上，當然不符。選項 C 說的是人的言語，但題目指的是某種奇怪聲音，所以也不符。正確答案為選項 A。

| 補充 | 說某人或某事很奇怪、奇特、怪異甚至不尋常，我們可以說 strange、weird、fishy 或 quirky。選項 A 中的 bug 是「蟲」，但當動詞時，可解作「煩擾，打擾」，例如：Would you stop bugging me?（你不要煩我，好嗎？）

Part 3 簡短對話

Question number 8.

W: I can't believe it! You eat with your dog and now even take it to the shower with you? 女：我無法相信耶！你跟你的狗吃飯就算了，現在還帶著牠跟你一起洗澡？

M: Come on! You know I'm crazy about dogs. It's just part of my family. 男：別這麼說！你知道我狂愛狗的。牠是我家人之一。

W: I understand, and I'm just worried about your health problems? 女：我了解，我只是擔心你的健康問題。

Question. What does the man mean? 男子的意思是什麼？

A. He doesn't understand why the woman is so sad. A. 他不懂為什麼女人這麼難過。

B. He doesn't consider it strange to take a shower with a dog. B. 他不認為和狗一起洗澡是件奇怪的事。

C. He's going to die with his pet. C. 他打算跟他的寵物一起死去。

| 詳解 | 從選項中可推測對話者聊關於寵物的事，女人說「I can't believe it（我無法相信），透露出她的驚訝，不是難過，所以選項 A 不符。男人很愛狗但沒有誇張到要跟自己的狗一起死，所以選項 C 也不符。所以正確答案為選項 B。

| 詳解 | 男人說他自己是「crazy about dogs」，意思是「對狗很瘋狂」。「crazy about/for（something / someone）」就是對「某事／某人很迷戀、瘋狂」。consider（認為）在「視…為…」的用法中，不帶有介系詞，不像 regard、view 等動詞，會跟介系詞 as 搭配。例如：I regard / view money as filth and dirt. = I consider money filth and dirt.（我視金錢如糞土。）

Question number 9.

W: How do you plan to celebrate the Lantern Festival? 女：你打算怎樣慶祝元宵節？

M: I'm thinking to have a DIY lantern competition. 男：我正在考慮舉辦一個自製花燈的比賽。

W: Cool! Girls are good at this. What about the prize? 女：酷啊！女生最會做這些了。獎品是什麼呢？

M: Uh, the winner will have my kiss! 男：嗯，贏的人可以獲得我的香吻一個！

Question. What is the two speakers' plan? 兩位說話者的計畫是什麼？

A. They're to decide the prize. A. 他們要決定獎品。

B. They're to take part in the Lantern Parade. B. 他們要參加燈會。

C. They're going to have a lantern making contest. C. 他們將舉行花燈比賽。

| 詳解 | 本題需注意兩位說話者的「決定」，因為三個選項都是關於 they 的描述。另外，當中兩個選項都提到 lantern，所以對話也必定跟此有關。男生提議獎品是香吻一個，所以選項 A 不符。選項 B 的 parade 是指遊行，但男生講的是花燈比賽，所以選項 B 也不符。故正確答案為選項 C。

| 補充 | DIY 是 Do It Yourself，也就是「自己動手做」，可以當動詞或形容詞用，例如：I want to have pasta for dinner. Let's DIY!（我想吃義大利麵當晚餐，我們自己動手做吧！）選項 C 的「take part in」是指「參與」的意思，相當於「participate in」。

Question number 10.

W: David, why did you turn down that excellent job offer in the States? You surprised me.
女：大衛，你為什麼回絕了美國那份優渥的工作？你讓我很訝異。

M: My wonderful sister, money isn't that important to me! I want to stay with my family.
男：我的好姐姐，錢對我來說沒有那麼重要！我想留在家人身邊。

W: Now I'm amazed.
女：現在我倒是對你另眼相看。

Question. What was the man's decision? 男人的決定是什麼？

A. He chose to live with his sister.
A. 他選擇跟姐姐住在一起。

B. He didn't accept a good job that is far from his home.
B. 他沒有接受一份離家很遠的優渥工作。

C. He is moving to the United States.
C. 他即將搬到美國。

| 詳解 | 選項都跟男生說話者有關，而且是關於工作、居住之事。男人因為想多陪家人而 turn down（拒絕，婉拒）了一份 excellent job（很棒的工作）。男人說的「stay with my family」不一定就是指跟姐姐住，也有可能是已結婚另組的家庭，所以選項 A 並不明確。他拒絕的工作在 States（美國）而不是他要搬去美國，所以選項 C 不符。故正確答案為選項 B。

Question number 11.

M: Mom, I have a sore neck.
男：媽咪，我的脖子酸痛。

W: That's because you didn't sleep on the pillow.
女：那是因為你都不用枕頭睡覺。

M: I feel uncomfortable with pillows.
男：睡枕頭很不舒服。

Question. What does the man mean? 男子的意思為何？

A. He didn't have enough sleep.
A. 他沒有足夠的睡眠。

B. He needs a better pillow to sleep well.
B. 他需要一個好一點的枕頭才能睡個好覺。

C. He doesn't like to sleep on the pillow.
C. 他不喜歡用枕頭睡覺。

| 詳解 | 三個選項都看得到 sleep（睡覺），可以推測對話跟睡眠有關；三個選項都以 he 作主詞，可知是男人的睡眠問題。男人說自己 sore neck（脖子很酸），所以選項 A 不符。而從男子說的「I feel uncomfortable with pillows. 」可知，選項 B 錯誤。所以正確答案為選項 C。

| 補充 | sore 表示「痠痛的」，常用在喉嚨、脖子等部委的不舒服，像是「get/have a sore throat/neck」。另外，也常用 ache 這個字表示「疼痛」，若是看到身體某個部位加上 -ache 這個字尾的話，就表示那個部位的痛感喔！例如：tooth 是「牙齒」，toothache 就是「牙痛」；stomach 是「胃」stomachache 就是「胃痛」。也可以用 achy 表示疼痛的持續，但是沒有很強烈。例如：My shoulders have been achy lately.（我的肩膀最

近一直隱隱作痛。）

Question number 12.

M: Brush your teeth before you go to bed.　男：睡覺前要刷牙。

W: OK, I'll do that later.　女：好啦，我待會兒會去。

M: Dear, I do this for your own good. I hate to keep asking you to do something you haven't done.　男：親愛的，我這麼做是為妳好。我不喜歡一直叫你去做你還沒做的事情。

W: I understand, but I'm a grown-up already.　女：我了解，但我已經是大人了。

Question. Who might be the two speakers? 這兩位說話者可能是什麼關係？

A. Teacher and student　A. 教師與學生

B. Dentist and patient　B. 牙醫與病人

C. Father and daughter　C. 父親與女兒

詳解 對話的類似內容的確可能發生在三個選項中所描述的關係，老師可以要求學生睡覺前刷牙，牙醫當然也可以這麼做。不過牙醫不會稱呼病人 Dear，而且還說「I do this for your own good」（我這麼做是為你好），已經太超過了，所以選項 B 不對。選項 A 的老師跟學生也是同樣的情況，而且女生的回答還顯得不耐煩，所以選項 A 不符。故正確答案為選項 C。

Part 4 短文聽解

Question number 13.

Please look at the following three pictures. Listen to the following announcement. Who is this for?

請看以下三張圖片。聆聽以下宣布。這是針對什麼樣的人宣布的？

Good news for mothers. We are having a special offer on kitchen utilities. Starting from today to the end of May, you can buy a microwave for only $1,000, a washing machine for $2,000 with a set of cutlery free! Get ready to shop or you'll regret it!

給媽媽們的好消息。我們的廚房用品大優惠。從今天起到五月底前，微波爐只要 1,000 元，洗碗機只要 2,000 元，再免費送你一套精美餐具組！馬上行動，否則你會後悔！

A

B

C

| 詳解 | 錄音中的短文有「you can buy ...」、「Get ready to shop...」等內容，即告訴考生這是針對消費者的宣傳內容，不過因為三張圖片似乎都能成立，所以廣告中的第一句就成了破題關鍵。「Good news for mothers.」也代表此特別優惠（special offer）是專門為媽媽們而設的，所以正確答案為選項 A。

Question number 14.

Please look at the following three pictures. Listen to the following short talk. What might Jenny probably do the whole morning?
請看以下三張圖片。聆聽以下簡短談話。珍妮整個早上可能都在做什麼？

Jenny has just started her own business last month. She is busy every day. Every morning Jenny needs to check the amount of goods available to sell. In the afternoon, she has to make sure the goods are ready for delivery by 4. It is not until 8 that Jenny can take a break before preparing for another day's hard work.
珍妮上個月才剛開始自己當老闆。她每天都很忙碌。每天早上珍妮要查看可以準備出售的貨品數量。下午，她得要確認所有貨品可在四點前送出。一直到晚上八點珍妮才可以休息一會，再為隔天辛勞的工作做準備。

| 詳解 | 本題問的是 Jenny 上午通常都在做什麼工作，所以對 morning（早上）前後所述說之事都要特別注意。內容中提到早上她要「check the stock and delivery list」（點貨和確認出貨單），所以三張圖中只有 B 最為符合。

| 補充 | 「開」的英文是 open，但中文說「開」，其實在不同情況代表不同意思。例如，「開店做生意」可以說成「open a store/shop to do business」，也可以說「start (up) a business」。另外，中文說「開車」可能有很多意思，英文則要用到對應的字：駕駛（drive）、發動（start）、開車門（open car door）...等。例如：He isn't able to start the car now because the engine is dead.（他現在沒辦法開車，因為引擎壞了。）而「打開電視」當然也不能用「open the TV」，否則是要把電視機的殼拆開來看了，電器用品的「開啟」及「關閉」，一般都用 turn on/off。

MEMO

Day 04

月　　日

我的完成時間＿＿＿＿分鐘
標準作答時間 10 分鐘

Part 1 看圖辨義

Questions 1-2

Part 2 問答

Questions 3-7

3. A. Well, I'm still considering.
   B. No, I can't afford it.
   C. Sure, it's a fat chance to win.

4. A. Sorry, I don't have the change.
   B. You need to change a bus at the next stop.
   C. I'm afraid we don't have the red ones.

5. A. I'm grad you've enjoyed the show.
   B. You can say that again.
   C. Tomorrow will be better.

6. A. Ok, I won't fool you anymore.
   B. No, I'm not a fool.
   C. All right. I'll go look for job tomorrow.

7. A. I did my best. Could you spare me three more days?
   B. I'm too weak to carry this.
   C. May I stay behind?

Part 3 簡短對話

Questions 8-12

8. A. The man is not telling the truth.
   B. The man's computer is better than hers.
   C. The man is happy with his computer.

9. A. She's going to move to Africa.
   B. Her husband is a Japanese.
   C. She's going to get married.

10. A. He forgot to bring his crown to the party.
    B. He was not allowed to the party.
    C. He missed his final exam.

11. A. Husband and wife
    B. Employer and employee
    C. Hotel staff and check-in guest

12. A. In a meeting room
    B. At an airport
    C. In a bank

Part 4 短文聽解

Question 13-14

13.

A

B

C

14.

A

B

C

上頁簡答

解答與詳解

1. (C) 2. (A) 3. (A) 4. (C) 5. (B) 6. (C) 7. (A) 8. (A) 9. (C) 10. (B) 11. (B) 12. (C) 13. (C) 14. (C)

Part 1 看圖辨義

For questions number 1-2, please look at the following picture.

Question number 1.

Where are these people? 這些人在哪裡？

A. They are in a gym. A. 他們在健身房。

B. They are at an airport. B. 他們在機場。

C. They are on an MRT train. C. 他們在捷運車廂內。

| 詳解 | 從圖片中最右邊的男子手抓著懸掛的手環，以最左邊女子的坐姿可推知，他們在大眾運輸工具上，可能是公車、火車或捷運等，所以正確答案是選項 C。A 的 gym 是「健身房」，C 的 MRT 是「Mass Rapid Transit」（在台灣稱作「捷運」）的縮寫。

Question number 2.

Who's the man in shorts? 穿短褲的男人是何人？

A. He's a thief. A. 他是一名小偷。

B. He's a robber. B. 他是一名搶匪。

C. He's a customer. C. 他是一名顧客。

| 詳解 | 本題測驗考生對於「與人有關」的字彙之認知，thief 可泛指一般「小偷」，只要是偷偷取走他人財物者，都可以稱為 thief，而 robber（搶劫犯）通常帶有暴力或恐嚇的手段，customer（則與圖片中人物毫無關聯），所以本題正確答案是選項 A。

Part 2 問答

Question number 3.

James, are you going to take part in the science competition?

詹姆士，你打算參加科學比賽嗎？

A. Well, I'm still considering. A. 這個嘛，我還在考慮。

B. No, I can't afford it. B. 不會，我負擔不起。

C. Sure, it's a fat chance to win. C. 當然囉，不太可能有機會贏。

| 詳解 | James 被問到是否要參加比賽，看似個 Yes/No 的問題，但可別一看到選項中有 No, ... 就閉著眼睛選下去了。選項 B 說「不，我負擔（afford）不起」，顯然不知所云，而選項 C 說「當然（會去參加），不太可能有機會贏。」也明顯不合邏輯，fat chance 是「機會渺茫」的意思，故正確答案為選項 A。

Question number 4.

I'd like to change this to a red one. 我想要換紅色的。

A. Sorry, I don't have the change. A. 不好意思，我沒有零錢。

B. You need to change a bus at the next stop. B. 你得在下一站換車。

C. I'm afraid we don't have the red ones. C. 恐怕我們沒有紅色的。

| 詳解 | 題目中的「change... to...」表示「將…換成…」，而選項 A 的 change 是個名詞，表示「零錢」，刻意用一樣的字來誤導答題；而 B 提到換車（轉搭）顯然與題目不相關，故正確答案是選項 C。

Question number 5.

Oh, no! This stage show is really terrible! 噢，不！這舞台秀真是糟糕！

A. I'm grad you've enjoyed the show. A. 我很高興你喜歡這表演。

B. You can say that again. B. 你說得沒錯。

C. Tomorrow will be better. C. 明天會更好。

| 詳解 | 題目的說話者認為舞台表演（stage show）很差（terrible），而選項 A 的回應顯然前後矛盾；C 說「明天會更好」也是雞同鴨講，不知所云，故正確答案是選項 B。「You can say that again.」在口語會話中很常聽到，字面意思是「你可以再說一次那句話。」用來表達認同對方所說的話，等同於「I agree with you.」。

Question number 6.

Will you stop fooling around? 你可以別再遊手好閒了嗎？

A. Ok, I won't fool you anymore. A. 好吧，我不再耍你了。

B. No, I'm not a fool. B. 不，我不是個呆子。

C. All right. I'll go look for job tomorrow. C. 好吧。我明天會去找工作。

| 詳解 | 題目的「fool around」是指「無所事事；遊手好閒」，但是 fool 當及物動詞時，表示「愚弄」，如選項 A 的用法，當名詞時表示「傻子」，如 B 的用法，因此 A 和 B 的回答都刻意以相同字 fool 試圖混淆，但回答皆不合邏輯，故正確答案是選項 C。

| 補充 | fool 在口語中也常見於「make a fool of + 某人」的用法，表示「使…（某人）出洋相或出醜」。例如：You made a fool of me in front of so many people!（你讓我在這麼多人面前出醜！）

Question number 7.

You are a week behind on your report. 你的報告已經拖一星期了。

A. I did my best. Could you spare me three more days? 我盡力了。你可以再通融我三天嗎？

B. I'm too weak to carry this. 我太虛弱了，提不動這個。

C. May I stay behind? 我可以留下來嗎？

｜詳解｜ behind 除了有「在後面」的意思外，也有「落後」的意思。two days behind 就是落後或拖了兩天。選項 B 的 weak（虛弱的）跟題目中的 week（星期），發音完全一樣，但意思差很遠，可別被誤導。C 的 stay behind 是指「留下來」，跟報告進度落後沒有關連。所以正確答案為選項 A。

｜補充｜ spare 當形容詞時，解作「備用的，剩餘的，空暇的，清瘦的，不豐富的」，例如 spare tire（備用輪胎）、spare figure（身材瘦削）、spare meal（不豐盛的一餐）。spare 當動詞時，解作「赦免，寬宥，提供（時間、金錢），分讓」，所以選項 A 的 spare me three more days 就是指「再通融三天」。

Part 3 簡短對話

Question number 8.

M: My second-hand PC is much better than a new one. 男：我的二手電腦比新機好太多了。

W: Come on, Peter! Your computer always shuts down for no reason. 女：拜託，彼得！你的電腦常無緣無故當機耶。

M: At least it's much cheaper than a new one. 男：至少它比新機便宜多了。

Question. What could the woman mean? 女人的意思可能為何？

A. The man is not telling the truth. A. 男人並沒有說實話。

B. The man's computer is better than hers. B. 男人的電腦比她的好。

C. The man is happy with his computer. C. 男人很滿意他的電腦。

｜詳解｜ 題目要聽清楚，本題問的是「女子的觀點」，從她的回應可推知，她並不認為男子的二手電腦有多好，即使男子真的認為很好且很滿意，所以她可能認為男子沒有說實話，正確答案為選項 A。

Question number 9.

W: I received Mary's wedding invitation card yesterday. 女：我昨天收到了瑪莉的喜帖。

M: Really? Who is the lucky guy? 男：真的嗎？那位幸運男子是誰啊？

W: An African businessman she met in Japan. 女：她在日本遇見的一位非裔商人。

M: Wow, cool! 男：哇，酷！

Question. What is true about Mary? 關於瑪莉，何者為真？

A. She's going to move to Africa. A. 她要搬到非洲去。

B. Her husband is a Japanese. B. 她丈夫是日本人。

C. She's going to get married. C. 她即將要結婚。

| 詳解 | 對話中「an African businessman she met in Japan」（一個她在日本遇見的非裔商人）是答題關鍵。Mary 即將要嫁給一名非洲商人但沒有提到她要搬到非洲，所以選項 A 錯誤。在日本遇見的非洲籍商人，不是日本人，所選項 B 也錯誤，故正確答案為選項 C。

Question number 10.

W: Hey, I didn't see you at the party last night. What's wrong?
女：嗨，我昨晚沒在派對上看到你。怎麼了？

M: Yeah, I failed my final exam so my dad grounded me.
男：是呀，我期末考不及格，所以我老爸下了禁足令。

W: No way! You're the party king.
女：不會吧！你是派對之王耶。

M: Well, looks like I should change my crown for some textbooks this time.
男：喔，看來我這次該把我的皇冠拿去換一些教科書了。

Question. What happened to the man? 男人發生了什麼事情？

A. He forgot to bring his crown to the party. A. 他忘了把皇冠帶去派對了。

B. He was not allowed to the party. B. 他被禁止去參加派對。

C. He missed his final exam. C. 他錯過了期末考。

| 詳解 | 從三個選項中可推測對話跟男生的期末考或他參加的派對有關。「failed my final exam」（期末考不及格）以及 grounded（禁足）是關鍵字，如果兩者都熟悉，那麼肯定可以找出正確答案。fail the exam 絕對是考生熟悉的片語，所以就算只聽懂這部分，考生也一樣可以推測出答案。女子問男子說，昨晚的 party 怎沒看到男子，所以選項 A 不符。男生說考試不及格，那表示有去考試，所以選項 C 不對。正確答案為選項 B。

| 補充 | miss 除了有想念之意，也是「錯過，錯失」的意思，例如：I missed the early bus.（我錯過了早班公車。）另外，口語中常聽見的「You can't miss.」就是「你一定可以（成功）的。」的意思。

Question number 11.

W: Good morning, Mr. Smith.
女：早安，史密斯先生。

M: Good morning, Julie.
男：早安，茱莉。

W: Nice tie. A gift from Mrs. Smith?
女：好漂亮的領帶，是史密斯太太送的禮物嗎？

M: Yes, it is my birthday this coming Sunday.
男：是的，這個星期日是我的生日。

Question. Who could be the speakers? 說話者們可能是誰？

A. Husband and wife	A. 丈夫與妻子
B. Employer and employee	B. 雇主與員工
C. Hotel staff and check-in guest	C. 飯店人員與入住旅客

｜詳解｜ 從女子稱呼男子「Mr. Smith」以及「A gift from Mrs. Smith?」可知，選項 A 錯誤；另外，一般情況下這一的對話內容也不會是飯店人員與入住旅客之間的對話，因此三個選項中只有雇主與員工比較有可能，所以正確答案為選項 B。

｜補充｜ coming Sunday 是「即將來臨的星期天」，coming weekend 則是「本週末」。此外，employer 和 employee 都是從動詞 employ（雇用）衍生出的兩個與「人」有關的名詞，-er 表示「動作的施作者」，-ee 表示「動作的接受者」。

Question number 12.

W: Good afternoon, what can I do for you?	女：午安，有什麼能為您效勞？
M: I'd like to apply for online banking.	男：我想申請網銀。
W: No problem. Please fill out this form.	女：沒問題。請填寫這張表格。
(A minute later...)	（1 分鐘過後）
M: Here you are. Can I get a loan at the same time?	男：在這裡。我可以同時辦個貸款嗎？
W: Sure. How much do you need?	女：當然可以。您需要多少？

Question. Where did the conversation take place? 這段對話的地點在哪？

A. In a meeting room	A. 在會議室
B. At an airport	B. 在機場
C. In a bank	C. 在銀行

｜詳解｜ 從選項中可推知要問的是這篇對話在哪裡進行。從對話中提到的「apply for online banking」以及「Can I get a loan at the same time?」可知，正確答案為選項 C。

｜補充｜ 對話中的兩個及物動詞片語「apply for」以及「fill out」分別是「申請」以及「填寫（完）」的意思。所以「申請…（金額）貸款」也可以說「apply for a loan of NT$...」。另外，雖然 in 與 out 意思相反，但「fill in」跟「fill out」用於表單或申請表時，都同樣是「填寫」的意思！若是硬要分，「fill in」比較偏向將小的空格填滿，而「fill out」的範圍比較大，像是整張申請表或是問卷。

Part 4 短文聽解

Question number 13.

Please look at the following three pictures. Listen to the following announcement. Where does it take place?

請看以下三張圖片。聆聽以下宣布內容。這會是在什麼地方？

This is the Captain speaking. We are going to land in 10 minutes. Please stay in your seat and have your seat belt fastened. Please do not turn on any electrical devices until the landing is completed. Thank you for your cooperation.

這是機長廣播。我們將在十分鐘後降落。請留在您的座位上並扣好安全帶。直到完全降落前，請不要開啟任何電子用品。謝謝您的合作。

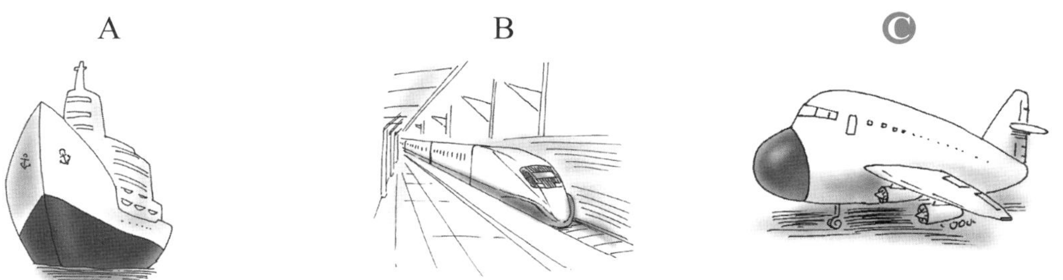

詳解｜本題出題率極高，但考生命中率也相當高。同樣是在飛機上聽到的廣播內容，本題考的是降落前的廣播，而非一般常考的起飛後「歡迎搭乘」之類的內容。廣播中的 captain，可以是船長或機長，而 have your seat belt fastened（扣上安全帶）也可以在三種交通工具中出現。所以最關鍵的字就落在 land 跟 landing（降落），因為這三幅圖中只有飛機能「降落」，所以答案為 C。

Question number 14.

Please look at the following three pictures. Listen to the following short talk. What might be the event?

請看以下三張圖片。聆聽以下簡短談話。這可能是什麼樣的場合？

Good morning, ladies and gentleman. I'm glad to talk about global warming with you. Climate change has been an important issue for years and I have been researching it since 1998. You may be interested in these figures shown here...

女士先生們，早安。很高興能與你們討論全球暖化現象。這幾年來，氣候改變已成為一個重要的議題，而我從 1998 年便著手研究。你可能對這些數據感到興趣⋯

詳解｜從三張圖中考生可以推測問題為「何種場合」。錄音內容中的「I'm glad to talk about ... with you」、「I have been researching...」是破題關鍵。辯論會的開場白不會是「很高興與你們討論⋯」，所以 A 不符。短文中雖然有出現 climate（天氣，氣候），但天氣播報員不會向觀眾或聽眾講授「自己的研究」，所以 B 也不符。故正確答案為 C（演講的場合）。

Day 05

月　　日

我的完成時間______分鐘
標準作答時間 10 分鐘

Part 1 看圖辨義

Questions 1-2

Part 2 問答

Questions 3-7

3. A. I'm good at playing this.
   B. Yes, I like to cook for myself.
   C. Good idea!

4. A. Just be patient. Why not take a different route?
   B. Take it easy! Taipei is not too far away.
   C. Please take a seat here.

5. A. I'm looking for a shortcut to the airport.
   B. Just follow me, please.
   C. Go down this road and come back here.

6. A. That's true. He's really mad about reading.
   B. He had a fight with Peggy.
   C. Me too. He must be mad at Peggy.

7. A. Never mind. Where there's a will, there's a way!
   B. Don't worry. We just started.
   C. Let's look at today's traffic.

Part 3 簡短對話

Questions 8-12

8. A. He lost a lot from his business.
   B. He started up business some time before.
   C. He works at a store.

9. A. At a dancing lesson
   B. In a cafeteria
   C. At a pub

10. A. Have a big meal
    B. Help prepare the dinner
    C. Do the dishes

11. A. He wants to go out with the woman.
    B. He agrees with the woman.
    C. He seldom watches movies on Netflix.

12. A. In a bookstore
    B. At a hotel
    C. In a library

Part 4 短文聽解

Questions 13-14

13.

A

B

C

14.

A

B

C

上頁簡答

解答與詳解

1. (B) 2. (B) 3. (C) 4. (A) 5. (B) 6. (B) 7. (B) 8. (B) 9. (C) 10. (B) 11. (B) 12. (C) 13. (B) 14. (C)

Part 1 看圖辨義

For questions number 1-2, please look at the following pictures.

Question number 1.

What time does the clock show? 時鐘顯示現在幾點幾分？

A. It's fifteen past six. A. 六點十五分。

B. It's a quarter to seven. B. 六點四十五分。

C. It's nine to seven. C. 六點五十一分。

| 詳解 | 看到圖片有時鐘，就可以預期考題跟「時間」有關。本題時鐘指示 6：45，所以英文說法可以是「six forty-five」、「a quarter to seven」或「15 minutes to seven」，所以正確答案是選項 B。

| 補充 | 用英文表達時間可以很簡單，也可以很複雜。例如現在是七點三十分，最常用的講法就是「seven thirty」，來點變化的說法就是「half past seven」。若是三點十五分，就是「three fifteen」，不一樣的說法是「a quarter past three」。不過通常考題的答案不會是最單純的講法。我們把時鐘分開一半，一到六的一半用「past」表達，七到十二的那一半就用「to」來表達，所以如果是一點十分，可以說「ten minutes past one」（一點鐘過了十分鐘）。如果是九點五十五分，可以說「five minutes to ten」（差五分鐘到十點）。

Question number 2.

What happened to the little boy? 小男孩發生了什麼事？

A. He is chasing a dog. A. 他正追著一隻狗。

B. A dog is running after him. B. 一隻狗正追著他跑。

C. He is running behind a dog. C. 他正跑在一隻狗的後面。

| 詳解 | 本題考的是「追著…跑」的動詞，基本上有兩種說法：chase 和 run after。圖片顯示狗追著小男孩跑，所以正確答案是選項 B。「run behind / in front of...」是「跑在…後面／前面」的意思。

| 補充 | chase 可以當及物或不及物動詞，要表示「追逐，追著…」時，可以說「chase...」或「chase after」（= run after），如果要表示抽象的「追逐夢想」，通常會用不及物動詞的「chase after」來表示。

Part 2 問答

Question number 3.

Tomorrow is good for an outdoor activity. 明天很適合戶外活動。

A. I'm good at playing this. A. 我很擅長玩這個。

B. Yes, I like to cook for myself. B. 是啊，我喜歡自己煮來吃。

C. Good idea! C. 好主意

｜詳解｜「(be) good at」是指「擅於」，而題目只說「明天適合戶外活動」，沒有提到什麼樣的活動或事情，所以 A 錯誤；B 的回答「I like to cook for myself」有不想外出的打算，但卻以 Yes, ... 來回應，顯然矛盾。題目這句話聽起來有建議明天去戶外走走的意思，所以正確答案為選項 C。

Question number 4.

I can't stand all the roadwork in Taipei. 我受夠了台北那些修路工程。

A. Just be patient. Why not take a different route? A. 耐點性子吧！何不走別的路線呢？

B. Take it easy! Taipei is not too far away. B. 放輕鬆點！台北並不是很遠。

C. Please take a seat here. C. 請這邊請坐。

｜詳解｜「can't stand」是指「無法忍受」，即使一時之間聽不出 roadwork，至少聽得出後面的 in Taipei 吧！從「無法忍受在台北的…」可知，選項 B 明顯錯誤（刻意一開始用「Take it easy!」來誤導答題），而 C 的回答也與情境不符，所以正確答案為選項 A。「take a... route」表示「走…路線」。

｜補充｜「受不了…」或「受夠了…」的說法有「can't stand...」、「be fed up with...」、「have had enough...」。例如：I'm fed up with these annoying mosquitos.（我受夠了這些討厭的蚊子。）、I have had enough with you.（我受夠你了。）

Question number 5.

How can I get to the parking lot? 我要怎麼到停車場？

A. I'm looking for a shortcut to the airport. A. 我正在找捷徑到機場。

B. Just follow me, please. B. 麻煩跟我走吧。

C. Go down this road and come back here. C. 順著這條路直走然後回到這裡。

｜詳解｜本題考問路，地點是停車場（parking lot），所以選項 A 不對。選項 C 的前半句沒什麼問題，但可別太急著就選它了，為後面的「come back here」完全是沒有道理的，所以正確答案為選項 B。「請跟我來」的回答也常用於對方問路的回答。

Question number 6.

I have never seen David so mad. 我從來沒有看過大衛這麼生氣。

A. That's true. He's really mad about reading. A. 真的。他確實對於閱讀非常著迷。

B. He had a fight with Peggy. B. 他跟佩琪吵架了。

C. Me too. He must be mad at Peggy. C. 我也是。他肯定是對佩琪很著迷。

| 詳解 | mad 這個形容詞有多種意思，主要看它接的介系詞，以及後面的受詞而定。題目句的 mad 意思是「生氣的」，而選項 A 的「mad about reading」卻是「對於閱讀非常著迷」，顯然完全扯不上關係；選項 C 看似正確，但題目句是否定句，所以如果改成 Me either 就正確了。因此正確答案為選項 B，指出 David 如此生氣的原因。

| 補充 | mad about/on 通常用來表示「對…著迷」，受詞可能是「人」也可能是「事物」。例如：My father is mad about baseball.（我父親很迷棒球。）但 mad at 則是「對…生氣」，例如：My father is mad at that liar.（我父親對這那個說謊的人很生氣。）

Question number 7.

I'm sorry, but the traffic is so heavy! 抱歉，交通實在太壅擠了！

A. Never mind. Where there's a will, there's a way! A. 不用介意。有志者事竟成嘛！

B. Don't worry. We just started. B. 別擔心，我們才剛開始。

C. Let's look at today's traffic. C. 我們來看今天的交通狀況。

| 詳解 | 聽到 traffic 就知道是與交通有關。「heavy traffic」就是「交通壅塞」，題目句的情境就是說話者塞在車陣當中，撥打電話給相關人士表示歉意（會遲到），因此選項 C 的回應不符。選項 A 與 B 的分別以「Never mind」、「Don't worry」開頭，符合正確的回答，但 A 的「Where there's a will, there's a way.」（有志者事竟成。）是不相關的回應，故正確答案為選項 B。

| 補充 | 英文裡的「塞車」可以說「get stuck in traffic」、「traffic jam/congestion」，jam 當名詞大家都知道有「果醬」的意思，果醬是黏稠的，汽車擁擠在一起就就有如堵成一團的果醬。但千萬別說成「The traffic was very crowded.（X）」了。

Part 3 簡短對話

Question number 8.

W: I heard that you opened a store downtown last month. How's it going?

女：我聽說你上個月在市區開了一家店。生意如何？

M: So far so good.

男：到目前為止還不錯。

W: That's great to hear! What kind of products are you selling?

女：那真是好消息！你賣的是什麼樣的產品呢？

Question. What can we learn about from the man?
從男人的話我們可以得知什麼？

A. He lost a lot from his business.　A. 他的生意讓他虧了很多錢。

B. He started up business some time before.　B. 他前一陣子創業了。

C. He works at a store.　C. 他在一家店裡上班。

| 詳解 | 從三個選項中可推知對話跟 business（生意）及男人有關，關鍵字是「open a store」以及 good。因為是「自行開店」，所以選項 C 不符。男人說到目前為止生意不錯（so far so good），所以選項 A 不符。故正確答案為選項 B。「start up business」就是「創業」的意思。

Question number 9.

M: Hey, want to dance?　男：嗨，要跳舞嗎？

W: Thanks for asking... but I'm not interested.　女：謝謝你的邀請。不過我沒有興趣。

M: No problem, maybe next time!　男：沒關係，也許下次吧！

Question. Where are the speakers? 說話者身在何處？

A. At a dancing lesson　A. 在舞蹈課

B. In a cafeteria　B. 在自助餐廳裡

C. At a pub　C. 在酒吧裡

| 詳解 | 看到選項應該知道本題考的是地點，關鍵字為 dance、not interested。聽到關於跳舞，考生可直接把選項 B 刪除。女生對男生的邀請回答「沒興趣」，此狀況不會發生在舞蹈教室，所以正確答案為選項 C。

| 補充 | 「Want to dance?」其實是「Do you want to dance?」之意。口語及日常對話中常忽略主詞，直接說出動詞，例如：Want a drink?（想喝點東西嗎？）、Want to go to the movies?（想看電影嗎？）另外，interest 是動詞也是名詞，是「興趣」的意思，在後面加上 in，為「對某人或某物有興趣」，例如：I am not interested in science.（我對科學沒有興趣。）

Question number 10.

M: Dear, I'm home. Wow, what's that smell?　男：親愛的，我回來了。哇，那是什麼味道？

W: I'm cooking pasta, and baking some grilled chicken in the oven.　女：我正在煮義大利麵，以及用烤箱來烤雞。

M: Wonderful! I'll go wash my hands to offer you a hand.　男：太棒了！我現在就去洗手幫妳忙。

Question. What is the man ready to do? 男人準備要做什麼？

A. Have a big meal　A. 大吃一頓

B. Help prepare the dinner　B. 幫忙準備晚餐

C. Do the dishes　C. 洗碗盤

| 詳解 | 三個選項提供的訊息是「做某事」，而題目問的是男子準備要做什麼，所以要注意男子所說的話。破題關鍵在「offer you a hand」（幫妳的忙），因此可知選項 A 不符。選項 C 以中文的角度來看似乎合理，「洗碗盤」的確可能是在用餐前先做，但英文的「do the dishes」則專指「用餐過後洗碗盤」，而不會有「把碗盤洗乾淨來盛飯菜」的狀況，所以不符，故正確答案是選項 B。

Question number 11.

W: Any plans tonight? What about watching a movie on Netflix at home?	女：今天晚上有什麼計畫嗎？在家看一部 Netflix 上面的電影怎麼樣？
M: Well, I prefer a relaxing night with you, too.	男：嗯，我也比較喜歡跟妳度過放鬆的一晚。
W: That sounds lovely. Let's make it a date then.	女：聽起來很貼心。那就這麼說定了喔。

Question. What does the man mean? 男子的意思為何？

A. He wants to go out with the woman.	A. 他想和女子外出。
B. He agrees with the woman.	B. 他同意女子的建議。
C. He seldom watches movies on Netflix.	C. 他很少用 Netflix 看電影。

| 詳解 | 單就三個選項來看，似乎彼此沒有太大關連，而答題關鍵點在「watching a movie on Netflix at home」、「prefer a relaxing night with you, too」，表示男子認同女子的建議，一起舒舒服服地在家上網看電影，所以正確答案為選項 B。選項 A「想和女子外出」明顯錯誤，選項 C「很少看上 Neflix 看電影」也跟「relaxing night with you, too」不符。

| 補充 | 「make it a date」字面意思是「敲定好一次約會」，類似商場上的「make it a deal」（成交）用法。例如：Let's escape the city for a day and go hiking in the mountains. What do you say? Make it a date?（我們逃離這個城市一天的時間，然後到山上去登山。如何？這麼說定囉？）

Question number 12.

W: Excuse me. I'd like to check out this book.	女：抱歉，我想借出這本書。
M: Sure, please wait.	男：沒問題，請稍等。
W: I still have three books I haven't returned yet. Can I still check out this book?	女：我還有三本書沒歸還。我還能借這本書嗎？
M: I'm afraid not.	男：恐怕不行。

Question. Where does the conversation take place? 這段對話在何處進行

A. In a bookstore	A. 在書店裡
B. At a hotel	B. 在飯店
C. In a library	C. 在圖書館

| 詳解 | 本題的破題關鍵是「check out this book」，意思是「登記借出這本書」，所以是在圖書館才有可能這麼說，正確答案為選項 C。雖然「check out」也會用在飯店住宿，表示「退房」，但不會是「check out this book」。另外，書店（bookstore）不會有借還書的服務，所以選項 A 錯誤。

| 補充 | check out 除了可在飯店住宿時表示「退房」之外，相反地，check in 則是指「在飯店辦理入住手續」或是「在機場辦理登機手續」。回到本題，check out 在此指「借出」，也可以用 borrow，當然如果本題用 borrow，答案就十拿九穩啦！

Part 4 短文聽解

Question number 13.

Please look at the following three pictures. Listen to the following short talk. Which picture is the best match?

請看以下三張圖片。聆聽以下簡短談話。哪一張圖片是最符合的？

This is my family. There are five of us. The two sitting are my mom and dad. I am standing in the middle, with my brother on my right and my sister on my left. My brother is a designer and he has long hair. My sister, who is an architect, prefers a boyish look.

這是我的家庭。共有五人。兩個坐著的人是我媽跟我爸。我站在中間，我哥在我的左邊，我姐在我的右邊。我哥是一位設計師，他留長髮。我姐是一位建築師，她喜歡男生的打扮。

A

Ⓑ

C

| 詳解 | 這種配對題目是比較簡單的，三張圖內容都差不多，只要一句句跟著短文內容便可以找出答案。內容通常會有幾個明顯的破題點，像是「my brother has long hair（我哥留長髮）」、「my sister prefers a boyish look（我姐喜歡男性打扮），都是讓考生可以確認答案的關鍵。所以本題正確答案為 B。

Question number 14.

Please look at the following three pictures. Listen to the following message. What will they have for dinner?

請看以下三張圖片。聆聽以下訊息。她們晚餐將吃什麼？

Hi, mum. I'm still in the office and might not be able to make dinner tonight. I'll get some pizzas on the way home. Would you mind making fruit salad? That will be great! See you tonight.

嗨，媽咪。我還在辦公室，今天晚上可能沒辦法煮飯。我回家時會順便帶披薩回來。你介意做水果沙拉嗎？那會很棒哦！晚上見。

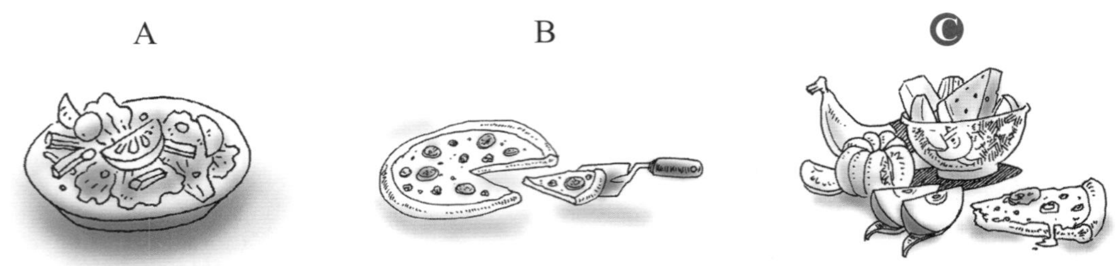

|詳解| 看到三張圖，考生可推知答案跟食物有關。留言者說她會「get some pizzas」（買些披薩），另外又請她媽媽「make fruit salad」（做水果沙拉），所以晚餐應該是披薩跟水果沙拉。故正確答案為 C。

Day 06

月　　日

我的完成時間＿＿＿分鐘
標準作答時間 10 分鐘

Part 1 看圖辨義

Questions 1-2

Part 2 問答

Questions 3-7

3. A. Too bad! It means that we are parting soon.
   B. Have a nice trip! When will you be back?
   C. So, you're leaving for Taiwan?

4. A. Thanks, I can go with my girlfriend.
   B. I'm not drunk yet. Give me another glass of wine.
   C. Sure, I need some fun after a hard day's work.

5. A. It's true though.
   B. Don't you think you expect too much?
   C. I believe what you said.

6. A. Ah, I was caught cheating again.
   B. Sorry, I was so sleepy after lunch.
   C. I need a nap. Wake me up at six.

7. A. Good. Then just go ahead.
   B. Just do your best. No pressure.
   C. Try this on. You're going to be great in it.

Part 3 簡短對話

Questions 8-12

8. A. The woman didn't send the contract.
   B. Miss White sent a package.
   C. The man has received the contract.

9. A. He's a mail carrier.
   B. He's a taxi driver.
   C. He's a ticket clerk.

10. A. She is on a business trip.
    B. She's going to marry Jake.
    C. She always smiles at Jake.

11. A. It is exciting for children.
    B. It is a romantic movie.
    C. It makes people feel moved.

12. A. His wife Mary has become seriously ill in hospital.
    B. He will propose a project to his boss the following day.
    C. He doesn't know whether Mary will promise to marry him.

Part 4 短文聽解

Questions 13-14

13.

A

B

C

14.

A

B

C

解答與詳解

上頁簡答 1. (C) 2. (B) 3. (A) 4. (C) 5. (A) 6. (B) 7. (B) 8. (A) 9. (B) 10. (A) 11. (C) 12. (C) 13. (B) 14. (A)

Part 1 看圖辨義

For questions number 1-2, please look at the following picture.

Question number 1.

Who could be the man sitting? 坐著的這名男子可能是誰？

A. A movie fan　A. 電影迷
B. A part-time worker　B. 計時工人
C. A famous singer　C. 知名歌手

|詳解| 圖片中坐著的人只有一位，就是坐在那邊寫東西（簽名）的男子，我們可以看到桌子前面有人在排隊等著拿這名男子的親筆簽名，右下角還有一個女孩很開心地拿到了簽名，所以正確答案是選項 C。

|補充| part-time 的字面意思是「部分時間」，引申為「臨時（工）的，兼職的」，而相對於這個字的是 full-time，字面是「完整時間」，引申為「全職的的」，這兩個字常與動詞 work 一起使用，work part-time/full-time 表示「打臨工／全職工作」。

Question number 2.

What are the people lining up for? 這些人排隊等什麼？

A. Free notebooks　A. 免費的筆記本
B. The man's signature　B. 男子的簽名
C. The famous singer　C. 這位知名歌手

|詳解| 圖片中的人在排隊等偶像簽名，即使無法聽出 signature（動詞 sign 的衍生字），也可以用「消去法」的方式確認正確答案是選項 B。選項 C 因為有 famous 一字，也許會讓考生有錯覺，但其實那位 famous singer 已經出現，就坐在那邊簽名，所以粉絲們並不是在他的出現，至於 A 的 notebook 則是明顯錯誤的答案。

|補充| 排隊有幾種說法，像題目的「line up (for)」，也可以說「queue up (for)」。「人們在排隊」可以說「People are queuing/lining.」。「大排長龍」可以說「People are waiting in a long line/queue.」。

Part 2 問答

Question number 3.

My family plans to move to the States. 我的家人打算移民到美國。

A. Too bad! It means that we are parting soon. A. 太糟了！那表示我們即將要分開。

B. Have a nice trip! When will you be back? B. 旅途愉快！什麼時候回來呢？

C. So, you're leaving for Taiwan? C. 那麼，你要出發到台灣去了嗎？

|詳解| the States = the United States = the USA（美國），加上「move to」，考生可以推知題目大意為「要搬去美國」，不是要去美國旅行，所以選項 B 的「Have a nice trip!」是錯誤的；選項 C 的「leaving for Taiwan」是陷阱，意思是「要去台灣」，所以不符，但考試時可能過於緊張，不小心把選項看成離開台灣（leaving Taiwan），所以要當心。但選項 A 的 parting 是破題字，指「分開」，所以可以確認正確答案為選項 A。

|補充| 「leave + 地方」以及「leave for + 地方」都是出現率極高的題型，前者是「離開原來的地方」，後者則是「離開原來的地方到另一個地方去」，所以多了一個 for 意思正好相反。例如：She leaves London.（她離開倫敦。）、She leaves for London.（她離開身處的地方去倫敦。）

Question number 4.

Let's have a drink after work. 我們下班後去喝一杯吧。

A. Thanks, I can go with my girlfriend. A. 謝啦，我可以跟我女朋友一起去。

B. I'm not drunk yet. Give me another glass of wine. B. 我還沒醉。再給我一杯酒。

C. Sure, I need some fun after a hard day's work. C. 沒問題，熬了一天後，我需要開心一下。

|詳解| let's 表示「提議一起去做某事或去某地」的意思，但它沒有請客的意思，所以選項 A 不對。選項 B 中的 drunk 是指「喝醉」，還沒開始喝就說還沒醉，要再來一杯，不合邏輯，故不選。所以正確答案為選項 C。「after a hard day's work」表示「在辛苦工作的一天之後」。

Question number 5.

What you just said is unbelievable. 你剛剛說的話令人難以置信。

A. It's true though. A. 但都是真的。

B. Don't you think you expect too much? B. 你不覺得你期望太多了嗎？

C. I believe what you said. C. 我相信你所說的。

|詳解| 題目句的 unbelievable 是動詞 believe 的衍生字，意思是「難以置信的」，理解本題句意之後，可以知道選項 C 的回應不符也不合邏輯；選項 B 的 expect 指「期待」，「期望太多」跟對方說的話令人難以置信也完全不相關，故正確答案為選項 A。破題字是 true（真實）及 though（但是）。

Question number 6.

Wake up, Tony! The teacher is staring at you! 起來了，湯尼！老師正盯著你看！

A. Ah, I was caught cheating again. A. 啊，我作弊又被抓包了。

B. Sorry, I was so sleepy after lunch. B. 對不起，我吃完午餐後就好想睡。

C. I need a nap. Wake me up at six. C. 我需要小睡一下。六點叫醒我。

｜詳解｜ 聽到 wake up，可推知 Tony 在睡覺，但場景可能是家裡或別的地方，再聽到 teacher 就可推知一定是在教室。不知道 staring 的意思沒有關係，因為我們有足夠的資訊可找到答案。既然是在教室睡覺，而且老師發現了，選項 C 一定不對。選項 A 中的 cheating 是「作弊」之意，跟睡覺無關，所以也不符。故正確答案為選項 B。

｜補充｜ stare 是「盯著看」。吃完午餐後特別想睡覺，我們可以說 got food coma（coma 是「昏睡」）。get / be caught 是「被抓到」，後面加上動詞-ing 就代表做某事時被抓包，例如：He was caught stealing.（他偷東西被抓到。）

Question number 7.

I can't handle it. 我應付不來。

A. Good. Then just go ahead. A. 很好。那麼就繼續吧。

B. Just do your best. No pressure. B. 盡力就好。不要有壓力。

C. Try this on. You're going to be great in it. C. 試穿這件。你穿起來一定很好看。

｜詳解｜ 關鍵字是 can't 以及 handle，合在一起是指「無法處理」或「做不來」。注意否定的 can't 及肯定的 can 在發音上會有明顯不同，若聽成「I can handle it.」可能就會把選項 A 當作是答案了。題目說「我應付不來」，表示需要對方幫忙，而選項 C 的 try 要小心，因為 try something on 是「試穿」的意思，而不是「試著做做看」的意思，所以也不對。故正確答案為選項 B。即使不懂 pressure（壓力）這個字也沒關係，只要可以聽懂「do your best」就知道正確答案了。

｜補充｜ 「go ahead」後面也常與介系詞 with 連用，表示「繼續進行...」，例如：The rain has stopped, so we can go ahead with moving the huge stones.（雨停了，所以我們可以繼續移動這些大塊石頭了。

Part 3 簡短對話

Question number 8.

M: Good afternoon. Are there any messages for me? 男：午安，有給我的留言嗎？

W: Good afternoon. Miss White just called. And here is a package for you. 女：午安，懷特小姐剛剛來電。還有這是給你的包裹。

M: Thanks. By the way, did you e-mail the contract? 男：謝謝。嗯，對了，妳把合約寄出去了嗎？

W: I'll send it right away. 女：我馬上寄。

Question. Which of the following is true? 以下何者為真？

A. The woman didn't send the contract.	A. 女子沒有寄出合約。
B. Miss White sent a package.	B. 懷特小姐寄了一個包裹。
C. The man has received the contract.	C. 男子已收到合約。

| 詳解 | 整理三個選項後，可得知除了一男一女的對話者外，還有 Miss White，另外還牽涉到合約及包裹。這種「何者為真」的題型在聽對話時要特別的注意，因為每一句都可能是線索。選項 B 說 Miss White 寄來了一個東西，但其實她只是打電話來，package（包裹）是誰寄來的我們不清楚，所以選項 B 不對。選項 C 說男子已收到合約，但對話中的合約無論是要寄給客戶的，或是要先寄給主管（也許是男子）審閱，我們並不清楚，但可以肯定的是，合約尚未寄出，所以選項 C 也不對。故正確答案為選項 A。

Question number 9.

M: Good morning, ma'am.	男：早安，女士。
W: Good morning. Could you please drop me off at Taipower Station, Exit 2?	女：早安。能否請你載我到台電大樓捷運站的二號出口
M: No problem. Just get in, please.	男：沒問題。請上車。
W: Thanks. I'm in a bit of a hurry, so if you could take the fastest route, I'd really appreciate it.	女：謝謝。我有點趕時間。要是你可以開最快的路徑，我將不勝感激。

Question. What does the man probably do? 男人可能是做什麼的？

A. He's a mail carrier.	A. 他是個郵差。
B. He's a taxi driver.	B. 他是個計程車司機。
C. He's a ticket clerk.	C. 他是個票務員。

| 詳解 | 從選項可清楚了解，題目問的是男人的職業，而關鍵字詞是「drop sb. off at + 地方」（讓某人在某處下車）。選項 A 的「mail carrier」就是 postman（郵差）的意思，選項 C 的「ticket clerk」是「售票處人員」，也許是在火車站、捷運站或是電影院門口等的售票員，都可以稱作「ticket clek」，都與對話內容不符，以正確答案為選項 B。

| 補充 | take 這個動詞後面常接「交通工具」，表示「搭乘…（某種交通工具）」，也可以接「行進／行走的路線」，像是對話中的「take the fastest route」（走開最快的路徑），或是「take a shortcut」（走捷徑）、「take the paths between mountains」（走山路）、「take the overpass」（走天橋）。

Question number 10.

M: Jean, what a surprise to see you here! 男：珍，真驚訝在這裡遇到妳！

W: Hi, Jake. I'm on business. How are you? 女：嗨，傑克。我來這裡出差。你好嗎？

M: Couldn't be better. I'm getting married. 男：再好不過了。我就要結婚了。

W: Congratulations! No wonder you are all smiles. 女：恭喜啊！難怪你春風滿面！

Question. What is true about the woman? 關於女子，何者為真？

A. She is on a business trip. A. 她正在出差。

B. She's going to marry Jake. B. 她就要嫁給傑克。

C. She always smiles at Jake. C. 她總是對著傑克微笑。

| 詳解 | 從選項可知，題目要問的是與女子有關的事情，應特別注意女子說的話。本題破題點在第二句，女子說「I'm on business.」，所以答案已經呼之欲出，正確答案為選項A。下一句男子說「I'm getting married.」，所以選項 B 錯誤；最後女子對男子說「No wonder you are all smiles.」並非女子總是對著傑克微笑，所以選項 C 也錯誤。

| 補充 | 女子問傑克過得好嗎，傑克回答說「Couldn't be better.」，等同於「It couldn't be better.」，字面意思是「不能再好了」，也就是「再好也不過了」。一般來說還可以這麼回答：Same old same old.（還是老樣子。）、I'm doing fine.（過得不錯。）、Not bad.（還過得去。）或 是 Terrible!（糟透了！）

Question number 11.

M: Where were you last night? 男：妳昨天晚上去哪裡啦？

W: Joe and I went to see that French movie. It was so touching. 女：我跟喬去看了那部法國電影。真的太感人了。

M: Is it the *Children in Heaven*? 男：是不是《天堂的孩子》？

W: Exactly. We couldn't hold back tears. 女：沒錯。我們都忍不住掉淚了。

Question. How is the movie? 那是部怎樣的電影？

A. It is exciting for children. A. 它令孩子們興奮。

B. It is a romantic movie. B. 它是一部浪漫的電影。

C. It makes people feel moved. C. 它讓人感動。

| 詳解 | 本題要考的是形容詞的分辨。選項中的 it 就是對話中討論的電影。女子說這部電影很touching（感人的），這是答題關鍵所在，最後她再補充說「couldn't hold back tears（忍不住掉淚），當中的 tears（眼淚）就是確認答案的第二個破題字。所以正確答案是選項 C。

| 補充 | moved 是過去分詞當形容詞用，表示「感動的」，相當於 touched，用來修飾「人」的感受。如果要形容「事物」令人感動，則要用 moving 或 touching。例如：I am moved / touched by his great love.（我被他的大愛感動了。）

Question number 12.

M: Pray for me. I'm going to propose to Mary tonight.	男：為我祈禱吧。我今天晚上要跟瑪莉求婚。
W: Way to go, my friend! I will cross my fingers tight.	女：太棒了，我的朋友！我會用力為你祈禱。
M: But I'm feeling so nervous now!	男：但是我現在好緊張！
W: Don't stress too much. Just be sincere and everything will be fine.	女：別壓力太大。只要拿出誠意，一切都會是好的。

Question. Why is the man feeling nervous? 男子為什麼感到緊張？

A. His wife Mary has become seriously ill in hospital.	A. 他住院的太太瑪麗已病入膏肓。
B. He will propose a project to his boss the following day.	B. 他隔天要向老闆提出一項專案。
C. He doesn't know whether Mary will promise to marry him.	C. 他不知道瑪麗是否會答應嫁給他。

| 詳解 | 對話一開始男子說「I'm going to propose to Mary」，這裡的 propose 是「求婚」，而不是「提議」的意思，所以正確答案是選項 C。對話中雖然有 pray（祈禱，祈求）、「cross my fingers」（為你祈禱），但並非是為了誰生病住院。propose 如果當及物動詞，後面的受詞必然是「事物」（也可能以 Ving 呈現），這時才解釋成「提議」，例如選項 B 中的用法。

| 補充 | propose 當「提議，提出」解時，為及物動詞，後面接 Ving 和 to-V 分別有不同的意思。例如：He proposed taking a taxi to the airport.（他建議搭計程車去機場。）、He proposed to take a taxi to the airport.（他打算搭計程車去機場。）另外，「Way to go.」是常見的口語用法，意思是「太棒了；幹得好」。也可用完整的句子表達：That's the way to go! You did it!（太棒了，你做到了。）

Part 4 短文聽解

Question number 13.

Please look at the following three pictures. Listen to the following announcement. Where can you hear it?

請看以下三張圖片。聆聽以下廣播。你可以在哪裡聽到？

Attention passengers, the next train to Hualien will be late 10 minutes due to a sudden system failure. Please wait behind the yellow line until the train arrives. We are sorry for any inconvenience and your patience is appreciated.

乘客們請注意，由於系統突然故障，下一班到花蓮的列車將晚十分鐘進站。請於黃線後等候直到列車抵達。很抱歉造成您的不便，也謝謝您的耐心等候。

| 詳解 | 從圖中可推知是問「什麼地點」的問題。廣播中提到 next train（下一班列車）可以確定選項 A 不對。但火車跟捷運的英文都稱作 train，所以 B 跟 C 都有可能是正確答案。不過當聽到 next train to Hualien 就可以確定圖三的捷運月台不可能是答案，因為捷運不會開到花蓮，而花蓮本身也沒有蓋捷運。所以本題正確答案為選項 B。

Question number 14.

Please look at the following three pictures. Listen to the following short talk. Which picture matches the talk?

請看以下三張圖片。聆聽以下簡短談話。哪一張圖符合談話內容？

I bought a big cake for Dad's birthday. Dad likes chocolate and therefore I chose the one with a chocolate base and strawberries on top. I also lit three candles, which means "I love you."

我買了一個大蛋糕慶祝父親的生日。爸爸喜歡巧克力，所以我選了一個上面有草莓的巧克力蛋糕。我也點了三根蠟燭，代表「我愛你」。

| 詳解 | 看完三張圖，腦中要有以下幾個單字：cake（蛋糕）、strawberry（草莓）還有 candle（蠟燭），這樣就可以很快找出正確答案。簡短談話中說 choose the one with chocolate base and strawberries on top，也就是「巧克力蛋糕上有草莓」，另外 lit three candles 代表蛋糕插上三根蠟燭。所以本題正確答案為選項 A。

Day 07

月　　　日

我的完成時間＿＿＿＿分鐘
標準作答時間 10 分鐘

Part 1 看圖辨義

Questions 1-2

Part 2 問答

Questions 3-7

3. A. Don't forget I'm a Taiwanese.
   B. I never put it to use.
   C. It's too expensive to travel to Japan.

4. A. It's a present from my dad.
   B. Well, it's been long we haven't watch movies together.
   C. Oh, no! What's wrong with it?

5. A. Yes, I tried to calm down.
   B. No, I don't mind.
   C. I didn't. I apologize.

6. A. There must be something wrong with it.
   B. You're telling me.
   C. It's actually unhealthy.

7. A. No, it's not mine.
   B. Sit down, please.
   C. Yes, my friend will be back soon.

Part 3 簡短對話

Questions 8-12

8. A. There's not enough sunshine for her to enjoy sunbathing.
   B. Her skin would be darkened.
   C. She might pass out under the big sun.

9. A. He will call in sick.
   B. He will visit Dr. Jones.
   C. He will do exercise for more sweat.

10. A. He has invited the woman to a party.
    B. He asked the woman a math question.
    C. He has just been to Lee's home.

11. A. To confirm an interview
    B. To know if she's accepted
    C. To ask for a job interview

12. A. A famous artist the speakers admire
    B. The son of the man and the woman
    C. A popular student who's going to graduate

Part 4 短文聽解

Questions 13-14

13.

A

B

C

14.

A

B

C

上頁簡答

解答與詳解

1. (B) 2. (C) 3. (B) 4. (A) 5. (C) 6. (B) 7. (C) 8. (B) 9. (A) 10. (A) 11. (C) 12. (B) 13. (C) 14. (B)

Part 1 看圖辨義

For questions number 1-2, please look at the following pictures.

Question number 1.

Which of the following is correct? 哪一張圖是正確的？

A. Meal No.1 contains a drink, a hamburger and a salad.
A. 一號餐有一杯飲料、一個漢堡和一份沙拉。

B. Meal No.2 contains a salad, French fries and chicken nuggets.
B. 二號餐有一份沙拉、薯條和雞塊。

C. Meal No.3 contains a drink, a drumstick and French fries.
C. 三號餐有一杯飲料、一支棒腿和薯條。

| 詳解 | 本題考的是速食店食品，相當生活化也很實用，只要掌握了速食店的單字就能輕鬆作答，但如果有些食物的單字可能不了解或不太確定，可以暫且保留，先聽聽其他選項中可以抓住單字，當你確定這個選項有一個項目是錯誤的，就可以用消去法的方式找到答案。例如，即使你不懂 nugget（雞塊）這個字，但可以確定 1 號餐中是沒有 salad 的，以及 3 號餐沒有 French fries，所以選項 A、C 都不可選。答案為 B。

| 補充 | 常常去速食店的你，是否都認識每一樣食物的英文名稱？「hash browns」是「薯餅」，nuggets 是「雞塊」，「milk shake」是「奶昔」，sundae是「聖代」，「一號餐」是「Meal/Combo No.1」，「內用」是「for here / dine in」，「帶走」是「to go / take away」，「打包的紙袋」是 doggie bag。

Question number 2.

What does the woman with a microphone probably do?

拿著麥克風的女子可能是做什麼的？

A. She's a tour guide.
A. 她是一名導遊。

B. She's a photographer.
B. 她是一名攝影師。

C. She's a journalist.
C. 她是一名記者。

| 詳解 | 圖片中左邊有兩人看著畫展，顯然這是在畫廊或博物館內，女記者對著其一位男性的攝影師工作人員在報導畫展，所以正確答案是選項 C。

| 補充 | 「記者」的英文，最簡單的說法是 (news) reporter，而這裡的 journalist 是比較正式的說法，專指「新聞記者」，-ist 是一個「與人有關」的字尾，而 journal 本身是「雜誌」或「期刊」的意思，可以想見 journalist 的工作除了報導之外，還得寫成文字，刊登在平面或電子媒體上。

Part 2 問答

Question number 3.

How come you can't speak simple Japanese after learning it for 5 years?
你怎麼在學了五年日語後還不會說簡單的日文呢？

A. Don't forget I'm a Taiwanese. A. 別忘了我是台灣人耶。

B. I never put it to use. B. 我從來都沒實際用過。

C. It's too expensive to travel to Japan. C. 去日本旅遊太貴了。

｜詳解｜ 本題的三個選項乍看之下無法理解其關聯性，這時候當然就得仔細聽清楚題目這句話了！「How come...?」就等於 Why...?。對於學了很久的一種語言，仍不會開口說，可能的原因當然跟你是哪裡人，或是去哪旅遊很貴完全扯不上關係，所以正確答案為選項 B。

｜補充｜ 「put... to use」也可以說成「put... into practical use」，是指「活用／實際運用⋯」。

Question number 4.

Wow! Look at that diamond watch on your hand! 天呀，看看你手上那支鑽錶！

A. It's a present from my dad. A. 這是我爸爸送我的禮物。

B. Well, it's been long we haven't watch movies together. B. 嗯，我們好久沒一起看電影了。

C. Oh, no! What's wrong with it? C. 噢，不！它怎麼了？

｜詳解｜ 根據題目說話者的用詞 Wow! Look at... 及語氣，可知這是在表達第一次看到這支鑽石手錶的驚訝，既然是有讚嘆的意思，選項 C 的回答就不適當了；題目問的是名詞的 watch，選項 B 則刻意以當動詞的 watch 來混淆，也是完全不知所云的回應，故正確答案為選項 A。

Question number 5.

You tried to make me embarrassed, didn't you? 你想讓我出糗，不是嗎？

A. Yes, I tried to calm down. A. 是的，我試著冷靜下來。

B. No, I don't mind. B. 不，我不介意。

C. I didn't. I apologize. C. 我沒有，我跟你道歉。

｜詳解｜ 只要先確認 apologize（道歉）一字，再仔細聽題目，就很容易選出答案。但由於本題是個附加問句，而前二個選項都以 yes 或 no 作開始，考生很容易被誤導，覺得不是 A 就是 B，而先刪去選項 C，但選項 A 的 calm down（冷靜下來）跟選項 B 的 don't mind（不介意）都與題目語意不相符，所以正確答案為選項 C。

｜補充｜ embarrassed 是「尷尬的，出糗的」的意思，例如：I feel embarrassed when speaking in public.（我在大家面前說話時會感到尷尬。）He was in an embarrassing situation.（他處於很尷尬的情況。）選項 B 的 mind 是指「介意」，mind 後面一定接「動詞＋-ing」，例如：Would you mind speaking louder?（你可以說大聲一點嗎？）

Question number 6.

Smartphones are too popular nowadays. 如今智慧手機太普及了。

A. There must be something wrong with it. A. 這其中一定有問題。

B. You're telling me. B. 這還用你說。

C. It's actually unhealthy. C. 這真的是不健康。

| 詳解 | 從選項 A 字尾的 it、選項 C 開頭的 It's... 可推知考題在講一種東西或一種現象，而題目句開頭的 Smartphones 就告訴你是在講智慧型手機的普及，這是大家都知道的事，故正確答案為選項 B。「You're telling me.」是常見的口語，表示認同對方的說法，意思是「這還用你說。」

| 補充 | 「對啊！／正是！／沒錯！／當然！／真的！／的確！／那還用說！」這些都是我們在口語會話中常常聽到或用到的話語，可別只會說「Sure. ／Of course...」喔！類似回答用語，你也可以說：「No doubt! 毫無疑問！/ 無庸置疑！」、「You bet! 當然！/ 的確！」、「Tell me about it! 還用你說！/ 可不是嗎？」、「You tell me! 還用你說！/ 可不是嗎？」、「You can say that again! 我完全同意！」

Question number 7.

Excuse me. Is this seat taken? 不好意思，這位子有人坐嗎？

A. No, it's not mine. A. 不，這不是我的。

B. Sit down, please. B. 請坐下。

C. Yes, my friend will be back soon. C. 有的，我朋友待會就回來。

| 詳解 | 相信大家都聽過「Take a seat.」，這是請對方就座的意思，但對於「Is this seat taken?」這個疑問句，雖然每一個字都超簡單，但很容易一時之間聽不出來是什麼意思！這句話的情境可能在餐廳、電影院或交通工具上，所以選項 A 是明顯錯誤，因為公共場所的椅子或座位，本來就不是「我的」或誰的；選項 B 通常是用在教室的課堂上，或是公司面試等正式場合，而且如果是在餐廳，椅子是可以移走的，那麼說「Sit down, please.」就變得很奇怪了，所以正確答案為選項 C。

| 補充 | 詢問對方「這位子有人的嗎？／可以坐這嗎？／」還可以說：「Is this seat taken／available／free?」、「Is anyone sitting here?」、「May I share your table?」、「Are you using this chair?」、「Do you mind if I use／take this chair?」

Part 3 簡短對話

Question number 8.

M: What are you putting on your skin?
男：妳擦什麼東西在皮膚上啊？

W: The hot sun almost burned my skin. I'm wearing some sunblock.
女：大太陽都快把我的皮膚烤焦了。我在擦防曬乳。

M: Skin protection is crucial, especially on such a hot summer day.
男：皮膚的保護很重要，尤其是在這炎熱的夏季裡。

Question. What is the woman worried about? 女人在擔心什麼？

A. There's not enough sunshine for her to enjoy sunbathing.
A. 陽光不夠充足，無法讓她享受日光浴。

B. Her skin would be darkened.
B. 她的皮膚可能曬黑。

C. She might pass out under the big sun.
C. 她在大太陽底下可能會暈倒。

| 詳解 | 題目問的是女子在擔心何事，所以應特別注意女子說的話。她表示「The hot sun almost burned my skin. I'm wearing some sunblock.」重點還是在第一句，即使你聽不出 sunblock 是什麼，女子擔心的是大太陽幾乎要把她的皮膚烤焦了，所以正確答案是選項 B。動詞 darken（使變黑／暗）是 dark（黑暗的）的衍生字。選項 A 的 sunbathing 是「日光浴」，以及選項 C 的「pass out」是「昏倒」，都是對話中沒有提及的。

Question number 9.

W: Honey, why are you still in bed? I'll go get your briefcase ready.
女：親愛的，你為什麼還在床上？我去幫你準備好公事包。

M: Leave it there, dear. I'm feeling strange.
男：親愛的，放著吧。我不太舒服。

W: You're sweating. Let me call Dr. Jones right now.
女：你在流汗。我現在就打電話給瓊斯醫生。

Question. What might the man do next? 男人接著可能會做什麼事？

A. He will call in sick.
A. 他會打電話請病假。

B. He will visit Dr. Jones.
B. 他會拜訪瓊斯醫生。

C. He will do exercise for more sweat.
C. 他會去運動以流更多的汗。

| 詳解 | 由於三個選項都是關於男子將要做的事，所以務必留意男子所說的話，並推斷發生在他身上之事，例如：他生病了、他去看醫生。本題只要聽懂 call for Dr. Jones（打電話給瓊斯醫生），答案就應該出來了，正確答案為選項 A。選項 C 明顯錯誤，而選項 B 是個可能讓你去選的陷阱，因為生病可能會去看醫生，但「看醫生」的英文說法是「go see / consult a doctor」，不會用 visit 這個動詞。

| 補充 | 對話裡的男子說自己「feeling strange」，就是指「feeling sick / ill」（感到不舒服）。

而「打電話請病假」可以用「call in sick (to work)」或「call to ask for a sick leave」，而「請幾天假」可以說「take (a)... day(s) off」或「take a 數字-day leave」。例如：I took two days' sick leave last week because of the flu.（我上禮拜因為流感請了兩天的病假。）

Question number 10.

M: There's a party at Lee's this Saturday night. Are you in?
男：這個星期六在小李家有派對。你要去嗎？

W: Of course!
女：當然要去！

M: I heard they're going all out with the decorations and music this time.
男：我聽說他們這次非常用心在做裝飾和音樂。

W: That sounds fantastic! I'll make sure to bring my new dancing shoes.
女：聽起很棒！我一定會把我新的舞鞋帶去。

Question. What has the man just done? 男人剛剛做了何事？

A. He has invited the woman to a party. A. 他邀請女子去參加一場派對。

B. He asked the woman a math question. B. 他問了女子一個數學題目。

C. He has just been to Lee's home. C. 他剛剛去過小李家。

| 詳解 | 本題破題點是「Are you in?」（你要參加嗎？）考生應該能聽懂 party 這個字，選項 B 說他問了一個數學問題，跟對話內容不符。男人說 party 在小李家舉行，但沒有說他剛去過小李家，所以選項 C 也不對。故正確答案為選項 A。

| 補充 | Are you in? 的意思是「你要去嗎」或「你要參加嗎」。另外「Count me in.」是很道地的英文，意思是「算我一份。」如果外國人問你 Are you in?，你可以說 I'm in. 或 Count me in.。

Question number 11.

W: This is Jessie Jones. I'm calling for an interview.
女：我是潔西瓊斯。我打來是想安排面試。

M: Yes, Miss Jones. Can you come by tomorrow at 10:30?
男：好的，瓊斯小姐。明天早上十點半妳可以來嗎？

W: Sure, thanks a lot.
女：當然可以，謝謝你。

M: Miss Jones, please bring along your resume. See you tomorrow.
男：瓊斯小姐，請攜帶妳的個人履歷。明天見。

Question. Why is the woman calling? 女子為何來電？

A. To confirm an interview A. 為了確認一場面試

B. To know if she's accepted B. 為了知道是否有錄取

C. To ask for a job interview C. 為了要求工作面試

| 詳解 | 從選項來看，要選出一個做某事的目的，且應與面試有關。答題關鍵就在對話第一句：I'm calling for an interview.（我為了面試而打電話來。）也就是詢問是否有工作面試的機會，所以故正確答案為選項 C。另外，也可以從男子的回答「Can you come by tomorrow at 10:30?」以及「please bring along your resume」確定，女子打電話來並非詢問是否已錄取。至於選項 A 的「確認面試」的意思是之前已經和公司聯繫過，要再次確認面試的時間、地點等，與對話內容不符。

| 補充 | resume 或 CV（curriculum vitae）都是「個人履歷表」，interview 有「面試，訪問」之意，可以當名詞及動詞，例如：The reporter is interviewing a political figure.（記者正在訪問一名政治人物。）本句的 interview 即為動詞。

Question number 12.

M: What did you pick out for our Johnny's graduation?	男：妳幫我們強尼挑了什麼畢業禮物？
W: I chose a painting for him.	女：我選了一幅畫給他。
M: That's good. I bet he'll be glad to have something unique hung in his new place.	男：那很好。我想有了這獨特的東西掛在他新的住處，他會很開心。
W: I hope so. It's a piece by a famous artist that I know he admires.	女：但願如此。那是一幅他欣賞的知名藝術家的畫作。

Question. Who could be Johnny? 強尼可能是誰？

A. A famous artist the speakers admire	A. 說話者們仰慕的一位知名藝術家
B. The son of the man and the woman	B. 男子和女子的兒子
C. A popular student who's going to graduate	C. 一名即將畢業、很受歡迎的學生

| 詳解 | 題目要問的是 Johnny 的身分，選項中有「famous artist」、admire、graduate 都是對話內容中出現過的字眼，不過考題往往就是喜歡用對話中出現的字詞來混淆你答題，必須特別注意。我們從一開始男子說的「our Johnny's graduation」可知，對話的男女可能是夫妻，所以 Johnny 可能是他們的小孩，正確答案是選項 B。選項 C 的「student who's going to graduate」是正確的，但多了 popular 這個對話中沒有提到的字眼，所以也是錯誤選項。

| 補充 | 「pick out something for somebody」是「為某人挑選了某物」。graduation 指「畢業」，「畢業典禮」是「graduation ceremony」或 commencement。「畢業旅行」則是 excursion。

Part 4 短文聽解

Question number 13.

Please look at the following three pictures. Listen to the following short talk. Which is Peter's schedule?

請看以下三張圖片。聆聽以下簡短談話。哪一個是彼得的行程表？

Peter has a busy schedule today. In the morning at 9:30, he has to teach a conversation class. In the afternoon at 2, he needs to attend a meeting with the principal. As the meeting ends at round a quarter to 5, he has another class from 6 to 9.
彼得今天行程相當緊湊。早上九點半，他得要教授會話課。下午兩點，他需要跟校長開會。隨著會議大約在四點四十五分結束，他接著有另一個六點到九點的課程。

｜詳解｜ 本題考的是行程，在看完三張圖後，應該要歸納出「Peter 早上有課，下午有會議，晚上有課」，接下來再依照聽到的內容逐一對照，就可以得出正確答案。選項 A 早上的時間不對，所以不符。選項 B 晚上的時間及事項都不對，「a quarter to 5」應該是 4：45，而非 5：15，所以選項 B 也不對。故正確答案為選項 C。

Question number 14.

Please look at the following three pictures. Listen to the following short talk. Where does it take place?
請看以下三張圖片。聆聽以下簡短談話。這是在什麼地方？

Good morning. Welcome to the Taipei Art Exhibition. I'm your guide, Jennifer. Please follow me to the lobby. The whole tour takes about 50 minutes. We'll start from the works of a well-known Italian painter.
早安。歡迎來到台北藝術展。我是你們的導覽員，珍妮佛。請大家跟我到大廳。整個導覽行程約五十分鐘。我們將從一位舉世聞名的義大利畫家的作品開始介紹。

｜詳解｜ 看完三張圖後，腦中要浮現 museum（博物館）、exhibition（展覽）和 hotel lobby

（飯店大廳），只要想出其中一個，就已掌握一半的命中率。考生可能不知道 exhibition，但 museum 跟 lobby 一定熟悉，所以聽到 Art Exhibition 時，A 就可以刪除。接著雖然有 lobby 甚至 guide 等字，但最後出現的關鍵字 painter 畫家，可以讓考生確定對話不會出現在飯店，所以選項 C 不符。故正確答案為選項 B。the works 在此指「作品」，works 為名詞。

Day 08

月　　日

我的完成時間＿＿＿＿分鐘
標準作答時間 10 分鐘

Day_08.mp3

Part 1 看圖辨義

Questions 1-2

Part 2 問答

Questions 3-7

3. A. I'm not hungry. I can eat on the plane.
   B. Here comes the train. It's almost an hour late.
   C. I suggest everybody wait for the train and get on it safely.

4. A. How about vegetable soup? Are they ready?
   B. Thanks. Give me two orders then.
   C. What you said doesn't make sense.

5. A. You never stay up late.
   B. Well, it's up to you.
   C. You see, I just finished one-third of tomorrow's exam.

6. A. E-commerce and General Psychology. Both are easy to pass.
   B. The main course here is excellent.
   C. I signed up during the break.

7. A. Sorry. I'll do my best next time.
   B. There might be a misunderstanding between us.
   C. I promise I will be on time tomorrow.

Part 3 簡短對話

Questions 8-12

8. A. She's a single parent.
   B. She has just given birth to a baby.
   C. She has beautiful hands.

9. A. She's one of the man's classmates.
   B. She is friendly.
   C. She is popular among the boys.

10. A. A stepfather beat a kid badly and was caught by the police.
    B. A kid was seriously hurt by a baby-sitter.
    C. A babysitter was blamed for leaving a kid alone in the car.

11. A. She is ordering something.
    B. She is choosing a present.
    C. She is trying on clothes.

12. A. Dry the clothes and buy some food.
    B. Walk the dog and dry the clothes.
    C. Walk the dog and buy some food.

Part 4 短文聽解

Questions 13-14

13.

A

B

C

14.

A

B

C

上頁簡答

解答與詳解

1. (B) 2. (B) 3. (C) 4. (B) 5. (C) 6. (A) 7. (C) 8. (B) 9. (C) 10. (B) 11. (B) 12. (C) 13. (B) 14. (A)

Part 1 看圖辨義

For questions number 1-2, please look at the following pictures.

Question number 1.

What do people do there? 人們去那裡做什麼？

A. Get a haircut　　A. 剪頭髮

B. See a movie　　B. 看電影

C. Ask for some information　　C. 詢問一些資訊

| 詳解 | 圖中 theater（電影院）是破題點。那是一張電影海報，所以人們去電影院當然是要看電影了，正確答案為選項 B。

| 補充 | 除了 theater 之外，「電影院」還有 cinema 這個英檢中級的單字，也很常出現在日常對話中。另外，theatre 是「英式英語」的說法，類似情況的還有「center → centre（中心）」、「meter → metre（公尺）」、「fiber → fibre（纖維）」、「luster → lustre（光澤）」…等。

Question number 2.

What are the things David is going to take for a picnic?
大衛將帶去野餐的是那些東西？

A. Some snacks, rollerblades, a blanket and a saucer　　A. 一些點心，直排輪，一條毛毯和一個盤子

B. Some Coke and a sandwich, rollerblades, and a frisbee　　B. 一些可樂和一份三明治，直排輪和飛盤

C. Some coke and a sandwich, rollerblades, and a blanket　　C. 一些可樂和一份三明治，直排輪和一條毛毯

| 詳解 | 看到本題的圖，要快速地把每樣東西用英文思考一遍：「籃子」是 basket，「可樂」是 coke，但選項中也可能是 drinks、soft drinks 等；「三明治」是 sandwich，「直排輪」是 rollerblades，如果不知道也沒關係，因為三個選項都有這個字；「飛盤」是 frisbee。當聽到圖中沒有的東西，就可以直接把選項刪除。比方說，選項 A 一開始出現的 snacks（零食）就是這種情況，所以選項 A 不符。而選項 C 中的初級單字 blanket 也是圖片中沒有的，故不可選。所以本題正確答案為選項 B。

Part 2 問答

Question number 3.

There's some twenty minutes before the train comes. Should we get something to eat? 距離火車到站還有二十幾分鐘。我們要不要買點吃的？

A. I'm not hungry. I can eat on the plane. A. 我不餓。我可以在飛機上吃。

B. Here comes the train. It's almost an hour late. B. 火車來了。它誤點快一小時了。

C. I suggest everybody wait for the train and get on it safely. C. 我建議所有人等到火車來，然後安全上車。

| 詳解 | 選項提供的提示有：飛機、火車、火車誤點。不用記 hungry（餓的）、eat（吃）的部分，因為關於飛機的只有一個選項，如果題目跟坐飛機有關，答案一定是它。當聽到 train 時，考生的選擇只剩下選項 B 跟 C。接著聽到 Should we ... eat?，就可確認答案是選項 C。如果能掌握到 some twenty minutes before the train comes（火車到站前還有二十多分鐘），就知道跟誤點完全沒有關係，所以選項 B 不對。故本題正確答為選項 C。

| 補充 | 選項 B 中「Here comes...」句型，意思是「…來了」或「…在這」，例如：Here is your receipt.（這是你的收據。）、Here are my parents.（我父母來了。）如果用代名詞，請記住代名詞所擺放的位置，例如：Here is your receipt. = Here it is. 或是 Here are my parents. = Here they are.。

Question number 4.

Sir, today's special is roasted chicken and pumpkin soup.
先生，今日特餐是烤雞和南瓜湯。

A. How about vegetable soup? Are they ready? A. 那麼蔬菜湯呢？都準備好了嗎？

B. Thanks. Give me two orders then. B. 謝謝，那麼就給我兩份。

C. What you said doesn't make sense. C. 你說的都沒道理。

| 詳解 | 選項 A 跟 B 明顯告知考生題目跟點餐有關，如果題目跟點餐主題完全無關，那麼答案應該就是選項 C。題目中出現 chicken（雞）跟 soup（湯），所以考生可以確定答案非 A 即 B。關鍵字詞「today's special」（今日特餐）意味著說話者是跟客人介紹餐點，所以正確答案為選項 B。

| 補充 | 「today's special」通常指「餐廳當天的推薦菜色或精選優惠菜餚」。選項 C 的「make sense」指「合理，符合常理」。

Question number 5.

David, why aren't you in bed yet? 大衛，你怎麼還沒睡覺？

A. You never stay up late. A. 你從來不會熬夜。

B. Well, it's up to you. B. 嗯，隨便你。

C. You see, I just finished one-third of tomorrow's exam. C. 你看，明天的考試我才讀了三分之一。

| 詳解 | 本題要考的是 up 當「醒著的（= awake）」的意思。三個選項中，A 跟 C 有微妙的關連，即「熬夜跟考試」。stay up 這個片語考生不會陌生，破題字是 still（仍然）。當問到「為什麼還沒睡覺」，選項 A 卻以 You 開頭，說「你從來不會（never）熬夜」，完全是不知所云的回答。題目問 why，比較選項 B 跟 C，後者帶出原因「just finished one-third of exam」（才讀完三分之一），所以正確答案為選項 C。

| 補充 | 除了「in bed」、「go to bed」之外，表示「去睡覺」還可以說「hit the hay / sack / pillow」、「turn in」、「catch some Z's」（這是一個輕鬆的口語表達方式，「Z's」是指睡眠時發出的打鼾聲。）

Question number 6.

What courses did you sign up for this semester? 你這學期選了什麼課？

A. E-commerce and General Psychology. Both are easy to pass. A. 電子商務跟大眾心理學，都是很好過關的。

B. The main course here is excellent. B. 這裡的主菜非常棒。

C. I signed up during the break. C. 我在下課休息時選課的。

| 詳解 | 選項的提示可整理為：談學校科目、談餐廳菜色、下課休息時去登記。聽到「What course ... sign up」時，我們可以先刪除選項 C，因為選項 C 的對應問題應該是「When did you ...」（何時⋯），所以選項 C 錯誤。選項 B 的 course 是故意誤導考生，這裡的 course 是指「菜色」，main course 是「主菜」，所以當聽到 semester（學期），就知道選項 B 不對。故正確答案為選項 A。

| 補充 | semester 是「學期」，也可以用 term 這個字。選項 C 的 break 指「下課休息時間」，在辦公室裡會有「coffee / tea break」，就是下午三點到四點間喝咖啡休息的時間。另外 recess 也指「短暫的休息時間」，議會的休會期或法院的休庭期，都可稱為 recess。在學校裡，一天課程中的中間休息時間（約十到十五分鐘）也可以叫 recess。

Question number 7.

This is the third time in a week you showed up late.
這已經是你這一個星期第三次遲到了。

A. Sorry. I'll do my best next time. A. 抱歉。我下次會盡力。

B. There might be a misunderstanding between us. B. 我們之間可能有誤會。

C. I promise I will be on time tomorrow. C. 我承諾我明天會準時。

| 詳解 | 本題三個選項沒有任何關連，建議考生理解重點就好：do my best（做到最好）、misunderstanding（誤會）、will be on time（會準時）。題目的重點在「show up late」，可以直接把 late 對應 on time，就能找出答案。因為是「the third time in a week」（這星期的第三次遲到），所以「promise... will be on time」（承諾會準時），正確答案為選項 C。

| 補充 | show up 是指「出現，現身」，例如：Show yourself (up).（你出來吧。）on time = punctual（準時的），例如：The train is never punctual. = The train is never on time.（火車不曾準時。）選項 A 的 promise 是「答應，承諾」，名詞也是 promise，make a promise 就是「做出承諾」。

Part 3 簡短對話

Question number 8.

M: How's my wife? 男：我太太怎麼樣了？

W: Congratulations. Both your wife and newborn daughter are safe. 女：恭喜。母女均安。

M: Many thanks, Dr. Wang. Can I go see my wife now? 男：非常感謝，王醫師，我現在可以去看我太太嗎？

W: She's tired now and needs a good rest. Don't worry. She'll be in good hands. 女：她現在很累，需要好休息一下。不用擔心，我們會好好照顧她的。

Question. What is true about the man's wife? 關於男子的太太，何者為真？

A. She's a single parent. A. 她是個單親媽媽。

B. She has just given birth to a baby. B. 她剛產下一個寶寶。

C. She has beautiful hands. C. 她的手很漂亮。

| 詳解 | 從三個選項可以推知題目問的是關於一個女子的事。不過要聽清楚問的是哪一個女子，可不一定是對話中的女子喔！聽出題目的「the man's wife」應該不是問題，所以選項 A 的「single parent」可以直接刪除了（男子第一句就問「How's my wife?」）；關鍵字詞是第二句，女醫師說的「Both your wife and newborn daughter are safe.」，可推知男子的太太剛生下一個女寶寶，所以正確答案是選項 B；另外，對話中最後一句「She'll be in good hands.」指的是產婦將會受到醫院很好的照顧，而不是手很漂亮，選項 C 也是錯誤的答案。

| 詳解 | be in good hands = be taken good care of = be looked after（獲得仔細的照料）。在生命過程中，很多時候我們必須把自己交託在某人手中，譬如生病的時候或決定嫁給某人的時候，自己是否「be in good hands」真的很重要呢！

Question number 9.

M: I want to ask Eliza out. What should I do? 男：我想約伊莉莎出去。我應該怎麼做？

W: Which Eliza? The blonde Eliza in my class? 女：哪一個伊莉莎？我班上那個金髮的伊莉莎嗎？

M: Bingo! What are my chances of dating her? 男：答對了，我跟她約會的機會有多少？

W: Not on your life! 女：下輩子吧！

Question. What can we know about Eliza? 關於伊莉莎，我們可以知道什麼？

A. She's one of the man's classmates. A. 她是男子的一位同學。

B. She is friendly. B. 她很友善。

C. She is popular among the boys. C. 她很受男孩們歡迎。

| 詳解 | 就選項內容來看，要注意對話中女性說話者的內容或被提到的女人。女子問「The blonde Eliza in my class?」然後男子回答說「Bingo!」，這表示 Eliza 並非男子的同學，選項 A 錯誤；選項 B 是對話中沒有提到的，所以不可選；最後男子又問他可以成功地約到 Eliza 的機會有多少，女子卻回答「Not on your life! 」也就是這輩子不可能，機會渺茫，所以可以推知正確答案是選項 C。

| 補充 | 對話中男子提到要「ask... out」。如果第一次成功約了對方出去，而且感覺不錯，那麼下一次就不是「ask her out」了，而是「date her」（跟她約會）了。blonde 是指「白膚金髮的」，blonde Eliza 就是「有一頭金髮的伊莉莎」

Question number 10.

M: What's the headline in today's paper? 男：今天報紙的頭條是什麼？

W: "Child Abused by Babysitter." 女：「小孩被保母凌虐」。

M: That's terrible. How's the baby now? 男：真恐怖啊！小孩現在還好嗎？

W: There're wounds on his whole body. And the babysitter has been arrested. 女：他全身都有傷口。且保姆已經被逮捕了。

Question. What are the speakers talking about? 說話者們在談論什麼？

A. A stepfather beat a kid badly and was caught by the police. A. 繼父把小孩打得很慘且已遭警方逮捕。

B. A kid was seriously hurt by a babysitter. B. 一個小孩被保姆嚴重傷害。

C. A babysitter was blamed for leaving a kid alone in the car. C. 一位保姆因獨留小孩在車子裡而受到責備。

| 詳解 | 從本題三個選項來看，對話內容肯定與保姆、小孩、照顧不當等有關，只要仔細聽取相關字詞即可。內容雖然有提到傷害小孩、被警方逮捕，但完全沒提到 stepfather，所以選項 A 錯誤；即使聽不懂 abuse 這個動詞，但最後提到保姆被警方逮捕，且小孩全身傷口，兩者連結在一起，可以推斷正確答案是選項 B；至於 C 的「leaving a kid

alone in the car」也是對話中沒有提到的。

|補充| abuse 可以當動詞和名詞，但兩者發音有點差異。當動詞時發 [ə`bjuz]，當名詞時唸成 [ə`bjus]。當動詞時，為及物動詞，後面的受詞如果是「人」，表示「凌虐，虐待」，受詞如果是「事物」，例如「藥物」、「權力」…等，則表示「濫用」。

Question number 11.

W: How about these? 女：這些怎麼樣？

M: These are all 30% off and we've got a lot of colors. 男：這些都打七折，而且我們有很多顏色。

W: Great. I want a purple one and please wrap it up for me. 女：太好了，我要一個紫色的，麻煩幫我包起來。

M: Sure, would you like a gift box for it? 男：當然，你要用禮盒裝起來嗎？

Question. What is the woman doing? 女人正在做什麼？

A. She is ordering something. A. 她在點東西。

B. She is choosing a present. B. 她在挑選禮物。

C. She is trying on clothes. C. 她在試穿衣服。

|詳解| 三個選項都在講關於 she，且都用現在進行式，所以要注意女性說話者的內容以及可能在做的動作。本題破題字為 wrap（包裝），如果聽不出這個字的意思，至少男子最後說的「gift box」（禮盒）要聽得出來，所以不是在點菜或試穿衣服，正確答案為選項 B。

|補充| 男店員說「we got a lot of colors」（我們有很多顏色），其實就是「we got a lot of colors you can choose from」（我們有很多顏色讓你選），也可以把它寫成「you can choose from a lot of colors」。

Question number 12.

M: Would you take Michael for a walk for me tonight, darling? 男：親愛的，今天晚上可以幫我帶小麥去散步嗎？

W: Sure, after I dry the clothes. 女：沒問題，先等我把衣服烘乾。

M: I can dry them for you so you can go and buy some food on the way home. 男：我可以幫妳烘乾衣服，那麼妳就可以去蹓狗順便在回家路上買些吃的回來。

W: That would be wonderful! Thank you, dear. 女：那很好！謝謝你，親愛的。

Question. What is the woman going to do? 女子即將去做何事？

A. Dry the clothes and buy some food. A. 烘乾衣服和買些食物。

B. Walk the dog and dry the clothes. B. 蹓狗和烘乾衣服。

C. Walk the dog and buy some food. C. 蹓狗和買些食物。

| 詳解 | 本題的選項有很多資訊，要馬上整理並不容易，但大概可推測對話內容可能會出現三件事：烘乾衣服（dry the clothes）、買些食物（buy some food）、蹓狗（walk the dog），所以要仔細聽對話中的人是否做了這些事件，或各自負責某些事情。就算考生只聽到最後一句 you can go and buy some food on the way home（妳可以去蹓狗順便在回家的路上買些吃的），也可以推出答案，此句代表女子將外出並且買東西，所以正確答案為選項 C。

| 補充 | 「on the way home 是慣用語，指「在回家的路上」。同樣的，「on the way to school」則是「在上學的途中」。注意 home 這個字可以當「地方副詞」，所以前面不需要再加介系詞了。

Part 4 短文聽解

Question number 13.

Please look at the following three pictures. Listen to the following short talk. Which is Katy?

請看以下三張圖片。聆聽以下簡短談話。哪一位是 Katy？

My best friend Katy is a lovely girl. She has big eyes and wears long, wavy hair. We have similar styles. We both love jeans and T-shirts. We love sports more than shopping.

我最好的朋友凱蒂是個很可愛的女孩子。她有雙大眼睛，留有又長又波浪捲的頭髮。我們的穿衣風格很類似。我們都喜歡牛仔褲跟 T 恤。我們比較愛運動多於逛街。

A

B

C

| 詳解 | 短文中說女生 wears long, wavy hair（留有長而直的頭髮），選項 A 的人是直髮，明顯不符；wavy 是 wave（波浪）的形容詞，表示「波浪狀的」，即使聽不出來這個字，也可確定它不是「直的」意思，一樣可以先將選項 A 剔除。。注意此句用的動詞是 wear，關於人的頭髮，我們可以用 have，也可以用 wear，但意思有點不太一樣，have 單純的表示「擁有」甚麼樣子的頭髮，而 wear 則是「刻意留成、做成」什麼樣的髮型。選項 C 的女生愛購物，但短文中說「love sports more than shopping」（愛運動多於逛街），所以選項 C 不符。且可以用穿衣風格來確認，因為凱蒂喜歡「jeans and T shirts」（牛仔褲跟 T 恤），所以本題正確答案為選項 B。

| 補充 | 「髮型（hairstyle）」可以說是人的「第二張臉」，選對髮型就能為整體裝扮大加分，常見與髮型有關的英文詞彙有：bob（齊短髮）、wavy hair（波浪捲髮）、curly hair（捲髮）、bangs / frings（劉海）、side-swept bangs（斜劉海）、straight hair（直髮）、perm（燙髮）、make one’s hair layered（剪層次）…等。

Question number 14.

Please look at the following three pictures. Listen to the following short talk. Who might Jack visit today?

請看以下三張圖片。聆聽以下簡短談話。傑克今天可能拜訪誰？

Jack is working on his final report. He spent days searching on the Internet and in the library. However, he needs more practical advice. To get this, he's going to see Professor John Lee today.

傑克正努力做他的期末報告。他花了好幾天在網路上及圖書館裡找資料。不過，他需要更實際的建議。為了獲得建議，他今天打算去見李約翰教授。

詳解 選項 A 給人的訊息是「talk with a teacher / professor」。選項 B 的訊息則是「seek help from a librarian」。至於選項 C 則有可能是「chat with a friend」。短文中主角 Jack 雖然因為要寫報告（report）而在圖書館（library）找資料，但問題是「他今天可能去拜訪誰」，所以不用考慮選項 B。儘管選項 C 不一定是在聊天，也有可能是在輕鬆的討論，但 John Lee 是男生的名字，所以答案一定是選項 A。

Day 09

月　　日

我的完成時間＿＿＿分鐘
標準作答時間 10 分鐘

Part 1 看圖辨義

Questions 1-2

Part 2 問答

Questions 3-7

3. A. You are truly my best friend.
   B. Only you can decide your life.
   C. Good, you finally made up your mind.

4. A. I am glad you said that.
   B. I'm having a new date.
   C. Don't make me wait so long next time.

5. A. I didn't see your ring. Is it stolen?
   B. OK, I'll call you on your cellphone.
   C. No problem. I'll drive you home.

6. A. What's the password to log in to the system?
   B. Do not enter the office after 9:00 p.m.
   C. We should call the police right away.

7. A. By keeping them away from work
   B. By creating a nice working environment
   C. By giving them a call twice a day

Part 3 簡短對話

Questions 8-12

8. A. Get some sleep
   B. Chat with the woman
   C. Keep surfing the Net

9. A. He shouldn't expect too much.
   B. He should have chosen a better restaurant.
   C. He should have suggested the food stall to his boss.

10. A. Lending him her computer
    B. Paying for his new computer
    C. Going with him to buy a new computer

11. A. He thinks himself to be too fat.
    B. He looks thin and tall.
    C. He has a strong will.

12. A. She took him to a yoga class.
    B. She came home with a birthday present.
    C. She ignored the man's birthday.

Part 4 短文聽解

Questions 13-14

13.

A

B

C

14.

A

B

C

上頁簡答

解答與詳解

1. (A) 2. (C) 3. (A) 4. (B) 5. (B) 6. (C) 7. (B) 8. (C) 9. (A) 10. (C) 11. (A) 12. (B) 13. (B) 14. (A)

Part 1 看圖辨義

For questions number 1-2, please look at the following pictures.

Question number 1.

What is true about the picture? 關於這張圖，何者為真？

A. The man was given a ticket for making a wrong right turn. A. 男子因違規右轉而被開罰單。

B. The policeman gave the man an alcohol test. B. 警察給男子進行了酒測。

C. There was a traffic accident and a policeman came to deal with it. C. 發生了一場交通事故，而一名警員到場處理。

| 詳解 | 看完圖片後可以先設想會出現的一些字詞：policeman（警察）、fine（罰款）、ticket（罰單）、not allowed to make a right turn（不允許右轉）、show one's ID/driver's license...等。根據這些資料，可知選項 B 的「alcohol test」不符，而圖片中的車子看不出來是發生交通事故，所以選項 C 也錯誤。故正確答案為選項 A。wrongful 是從 wrong 衍生出的形容詞，可以表示「不正當的，違法的」。

Question number 2.

What are the men doing? 這些人在做什麼？

A. They are hiking in the mountains. A. 他們正在山區健行。

B. They are having a running race. B. 他們正在賽跑。

C. They are jogging pleasantly. C. 他們正愉快地慢跑。

| 詳解 | 從圖中考生可知男人在公園裡跑步，所以選項 A 說在山區就與圖不符。比較有可能的是選項 B 跟 C。而就圖的表現來看，裡面的男人看起來像是在悠閒的慢跑，而非拼命地賽跑，故選項 C 比選項 B 更合適。

| 補充 | 本題考的是對於運動類單字的認識，其他相關字彙還有：biking 騎單車、camping 露營、mountain climbing 爬山、rock climbing 攀岩、skiing 滑雪、grass skiing 滑草、scuba diving 潛水、sky-diving 跳傘、swimming 游泳、surfing 衝浪、skating 溜冰、skateboarding 滑板、kayaking 皮划艇、canoeing 划船、sowing 划艇、cycling 騎自行車、paragliding 滑翔傘飛行、bungee jumping 高空彈跳...。

Part 2 問答

Question number 3.

Whatever decision you make, you have all my support.
不管你做什麼決定，我都全力支持你。

A. You are truly my best friend. A. 你真是我最要好的朋友。
B. Only you can decide your life. B. 只有你能決定自己的人生。
C. Good, I finally made up my mind. C. 很好，我終於決定了。

| 詳解 | 本題關鍵在於對於題目後半句「you have all my support」的適當回應。當對方跟你說「我全力支持你」時，你卻以選項 B 的「只有你能決定自己的人生」或是選項 C 的「很好，我終於決定了。」都是不知所云、毫無邏輯的回答，所以正確答案是選項 A 的「你真是我最要好的朋友。」這種回以感激的話。

| 補充 | 「have all my support」也可以說成「put my full weight behind somebody」或「be at somebody's side」（支持某人）。這裡的「full weight」不是「全部的體重」，而是「全部的力量」，把自己的力量作為別人的後盾，意思就是「全力相挺」。「下決定」或「做決定」，英文習慣說法是「make a decision」。選項中還有一個常用的片語「make up your mind」是「下定決心」的意思。

Question number 4.

It's rare to see you hang out so late. 很少看你在外面玩得這麼晚。

A. I am glad you said that. A. 我很高興你那樣說。
B. I'm having a new date. B. 我有新的約會對象。
C. Don't make me wait so long next time. C. 下次別再讓我等這麼久了。

| 詳解 | hang out 指「在外面玩，鬼混」，跟朋友出去我們可以說「hang out with friends」。既然是跟外出有關，只有選項 B 的「having a new date」（有新的約會）跟「外出，在外面」有關係。所以本題正確答案為選項 B。

| 補充 | 本題的句型是「It is + 形容詞 + to-V」，這裡的不定詞（to-V）是所謂「真主詞」，而句首的 It 是「虛主詞」，所以形容詞是「主詞補語」，用來修飾後面的 to-V 這個真主詞。例如：It is pleasant to have you by my side.（很高興有你在身旁。）

Question number 5.

Give me a ring when you are home. 你到家時打個電話給我。

A. I didn't see your ring. Is it stolen? A. 我沒有看見你的戒指。它被偷了嗎？
B. OK, I'll call you on your cellphone. B. 好的，我會打手機給你。
C. No problem. I'll drive you home. C. 沒問題，我會開車送你回家。

| 詳解 | 「give somebody a ring」並不是給某人戒指，而是打電話給某人的意思，這時候的 ring 可以用 call 取代。選項 A 刻意以 ring 當「戒指」解來造成讓考生混淆的句子。選項 C 刻意以相同的 home 混淆答題，但也是一個不知所云的回答。所以正確答案為選項 B。

| 補充 | 「打電話給某人」，最簡單、直接的說法就是「call + 人」，如果要表達透過手機、市話還是其他通訊軟體等，就加一個介系詞 on，例如「Please call me on LINE.」（請打 LINE 電話給我。）如果要表示撥打一個電話號碼，可以用 at，例如：Call / Contact use at 0800-xxx...（撥打 0800-xxx... 與我們聯繫。）但要注意的是，「打我手機」千萬別說成「Call my cellphone.」了。

Question number 6.

Somebody entered our office and logged in to the system.

有人進入了我們的辦公室然後登入了系統。

A. What's the password to log in to the system? A. 登入系統的密碼是什麼？

B. Do not enter the office after 9:00 p.m. B. 晚上九點過後不可以進入辦公室。

C. We should call the police right away. C. 我們應該馬上報警。

| 詳解 | 選項中有「password to log in to the system」、「enter the office」、「call the police」，可以推知題目可能與「steal into the office and illegally enter into the system」（溜進辦公室並違法進入系統）有關，且說話者認為這個 somebody 做了一件非法的事情，所以正確答案為選項 C。

| 補充 | 「log in/on to」一般用在電腦、網路系統、網頁方面的「登入」，也可以用「sign in」。而 access 指「進入」或「存取」，當名詞時後面需加 to，例如：The only access to this building is the back door.（唯一能進入這棟大樓的地方是後門。）You access to the system is denied.（您已被拒絕進入本系統。）

Question number 7.

How do you keep your employees active and positive?

你如何讓你的員工們保持主動積極？

A. By keeping them away from work A. 讓他們遠離工作。

B. By creating a nice working environment B. 創造愉快的工作環境。

C. By giving them a call twice a day C. 每天跟他們通兩次電話。

| 詳解 | A 跟 B 兩個選項跟工作（work）有關，要注意「working environment」一詞，指「工作環境」。題目問要如何讓員工（employees）保持有主動積極（active and positive），選項 A 叫他們不用工作（keep them away from）顯然不適合，老闆打電話給他們也不是一個適切的做法，所以選項 C 也不對。選項 B 的「nice working environment」是正面的詞彙，除了呼應「active and positive」，我們可以理解為「好的工作情緒，好的工作條件，好的工作狀況」，不管那一個都符合題目。所以本題正確答案是選項 B。

｜補充｜ 選項 A 的 keep 這個字很好用，它本身是「保持」的意思，也有「保存」之意。這裡的「keep away from」是「讓…遠離」。另外，「keep something secret」是「保密」。「keep the room tidy」是「保持這個房間整潔」。

Part 3 簡短對話

Question number 8.

W: You've been surfing the net for four hours. Don't you have any other things to do? 女：你已經掛在網上四小時了。你沒有別的事情可以做嗎？

M: Suggest something. I'll be really thankful. 男：給我些提議啊。我會很感謝妳。

W: Like reading or chatting. 女：比如說看書或聊天。

M: I can do that on the Internet! 男：我可以在網路上做那些事啊！

Question. What might the man do next? 男子接下來可能會做什麼？

A. Get some sleep A. 去睡覺

B. Chat with the woman B. 跟女子聊天

C. Keep surfing the Net C. 繼續上網

｜詳解｜ 三個選項都是與「做什麼事」有關，包括睡覺、上網、聊天。對話中出現的行為有「surfing the net」（上網），reading（閱讀）以及 chatting（聊天）。破題點為男人說「I can do that on the Internet!」（我可以在網路上做那些事啊！）那些事是指女人說的 reading 跟 chatting，所以他還是會繼續上網。故本題正確答案為選項 C。

｜詳解｜ 常聽到「上網」的英文說法主要有「go online」以及「surf the Net/Internet」，注意這裡的 Net 和 Internet 都要大寫。例如：I'll go online later to take a look at what's new there.（我等會兒上網看看有什麼新的消息。）Nowadays people tend to surf the Net on their cellphones to kill time once they have nothing to do.（現在大家沒事做的時候都傾向於滑手機打發時間。）

Question number 9.

W: How was the dinner with your boss last night? 女：昨晚和老闆吃晚餐如何？

M: Awful, I'd rather eat at the food stall downstairs. 男：糟透了，我寧可到樓下的小吃店吃。

W: What did you expect for a $100 meal? 女：你對於一餐 100 塊的能期待什麼？

Question. What does the woman want to tell the man? 女子想告訴男子什麼？

A. He shouldn't expect too much. A. 他不應期待太多。

B. He should have chosen a better restaurant. B. 他應該選一家比較好的餐廳。

C. He should have suggested the food stall to his boss. C. 他應該建議他老闆去吃那家小吃攤。

| 詳解 | 從選項 B、C 的內容可推測對話應與吃東西有關，且是 restaurant（餐廳）及 food stall（小吃店）的選擇比較。男子說「I'd rather eat at the food stall」（我寧願吃小吃攤），第一個破題字就在 would rather，指「寧願」。女子接著說「what did you expect」（你要期待什麼），因為只是一頓 100 元的晚餐，所以不應期待會有多豐盛或美味，expect 為第二個破題字。故本題正確答案為選項 A。

| 補充 | 男子說「I'd rather (= I would rather)...」（我寧願...）後面要接原形動詞，因為前面有 would 這個助動詞；另外一個表示「寧願」的動詞是 prefer，但後面要接不定詞或動名詞。例如這裡的「I'd rather eat at the food stall downstairs. 」=「I prefer to eat at the food stall downstairs.」。在選項 C 的「suggested the food stall to his boss」當中，suggest 有一個比較罕見的「授予動詞」用法，也可以說成「He should have suggested his boss the food stall.」

Question number 10.

W: Looks like you need a new computer.	女：看來你好像需要一台新電腦。
M: You bet. I'm looking for a cheap but good one. It would be a great help if you go along with me.	男：沒錯。我正在找一台物美價廉的。如果妳跟我一起去，可以幫我一個大忙。
W: OK. Let's start by checking out some options online and comparing prices and specs.	女：好的。我們先上網查看一些選擇並比較價錢與規格吧。

Question. What's does man want the woman to help him with?
男子想要女子幫他什麼？

A. Lending him her computer	A. 把她的電腦借他用
B. Paying for his new computer	B. 為他支付新電腦的費用
C. Going with him to buy a new computer	C. 跟他一起去買新電腦

| 詳解 | 對話中男子說的「You bet.」是會話中常聽到，表示同意對方的說法，白話的意思是「你說的沒錯。」既然認同女子所說應該去買新的電腦，則選項 A 不對。男子又說「It would be great help if you go along with me.」（如果你跟我一起去，會是幫我很大的忙），所以正確答案為選項 C。男子並沒有要女子買給他，所以選項 B 錯誤。

Question number 11.

M: Jimmy lost 10kg within a month. How did he do that?	男：吉米一個月內瘦了十公斤。他怎麼做到的？
W: Eat less and exercise more, but most important of all, will power.	女：少吃多運動，不過最重要的是，意志力。
M: I'll start to make a diet plan today.	男：我今天就開始訂定節食計畫。

Question. What can be true about the man? 關於男子，何者可能為真？

A. He thinks himself to be too fat. A. 他認為自己太胖了。

B. He looks thin and tall. B. 他看起來瘦瘦高高的。

C. He has a strong will. C. 他意志堅定。

| 詳解 | 三個選項都是關於男說話者，且描述他的外表是 fat（胖的），thin and tall（瘦瘦高高的）及內在 strong will（意志堅定）。而本題破題點為男子最後一句「start to make a diet plan」（開始訂定節食計畫），既然男子要減肥，可見他本身並不瘦，所以選項 B 不符。至於他意志力是堅強還是薄弱，我們無從得知，而女子說的「most important of all, will power」（最重要的是，意志力）只是在提醒他減肥需要意志力，同時也暗指 Jimmy 是有意志力的，而非對話中的男子，故選項 C 錯誤。所以本題正確答案為選項 A。

| 補充 | 要說別人瘦了幾公斤，我們會說「lost + 數字 + kg」，因為已經瘦了，所以要用 lose 的過去式 lost 來表達。由此可知，「減肥」是「lose weight」，而「增肥」則是「gain weight」。女人說 most important of all，most important 是用最高級，表示最重要之意，加上 of all 是指全部裡面最重要的，也就是 will（意志力）。

Question number 12.

M: Where have you been all day? 男：妳整天去哪裡了？

W: I went to yoga class this morning, then went to the bookstore after lunch, and bought you a present for your birthday. Happy Birthday, dear! 女：我早上去上瑜伽課，午餐後去了書店，然後就買了生日禮物給你。親愛的，生日快樂！

M: Thank you, my love. You always surprise me! 男：謝謝，我的愛人！妳總是給我驚喜！

Question. What did the woman do? 女子做了何事？

A. She took him to a yoga class. A. 她帶他去上了瑜伽課。

B. She came home with a birthday present. B. 她帶著一個生日禮物回家。

C. She ignored the man's birthday. C. 她忽略了男子的生日。

| 詳解 | 選項 B 跟 C 分別提到 birthday，可推測本題對話內容跟生日有極大的關係，而且是與男子的生日有關。選項 A 的 yoga 指瑜伽，女子回答男子說「I went to yoga class this morning」（我早上去上了瑜伽課），代表男子沒有去，所以選項 A 不對。而本題關鍵點在女子中間說了一串今天去做了什麼是之後的「Happy Birthday」，表示她沒有忘記或忽略男子的生日，所以選項 C 也不對，而在連串的話語中，女子說到「bought you a present」（買了生日禮物給你），所以可以更確定正確答案是選項 B。

| 補充 | 「對話第一句的「Where have you been...」表示「你去了哪裡」，如果改成「Where have you gone...」，也是同樣的中文解釋，不過意思就稍有不同了，後者表示女子現在還沒回到家，也許兩人正在講電話。「have been」指「去過」，例如：I have been to France.（我去過法國。）而 have gone 是指「（已經）去了」，例如：My dad has gone to Europe.（我爸爸去歐洲了。）也就是說，他現在人不在這裡，而是在歐洲。

Part 4 短文聽解

Question number 13.

Please look at the following three pictures. Listen to the following short talk. What place is talked about?

請看以下三張圖片。聆聽以下簡短談話。談論的是哪個地方？

KID's Paradise is a newly open amusement park in town. Kids and adults can enjoy the wonderful scenery in the country's longest cable car. And there's also the first man-made beach where you can cool off.

「孩子天堂」是鎮上新開的遊樂園。小朋友跟大朋友們可以坐在全國最長的纜車上欣賞優美的風景。另外還有第一座你可以消暑的人工海灘。

| 詳解 | 可以先試著將三張圖片裡面的遊樂設備的英文想一遍，有 merry-go-round（旋轉木馬）、roller coaster（雲霄飛車）、cable car（纜車）、beach（海灘）及 surfing（衝浪）。接下來注意聽遊樂場的設備內容。本題關鍵字詞是 cable car（纜車），所以 A、C 都不對。最後的 man-made beach（人造海灘）幫考生確定答案，故本題正確答案為選項 B。也許談話內容中有一些字詞聽不出來（像是英檢中級的 paradise 天堂、amusement 娛樂、scenery 風景），不過沒關係，重點抓住關鍵字詞即可。

| 補充 | 常見的遊樂園備有：旋轉木馬 merry-go-round、雲霄飛車 roller coaster、纜車 cable car, gondola、碰碰車 / 船 bumper car / boat、摩天輪 Ferris wheel、滑水道 water slide、鬼屋 haunted house、賽車 go-kart、海盜船 pirate ship、自由落體 / 大怒神 freefall、咖啡杯 teacups、旋轉鞦韆 swing ride、海盜船 pirate ship…等。

Question number 14.

Please look at the following three pictures. Listen to a message Betty left her brother. Where might her brother be?

請看以下三張圖片。聆聽 Betty 留給她弟弟的訊息。她弟弟可能在哪裡？

Hey Dave, it's sis. I know you are about to get off work so I'm going to give you a ride. I booked a table at the Sunday's. See you later.

嗨，大衛，是老姐啦。我知道你快下班了，所以我待會來載你。我在星期天餐廳訂了位。待會見囉。

｜詳解｜ sis 是 sister 的簡稱。本題破題關鍵在「you are about to get off work」（你快下班了）。「be about to-V」是「就要去做…」。因此，Betty 留言時，弟弟 Dave 還沒下班，人還在辦公室，所以答案是選項 A。再加上 Betty 說要去載他，代表 Dave 沒有在開車，故選項 B 也不對。

Day 08
Day 09
Day 10
Day 11
Day 12
Day 13
Day 14

Day 10

月　　日

我的完成時間＿＿＿＿分鐘
標準作答時間 10 分鐘

Day_10.mp3

Part 1 看圖辨義

Questions 1-2

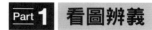

Name/Subject	Michael	Ruby	Wendy
English	89	99	76
Math	91	80	72
Chinese	97	50	100

Part 2 問答

Questions 3-7

3. A. No, I haven't. Is it serious?
   B. Yeah, that really made me laugh so hard!
   C. Not yet, I'm expecting his call.

4. A. Cool idea! What do you plan to sell?
   B. How much is it? Perhaps we can share the apartment.
   C. Are you kidding? You might get famous.

5. A. Why do you cover your face?
   B. You look great the way you are.
   C. Make a wish then.

6. A. I think the cat bit it open and escaped.
   B. I don't know, and that's not my bag.
   C. It might be Lily. She likes to gossip.

7. A. Let's make it half an hour earlier. I don't want to be late.
   B. I'll be there by 6:15. Be on time.
   C. Sure, here you are.

Part 3 簡短對話

Questions 8-12

8. A. She didn't treat her assistant well.
   B. She is not responsible enough.
   C. She ignored what the man had reminded her of.

9. A. Millions of dollars are stolen.
   B. Some information is gone.
   C. He fired the woman.

10. A. He shouldn't drive too often.
    B. Yesterday was really not his day.
    C. He should have the bad luck.

11. A. At a museum
    B. At the office
    C. At a bookstore

12. A. She's not satisfied with the hair dresser.
    B. She prefers straight hair.
    C. She wants to grow her hair.

Part 4 短文聽解

Questions 13-14

13.

A

B

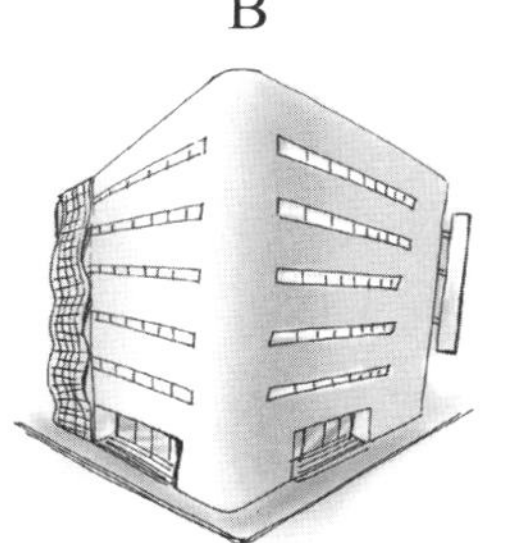

C

14.

A

B

C

上頁簡答

解答與詳解

1. (C) 2. (C) 3. (B) 4. (A) 5. (B) 6. (C) 7. (A) 8. (B) 9. (B) 10. (C) 11. (C) 12. (C) 13. (B) 14. (A)

Part 1 看圖辨義

For questions number 1-2, please look at the following picture.

Question number 1.

Who got a full mark on one of his or her subjects? 誰的其中一個科目獲得滿分？

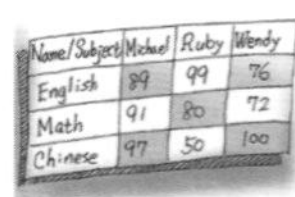

Name/Subject	Michael	Ruby	Wendy
English	89	99	76
Math	91	80	72
Chinese	97	50	100

A. Michael　　A. 麥可
B. Ruby　　B. 露比
C. Wendy　　C. 溫蒂

| 詳解 | 本題關鍵在於聽懂「full mark」是「滿分」，也可以說成「full score」或是「an ace」，「one of his or her subjects」是「他／她們的其中一科」，所以正確答案為選項 C。

| 補充 | 如果要問人家「（某一科）考幾分？」可以這樣問：

What did you get?（你拿幾分？）

What was your score?（你分數多少？）

回答的方式可能有：

I got really good grades.（我考超高分的。）

I got 80 points in English.（我英文考了 80 分。）

I scored 90 marks in Mandarin Chinese.（我國文考了 90 分。）

I got an A in history!（我歷史拿到 A 耶！）

I screwed up on the test.（我考試考砸了。）

I didn't do well in Match.（我數學成績不太好。）

I failed the test.（我考不及格。）

Question number 2.

Which subject did Ruby do the worst on? 露比考最差的是哪一科？

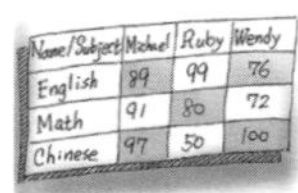

Name/Subject	Michael	Ruby	Wendy
English	89	99	76
Math	91	80	72
Chinese	97	50	100

A. English　　A. 英文
B. Math　　B. 數學
C. Chinese　　C. 中文

| 詳解 | 本題關鍵在 worst 這個字，搭配後面介系詞的發音是 [ˋwɝstʌn]，「do the worst on + 科目」表示「（某一科）…考最差」，對照圖中 Ruby 考的三個科目中，中文考 50 分是

最差的，所以選項 C 是正確答案。

| 補充 | 這樣的圖表，在「看圖辨義」的考題中可以有很多種考法，也可能問你「Who got the lowest grade in which subject?」（誰哪一科拿到最低的分數？）、「Who got the highest grade in which subject?」（誰哪一科拿到最高的分數？）、「Who got the highest point in English?」（英文考最高的是誰？）…。

Part 2 問答

Question number 3.

Rick, have you watched that funny show? 瑞克，你看過那場滑稽表演了嗎？

A. No, I haven't. Is it serious? A. 不，還沒有耶。很嚴肅嗎？

B. Yeah, that really made me laugh so hard! B. 有啊，那真的讓我笑翻了。

C. Not yet, I'm expecting his call. C. 還沒，我在等他的電話。

| 詳解 | 選項 A 的 serious 以及 B 的「made me laugh」給了我們一些線索，可能是在講某件事情給人的感受。相對於選項 C 跟「回電話」有關，考生聽到 watch 時，就知道選項 C 不對。接下來對照題目句的「funny show」（有趣的表演），可以確定正確答案為選項 B。

| 補充 | 選項 C 的 expect 是「期待」，expecting 是進行式，表示「正等待著，正期待著」。

Question number 4.

I'm going to rent an area in the night market. 我打算去夜市租一個位置。

A. Cool idea! What do you plan to sell? A. 很讚的主意哦！你打算賣什麼呢？

B. How much is it?
Perhaps we can share the apartment. B. 要多少錢？
或許我們可以合租那間公寓。

C. Are you kidding? You might get famous. C. 你在開玩笑嗎？你可能會出名哦。

| 詳解 | 三個選項的內容並不困難，也沒有太難的單字，所以一定得掌握題目。rent 以及 night market 是破題關鍵，不管是租什麼，在夜市裡主要就是買跟賣的行為，而從選項 A 的「plan to sell」可知，本題正確答案為選項 A。

| 補充 | 題目句中的 area（區域）其實就是指「攤位」，可以用英檢中級的 booth 或 stall 取代，在 exhibition（展覽）或 bazaar（市集）擺放的攤位，也稱為 booth。

Question number 5.

I wish I had a face and a figure like a movie star. 我希望我有明星般的臉蛋跟身材。

A. Why do you cover your face? A. 為什麼要遮住你的臉？

B. You look great the way you are. B. 你這樣看來就很好了。

C. Where can I make a wish? C. 我可以去哪許個願呢？

| 詳解 | 聽到「I wish...」時，三個選項中最不相關的就是選項 A。另外，「I wish I had...」其實聽起來就是正在做許願這個動作了，所以選項 C 的回應不符，「You look great the way you are.」（你現在這樣子看來就很棒了。）是本題中最適當的回答，故正確答案為選項 B。

| 補充 | 「I wish I had...」是假設語氣用法，wish 後面的名詞子句動詞時態，比照「if 假設語氣」中的動詞用法，表示與「現在事實相反」時，動詞要用過去式。例如：I wish I had told him my feelings.（我希望我告訴了他我的感覺。）但實際的狀況是「我沒有告訴他」。

Question number 6.

Who let the cat out of the bag? 是誰把祕密洩漏了出去？

A. I think the cat bit it open and escaped. A. 我想貓自己把它咬開然後逃了出去。

B. I don't know, and that's not my bag. B. 我不知道耶，而且那不是我的袋子。

C. It might be Lily. She likes to gossip. C. 有可能是莉莉。她很喜歡講八卦。

| 詳解 | 如果不知道題目的「let the cat out of the bag」是一句經常聽到的俚語（指「洩露祕密」），可能就會在選項 A、B 之間難以抉擇了。而題目是問誰洩漏了祕密，故本題正確答案為選項 C。知道這個俚語的意思之後，選項 C 只要聽懂「It might be Lily.」就可以確定答案是它了，gossip 是個中級的單字，意思是「聊八卦」。

| 補充 | 「let the cat out of the bag」背後有個有趣的故事。話說以前的人在歐洲市場買小豬，都是放在布袋裡帶回家。然而黑心的商人會把體重接近的野貓放進布袋裡，等不知情的客人回家打開袋子，跑出來的是貓咪而不是豬，才發現自已被騙了。日後這個「貓」也代表著不好的消息或是祕密的意思。

Question number 7.

Could you pick me up at 5:45? 你可以五點四十五分來接我嗎？

A. Let's make it half an hour earlier. I don't want to be late. A. 我們提早半小時好了。我不想遲到。

B. I'll be there by 6:15. Be on time. B. 我六點十五分到那裡。要準時哦。

C. Sure, here you are. C. 沒問題，給你。

| 詳解 | 選項 A 跟 B 分別都有提到時間，考生要注意題目中出現的時間。題目說在 5:45，選項 B 說 6:15，而且還加一句「Be on time.」（要準時那裡。）可見得語意不符，故選項 B 不對。選項 C 的「here you are」（在這，給你）是文不對題的回答。其實本題破題字詞為「pick me up」（接我），所以正確答案為選項 A。

| 補充 | 我們說「make it」時，可以指「把某事情做成…」或「讓某事變成…」，像選項 A 中「Let's make it ...」就是說「把原來約定的時間改成…」。又例如去餐廳當服務生問你幾位時，你可以回答說」A table for three please. Oh, let's make it four.」（麻煩三位。哦，改四位好了。）

Part 3 簡短對話

Question number 8.

M: The titles on these papers are all wrong. 男：這些文件上的標題全都是錯的。

W: But I had my assistant double check it. 女：但我已請助理再三檢查過了。

M: Did you do it yourself again? 男：妳自己有檢查嗎？

W: Sorry, it's my mistake. 女：對不起，是我的失誤。

Question. What mistake did the woman make? 女子犯了什麼錯誤？

A. She didn't treat her assistant well. A. 她沒有好好對待她的助理。

B. She is not responsible enough. B. 她不夠盡責。

C. She ignored what the man had reminded her of. C. 她忽視了先前男子提醒過她的事。

｜詳解｜三個選項都與女子做了什麼不該做的事有關，所以本題在還沒聽到題目句之前，應該很容易設想到要問的是什麼。對話中提到 assistant 的部分只有女子說的「I had my assistant double check it.」而選項 A 的敘述完全不相關；答題關鍵在最後兩人的對話：Did you do it yourself again? W: Sorry, it's my mistake.。這表示女子沒有做到自己 double-check 這個動作，意味著她不夠負責任，所以正確答案為選項 B。選項 C 的部分，因為對話中並沒有提到男子先前提醒過她什麼，所以並不是最適當的答案。

｜詳解｜女子在對話中說「I had my assistant double check it.」當中的 had 在此是使役動詞，跟 make、let 等動詞用法相同，例如：I had the maid clean the floor.（我讓傭人清洗地板。）或 The boss made the secretary retype all the letters.（老闆要祕書把所有的信重打。）

Question number 9.

W: I made a mistake. Forgive me, please. 女：我出錯了。請原諒我。

M: What kind of mistake? 男：出了什麼樣的錯？

W: I... I deleted your file without saving it. 女：我…我沒有幫你存檔就把檔案刪掉了。

M: What? That's my client's information. It's worth millions! 男：什麼？那是我的客戶資料耶。價值好幾百萬啊！

Question. What has actually happened? 究竟發生了何事？

A. Millions of dollars are stolen. A. 幾百萬元被偷了。

B. Some information is gone. B. 有些資料不見了。

C. He fired the woman. C. 他把女子開除了。

｜詳解｜從選項 A 與 B 可推知有東西不見了，可能是錢被偷（money is stolen）、某些資料不見（certain information is lost）或因為東西不見而女子被炒魷魚（being fired）。女子在說完她做的錯事後，男子的回應是「It's worth millions!」（那價值好幾百萬啊！）沒有提到開除之事，而且我們不確定他們是否為僱主關係，所以選項 C 不對。另外 millions 指的是客戶資料（client's information）的價值，不是真的被偷了現金幾百萬，所以選項 A 也不對。故本題正確答案為選項 B。

｜補充｜說某人出錯了，我們習慣用「make a mistake」。女子說她「deleted your file without saving it」，without 指「沒有」，整句意思是「沒有存檔就把檔案刪掉」。without 是介系詞，後面接動詞-ing，所以 save 要用 saving。

Question number 10.

M: I got a ticket for running a red light yesterday. What a bad day!	男：我昨天闖紅燈被開了一張罰單。真是倒楣的一天！
W: But I think it served you right, because you're always such a careless driver.	女：但我認為你活該，因為你總是開車很不用心。
M: Yeah, I know. I need to be more careful next time.	男：是的，我知道。我下次得更加小心。
W: It's important to follow traffic rules for everyone's safety.	女：為了每個人的安全，遵守交通規則很重要。

Question. What does the woman think about the man? 女子對男子有何看法？

A. He shouldn't drive too often.	A. 他不該太常開車。
B. Yesterday was really not his day.	B. 他昨天確實運氣不好。
C. He should have the bad luck.	C. 他活該倒楣。

｜詳解｜從選項內容可推知對話內容與男子的行為或發生在他身上的事有關，而題目問女子對男子的看法，所以應特別注意女子所說的話。另外，選項 C 的「serve him right」值得注意，它指「你活該／罪有應得」。本題破題點為女子說的「But I think it served you right, because...」，所以她覺得男子今天被開罰單是應該的。故本題正答案為選項 C。

｜補充｜男子說「I got a ticket for...」，這裡的 for 是指「因為」。run 本來是「跑」的意思，而「run a traffic/red light」是指「闖紅燈」。serve 本來是「服務」的意思，「serve somebody right」字面意思是「把你服務得相當正確」，也就是「...是你應得的」，換個說法是「You deserve it!」

Question number 11.

W: Should we go now? I feel sleepy.	女：我們該走了嗎？我有點睏。
M: We have been here for only half an hour. I thought you wanted to do more reading.	男：我們才來這裡半小時。我以為妳想多看一點書。
W: Right, but I feel sick picking up a book again after reading a 500-page report.	女：是沒錯，不過在我讀完一份五百頁的報告後，要再拿起一本書真的很受不了。

Question. Where are the speakers? 說話者身在何處？

A. At a museum　　A. 在博物館

B. At the office　　B. 在辦公室

C. At a bookstore　　C. 在書店

| 詳解 | 三個選項很明顯已經告訴你題目問的是地點。本題破題字為 reading，第一個出現的 reading（I thought you wanted to do more reading）是名詞，這裡指「書籍」或「讀物」。男子 說他們在那個地方才半小時，所以選項 B 不可能。接著他說「我以為妳想多看書」，代表他們身處的地方有很多書籍可閱讀，所以選項 A 也不對。故本題正確答案為選項 C。

| 補充 | 「pick up a book」是「拿起一本書來看」，「pick up」原意為「撿起」，此處是一種延伸的含意，例如：What did you pick up at the supermarket? 應該要翻譯為「你在超級市場買了什麼」而不是「你在超級市場撿到了什麼」。「pick someone up」是指「接送某人」，而非把某人撿起來。

Question number 12.

W: My dad wants me to get my hair cut short, but I only want small amounts of it.　　女：我爸要我把頭髮剪短，不過我只想些微修一下就好了。

M: I see. So how do you want me to do your hair?　　男：了解。所以你希望我怎麼剪呢？

W: Cut it shorter on the sides but not too much on the back.　　女：旁邊可以修短一點，但後面不要太短。

Question. What's true about the woman? 關於女子，何者為真？

A. She's not satisfied with the hair dresser.　　A. 她對這名理髮師不滿意。

B. She prefers straight hair.　　B. 她比較喜歡直髮。

C. She wants to grow her hair.　　C. 她想把頭髮留長。

| 詳解 | 從三個選項考生可推知對話內容與女子理髮有關，且應特別注意聽女子所說的話。答題關鍵在第一句後半的「but I only want small amounts of it」，這裡的 it 當然是指前半句提到的 haircut（剪髮），也就是「修剪一點點」的意思。而對話內容並未提及或暗示女子對理髮師（hairdresser）不滿，或是她比較喜歡直髮（straight hair），所以選項 A、B 均不可選，只有選項的「想把頭髮留長」是比較合適的答案，故正確答案是選項 C。

| 補充 | 「去剪頭髮」可以說「have / get a haircut」或是「have / get one's hair cut」，但可別說成「I want to cut my hair.」了，因為這表示自己剪自己的頭髮。另外，「稍微修一下」也是我們常常會對理髮師（hairdresser / barber）說的話，通常會用 trim 這個字，用法和 haircut 一樣，可當名詞或動詞，而常聽到的「燙髮」、「染髮」、「挑染」、「離子燙」等的英文分別是 perm、dye、highlight、straight perm。

Part 4 短文聽解

Question number 13.

Please look at the following three pictures. Listen to the following announcement. Where might you hear this?

請看以下三張圖片。聆聽以下宣布。你可能會在哪裡聽到這些話？

Dear customers, thank you for shopping at Flowers. We are having a special event today. Flowers offer you a free gift-wrapping service on the 5th floor, so you can add a little surprise to your presents. Go and check it out at the gift section, 5th floor.

親愛的顧客，感謝您蒞臨花之都購物。今天我們有一項特別的活動。花之都在五樓提供您免費的禮物包裝服務，您可以替您的禮物增添一點驚喜。請到五樓禮品部來接受此項服務。

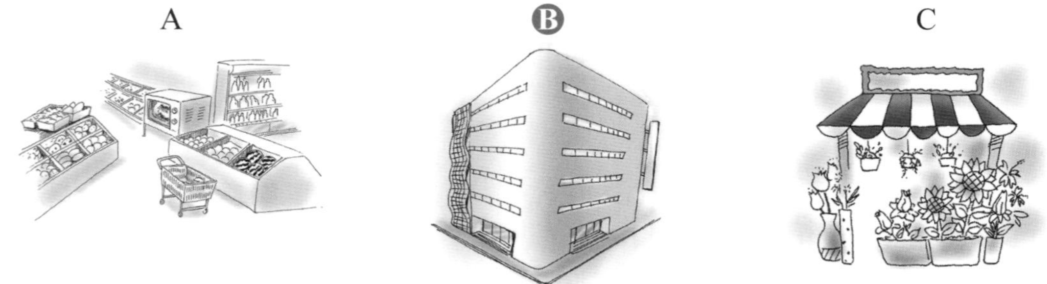

| 詳解 | 聽到 shopping 時，對照三張圖片，其實都有可能是答案。at Flowers 會誤導考生，這裡的 Flowers 是一家店的名稱，而非花店，「花店」的英文說法是 florist's，所以選項 C 可能不符。本題破題字在 5th floor（五樓），三張圖中只有選項 B 有樓層，而 gift section 是指「禮品部」，相信只有較大的購物中心或百貨公司才有分部門，所以本題正確答案為 B。

| 補充 | 「gift-wrapping service」是「禮物包裝服務」。free 有多種用法，形容「人」時可以指「自由的，有空的」，形容「物」時可以解釋為「免費的」，例如：People are free to borrow books from a library.（人們自由地在圖書館裡借書。）或 The drink goes with the set. It's free.（飲料跟著套餐，是免費的。）以及 The products here are duty free.（這裡的商品都是免稅的。）duty 在此指「稅金」。

Question number 14.

Please look at the following three pictures. Listen to the following message. What would Jenny probably do after listening to her boss's message?

請看以下三張圖片。聆聽以下訊息。珍妮在聽完她老闆的訊息之後可能會去做什麼？

Jenny, I won't be back to the office till 1:30. Mr. Peterson is visiting this afternoon. I would like you to prepare the meeting room first and go get him at the hotel at 1:00. Call me if necessary.

珍妮，我要到下午一點半才會回辦公室。彼得森先生今天下午將來訪，我希望妳先準備好會議室，然後一點鐘去飯店接他。如有必要請撥電話給我。

A

B

C

| 詳解 | 仔細看這三張圖，考生可能發現它們似乎是照順序排列，這絕對有助於選出正確答案，不過我們還是先想想可能會出現在留言的內容：圖 A cleaning up the meeting room（清理會議室），圖 B calling Mr. Peterson（致電給彼得森先生），圖 C driving Mr. Peterson to certain place（載彼得森先生到某處）。留言者是珍妮的老闆或上司，他沒有請 Jenny 打給 Mr. Peterson，只告訴她 he is visiting（他將來拜訪），所以選項 B 不對。雖然老闆要 Jenny 去接 Mr. Peterson，但破題點在 prepare the meeting room first（先準備好會議室），先後順序出來了，所以正確答案為選項 A。

Day 11

月　　日

我的完成時間＿＿＿＿分鐘
標準作答時間 10 分鐘

Day_11.mp3

Part 1 看圖辨義

Questions 1-2

Part 2 問答

Questions 3-7

3. A. You're welcome! It's my pleasure to meet you.
   B. Thank you for letting me know.
   C. Of course. I know it must be going to work.

4. A. Just say it.
   B. What's so funny?
   C. Keep your word.

5. A. It's my turn.
   B. Let's talk about that now.
   C. I feel the same way.

6. A. Not really. The power supply must have been turned off.
   B. I think we'd better call the police right now.
   C. You should buy yourself a new house.

7. A. No, you can't force me to do so.
   B. Seeing is believing.
   C. I only believe in myself.

Part 3 簡短對話

Questions 8-12

8. A. He is a changed boy.
   B. He cheated on his test.
   C. He didn't get a passing mark.

9. A. HSR Taoyuan Station
   B. The taxi stand
   C. The bus stop

10. A. At the airport
    B. At the meeting room
    C. At the train station

11. A. Washing his clothes
    B. Cleaning all the windows
    C. Making his room free from dirt

12. A. Ted
    B. Mike
    C. Wendy

Part 4 短文聽解

Questions 13-14

13.

A

B

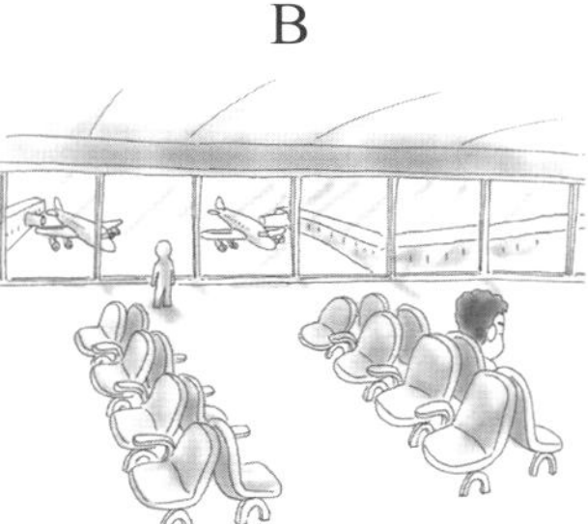

C

14.

A

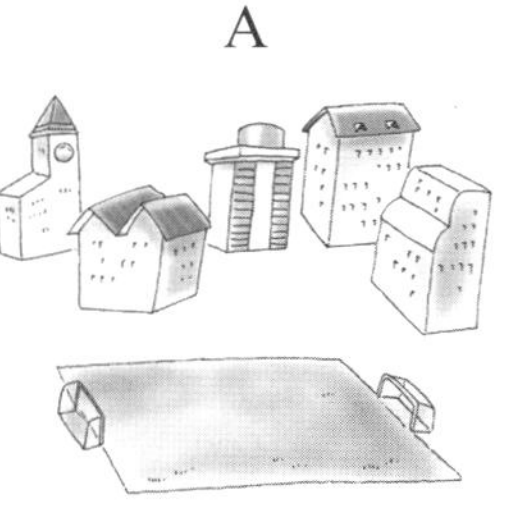

B

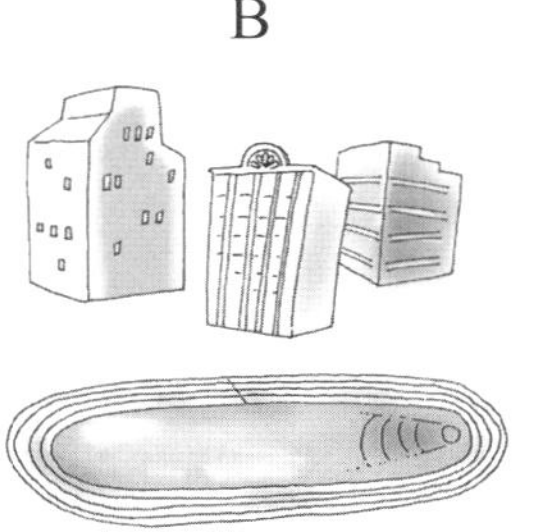

C

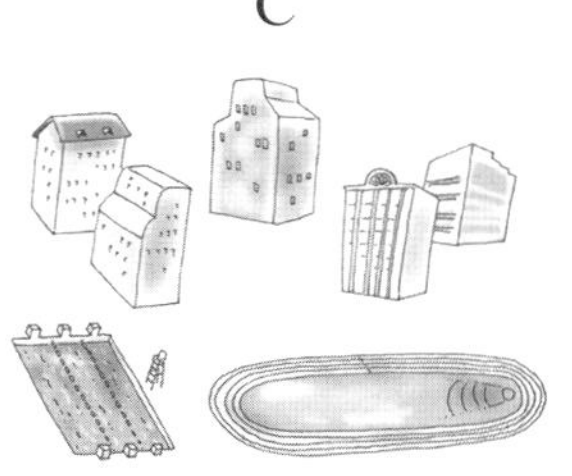

上頁簡答

解答與詳解

1. (A) 2. (C) 3. (B) 4. (A) 5. (C) 6. (B) 7. (B) 8. (C) 9. (C) 10. (A) 11. (B) 12. (A) 13. (C) 14. (C)

Part 1 看圖辨義

For questions number 1-2, please look at the following pictures.

Question number 1.

What can be told from the picture? 從這張圖可以推知什麼訊息？

A. The longer you work out, the thinner you become. A. 你運動的時間越久，你就會越瘦。

B. The more weight you gain, the less time you can waste. B. 你增加越多體重，你能浪費的時間就越少。

C. Swimming is the best way to keep fit. C. 游泳是保持窈窕最好的方法。

| 詳解 | 上面第一排文字「amount of exercise」是「運動量」的意思，而第二排文字「reduce in weight」是「減少的體重」的意思，上下對照可知，運動時間越久，能夠減去的體重會越多，所以正確答案為選項 A。

| 補充 | 選項 A 的 the longer you ..., the thinner you ... 即「你…時間越久，你就…越瘦」，這是相當常見的「越…，越…」句型：「The + 比較級..., the + 比較級...」，例如：The harder you learn, the smarter you are.（你越努力學習，你就越聰明。）

Question number 2.

What might the man be? 這位男士可能是做什麼的？

A. A professor A. 教授

B. A movie star B. 影星

C. A writer C. 作家

| 詳解 | 本題關鍵在男子背後的 BESTSELLER（暢銷書），所以這位坐著為人們簽名的人當然不會是影星或歌星，而是一名 writer 或 author（作家），故正確答案為選項 C。

| 補充 | 「問對方做什麼」最直接的詢問方式當然就是「What is your job?」 或是「What are you?」，但美國人基本上不會這麼問。雖然文法上沒有錯誤，但對美國人來說，這樣的問法既不禮貌，也不自然。那該怎麼問才對呢？美國人多用「What do you do for a living?」，或者更簡短的「What do you do?」另外，還有兩種比較友好的詢問方式：「What kind of work do you do?」以及「What line of work are you in?」

Part 2 問答

Question number 3.

I'm sorry but our manager didn't accept your suggestion.
很抱歉我們經理並未接受你的建議。

A. You're welcome! It's my pleasure to meet you. A. 不客氣！跟你見面是我的榮幸。

B. Thank you for letting me know. B. 感謝您的告知。

C. Of course. I know it must be going to work. C. 當然。我就知道這行得通。

| 詳解 | 對於「I'm sorry but...」的回應方式，用「You're welcome!」顯然是雞同鴨講了，所以選項 A 錯誤；在告知對方的提議沒有被接受之後，坦然面對結果而表示「感謝您的告知」，這是最適當的回答，故正確答案是選項 B。既然提議被拒絕了，就不可能回答說「這行得通」了，所以選項 C 錯誤。

| 補充 | 選項 C 中「it's going to work」的 work 在這裡不是指「工作」，而是指「運作」，譬如說「The toaster doesn't work.」（烤吐司機壞了。）意思就是機器無法運作。而在本題裡 work 則翻譯為「行得通」，提議若可以「運作」當然就表示「行得通」囉！

Question number 4.

Sally, there's something important I want to tell you.
莎莉，有些重要的事我想告訴你。

A. Just say it. A. 就直說吧。

B. What's so funny? B. 什麼事那麼好笑？

C. Keep your word. C. 你要守承諾。

| 詳解 | 本題題目容易理解，反而選項 A 跟 C 是本題的關鍵。選項 A 的 it 就是指題目句的「something important」，而選項 C 的 keep 原指「保持，保有」，「保有你說過的話」就表示「信守承諾」，本題正確答案為選項 A。

| 補充 | 表示「守承諾」的「keep one's word」，也可以用 promise 取代 word。相反地，「違背承諾，食言」可以用 break 這個動詞，例如：You broke your word to me! I'll never believe you again!（你不遵守對我的承諾！我絕對不會再相信你了！）

Question number 5.

It's nice to have talked with you. It's inspiring. 很開心跟你聊天。很有啟發性。

A. It's my turn. A. 換我了。

B. Let's talk about that now. B. 我們現在就來討論吧。

C. I feel the same way. C. 我也這麼覺得。

| 詳解 | 根據選項可推知某人剛提出某個想法或感覺，三個選項則是相對的回應。It's nice to

have talked with you.（很高興跟你聊天。）就是對方的感覺，所以最適當的回應是選項 C。

|補充| inspiring 是現在分詞當形容詞用，指「有啟發性的」，名詞為 inspiration。選項 B 的「I feel the same way.」意思很容易懂，就是「我的感覺跟你一樣。」如果是「我剛好跟你相反」，我們可以說 I feel the opposite.

Question number 6.

What happened? I think our house was robbed.
發生什麼事了？我們家好像遭小偷了。

A. Not really. The power supply must have been turned off.　A. 不盡然。我們的供電一定是被切斷了。

B. I think we'd better call the police right now.　B. 我想我們最好馬上報警。

C. You should buy yourself a new house.　C. 你應該為自己買間新的房子。

|詳解| 本題關鍵是題目中 rob 這個動詞，在被動式中，它的過去分詞是 robbed，表示「被搶了」，「房子被搶了」的概念就是家裡遭小偷了，所以最適當的回應是選項 B。

|補充| rob 常與介系詞 of 搭配使用，句型是「rob + 人 + of + 財物」。例如：The man was robbed of his wallet when he walked on the street last night.（這名男子昨晚走在街道上時被搶了皮包）另外，rob 也有「剝奪」的意思，因此介系詞 of 後面的名詞，可能是抽象的概念。例如：I broke my leg on the last day of school, so I was robbed of a fun summer holiday.（在學期的最後一天摔斷了腿，因此暑假能開心玩樂的權利也被剝奪了。）

Question number 7.

Do you believe in ghosts? 你相信有鬼嗎？

A. No, you can't force me to do so.　A. 不，你不能強迫我這樣做。

B. Seeing is believing.　B. 眼見為憑。

C. I only believe in myself.　C. 我只相信我自己。

|詳解| 本題關鍵字是 believe 和 ghost，對於「相不相信有鬼」這個問題，只要是親眼看到過的人，自然會說相信了，所以選項 B 是最適當的回答。題目句雖然以「Do you...?」開頭，是個以 Yes/No 來回答的問題，但可別直接就選 A 了喔！因為對方只是問你信不信，而你要是回答「不能強迫我去信」的話，就完全走鐘了喔！至於選項 C 刻意以相同動詞 believe 來混淆，但也是完全離題的回應。

Part 3 簡短對話

Question number 8.

W: How was your test yesterday, Bob?
女：你昨天的考試如何，鮑伯？

M: Well, not so good and not so bad...
男：這個嘛，不怎麼好，也不怎麼壞…

W: Tell me, Bob.
女：鮑伯，告訴我。

M: I failed it.
男：我考不及格啦。

Question. What actually happened to Bob? 鮑伯究竟發生了何事？

A. He is a changed boy.
A. 他已經脫胎換骨。

B. He cheated on his test.
B. 他考試作弊。

C. He didn't get a passing mark.
C. 他考試沒過關。

| 詳解 | 從選項 B 與 C 可推知對話內容跟學校考試有關，可能是男孩考試作弊，或男孩考試不及格。選項 A 的 changed 指「改變的，不一樣的」，也就是他變得不一樣了。本題破題字為 fail，原本是「失敗」的意思，後面搭配「考試」等名詞時，引申為「不及格」，所以與「考試作弊」無關，故本題正確答案為選項 C。「passing marking」就是指「通過／及格的分數」。

| 詳解 | 「考不及格，被當掉」一般會用到中級的 flunk 這個動詞，當及物動詞時後面接「人」或「考試，測驗」，常用於被動式，例如：I got flunked by my Math teacher.（我被數學老師當掉了。）I flunked my Math test.（我數學考試不及格。）

Question number 9.

W: Where are you going, Mr. Lin
女：林先生，您要去哪？

M: I'm going to HSR Taoyuan Station.
男：我要到桃園高鐵站。

W: Are you going by taxi?
女：你要搭計程車過去嗎？

M: No, I'm going to take a bus.
男：不，我要搭公車。

Question. Where is Mr. Lin going the next? 接下來林先生要去哪裡？

A. HSR Taoyuan Station
A. 桃園高鐵站

B. The taxi stand
B. 計程車招呼站

C. The bus stop
C. 公車站

| 詳解 | 對話第二句中提到的「桃園高鐵站（HSR Taoyuan Station）」是最終目的地（HSR 是 High Speed Rail），但 Mr. Lin 必須先搭上交通工具，也就是他選擇搭乘的「公車（bus）」，才能到達 HSR Taoyuan，因此正確答案是選項 C。

| 補充 | 關於「搭乘交通工具」的用法，可以用介系詞 by 或是動詞 take 來表達。例如：Jenny went to the museum by bus yesterday.（Jenny 昨天搭公車去博物館。）或是 Jenny took a bus to the museum.。當然，其他的交通工具也可用 take，例如：take a(n) taxi / train /

ship / boat / ferry / airplane（搭計程車／火車／船／小船／渡輪／飛機。另外，在表示捷運與高鐵時，只可使用 the，不能用 a：take the MRT「搭捷運」、take the HSR「搭高鐵」。

Question number 10.

M: We can't board the flight. There's a strong typhoon.
男：我們不能登機了。有個強烈颱風來襲。

W: So, we might be absent from the meeting tomorrow?
女：所以，我們可能無法出席明天的會議嗎？

M: I'm afraid so.
男：恐怕如此。

Question. Where does the conversation take place? 對話是在何處進行的？

A. At the airport	A. 在機場
B. At the meeting room	B. 在會議室
C. At the train station	C. 在火車站

| 詳解 | 本題考生只要聽到 flight（班機，航班），就可以確定答案了，故本題正確答案為選項 A。選項 B 以對話中出現的相同字彙 meeting 刻意造成混淆，務必小心理解。

| 補充 | board the flight 意思是「登機」，除了「上飛機」以外，「上船」、「上火車」、「上公車」，只要是「可以在上面走動的交通工具，都可以使用 board 這個動詞，例如：board the ship（上船），但你不能說「board the car / motorcycle」。另一個簡單的動詞片語可以代替 board 的則是 get on。對話中的 absent 是「缺席」，常用於「be absent from...」這個片語。

Question number 11.

W: Do you feel like shopping today with us?
女：你今天想跟我們去逛街嗎？

M: I'm too tired to join you.
男：我很累，不跟你們去了。

W: What have you done today?
女：你今天做了什麼？

M: I did all of my laundry, tidied up my room and helped clean the yard.
男：我洗了所有的衣服，整理了房間，還有幫忙清理院子。

Question. What didn't the man do? 男子沒有做何事？

A. Washing his clothes	A. 洗衣服
B. Cleaning all the windows	B. 清洗所有窗戶
C. Making his room free from dirt	C. 清除房間的塵垢

| 詳解 | 三個選項都與做家務（housework）有關，而問題可能是問「做了什麼家務」或「沒做那一項家務」。男子說他今天洗了所有衣服（did all the laundry），整理了房間（tidied up the room），還有幫忙清理院子（helped clean the yard），但未提到清潔窗戶，故本題正確答案為選項 B。

| 補充 | 大家買東西時最喜歡看到 free 吧！這表示有東西可以不用花錢「免費」拿或吃，而當 free 與 from 搭成片語時，則有「免去...」的意思，例如：My grandpa had lots of health problems before he passed away, but now I think he's free from pain.（爺爺在過世之前有許多健康上的問題，但我想他現在已經不痛了。）

Question number 12.

M: Do you know where Ted is?
男：妳知道泰德在哪裡嗎？

W: He's in the library, Mike.
女：他在圖書館，麥可。

M: Thanks, Wendy. I'll go find him there.
男：謝謝你，溫蒂。我會過去那找他。

W: Sure, let me know if you need any help.
女：當然，有需要任何協助的話請讓我知道。

Question. Who are the man and woman talking about?
男子與女子正在談論誰？

A. Ted A. 泰德
B. Mike B. 麥可
C. Wendy C. 溫蒂

| 詳解 | 先看過三個選項之後，可確定本題是問「什麼人」（who）的問題，選項中有三個名字，而題目要問的是這對男女正在談論誰，所以必須仔細聆聽提到人名的時候。雖然對話的第一句「Do you know where Ted is?」已經點出答案是誰了，但句尾 Ted 和 is 會連音（唸成 [tɛ-dɪs]），考生一不小心可能會聽成別的單字而選錯答案，因此要特別注意，本題正確答案是選項 A。

| 補充 | 在對話第一句「Do you know where Ted is?」中，疑問詞 where 引導了一個名詞子句，作 know 的受詞，但要注意的是，這個名詞子句的主詞與動詞擺放順序，應依肯定句，而非疑問句的原則。例如：A: Where is Ted? Do you know? = Do you know where Ted is?

Part 4 短文聽解

Question number 13.

Please look at the following three pictures. Listen to the following announcement. Where might you hear this?
請看以下三張圖片。聆聽以下宣布。你可能會在哪裡聽到這些話？

The next station is Zhongxiao Fuxing station. Passengers heading for the Taipei Zoo, please change trains at this station. The doors are closing. Please mind the platform gap.
下一站是忠孝復興站。往台北動物園的乘客請在本站換車。列車門即將關閉。請注意月台間隙。

｜詳解｜ 本題破題字相當多且出現頻繁，光是 station（站）就出現三次。三張圖中唯一不可能聽到 station 的就是選項 B 的機場候機室，所以 B 不對。公車的車站也稱為 station，但廣播內容的最後兩個字 platform gap（月台間隙）讓考生確認答案，本題正確答案為選項 C。

｜補充｜ 「be head for + 地方」是「前往…」的意思。這裡的 mind 是指「注意，小心」，例如：Mind your behavior.（注意你的行為。）gap 是個中級的單字，意思是「間隙，縫隙」，我們常聽到別人說的 generation gap 就是指「代溝」。

Question number 14.

Please look at the following three pictures. Listen to the following short talk. Which picture matches the talk?

請看以下三張圖片。聆聽以下簡短談話。談話內容是在講哪一張圖？

East High School is one of the most famous schools in town. With five large buildings, a standard track field and a swimming pool, it is the 2nd largest high school.

東方高中是鎮上最知名的高中之一。有著五座大樓，一個標準操場以及一個游泳池，它也是第二大的高中。

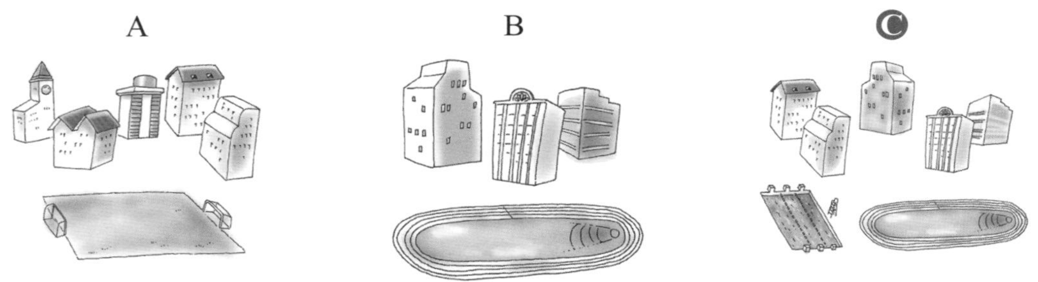

｜詳解｜ 三張圖都是學校，所以題目應該是問所講的是哪一間學校。聆聽時，考生要仔細抓到這些相關字：building（大樓）、track field（操場）、swimming pool（游泳池）、soccer / football field（足球場），另外還要注意數目。談話中的「five large buildings」和「a swimming pool」都是破題點。本題正答案為選項 C。

Day 12

月　　　日

我的完成時間＿＿＿＿分鐘
標準作答時間 10 分鐘

Part 1 看圖辨義

Questions 1-2

Part 2 問答

Questions 3-7

3. A. It's sad that you lost the final!
   B. I'm sorry to hear that.
   C. Of course, we are the best.

4. A. Stop smoking! It'll ruin our health.
   B. Come on, you are barking up the wrong tree.
   C. Sorry, he was not at home yesterday.

5. A. I've just finished my homework.
   B. We're sharing some silly old stories.
   C. Watch your mouth! That's rude.

6. A. There must be a pipe that burst.
   B. No problem. I'll fill in the form.
   C. That's terrible! We need to call the police.

7. A. Will you stop being a backseat driver?
   B. I can't tell between left and right.
   C. Stop bothering me. I need to focus on my work.

Part 3 簡短對話

Questions 8-12

8. A. Their mutual friend
   B. A popular actress
   C. A famous singer

9. A. She moved into a new apartment.
   B. It is her birthday.
   C. The man likes the woman.

10. A. Employer and employee
    B. Principal and teacher
    C. Teacher and student

11. A. The woman has booked a table.
    B. They will sit outside the restaurant.
    C. Three people are going to have dinner.

12. A. The way the woman talked bothers him.
    B. A customer is not happy about him.
    C. He wasted too much time on a difficult customer.

Part 4 短文聽解

Questions 13-14

13.

A

B

C

14.

A

B

C

上頁簡答

解答與詳解

1. (C) 2. (B) 3. (C) 4. (B) 5. (B) 6. (A) 7. (A) 8. (C) 9. (A) 10. (C) 11. (C) 12. (B) 13. (B) 14. (C)

Part 1 看圖辨義

For questions number 1-2, please look at the following pictures.

Question number 1.

What are the people probably watching? 這些人可能正在觀看什麼？

A. A fantastic road show　A. 精彩的街頭表演

B. A terrible TV program　B. 糟糕的電視節目

C. A horror movie　C. 恐怖片

詳解　本題其實是在問什麼地方。圖片的背景很明顯是在電影院，不會是在家裡或是街頭，所以選項 A 的「road show」，以及選項 B 的「TV program」都已經透漏了不是在電影院的訊息，即使不知道 horror（恐怖）的意思，至少聽得出 movie 吧，所以正確答案是選項 C。

補充　「表演」的英文，除了初級的 show，一般也很常見英檢中級的 performance，例如「街頭表演」也可以說成「street performance」，而「畢業公演」則是「graduation performance / play」。

Question number 2.

What can you tell from the man? 從圖中的男人你可以得知什麼？

A. He's having a cup of coffee made by his wife.　A. 他在喝妻子為他泡的咖啡。

B. He's reading a newspaper.　B. 他正在看報紙。

C. He usually prefers jeans but wears a suit today.　C. 他平常喜歡穿牛仔褲但今天他穿了西裝。

詳解　從圖片能想到的單字、片語應該有：a man in suit（穿西裝的男人）、having a cup of coffee / eating breakfast in the living room（在客廳吃早餐）、reading a newspaper（看報紙）。因為題目問的是，你可以「從這張圖片」得知什麼事，而圖中沒有任何女人，所以無法確定早餐是誰做的還是買回來的，所以選項 A 錯誤。接著，男子穿著西裝沒錯，但無法從圖中得知他平常愛穿什麼，所以選項 C 也不對。只有「看報紙」是可以確定的，故正確答案為選項 B。

補充　newspaper 是「報紙」。「早報」我們會說 morning paper，「晚報」就是 evening paper，而「號外」則是 (an) extra。

Part 2 問答

Question number 3.

Our team will win in the final. 我們的隊伍一定會贏得總決賽。

A. It's sad that you lost the final! A. 很遺憾你們輸了總決賽！

B. I'm sorry to hear that. B. 我很遺憾聽到這件事。

C. Of course, we are the best. C. 當然囉，我們是最棒的。

| 詳解 | 根據三個選項中的 final（總決賽）跟 team（隊伍）可推知跟比賽有關。總決賽還沒開始，怎麼會先輸了（lost），所以選項 A 不對，而對於一句自信、樂觀的話，選項 B 的回應完全是不盡情理。故本題正確答案為選項 C。

| 補充 | 在一些像是球類的比賽過程中，有所謂「資格賽」（a qualifying tournament）、「淘汰賽」（a knockout）、「半準決賽」（a quarter-final）、「準決賽」（a semi-final）、「決賽」（the final / the championship match） 等重要的比賽階段，另外，「友誼賽」是 friendly (competition / match)。

Question number 4.

You ruined the garden when I was not at home. 我不在家時你把花園搞得亂七八糟。

A. Stop smoking! It'll ruin our health. A. 別再抽菸了！它會毀了你的健康。

B. Come on, you are barking up the wrong tree. B. 拜託，你罵錯人了。

C. Sorry, he was not at home yesterday. C. 抱歉，他昨天不在家。

| 詳解 | 本題考生要非常注意的是選項 B，一般 bark 我們知道用在狗身上，指「吠叫」，但這裡的 bark 延伸指「罵，臭罵」。「barking up the wrong tree」表面意思是狗狗對著錯誤的樹吠叫，但其延伸的涵意是「罵錯人」。題目的 ruin 是關鍵字，指「毀掉，弄得亂七八糟」，而選項 A 刻意用了相同字彙 ruin，但完全與題目扯不上關係。若要推掉責任，則要說自己不在家而非他人，所以選項 C 也不對。故本題正確答案為選項 B。

| 補充 | ruin 也可以當名詞用，表示「毀壞，破產，墮落，徹底毀掉」，例如：in a state of ruin（處於破敗不堪的狀態）、fall or go into ruin（陷入毀滅狀態）。另外，慣用複數形的 ruins 表示「廢墟」。例如：A big earthquake left the whole town in ruins.（一場大地震讓整個城鎮成為廢墟。）

Question number 5.

What's so funny? 什麼事那麼好笑？

A. I've just finished my homework. A. 我剛做完了家庭作業。

B. We're sharing some silly old stories. B. 我們正在分享一些從前做的蠢事。

C. Watch your mouth! That's rude. C. 注意你的言語！那很不禮貌。

| 詳解 | 就選項來看似乎猜不到題目要問什麼，不過還好聽懂「What's so funny？」（什麼事那麼好笑？）不是太困難。這句代表在做或講某些有趣的事，跟做完了家庭作業無關，所以選項 A 不對。選項 C 的 rude 指「沒禮貌」，才問一句「有什麼好笑的？」並沒那麼嚴重，所以選項 C 也不合邏輯。故本題正確答案為選項 B。

| 補充 | rude 形容「人」時表示「粗魯的，無理的」，如果用來形容「物」呢？像是「use rude tools」（使用粗糙簡陋的工具）、buy rude cotton（購買天然未加工的棉）、tell a rude joke（講了一個粗俗的笑話）

Question number 6.

The bathroom is filled with water! 浴室淹水了！

A. There must be a pipe that burst. A. 一定是有一根管破裂了。

B. No problem. I'll fill in the form. B. 沒問題。我會把表格填寫好。

C. That's terrible! We need to call the police. C. 真糟糕！我們得報警才行。

| 詳解 | 本題關鍵是題目中「filled with...」這個片語，它等於「full of...」，表示「充滿⋯的」，回到家看見浴室淹水，想必會有點崩潰的感覺，那麼選項 C 前半句的「That's terrible!」就是相當正常的回應，不過，也不能勞煩警察來處理吧！所以選項千萬不要只看一半就選定了；選項 B 則刻意以相同動詞 fill 來混淆一下，但「填寫表格」跟浴室淹水完全扯不上關係。故本題正確答案是選項 A。pipe（管子，水管）和 burst（爆裂，爆開）都是初級單字，動詞 burst 的三態都是 burst。

Question number 7.

You should turn left before that block. And you drive too fast.
你應該在那個街區之前就右轉。而且你開太快了

A. Will you stop being a backseat driver? A. 你可以不要再指手畫腳了好嗎？

B. I can't tell between left and right. B. 我無法分辨左右。

C. Stop bothering me. I need to focus on my work. C. 別煩我了。我必須專心在我的工作。

| 詳解 | 本題答題關鍵是選項 A 的「backseat driver」，意思是「一直指使駕駛如何開車的後座乘客」。聽到題目的 drive，可知是在「開車」，所以選項 C 不對。分不清左右（can't tell between left and right）的人是不可能開車的，所以選項 B 也不對。所以即使你一時聽不出或沒學過什麼叫「backseat driver」，也能輕易地以刪除法確定正確答案為選項 A。

Part 3 簡短對話

Question number 8.

W: Look, who's that handsome guy wearing a pair of sunglass?
女：你看，那個戴著墨鏡的帥哥是誰？

M: I have no idea. But I seem to see him somewhere.
男：我不知道。不過我似乎在哪見過他。

W: Oh, I got it! On TV! He is Jay Chou.
女：啊，我知道了！在電視上嘛！他是周杰倫。

Question. Whom did the speakers come across? 說話者碰到了誰？

A. Their mutual friend　A. 他們共同的朋友

B. A popular actress　B. 一位受歡迎的女演員

C. A famous singer　C. 一位知名歌手

詳解 本題的選項可以讓考生直接推測問題是「說話者遇見了誰」，而破題關鍵有二：1. handsome guy；2. On TV!。首先，即使不懂 mutual（相互的），看到 friend 也可以直接剔除掉選項 A，而女子說的「handsome guy wearing...」也可以確定選項 B 是錯誤的，故本題正確答案為選項 C。

Question number 9.

M: Hello, Catherine.
男：哈囉，凱撒琳。

W: Hello, Robert. Welcome to my housewarming party. Just make yourself comfortable.
女：哈囉，羅勃。歡迎參加我的喬遷派對。當自己家一樣，別客氣。

M: This is for you.
男：這是給妳的。

W: Thank you, you are so sweet.
女：謝謝，你真好。

Question. Why is the woman given a present? 為什麼女子會收到禮物？

A. She moved into a new apartment.　A. 她搬進了一間新公寓。

B. It is her birthday.　B. 那是她的生日。

C. The man likes the woman.　C. 男子喜歡那女人。

詳解 三個選項都比較跟女說話者有關，因此須注意女子說的話。如果是選項 B，應該會聽到 happy birthday、birthday gift 等字詞。如果是選項 A，應該會聽到 move to a new house / an apartment 等。本題的破題點為「housewarming party」，指「喬遷派對」，很明顯女人搬了新家，男人到她家作客並送上禮物，所以正確答案為選項 A。至於男子是否因為喜歡女子很前來參加 party 以及送禮物，理論上只是有可能，但無法從對話中確定，所以 C 並非是最好的答案。

補充 外國人搬新家後，通常會找朋友到新家開個派對熱鬧熱鬧，這種派對就叫「housewarming party」。本題女人搬進新家，好朋友來慶祝她喬遷之喜，女人對朋友說 Make yourself comfortable. 就是請他們當作自己家就可以了。只要是朋友到我們家來或我們所舉行的宴會，我們都可以說 Make yourself comfortable / at home.。

Question number 10.

W: You're late again. Give me a reason. 女：你又遲到了。給我一個理由。

M: I overslept. 男：我睡過頭。

W: And you didn't hand in your homework. Why? 女：而且你沒有交作業。為什麼？

M: I left it on my desk. 男：我放在書桌上忘了帶來。

Question. Who are the speakers? 對話者是誰？

A. Employer and employee A. 僱主與員工

B. Principal and teacher B. 校長與老師

C. Teacher and student C. 老師與學生

詳解 看到選項內容，便可確定問題是問「兩位對話者是什麼關係」。對話中的破題關鍵就是 homework（家庭作業），公司的員工不會有家庭作業，所以選項 A 不對。老師不會有什麼家庭作業，校長也不可能這樣跟老師說話，所以選項 B 錯誤。故本題正確答案為選項 C。

補充 「hand in」是指「繳交」，是老師常用的說法。發下考卷一般會說「give out the test paper」。

Question number 11.

M: Two for dinner? 男：兩位用餐嗎？

W: No, a table for three. 女：不，請給我三個人的座位。

M: This way, please. I'll let you sit by the window. 男：這邊請。我讓你們坐靠窗的位子。

W: Thanks. 女：謝謝你。

Question. What is true? 何者為真？

A. The woman has booked a table. A. 女人有預訂位子。

B. They will sit outside the restaurant. B. 他們將坐在餐廳外。

C. Three people are going to have dinner. C. 有三人要吃晚餐。

詳解 從選項可預測對話內容跟餐廳用餐有關。服務生問「Two for dinner?」（兩位用餐嗎？）代表客人沒有訂位，所以選項 A 不對。女人回答說「a table for three」（要三個人的座位），所以正確答案就是選項 C。

補充 當我們出國要搭飛機時，航空公司人員也會問你是否要「sit by the window」（坐靠窗座位）或是「sit by the aisle」（坐靠走道座位）。另外我們說「訂位」，英文可以用「make a reservation」或者說 booking。

Question number 12.

W: Hey, what's bothering you?　女：嗨，你在煩什麼？

M: Well, a customer called to complain about me.　男：嗯，一個客人打電話來投訴我。

W: That's sure to be bothering. Did you know why?　女：那的確很煩人。你知道原因嗎？

M: I'm trying to figure it out.　男：我還在試著了解。

Question. Why is the man unhappy? 男子為什麼不開心？

A. The way the woman talked bothers him.　A. 女子說話的方式讓他覺得煩。

B. A customer is not happy about him.　B. 一個客人對他不滿。

C. He wasted too much time on a difficult customer.　C. 他浪費太多時間在一個奧客身上。

| 詳解 | 根據選項 B 跟 C，對話內容應該是男人跟他 customer（客人）之間的事，破題字為 complain（抱怨）。因為一名客人打電話來抱怨他，導致他 unhappy（不開心），故正確答案為選項 B。

| 補充 | 在奉行顧客至上（customer first）的服務業中，「奧客」總是最讓人心累。奧客專指很難應付或惡劣的客人，英文就會直接說 difficult customer，其中 difficult 在這邊是指「難搞的」，千萬別說成「bad customer」了。

Part 4 短文聽解

Question number 13.

Please look at the following three pictures. Listen to the following short talk. Which is the speaker's house?

請看以下三張圖片。聆聽以下簡短談話。哪一間房子是說話者的家？

My family and I live in the countryside. It might not be as convenient as living in the city but we are closer to nature. We grow flowers in our front yard and keep a dog in the back yard. It is much more fun than living in the city.

我和我的家人住在鄉間。這可能沒有跟住在城市一樣方便，不過我們更接近大自然。我們在前院裡種花，在後院裡養一隻狗。住在這裡比住在都市有趣多了。

A

B

C

| 詳解 | 選項 A 是大部分都市人住的 apartment，選項 B 是 house with yards（有院子的房子），選項 C 是開放式的 villa / summer house。大概整理出這些資訊後，聽到短文中出現 front yard（前院）跟 back yard（後院）時，我們就可以確定正確答案為選項 B。

Question number 14.

Please look at the following three pictures. Listen to the following short talk. What might Tina buy?

請看以下三張圖片。聆聽以下簡短談話。蒂娜可能買什麼？

Tina is making a cheesecake for her mother. She checked her refrigerator and found she had run out of butter and sugar. Yet she had lots of flour and enough cheese.

蒂娜正在為媽媽做起司蛋糕。她查看了一下冰箱，發現已經沒有奶油和糖了。不過她有許多的麵粉跟足夠的起司。

| 詳解 | 本題考烹煮材料的單字，請務必盡力掌握圖中所有材料的英文。蒂娜是要做蛋糕，不是要去買，所以選項 B 已經不符。本題的破題點是 had run out of butter and sugar（已經沒有奶油跟糖），run out of 指「耗盡，用光」，所以蒂娜要買的就是這兩種材料（ingredients）。故正確答案為選項 C。

| 補充 | run out of 是「耗盡，用完」，例如：My car ran out of fuel.（我的車沒油了。）、We are running out of time.（我們快沒時間了。）

Day 13

月　　日

我的完成時間______分鐘
標準作答時間 10 分鐘

Part 1 看圖辨義

Questions 1-2

Part 2 問答

Questions 3-7

3. A. I'm getting on the bus.
   B. As usual, and you?
   C. I appreciate your help.

4. A. Yes, I believe you can do it yourself.
   B. Yes, please. This box is so heavy.
   C. Just take it easy.

5. A. It's 10:15 a.m. now.
   B. I'm afraid not.
   C. What do you want me to do?

6. A. What's the matter?
   B. Don't worry. Be happy!
   C. Thank you.

7. A. It was September 8.
   B. It was Tuesday.
   C. It was an important day.

Part 3 簡短對話

Questions 8-12

8. A. Two
   B. Three
   C. We don't know.

9. A. The woman did.
   B. The man did.
   C. Neither of them went mountain climbing yesterday.

10. A. He's driving on the road.
    B. He's getting out of his car on the parking lot.
    C. He's starting up the engine.

11. A. She works with John in a same company.
    B. She's a fellow worker of Sandy.
    C. She moved into a new house recently.

12. A. David guesses he's younger than Mary.
    B. Mary is 5 years younger than David.
    C. They look the same age.

Part 4 短文聽解

Questions 13-14

13.

A

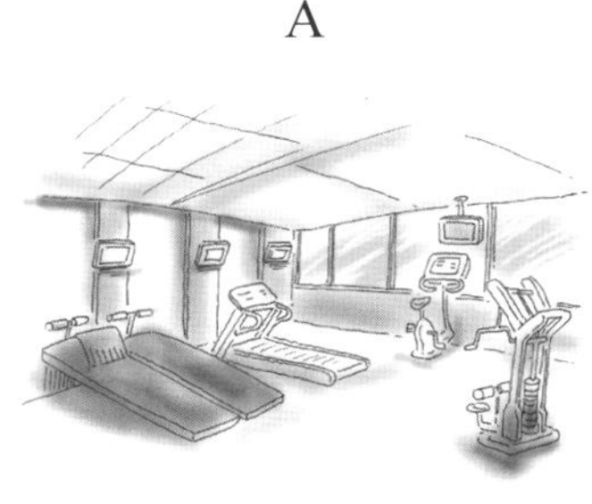

B

C

14.

A

B

C

上頁簡答

解答與詳解

1. (B) 2. (B) 3. (B) 4. (B) 5. (A) 6. (C) 7. (B) 8. (A)
9. (C) 10. (A) 11. (B) 12. (B) 13. (A) 14. (B)

Part 1 看圖辨義

For questions number 1-2, please look at the following pictures.

Question number 1.

What happened to the girl? 女孩發生了什麼事？

A. She found a key on her way home. A. 她在回家途中發現了一把鑰匙。
B. She was locked outside of her home. B. 她被鎖在家門外了。
C. Her key was in the garbage. C. 她的鑰匙在垃圾裡。

| 詳解 | 從圖片可知女生出門時把鑰匙放在家裡，所以選項 A 不對。女生提著的是 garbage（垃圾）沒錯，但 key（鑰匙）其實在家裡桌上，所以選項 C 也不對。故正確答案為選項 B。

| 補充 | lock 當名詞為「鎖頭」，當動詞則為「鎖住，鎖上」，unlock 就是「解鎖」，例如：Please unlock the door. I can't get in.（請把門鎖打開。我進不去。）Lock the door carefully when you are away.（你不在家時請把門小心鎖上。）

Question number 2.

What is the woman trying to do? 女子正試著做什麼？

A. Order dessert A. 點甜點
B. Foot the bill B. 付帳
C. Blame the waiter C. 責怪服務生

| 詳解 | 請用英文思考圖中內容：a man and a woman (are) in the restaurant（一男一女在餐廳裡）、finished their meals（用完他們的餐點）、the woman took the bill（女人拿了帳單）、she paid（她付了錢）。圖中兩人表情愉快，所以應該沒有對誰生氣，故選項 C 不符。女人手拿帳單，有付錢的意思，所以選項 A「她想點甜點」也不對。故本題正確答案為選項 B。

| 補充 | foot the bill = pay the bill（買單，付帳）。跟服務生要帳單，我們可以說：May I have / take the bill?

Part 2 問答

Question number 3.

How are you getting on? 最近如何？

A. I'm getting on the bus. A. 我正要上公車了。

B. As usual, and you? B. 一如往常，你呢?

C. I appreciate your help. C. 感謝你的幫忙。

| 詳解 | 從三個選項來看，彼此似乎關聯性不大，各自為針對不同話語的回應，所以必須仔細聽好題目這句了！題目的「How are you...?」已經點出是一句「問候語」，所以即使不確定「How are you getting on?」真正的意思，大約也能抓到十之八九的語意。對於「你最近好嗎？」的回答，最適當的回應就是選項 B 了。選項 A 刻意以相同的「getting on」混淆答題，請特別注意。

| 補充 | how 也常用來詢問對方對於某事物的感覺（例如 How was your test?），或者問對方做某件事情的過程與方法（例如：How do you go to work every day?）。

Question number 4.

Is there anything I can help with? 有什麼我能幫忙的嗎？

A. Yes, I believe you can do it yourself. A. 是的，我相信你可以自己搞定。

B. Yes, please. This box is so heavy. B. 是的，麻煩一下。這箱子好重啊。

C. Just take it easy. C. 放輕鬆點就好了。

| 詳解 | 從三個選項來爛，(A) 是用來表達「鼓勵對方」，但完全與題目問句不相關。(C) 通常用來請對方放鬆一下，不要太拘束等，所以聽到「有什麼我能幫忙的嗎？」時，選項中最適當的回應自然是 B 了，故正確答案是選項 B。

| 補充 | 經常被用錯的一句話是「Is there anything I can help you?」因為還原成肯定句時是「I can help you something.」something 是一件事情，若要表達「幫助你做某事」，應該是「help you with something」，須加上介系詞 with，因此在問句中 with 當然也不能省略。另外，本題在 help 和 with 中間加進 you（= Is there anything I can help you with?）也是一樣的意思。

Question number 5.

Mary, do you have the time? 瑪莉？現在幾點了？

A. It's 10:15 a.m. now. A. 現在早上 10 點 15 分。

B. I'm afraid not. B. 我恐怕沒空。

C. What do you want me to do? C. 你要我做什麼？

| 詳解 | 本題考你懂不懂「have time」和「have the time」的差別！time 前面加了一個定冠詞 the，表示特定的時間，其實也就是在問此時此刻、當下的時間。所以題目這句相當於

「What time is it now?」、「What time do you have now?」所以正確答案是選項 A。

｜補充｜ time 這個字在英文裡可謂千變萬化，且一不小心很容易被誤解。例如和朋友一起去酒吧，大家談天很盡興，聊得忘了時間。不一會兒酒吧老闆可能走過來跟大家說：「**Time, please!**」這時候可別誤以為人家在問你現在幾點喔！那是「抱歉，我們要打烊了。」的意思。

Question number 6.

Have a safe flight! 祝你旅途順利！

A. What's the matter? A. 怎麼了？

B. Don't worry. Be happy! B. 別擔心。開心點！

C. Thank you. C. 謝謝你。

｜詳解｜ 從三個選項可以很容易猜到題目一定和是電話用語有關。「This is... speaking.」通常是接電話時的第一句話，接著打電話的人第一句話會說什麼，就是本題的答案了。通常電話的另一端應該會說「我是…（某某人）」、「請找…某某人」等，選項 A 通常是接電話者的用語，明顯錯誤；選項 B 這句也是接電話的人說的話，通常是在確認對方要找誰時，所以也不對。「May I speak to..., please?」就是打電話的人要找某某人會說的話，所以正確答案是選項 C。

｜補充｜「旅行祝福」的話，還可以說：Have a nice trip!（祝你旅途愉快！）、Wish you a good journey!（願你有一個美好的旅程！）、Bon voyage!（祝你旅途愉快！）→ 原為法文，已在英文使用中形成流行用語。

Question number 7.

What day was it yesterday? 昨天是星期幾？

A. It was September 8. A. 昨天是 9 月 8 日。

B. It was Tuesday. B. 昨天是星期二。

C. It was an important day. C. 昨天是個重要的日子。

｜詳解｜ 本題其實考的不是句意的理解，而是發音的辨認。由於 day 和 date 在一個句子裡辨認不易，所以要特別留意它們的「連音」。day 是母音 [e] 結尾，而 date 是無聲子音 [t] 結尾，所以在「What day / date was...?」當中，兩者就很容易可以分別得出來，前者是 [(h)wɑ de wɑz...]，後者是 [(h)wɑ de twɑz...]。以 What day 開頭的問句是在問「星期幾」，所以選項 B 回答星期二，就是正確答案。選項 A 回答的是「日期」，選項 C 最後也有個 -day 的音，讓你覺得好像也是針對問題在回答，但根本是答非所問。

Part 3 簡短對話

Question number 8.

M: Those snacks on the table look delicious.
男：桌上那些零食看起來很好吃。

W: I just bought them from the night market.
女：那是我在夜市剛買回來的。

M: You must have stood in a long line to get them, huh?
男：你肯定得排了很長的隊才買到吧？

W: Yeah, I spent almost an hour for both.
女：對啊，我花了差不多一個小時才買到這兩樣。

Question. How many kinds of food did the woman purchase?
女子買了幾種食物？

A. Two A. 兩種

B. Three B. 三種

C. We don't know. C. 我們不知道。

詳解 題目問的是女子買了幾種食物，對話的第一句雖然有提到食物（snacks），但未提及買了幾樣，所以應注意接下來女子的發言部分，以及與數字有關的字詞。對話最後：I spent almost an hour for both.（我花了差不多一個小時才買到這兩樣），聽到會後這裡，答案也就出來了。本題正確答案為選項 A。

Question number 9.

W: I didn't go mountain climbing yesterday.
女：我昨天沒有去爬山。

M: I didn't, either.
男：我也沒有去。

W: Why? Are you still busy with your entrance exam?
女：為什麼？你還在忙著準備入學考試嗎？

M: That's right. I spent almost 8 hours every day preparing the exam.
男：沒錯。我每天花差不多八個小時準備考試。

Question. Who went mountain climbing yesterday? 昨天誰去爬山了？

A. The woman did. A. 女子去了。

B. The man did. B. 男子去了。

C. Neither of them went mountain climbing yesterday. C. 昨天沒有人去爬山。

詳解 從三個選項來看就知道題目要問的是男子或女子，或是兩人都沒有去做什麼事，而答題關鍵就在於是否聽出 either 這個字。either 表示「也不～」，用於否定句，男子表示，他昨天「也沒有」去爬山。對話裡面只有兩個人，而其中一人說出「..., either.」，就表示「兩個人都沒去」，那麼答案就出來了，正確答案是選項 C。反之，如果聽到的是 So... 或 ..., too，那就表示「兩個人都有去」。

| 補充 | busy 這個形容詞用法是「be busy + Ving」（忙著做某件事）。例如：We're busy preparing for our trip over vacation.（我們忙著準備假期的旅行。）不過 busy 還有另一個用法是「be busy with + 名詞」（忙於某事）。例如：She has been so busy with work recently that she doesn't have time to sleep.（她最近工作超忙，導致她都沒時間睡覺。）

Question number 10.

W: Don't you hear the sound of the ambulance? 女：你沒有聽到救護車的聲音嗎？

M: Oh, I really don't. I need to turn down the volume a bit. 男：哦，我真的沒有。我得把音量調低一點。

W: And you need to quickly give way for the ambulance, or you'll be fined. 女：而且你得趕快讓路給救護車，不然你會被罰款。

M: You're right. 男：你說得對。

Question. What is the man probably doing? 男子可能在做什麼？

A. He's driving on the road. A. 他正在路上開車。

B. He's getting out of his car on the parking lot. B. 他在停車場且正要從他的車子裡出來。

C. He's starting up the engine. C. 他正要發動引擎。

| 詳解 | 從三個選項來看，可以知道這題要問的是「男子正在做什麼？」，本題主要關鍵就在於是否聽出且聽懂 give way（讓道）這個片語，因為它不可能用在從車子裡出來（getting out of his car）或是正在發動引擎（starting up the engine）時，固本題正確答案是選項 A。

| 補充 | 「give way」照字面意思「給路」，所以「give way for...」可以用來表示「讓路給…」，不過這裡的介系詞 for 也可以換成 to，且除了「讓道，讓路，讓步」之後，也常被引伸為「被…取代」。例如：His calmness gave way to his anger when he saw his girlfriend walking with another man.（當它到他女朋友和別的男人走在一起時，他內心的平靜被一陣怒火所取代。）另外，「give way」也可以不接介系詞，表示「讓步，屈服」。例如：Neither of them is willing to give way, so they could be arguing for a very long time.（他們兩個誰也不願意讓步，所以他們會吵好長時間。）

Question number 11.

M: Hi, Helen! Welcome to my housewarming party. 男：嗨，海倫！歡迎來到我的新居喬遷派對。

W: It's been long, John. How's going? 女：好久不見，約翰。最近如何？

M: Pretty good. By the way, who are the pretty girls? 男：挺好的。對了，這兩位漂亮的女孩是誰？

W: Sandy and Rube. They are my colleagues. 女：是仙蒂和盧比，她們是我的同事。

M: Sandy and Rube, nice to meet you two. 男：仙蒂、盧比，很高興認識你們。

Question. What is true about Helen? 關於海倫，何者為真？

A. She works with John in a same company.　A. 她和約翰在同一家公司工作。

B. She's a fellow worker of Sandy.　B. 她是仙蒂的一位同事

C. She moved into a new house recently.　C. 她最近搬進了新房子。

| 詳解 | 本題應盡可能記住三個選項的內容，然後仔細聆聽對話，有提到 Helen 以及她的發言部分，應多加注意。首先，從對話一開始的「M: Hi, Helen!」及「It's been long, John.」，我們知道對話男女分別是 John 和 Helen，且他們很久未見了，所以確定選項 A 是錯誤的。男子一開始說「Welcome to my housewarming party.」表示他剛搬新家，所以選項 C 是錯誤的。女子（Helen）說「Sandy and Rube. They are my colleagues.」所以正確答案是選項 B。

| 補充 | 初次見面時的打招呼用語，通常會說 Nice to meet/see you.，但如果是再次遇見對方就不能說 Nice to meet you.，而是要說 Nice to see you again.。另外，當彼此初次見面後要道別時，可以說 Nice meeting you. 或 Nice to have met you.。

Question number 12.

M: May I have your name, please?

W: Sure, just call me Mary, and I'm twenty-six years old.

M: My name is David. I'm older than you by 5 years.

W: Are you kidding? I think you look younger than me.

男：可以請問您的名字是？

女：當然，你可以叫我瑪麗，我二十六歲。

男：我叫大衛。我比你大五歲。

女：你在開玩笑嗎？我覺得你看起來比我年輕。

Question. What's true about the speakers? 關於說話者，哪一項是正確的？

A. David guesses he's younger than Mary.　A. 大衛以為他比瑪麗年輕。

B. Mary is 5 years younger than David.　B. 瑪麗比大衛小五歲。

C. They look the same age.　C. 他們看起來同年齡。

| 詳解 | 本題是問年齡大小的問題，就文法觀點來說，是在考比較級的用法。David 說「I'm older than you by 5 years.」所以瑪麗比大衛小五歲，正確答案是選項 B。

| 補充 | 在英文裡，「比…大／小幾歲」的表達方式，一般都使用下列幾種說法（以「我比你大 5 歲」為例）：

I'm 5 years older than you.

I am your senior by five years.

I am five years your senior.

I am older than you by five years.

Part 4 短文聽解

Question number 13.

Please look at the following three pictures. Listen to the following message. Where is Sally?

請看以下三張圖片。聆聽以下訊息。莎莉現在在哪裡？

Martin, this is Sally. I've been waiting for you for almost an hour. I was here at 3 and worked out till now. I'm really tired and I'm heading for the showers. I'll wait for your call at home.

馬丁，我是莎莉。我幾乎等了你快一小時了。我三點就在這裡了，且我一直運動到現在。我真的累了，要去沖澡了。我在家等你的電話囉。

｜詳解｜ 選項 A 是 gym / fitness center，選項 B 是 home，選項 C 是 bathroom。圖二跟圖三可以視為同一個場所，即家裡和家裡的浴室。破題字為 work out，在此指「運動，健身」。莎莉說她三點到現在都在這裡健身（was here at 3 and worked out till now），所以她不可能在家，也就是說答案不可能是選項 B 跟 C，故正確答案為選項 A。

｜補充｜ head for 指「前往…，去做…」，例如：Martin is heading for an interview.（馬丁正要去面試。）head to 指「前往」，例如：Martin is heading to Taichung.（馬丁正要去台中。）I am heading home.（我正要回家。）

Question number 14.

Please look at the following three pictures. Listen to the following short talk. Where would Mary go?

請看以下三張圖片。聆聽以下簡短談話。瑪麗可能去哪裡？

For days, Max didn't eat and play much. Max used to bark happily at Mary whenever she bought him his favorite can. But today, Max gave the canned food a sniff and moved away. Mary decided to take him to a place.

小邁好幾天都吃不多，也不愛玩耍。以前每當瑪麗買小邁最愛的罐頭給牠時，牠都會開心的汪汪叫。不過今天，小邁聞了一下罐頭就走開了。瑪麗決定要帶牠到一個地方。

|詳解| 簡短談話中的 Max 是一隻狗，關鍵字為 bark（吠叫），因為只有狗發出的聲音我們會用 bark。Max 這幾天「didn't eat and play much」（吃不多也不愛動），甚至連牠最愛的「canned food（狗罐頭）也引不起牠的興趣，而且「gave the canned food a sniff and moved away」（聞了聞便走開），所以正常狀況下，瑪莉應該會決定帶 Max 去看醫生。故本題正確答案為選項 B。

Day 14

月　　日

我的完成時間______分鐘
標準作答時間 20 分鐘

Part 1 看圖辨義

Questions 1-5

1. 2. 3. 4. 5.

Part 2 問答

Questions 6-15

6. A. You mean now?
   B. Thanks for your effort.
   C. No, I want to ride the U-bike there.

7. A. Yes, my daddy is cooking in the kitchen.
   B. No, my mommy is in the bedroom.
   C. Come in, please.

8. A. Tell me when you're ready.
   B. Sure, it's quite special.
   C. No, it's been several years.

9. A. I work as an waitress in a restaurant.
   B. I get paid by hour and receive my paycheck every month.
   C. I only earn thirty thousand dollars a month.

10. A. I'm going out for lunch later.
    B. I'm going to the library for some useful books.
    C. I'll look for a job and save some money.

11. A. Just take your time.
    B. I see, but I don't know what you mean.
    C. Yes, I'm now in a hurry to take a break.

12. A. No worries, just make sure you do it right.
    B. That's great! Don't care about me anymore.
    C. OK. Let me know if anything comes up.

13. A. No way! Will you be absent tomorrow?
    B. Thanks for letting me know.
    C. We should respect one another.

14. A. Don't cheat on your wife.
    B. You doubt whether it's true or not?
    C. Really? It seems out of character for him.

15. A. Definitely! I've got a lot of fun activities lined up.
    B. I wonder how you know summer vacation is coming soon.
    C. Yes, I can't wait to go skiing on high mountains.

Part 3 簡短對話

Questions 16-25

16. A. Making more friends
    B. Always keeping his promises to her
    C. Giving up on his friend

17. A. He has bad luck on the exam day.
    B. He studies hard for just a few days before the exam.
    C. He fails to get enough sleep before the exam.

18. A. He made a fool of himself.
    B. He was turned down by a pretty girl.
    C. He made a girl fall down at the party.

19. A. It gives her good working experience.
    B. It can protect some people from hunger.
    C. It can make a big difference.

20. A. The man keeps in contact with her.
    B. The man spends more time with her.
    C. The man stops being angry with her.

21. A. Teach the kid to know about safety signs
    B. Watch out for the kid at any time
    C. Remember to remind the boy not to run through the road

22. A. He pushed the chair over on purpose.
    B. She was sure that he is not angry anymore.
    C. He is very polite and helpful.

23. A. He likes to eat meat and fish.
    B. He goes to the gym every week.
    C. He makes it a rule to work out and eat healthy.

24. A. He's the best they have ever seen.
    B. The woman thinks the teacher is better than any in the past.
    C. The man also likes the new teacher very much.

25. A. To help with preparing the party
    B. Not to say a word about the party
    C. Not to tell Jack they've known about the surprise party

Part 4 短文聽解

Questions 26-30

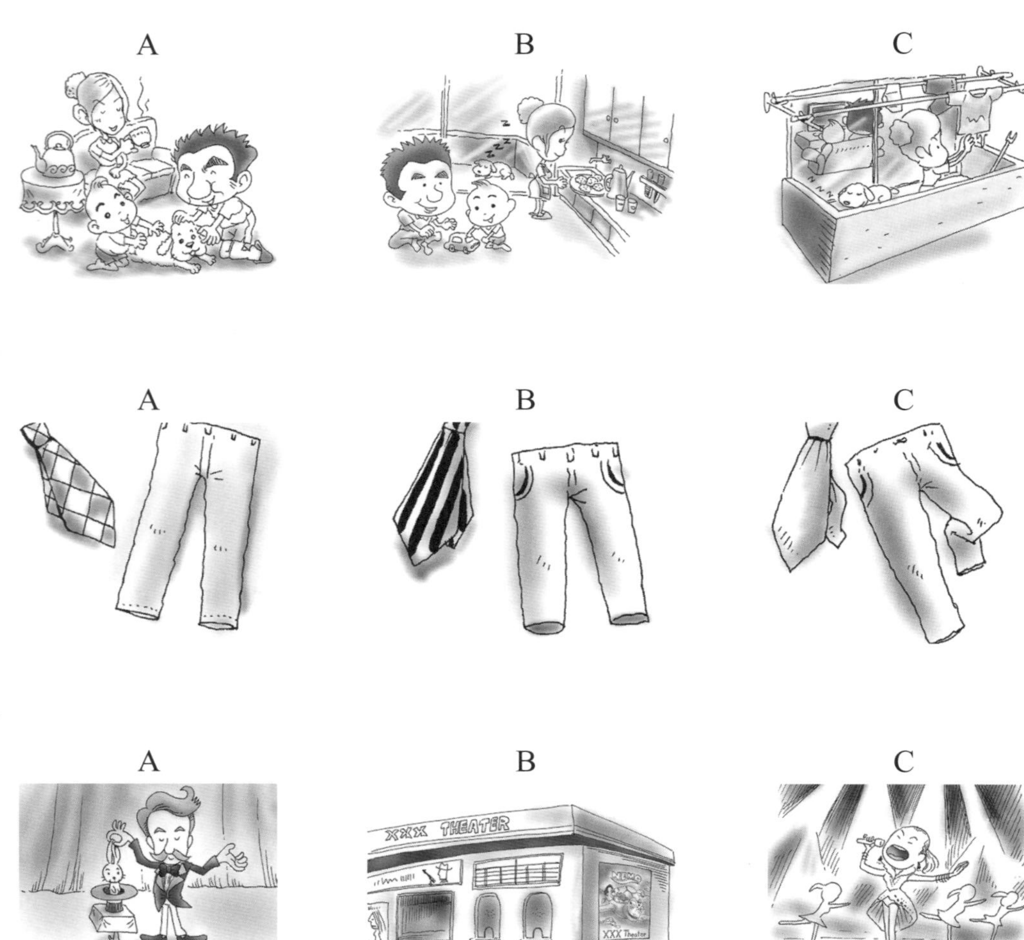

29.

A

B

C

30.

A

B

C

1. (C) 2. (B) 3. (C) 4. (A) 5. (C) 6. (A) 7. (A) 8. (B) 9. (B) 10. (C) 11. (A) 12. (C) 13. (B) 14. (C) 15. (A) 16. (C) 17. (B) 18. (A) 19. (C) 20. (A) 21. (B) 22. (A) 23. (C) 24. (B) 25. (B) 26. (B) 27. (B) 28. (A) 29. (B) 30. (B)

Part 1 看圖辨義

For questions number 1-5, please look at the following pictures.

Question number 1.

What is true about the picture? 關於這張圖，何者為真？

A. There are two light trucks waiting for the traffic light. A. 有兩部小貨車在停等紅燈。

B. An ambulance is running through the red light. B. 一輛救護車正闖過紅燈。

C. We can't see any passengers on the sidewalk. C. 人行道上看不到任何行人。

｜詳解｜ 本題純粹是考你對於一些交通相關字詞能否分辨出來，包括（light）truck、traffic light、ambulance、red light、run through、passenger、sidewalk 等。就算你不知道「light truck」的意思，也應該要知道圖中停等紅燈的一大一小貨車不可能都一樣叫作「light truck」（light 輕的／heavy 重的），所以 A 顯然錯誤。圖中看不到任何救護車，所以 B 也錯誤，故正確答案是選項 C。

｜補充｜ 「小型貨車」除了可以用「light truck」表示之外，也可以說 pickup 或 pickup truck 。「貨車」一般可以說 「delivery car」甚至 truck。有蓋的小型貨車，我們可以用 van（載人的小巴也可以叫 van。）表示。另外，「拖車」是 trailer 或 trolley，「牽引機」是 tractor。

Question number 2.

What can we tell from the picture? 從圖片裡我們可以得知何事？

A. A lion has escaped from the zoo. A. 一隻獅子從動物園逃跑出來了。

B. People are celebrating a festival. B. 人們在慶祝某個節日。

C. Some Chinese are performing a drama in front of a crowd. C. 一些中國人在人群前表演戲劇。

｜詳解｜ 看到圖就知道跟 festival（節日，節慶）有關，可以聯想到「Chinese New Year」（農曆新年）、festival（節慶）、lion dance（舞龍舞獅）、celebrate （慶祝）。因為舞獅的獅子是假的，所以選項 A 的活獅子跑到街上不對。舞龍舞獅、打鼓可以是一種表演（performance）但不是戲劇（drama），所以選項 C 不對。故本題正確答案為選項 B。

| 補充 | 有關中國人過新年的相關英文有：鞭炮（fire cracker），放鞭炮（play the fire cracker），春聯（couplets），紅包（red envelope / lucky money）。Chinese people give out money in red envelopes on Chinese New Year to wish each other good luck and fortune.（中國人在農曆新年發紅包，祝彼此財運當頭。）

Question number 3.

What do we use this for? 我們用這個做什麼？

A. Repairing the roof	A. 修理屋頂
B. Mopping the floor	B. 拖地板
C. Cutting grass of an area	C. 割除一個區域的草

| 詳解 | 本圖是一台割草機，不知道割草機的英文沒關係，總會知道它是用來「割草」（cut grass）的吧！所以正確答案是選項 C。選項 A 的 repair（修理）、roof（屋頂），選項 B 的 mop（拖地）、floor（地板）都是初級的基本單字，要能夠聽得出來喔！

| 補充 | 「割草機」的英文是 mower、lawnmower 或是 mowing machine。「除草」這個動詞就是 mow，lawn 是「草坪」的意思。

Question number 4.

What are the people doing? 這些人在做什麼？

A. Playing cards	A. 打牌
B. Playing chess	B. 下棋
C. Building blocks	C. 堆積木

| 詳解 | 圖片很清楚告訴你，這些人在打牌（playing cards），且 cards 也是很容易聽得出來的單字，所以正確答案為選項 A。chess（西洋棋）和 blocks（積木）都是初級單字，也都可以搭被動詞 play 來表達，不過一般來說，「玩積木」要說「(playing with) building blocks」，另外，積木也可以用 bricks 表示。

Question number 5.

Where was the photo taken? 這張照片是在何處拍的？

A. In front of a waterfall	A. 在瀑布前方
B. At the top of the mountain	B. 在山頂上
C. Near a tall building	C. 在一棟高聳建築物附近

| 詳解 | 圖片中人物後方顯然是一棟很高的建築物，而從三個選項中聽到的單字 waterfall（瀑布）、mountain（山）、tall building（大樓）來判斷，正確答案就是選項 C 了。

| 補充 | 一樣都是「高」，high 和 tall 的主要差別在哪呢？tall 強調事物本身從「頭」到「腳」之間的距離「很長」，而 high 則強調事物最高點到某一個表面之間的距離「很遠」。另外，還要記住這個原則：形容「一個人個子高」，不能用 high，只能用

tall。比如：Emily is very tall. 而不能說：Emily is very high.。所以我們在描述又「瘦」又「高」的事物時，應該用 tall。比如 tall buildings（高樓）、a tall tree（一顆大樹）。因為不論是高聳入雲的摩天大樓，還是高大的樹木，它們本身從頭到腳之間的距離都很長。

Part 2 問答

Question number 6.

Why not join us to go biking? （何不跟我們一起去騎單車？）

A. You mean now? A. 你是說現在嗎？

B. Thanks for your effort. B. 感謝你的辛勞。

C. No, I want to ride the U-bike there. C. 不，我想騎 U-bike 去那裡。

｜詳解｜ Why not...? 常用來表達「提議、建議」，對於這項提議，如果願意去但當下還有一點事情不能馬上去，也許就會反問「是現在就要去嗎？」，所以正確答案是選項 A。B 完全是不知所云、不合邏輯的回答，而 C 說「想騎 U-bike」似乎也沒什麼不對，但就錯在句首的「No, ...」了。

｜補充｜ 除了「Why not + 原形動詞」的句型，還有「What/How about + Ving」也可以用來提出建議喔！例如：What/How about going shopping now?（我們逛街購物如何？）

Question number 7.

Are there any adults in? 有大人在家嗎？

A. Yes, my daddy is cooking in the kitchen. A. 是的，我爸正在廚房煮飯。

B. No, my mommy is in the bedroom. B. 不，我媽在臥室裡。

C. Come in, please. C. 請進。

｜詳解｜ 本題關鍵在於 adults 及與其連音的 in，因為 in 屬於「功能性」字眼在收聽錄音時不容易聽得出來，且這裡的 in 後面沒有名詞，所以它並不是介系詞，而是個副詞，表示「在家，在屋子裡」，相當於 at home，與它相反意思的是 out。選項 B 雖然說「my mommy」以及「in the bedroom」，但前面卻說「No,...」，形成矛盾，故 B 錯誤；C 的回答似乎也沒什麼不對，直接請對方進來就表示有大人在，不過題目這句如果是在電話中，那麼 C 就不可選了，所以最適當的答案是選項 A。

Question number 8.

Have you been there before? 你去過那裡嗎？

A. Tell me when you're ready. A. 你準備好時跟我說。

B. Sure, it's quite special. B. 當然，它相當特別。

C. No, it's been several years. C. 不，已經好幾年了。

| 詳解 | 題目句子問「是否去過」某個地方，回答「你準備好時跟我說」很明顯都是答非所問，選項 A 錯誤；C 回答的「已經好幾年了」就表示「有去過」的肯定回答，但前面卻是「No, ...」，所以 C 也錯誤；故正確答案是選項 B。

| 補充 | been 和 gone 分別是動詞 be 和 go 的過去分詞，用於完成式中。雖然過去分詞 been 和 gone 都可以用來談論一段經歷或旅程，但它們所表達的意思不同。been 暗示旅程已結束，並已返回出發地；而 gone 則暗示旅程仍在進行中，未返回出發地。例如：I've been to Paris.（我去過巴黎）、She's gone to Paris.（她已經去了巴黎。）

Question number 9.

How do you get paid? 你是如何領薪的？

A. I work as an waitress in a restaurant. A. 我在一家餐廳擔任女服務生

B. I get paid by hour and receive my paycheck every month. B. 我以時薪計，每個月領一次薪水。

C. I only earn thirty thousand dollars a month. C. 我一個月只賺三萬元。

| 詳解 | 「How do you get paid?」（如何領薪）這個問題的範圍很廣，可能問對方是月領、週領、雙週領或是日日領，也有可能是指領現或轉帳或領支票的方式。選項 A 的回答完全不相關，可直接排除；問你如何領，卻回答一個月領多少，也是文不對題，選項 C 也錯誤；故正確答案是選項 B。

| 補充 | paycheck 就是 pay（薪資）和 check（支票）合成的一個字，原指「付薪水的支票」，一般就是指 salary（薪水）。

Question number 10.

What are you going for after you quit school? 你休學之後有什麼打算？

A. I'm going out for lunch later. A. 我等一下要出去吃午餐。

B. I'm going to the library for some useful books. B. 我要去圖書館找些有用的書。

C. I'll look for a job and save some money. C. 我會去找份工作並存點錢。

| 詳解 | 本題主要考你知不知道「go for」是什麼意思，一般來說，應以「（接下來或將來）要做什麼」為方向來思考。題目問「What are you going for」，選項 A 卻用「going out for」回答，顯然錯誤；問你未來的計劃，選項 B 卻回答「要去圖書館找書」，文不對題，故本題正確答案為選項 C。

| 詳解 | 「quit school」字面意思是「放棄學校」，其實就是中途棄學且沒有完成學業，即「退學」或「輟學」之意。另外，也可以衍生出「quit university」或「quit one's studies」等片語。例如：Here is a list of questions to ask yourself before you quit your studies.（在你休學之前，好好思考清單上的幾個問題吧。）

Question number 11.

Let's do it right now. Hurry up! 我們現在就來做。快點！

A. Just take your time. A. 慢慢來沒關係。

B. I see, but I don't know what you mean. B. 我知道了，不過我不知道你在講什麼。

C. Yes, I'm now in a hurry to take a break. C. 是的，我現在急著要休息一下。

| 詳解 | 題目的「Let's...」有提出建議之意，且「Hurry up!」是用來催促對方加快腳步，因為趕時間，A 的回答表示不認同對方所說，可以慢慢來沒關係，當然也是一種正常的回答，所以正確答案就是選項 A。B 回答「我了解」卻又說「我不你知道在講什麼」，顯然前後矛盾；C 用 Yes 開頭表示認同，接著卻說「要休息一下」，不知所云，當然也是錯誤選項。

| 詳解 | 「Hurry!」和「Hurry up!」都可以用催促對方趕快去做某事，但「Hurry up!」語氣更為強烈，且強調的是要趕上一個目標。例如：Hurry up! We're running out of time!（趕快！我們的時間快沒了。）

Question number 12.

Don't worry. I can take good care of myself. 別擔心。我能照顧好自己。

A. No worries, just make sure you do it right. A. 不用擔心，只要確定你做的是正確的。

B. That's great! Don't care about me anymore. B. 那很好。不用再管我了。

C. OK. Let me know if anything comes up. C. 好吧。有任何事情的話要讓我知道。

| 詳解 | 題目這句以「Don't worry.」開頭，要對方放心，但 A 卻回答「你不用擔心」（No worries, just...）顯然不對；同樣地，B 回答「不用再在乎我了」（Don't care about me anymore）也是矛盾的回答，所以正確答案就是選項 C。「come up」就是「出現」的意思。

| 詳解 | 「take care of」也有「處理，負責」的意思。當「照顧」解時，其後接有生命的人或動物等，當「處理」時，後接沒有生命的事物。例如：You clean the tables, and I'll take care of sweeping the floor.（你清理桌子，我來負責掃地板。）

Question number 13.

Jay is absent from his work today. Jay 今天沒來上班。

A. No way! Will you be absent tomorrow? A. 不會吧！你明天不來嗎？

B. Thanks for letting me know. B. 謝謝你讓我知道。

C. We should respect one another. C. 我們應彼此互相尊重。

| 詳解 | 「absent from...」就是「缺席…」，後面接 work 是「沒來上班」，接 school 則是「沒來上學」。題目說某人沒來上班，選項 A 刻意以相同字彙 absent 混淆答題，回答卻說「你明天也不來嗎？」，這是毫不相關的回答；別人告知一個消息，選項 C 卻回答應彼此互相尊重，也是不知所云的回答，所以正確答案就是選項 B。

Question number 14.

I know for certain that Gary has two girlfriends. 我當然知道蓋瑞有兩位女友。

A. Don't cheat on your wife. A. 別對你太太不忠。

B. You doubt whether it's true or not? B. 你懷疑這件事是真是假嗎？

C. Really? It seems out of character for him. C. 真的嗎？這似乎不像他的個性。

| 詳解 | 題目這句的說話者表示自己相當確定某人腳踏兩條船（has two girlfriends），結果 A 卻回答別對你太太不忠，感覺前面少了一句，應先對於這件消息表示看法，所以不對；而題目已經說「for certain」了，B 還回答說「You doubt...」，這是不合理的回應，所以正確答案就是選項 C。「out of character」是「不符個性／人格特質」的意思。

| 詳解 | 名詞 character 除了可以表示「（故事或電影裡的）角色」以外，還可以指「個性」和「（事物的）特色」。例如：Who is your favorite character in *Star Wars*?（你最喜歡《星際大戰》裡的哪個角色？）The furniture is what gives that house character.（這些家具讓那間房子展現出最大的特色。）

Question number 15.

Are you looking forward to the coming of summer vacation?
你期待暑假即將到來嗎？

A. Definitely! I've got a lot of fun activities lined up. A. 當然！我已經想好一堆有趣的活動了。

B. I wonder how you know summer vacation is coming soon. B. 我好奇你怎麼會知道暑假快到了。

C. Yes, I can't wait to go skiing on high mountains. C. 是的，我等不及要到高山上去滑雪了。

| 詳解 | 暑假即將來到，顯然是大家都會知道的事，所以 B 的回答不合邏輯；既然是暑假要到了，就不可能跟冬天的滑雪（skiing）有關，所以 C 也是明顯錯誤，故本題正確答案是選項 A。「line up」本來是「排隊」的意思，這裡的「got... lined up」就是指「將…依順序排定好」。

| 詳解 | 很多人一看到 to 就會反射動作加上原形動詞，但是「look forward to」的 to 是介系詞，後面如果遇到動詞要加上 ing。既然是介系詞，後面當然也可以接名詞，例如：Are you looking forward to the graduation trip?（你們期待這次的畢業旅行嗎？）

Part 3 簡短對話

Question number 16.

M: I feel so sad. 男：我感到很難過。

W: Why? What happened? 女：為什麼？發生了什麼事？

M: My friend kept breaking promises and never listened to me. 男：我朋友一直違背承諾，從不聽我的話。

W: That's tough. Sometimes it's best to let go of bad relationships. 女：那真是難受。有時候，最好放棄不好的關係。

Question. What does the woman suggest the man do? 女子建議男子做什麼？

A. Making more friends A. 結交更多朋友

B. Always keeping his promises to her B. 永遠對她守承諾

C. Giving up on his friend C. 放棄他的朋友

| 詳解 | 從女子的回答中可以知道，她認為有時候最好放下不好的關係，因為「let go of...」是「讓…離開，放下…」的意思。這暗示她建議男子放棄他的朋友（give up on his friend），因為他描述的朋友行為不佳，持續違背承諾（kept breaking promises）並不聽從男子的話。因此，選項 C 是最合適的答案。

| 補充 | promise 可以當動詞或名詞，意為「承諾」或「保證」。作為名詞時，表示一個人對他人做出的承諾，例如：He made a promise to help her.（他承諾會幫助她。）作為動詞時，表示承諾去做某事，後面接不定詞（to-V），例如：I promise to be there on time.（我保證會準時到達。）而「break a promise」是指違背承諾或食言，例如：He broke his promise to call me every day.（他違背了每天給我打電話的承諾。）

Question number 17.

M: I failed the Midterm exam. Maybe it has something to do with bad luck. 男：我期中考試沒考好。也許是運氣不好。

W: No, I don't think you study hard enough at ordinary times. 女：不，我認為你平時就不夠用功。

M: What? I spent almost 8 hours studying for the exam and I only slept 5 hours a day last week! 男：什麼？我上星期為了這考試每天念書將近八個小時，每天只睡五個小時！

Question. What seems to be the matter with the man? 似乎男子的問題何在？

A. He has bad luck on the exam day. A. 他考試當天運氣不好。

B. He studies hard for just a few days before the exam. B. 他僅在考前幾天努力用功。

C. He fails to get enough sleep before the exam. C. 他考前沒有獲得足夠的睡眠。

| 詳解 | 從對話中可以看出，女子認為男子平時（at ordinary times）不夠用功，而男子辯解說他在考試前一週花了很多時間學習。這表示男子的問題在於他平時就不努力學習，只在考試前集中用功。因此，正確答案是選項 B。

| 補充 | 「have something to do」和「have nothing to do」是用來表示某事與另一事有關或無關。例如：His success has something to do with his hard work.（他的成功與他的努力有關）。相反，當 something 換成 nothing 時，則表示完全無關，例如：This issue has nothing to do with me.（這件事與我無關）。

Question number 18.

M: I spilled my drink on a pretty girl's skirt and fell down at the party last night.
男：我昨晚在派對上把飲料灑在一位漂亮女孩的裙子上，然後摔倒了。

W: Oh no, that sounds embarrassing.
女：哦不，那聽起來很尷尬。

M: Yes, everyone laughed at me.
男：是的，大家都笑我。

W: Don't keep that in mind. It happens to everyone sometimes.
女：別放在心上，這種事有時候人人都會遇到。

Question. What happened to the man last night? 男子昨晚發生了什麼事？

A. He made a fool of himself.
A. 他出糗了。

B. He was turned down by a pretty girl.
B. 他被一位漂亮女孩拒絕了。

C. He made a girl fall down at the party.
C. 他讓一個女孩在派對上摔倒了。

| 詳解 | 男子描述他在派對上把飲料灑在（spilled my drink on...）一位漂亮女孩的裙子上，然後自己摔倒（fell down）了。女子回應這是很尷尬的（embarrassing）事情，男子也提到大家都在笑他。因此，這個事件讓男子確實是出糗了，所以正確答案是選項 A。對話中並沒有提到男子被一位漂亮女孩拒絕，所以 B 錯誤；男子提到他自己摔倒了，而不是讓一個女孩摔倒，所以選項 C 不正確。

| 補充 | 在英文裡，除了「make a fool of oneself」，還有「make a spectacle of oneself」有類似的意思，表示「讓自己成為眾人注目的焦點」。另外，「make a scene」也是一個常用的片語，意思是在公共場合或社交場合中制造或引起騷動、吵鬧或尷尬的情況。例如：He made a scene at the party and embarrassed everyone.（他在派對上大吵大鬧，讓所有人都感到尷尬。）

Question number 19.

W: Helping at the food bank really changed me.
女：在食物銀行幫忙真的改變了我。

M: How come?
男：怎麼說？

W: It made me feel good inside. Besides, it showed me how important kindness is.
女：這讓我感到內心愉悅。而且，它讓我明白了善良的重要性。

M: That's nice. Helping others can be really special.
男：太好了。幫助他人真的很特別。

Question. What does the woman think about what she has done to the food bank? 女子對於自己為食物銀行做的事有何看法？

A. It gives her good working experience. A. 它給了她良好的工作經驗。
B. It can protect some people from hunger. B. 它可以保護一些人免於飢餓。
C. It can make a big difference. C. 它可以產生重大影響。

| 詳解 | 女子在對話一開始就說「Helping at the food bank really changed me.」表示這樣的善舉經驗改變了她，接著補充說讓她內心感到愉悅（feel good inside），並且讓她明白了善良的重要性（how important kindness is）。這顯示她認為她的行動對他的人生可以產生重大影響（make a big difference），所以正確答案是選項 C。對話中並沒有提到女子認為她的工作給了她良好的工作經驗，她的焦點在於行動對她個人的影響和改變，所以 A 錯誤；選項 B 的敘述也是女子沒有提到的。

| 補充 | 「make a difference」字面意思是「製造出不同的東西」，其實就是「產生影響」、「有所不同」。例如：Even small donations can make a difference in poor areas.”（小額的捐款也可以對於貧困地區產生重大影響有所不同。）其他類似用法還有：Have an impact、make a contribution、bring about a change、make a positive/negative effect、play a part...等。

Question number 20.

W: I haven't heard from you in a while. Are you still angry with me? 女：我有一段時間沒有你的消息了。你還生我的氣嗎？

M: No, I've just been really busy lately. 男：不，最近我真的很忙。

W: But you could still drop me a line once in a while, right? 女：但你有時候還是可以寫個訊息給我，對吧？

M: I know, I'm sorry. I'll try to make more time for it. 男：我知道，對不起。我會盡量抽出更多時間的。

Question. What does woman expect? 女子期待什麼？

A. The man keeps in contact with her. A. 男子與她保持聯繫。
B. The man spends more time with her. B. 男子多花點時間跟她在一起。
C. The man stops being angry with her. C. 男子別再對她生氣。

| 詳解 | 女子在對話中表示她有一段時間沒有收到男子的消息，這暗示她期待男子能夠保持聯繫（keep in touch/contact），即偶爾給她留言或傳訊息（drop me a line）。因此正確答案是選項 A。雖然女子可能會希望與男子花更多時間在一起，但這並不是她在對話中明確表達的期待，所以 B 不可選；女子問男子是否還在生她的氣，但男子否定了這一點，所以 C 也是錯誤的。

| 補充 | 「drop someone a line」中的 drop 本指「使落下」，而 line 就是「一行字句」，大多用來指寫信給某人，不過在口語中，也常被用來表示「打電話給某人」、「寄電子郵

件給某人」或「傳簡訊給某人」的意思。

Question number 21.

M: Make sure to keep an eye on your son while he's playing outside.

男：當你兒子在外面玩耍時，一定要顧好他。

W: I will. Safety first, right? I'll make sure he stays out of trouble.

女：我會的。安全第一，對吧？我會確保他不惹麻煩。

M: And don't forget to remind him to be careful when he's near the road.

男：而且不要忘記提醒他在靠近馬路時要小心。

Question. What does the man want the woman to do? 男子希望女子做什麼？

A. Teach the kid to know about safety signs

A. 教導孩子認識安全標誌

B. Watch out for the kid at any time

B. 隨時注意孩子的安全

C. Remember to remind the boy not to run through the road

C. 記得提醒男孩不要穿越馬路

| 詳解 | 答題關鍵是對話一開始男子說的「keep an eye on...」。男子告訴女子在她的兒子在外面玩耍時要保持警覺，並提醒她要確保他不惹麻煩（stays out of trouble）。這表示男子希望女子隨時（at any time）注意孩子的安全，而不是只有遊戲或接近馬路時，所以正確答案是選項 B。對話中男子並沒有提到教導孩子認識安全標誌，所以 A 錯誤；男子雖然提到提醒孩子在靠近馬路時要小心，但這只是他在對話中提到的一件事情，並非全部，所以 C 不對。

| 補充 | 「keep an eye on」是一個常見的片語，意思是「密切注意」或「留意」，通常用來描述持續監視、觀察或注意某人或某物的行為或情況。例如，你可以說「請保持對孩子的注意，不要讓他們走到危險的地方。（Please keep an eye on the children and make sure they don't go to dangerous places.）」類似表達方式還有「keep watch over」、「keep a close watch on」、「keep tabs on」、「monitor」等。

Question number 22.

W: Did you really push the chair over?

女：你真的把椅子推倒了嗎？

M: No, I didn't mean to. It just happened.

男：沒有，我不是故意的。它只是碰巧發生。

W: Oh, I see. I thought you did it because you were angry.

女：嗯，我了解。我以為你是因為生氣才這麼做的。

M: No, I'm not angry at all. It was just an accident.

男：不，我一點也不生氣。這只是個意外。

Question. What did the woman think about the man?
女子對於男子有什麼看法？

A. He pushed the chair over on purpose.
B. She was sure that he is not angry anymore.
C. He is very polite and helpful.

A. 他故意推倒椅子。
B. 她確定他不再生氣了。
C. 他非常有禮貌且樂於助人。

| 詳解 | 對話中男子解釋說他不是故意推倒椅子的，關鍵字詞是「didn't mean to」，接下來女子說她原本以為他是因為生氣才這麼做的，所以她以為他是故意的，故正確答案是選項 A。「S + mean to-V」=「S + V... on purpose」（故意做某事）。最後男子澄清說他一點也不生氣，並沒有說女子的看法，也沒有提到男子有禮貌或樂於助人，所以 B、C 皆錯誤。

| 補充 | purpose 是「目的」的意思，而「on purpose」就字面意思來說是「基於有所目的」，所以解釋成「故意地」，也可以用 purposely 表示。

Question number 23.

W: Do you exercise every day?
M: Yes, I go jogging every morning, and go to the gym to work out twice a week.
W: Very good. Do you also eat healthy?
M: Ah..., I prefer meat and fish, and...
W: You should try to eat more fruits and vegetables.

女：你每天都有運動嗎？
男：是的，我每天早上慢跑，每週還會去健身房鍛鍊兩次。
女：很好。你吃得很健康嗎？
男：嗯…我比較喜歡吃肉和魚，還有…
女：你應該試著多吃些水果和蔬菜。

Question. What is NOT true about the man? 關於男子，哪一項是不正確的？

A. He likes to eat meat and fish.
B. He goes to the gym every week.
C. He makes it a rule to work out and eat healthy.

A. 他喜歡吃肉和魚。
B. 他每週去健身房。
C. 他固定做運動且健康飲食。

| 詳解 | 男子說他每天早上慢跑（go jogging every morning），每週還會去健身房兩次（go to the gym to work out twice a week），但是被問到是否健康飲食時，他回答說他比較喜歡吃肉和魚（prefer meat and fish），並沒有提到他有固定健康飲食的習慣，因此選項 C 是錯誤的敘述，故正確答案是選項 C。

| 補充 | 「make it a rule to-V」是個常見的句型，表示「依照慣例會去做某事」，以文法結構來說，it 是個「虛受詞」，真正受詞是後面的不定詞（to-V）。

Question number 24.

M: What do you think about our new English teacher?
男：你覺得我們的新英文老師怎麼樣？

W: He explains things very well. I think he's second to none.
女：他講解得很好。我覺得他是最好的。

M: I don't really agree. I've had better teachers in the past.
男：我不太同意。我以前有過更好的老師。

W: What do you think makes them better?
女：你覺得那些老師哪裡更好？

Question. What do the speakers think about the new English teacher?
關於新來的英文老師，兩位說話者是怎麼看的？

A. He's the best they have ever seen.
A. 他是他們見過最好的老師。

B. The woman thinks the teacher is better than any in the past.
B. 女子認為這位老師比過去任何老師都好。

C. The man also likes the new teacher very much.
C. 男子也非常喜歡這位新來的老師。

| 詳解 | 對話中女子認為新老師講解得很好，並說他是最好的，這裡用了「second to none」這個慣用語，字面意思是「稱第二沒人敢稱第一」，也就是「最佳的，首屈一指的」，因此，正確答案是選項 B。而男子不太同意，並提到他以前有過更好的老師，所以 A、C 選項都是不正確的。

Question number 25.

M: Do you know that Jack is preparing a surprise party for his girlfriend?
男：你知道嗎，傑克正在為他的女朋友準備一場驚喜派對？

W: Really? When will be the party, and where will it take place?
女：真的嗎？派對什麼時候舉行，地點在哪裡？

M: Next Saturday, at Jack's home. Remember to keep it a secret, OK?
男：下週六，在傑克家裡。記得保密，知道嗎？

W: No problem.
女：沒問題。

Question. What does the man want to woman to remember?
男子希望女子記住什麼？

A. To help with preparing the party
A. 去幫忙派對的準備工作

B. Not to say a word about the party
B. 不要說出關於派對的任何消息

C. Not to tell Jack they've known about the surprise party
C. 不要告訴傑克他們已經知道這場驚喜派對

| 詳解 | 題目問的是男子希望女子記住什麼，所以要注意的是男子說過的話，以及關鍵字 remember 的出現。男子提到派對的時間和地點後，特別要女子記得保守祕密（keep it

a secret），也就是不要說出關於派對的任何消息，所以正確答案是選項 B。對話中並沒有提到需要女子幫忙準備派對，男子只是要求女子保密，所以 A、C 錯誤。

| 補充 | 在英文裡，要求對方不要洩密或說溜嘴有哪些常見的表達用語呢？你也可以這麼說：

Keep it to yourself.
Don't spill the beans.
Mum's the word.
Keep your lips sealed.
Don't let the cat out of the bag.
Keep this under wraps.
This is between you and me.

Part 4 短文聽解

Question number 26.

Please look at the following three pictures. Listen to the following short talk. Which picture matches the talk?

請看以下三張圖片。聆聽以下簡短談話。談話內容指的是哪一張圖？

It was a Sunday afternoon. The Wang family all relaxed at home. Mr. Wang was having fun with his son in the living room. Mrs. Wang was busy making snacks. And Pitt, their puppy was sleeping soundly under the sun.

這是一個星期天的下午。王家一家人都在家中休息。王先生跟兒子在客廳玩樂。王太太正忙著做點心。而他們的小狗小畢則在陽光下睡得正香甜。

| 詳解 | 從三張圖可推知這一家共有三人，father、mother、son 以及一隻狗。請先把圖中的行為整理：play with the dog（跟狗玩）、drink tea（喝茶）、cook in the kitchen（在廚房煮東西）、watch TV in the living room（在客廳看電視）、dry clothes（晒衣服），然後再仔細聽誰在做哪一件事，便可找出答案。their puppy was sleeping under the sun（他們的狗在陽光下睡覺），所以選項 A 不符。Mrs. Wang was making snacks（王太太在做點心）而不是在曬衣服，所以選項 C 也不符。故本題正確答案為選項 B。

| 補充 | sound 當名詞時是「聲音」的意思，它可以指任何聽到的聲音，如雷聲、風聲、流水聲，也可以是人造的聲音（如音樂、機器運轉聲、門鈴聲。例如：I heard a strange sound coming from the basement.（我聽到地下室傳來一個奇怪的聲音。）另一個表示「聲音」的名詞是 voice，它特指人類或動物的嗓音，主要用於描述說話、唱歌等活動中發出的聲音。例如：I recognized his voice immediately.（我立刻認出了他的聲

音。）不過，本題談話中的 soundly 衍生自形容詞 sound，表示「安好的，健全的」，屬於英檢中級單字。例如：She is sound in body and mind.（她身心健康。）

Question number 27.

Please look at the following three pictures. Listen to the following short talk. What did the speaker buy?

請看以下三張圖片。聆聽以下簡短談話。說話者買了什麼？

I bought my boyfriend a tie and a pair of pants as his birthday gift. The tie is a stylish one with long lines whose color is different from the areas next to it. And the pants are best for work. There are pockets at both sides.

我買了一條領帶和一條褲子給我男朋友作為生日禮物。領帶是時尚款式的，有長條紋，顏色與旁邊的區域不同。褲子則非常適合上班穿，兩邊都有口袋。

A

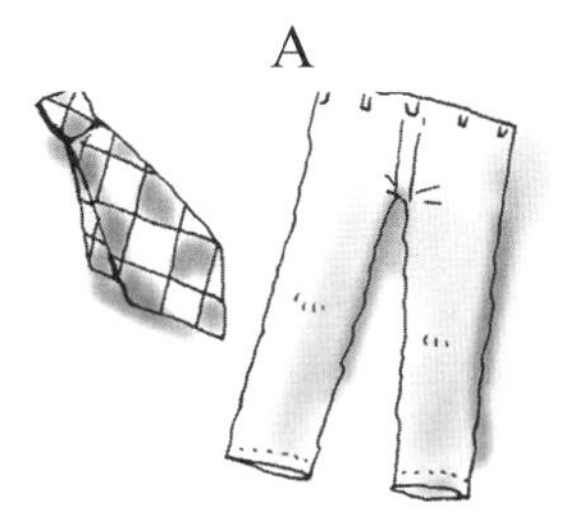

B

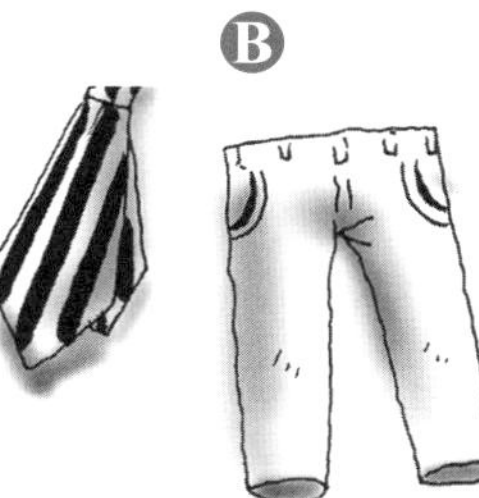

C

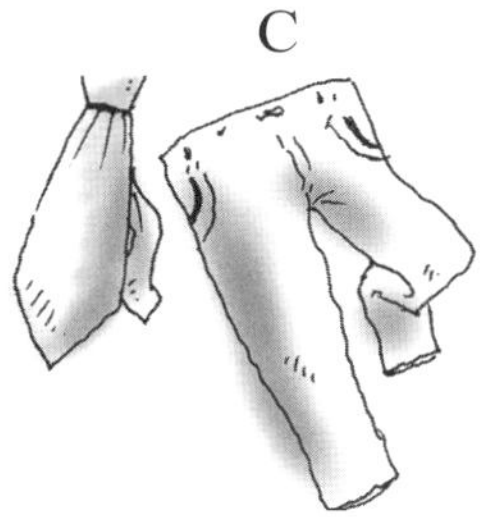

| 詳解 | 三張圖裡的物件幾乎都一樣，本題要考的是領帶（tie）款式的不同，破題關鍵在「long lines」（長線條），所以本題正答案為選項 B。

| 補充 | 「領帶」是 tie，領帶上的「條紋」可以用 stripe 表示，這是個英檢中高級單字。而「條紋領帶」就是「tie with stripes」，「格子領帶」是 tie with checks，只有顏色沒有圖案的「素面領帶」可以是「a (color) tie、a plain (color) tie」，例如：a black tie、a plain black tie。「褲子兩旁有口袋」是 pockets at both sides，「前面有口袋」是 pockets in front，「後面有口袋」是 pockets at the back。

Question number 28.

Please look at the following three pictures. Listen to the following opening speech. Where does it take place?

請看以下三張圖片。聆聽以下公開性談話。談話是哪個地方發生的？

Good evening, ladies and gentleman. Welcome to the century's most mysterious magic show. For the next second, sit tight as you will be amazed by surprises and more surprises.

女士先生們晚安。歡迎來到本世紀最神祕的魔術表演。從下一秒鐘開始，請務必坐好，因為一波又一波的驚喜將讓你驚豔無比。

｜詳解｜ 可從三張圖中推測題目可能是在問場所，聽不懂 mysterious（神祕的）沒關係，只要你聽懂了「magic show」（魔術表演），自然就知道要選哪一張圖了，所以正確答案為選項 A。

Question number 29.

Please look at the following three pictures. Listen to the following message. What might Rose be going to do later?

請看以下三張圖片。聆聽以下訊息。蘿絲等一下可能會做什麼？

Rose, this is David. I guess your cellphone battery might be dead, because I called you a few times and your phone kept turned off. I've just sent by express delivery the three samples you said you want to see yesterday. Let me know your final decision as soon as possible. Thanks.

蘿絲，我是大衛。我想你的手機應該是沒電了，因為我打了幾次電話給妳，而妳的手機一直處於關機狀態。我剛剛已經用快遞寄出了妳昨天説想看的三個樣品。請儘快告訴我妳的最終決定。謝謝。

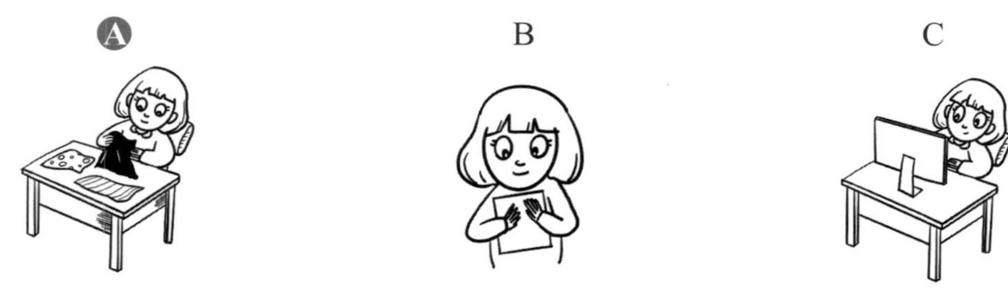

｜詳解｜ 訊息的留言者提到，已將 3 份樣本用快遞（express delivery）的方式送過去給 Rose 看，並請他盡快（as soon as possible）做出最後決定，所以 David 接下來要做的事，就像圖 A 品鑒寄來的三個樣品，所以正確答案是選項 A。

｜補充｜ 在這個智慧型手機當道的時代，手機沒電可是件大事，讓人覺得很恐慌呢！如果要表示「手機沒電」，除了可以用 dead 這個形容詞之外，有可以用動詞 die，例如：My phone battery died. =My phone battery is dead.。如果要說「手機快沒電」，可以用 die 的進行式「is dying」來表示。

Question number 30.

Please look at the following three pictures. Listen to the following news report. What will be the weather like in most areas tomorrow?

請看以下三張圖片。聆聽以下新聞報導。明天大部分地區的天氣如何？

Now let's look at the weather forecast tomorrow. It's going to be a cloudy rainy day in most areas. But there will be lower chance of rainfall in some southern areas, and it's going to be warmer there, but not hot, thanks to the rains.

現在讓我們來看看明天的天氣預報。大部分地區將會是多雲有雨的一天。不過，在一些南部地區，降雨的機率會較低，天氣會比較溫暖，但由於下雨的關係，不會感到炎熱。

| 詳解 | 題目問的是「大部分地區的天氣」，所以要注意聽取關鍵字詞「in most areas」，氣象報導中提到大部分地區將會是多雲有雨（cloudy rainy）的一天，只有南部部分地區（some southern areas）降雨機率較低，所以正確答案是選項 B。

Day 15

月　　日

我的完成時間______分鐘
標準作答時間 10 分鐘

Part 1 看圖辨義

Questions 1-2

Part 2 問答

Questions 3-7

3. A. I'm not sure, but I'm willing to try.
   B. Yes, you know I'm always a real problem.
   C. Can you also solve my problem?

4. A. I'll try to set aside more time for fooling around.
   B. That's right. I'll enter the 6th year grade this fall.
   C. Thanks for the advice.

5. A. Sorry, I don't know he's our project manager.
   B. Thanks for letting me know.
   C. Wait a minute. I'll pull over.

6. A. Thanks, I'll do my best to stay confident.
   B. Trust me. You can give it a try.
   C. When will the speech be open to the public?

7. A. We owe a great deal to our parents.
   B. Let me check the total for you.
   C. I should pay you 500 dollars in all.

Part 3 簡短對話

Questions 8-12

8. A. Seeking help from her teacher
   B. Practicing regularly
   C. Keeping confident

9. A. They met because of a car accident.
   B. They did not expect to meet with each other.
   C. They are unhappy about how they met.

10. A. His secret love for the woman
    B. A misunderstanding between them
    C. A secret about David

11. A. Worried and nervous
    B. Out of breath
    C. Very comfortable

12. A. To a park
    B. To a beautiful garden
    C. To a library

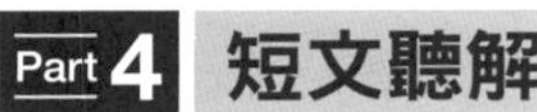

Part 4 短文聽解

Questions 13-14

13.

A

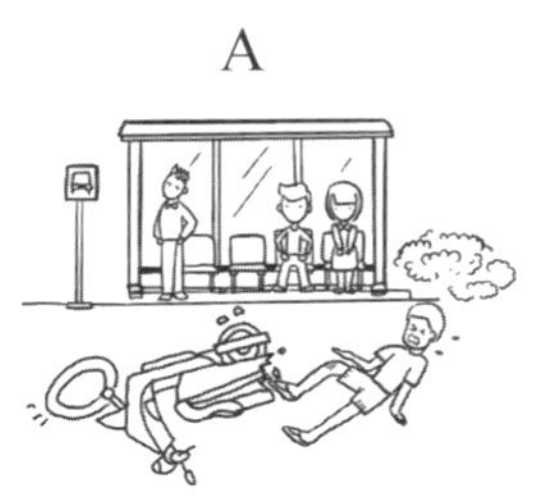

B

C

14.

A

B

C

上頁簡答

解答與詳解

1. (A) 2. (C) 3. (A) 4. (C) 5. (B) 6. (A) 7. (B) 8. (A) 9. (B) 10. (C) 11. (B) 12. (C) 13. (B) 14. (B)

Part 1 看圖辨義

For questions number 1-2, please look at the following pictures.

Question number 1.

Which items did the woman choose? 女子選了哪些東西？

A. Clothes and shoes A. 衣服及鞋子

B. Shoes and watches B. 鞋子及手錶

C. Necklaces and earrings C. 項鍊及耳環

| 詳解 | 圖中的女人在 trying on shoes（試穿鞋子），椅子上有衣服，表示女人選了（choose）可能會買的鞋子跟衣服。店裡有的貨品考生也必須知道，例如：包包（bags）、飾品（accessories）等。店裡沒有賣手錶（watch），所以選項 B 不對。女人沒有拿任何飾品，所以選項 C 也不對。故正確答案為選項 A。

| 補充 | try 加上 on，表示試穿衣物、鞋子，看看好不好看、尺寸對不對。例如：Can I try these dresses on somewhere please？（請問我可以在哪裡試穿這些洋裝？）如果是在點餐時，想試吃哪一樣食品，直接用 try 就可以了。例如：I'll try a piece of that mint apple rose pie, please.（請給我一個薄荷蘋果玫瑰派試試。）

Question number 2.

What happened in the picture? 圖中發生了什麼事？

A. A man-made accident A. 一場人為意外

B. A terrible snowstorm B. 一場可怕的暴風雪

C. A forest fire C. 一場森林大火

| 詳解 | 看到本圖，想到的應該是：a fire（一場火警）、lots of firemen and fire engines help putting out the fire（許多消防員及消防車幫忙滅火）。圖中顯然是一場森林大火（forest fire），故本題正確答案為選項 C。snowstorm 是「暴風雪」，所以選項 C 錯誤；man-made 是「人為的」意思，因為我們無從得知森林大火是天然的（natural）還是人為的，所以相較於 C，選項 A 不是最好的答案。

Part 2 問答

Question number 3.

Do you know how to solve this problem? 你知道如何解決這問題嗎？

A. I'm not sure, but I'm willing to try. A. 我不確定，但我願意試試。

B. Yes, you know I'm always a real problem. B. 是的，你知道我一直都是個難搞人。

C. Can you also solve my problem? C. 你也可以解決我的問題嗎？

| 詳解 | 題目這句詢問對方是否知道解決問題的方法，回答「我不確定，但願意嘗試」，展現自己肯定的意願和積極性，所以正確答案是選項 A。選項 B 的回答並沒有提供解決問題的意圖或方法，而是轉移話題到對自己的描述，所以錯誤。選項 C 沒有正面回答問題的詢問，反而提出了另一個問題，這並不是對原始問題的適當回應。

Question number 4.

As long as you study harder, you will get better grades.
只要你用功讀書，你的成績就會變好。

A. I'll try to set aside more time for fooling around. A. 我會試著挪出更多時間玩耍。

B. That's right. I'll enter the 6th year grade this fall. B. 沒錯，我今年秋天就要升上六年級了。

C. Thanks for the advice. C. 謝謝你的建議。

| 詳解 | 題目這句話是給對方一個良心的建議，而選項 A 要考你知不知道「set aside」（騰出，挪出）的意思，選項 A 說「我會試著挪出更多時間玩耍。」顯然是顛倒是非的回答；選項 B 則以相同的 grade 這個字意圖造成混淆，選項 B 說「我今年秋天就要升上六年級了」這個回應與原句的建議沒有直接關係。所以正確答案是選項 C。

| 補充 | grade 當名詞時，可以表示「學業成績」、「學生在考試或課程中的評分」，例如「A grade」代表優異成績。grade 也有「年級」的意思，如「sixth grade」指「六年級」。grade 還有「等級」之意，指某物或某人的品質或等級，如「high grade materials」指「高檔的材料」。

Question number 5.

As to the project, the boss didn't like it. 關於這個專案，老闆不喜歡。

A. Sorry, I don't know he's our project manager. A. 抱歉，我不知道他是我們的專案經理。

B. Thanks for letting me know. B. 謝謝你讓我知道。

C. Wait a minute. I'll pull over. C. 等一下，我會把車停靠路邊。

| 詳解 | 題目這句是告知對方一件壞消息，而選項 A 回應是對專案經理（project manager）身份的困惑，並沒有直接回應老闆對專案的意見。選項 C 則是把車停靠路邊（pull over）相關的動作，與專案或老闆的意見無關，因此正確答案是選項 B。「謝謝你讓我知道」是一個適當且禮貌的回應。這表示對方理解並接受，且表達了感謝之意。

| 補充 | project 當名詞可表示「專案」，指一項計畫或任務，例如「science project」指「科學專案」。project 還有「工程」的意思，例如「construction project」指「建設工程」。project 當「動詞」時，為中高級程度用字，可以指「投射」，指將影像、聲音等傳送到某處，例如「project the image on the screen」指將影像投射到螢幕上，也可以表示「預測」，指對未來進行預測，例如「project the sales figures」指「預測銷售數字」。

Question number 6.

Don't be afraid to give a speech in public. 不要害怕在公開場合演說。

A. Thanks, I'll do my best to stay confident. A. 謝謝，我會盡力保持自信。

B. Trust me. You can give it a try. B. 相信我，你可以試試看。

C. When will the speech be open to the public? C. 這場演講什麼時候對外開放？

| 詳解 | 原句是給予鼓勵，告訴對方不要害怕在公開場合演說，B 的回應「相信我，你可以試試看。」變成倒過來鼓勵「正在鼓勵你的人」，邏輯上完全錯誤；C 問及演講何時對外開放，與「給予建議」的主旨無關，所以正確答案是選項 A，是對建議的正確回應，表達了接受建議的態度並承諾努力保持自信。

| 補充 | 「stay + 形容詞」結構用於描述保持某種狀態。例如：「stay calm」保持冷靜。「stay focused」保持專注。這結構通常表示持續狀態，用於鼓勵、指示或描述。

Question number 7.

How much do I owe you in all? 我總共欠你多少錢？

A. We owe a great deal to our parents. 我們深受父母之恩。

B. Let me check the total for you. B. 讓我為你查看一下總額是多少。

C. I should pay you 500 dollars in all. C. 總共我應該支付你 500 美元。

| 詳解 | 選項 A 刻意以與題目相同的動詞 owe 回答，意圖混淆答題，「我們深受父母之恩。」這回答與原問題無關；題目問我該給你多少，C 卻回答我該支付你多少，答非所問，所以正確答案是選項 B，表明為對方確認總額該給多少錢。

| 補充 | owe 當動詞時表示「欠債，欠款」，也可用來表示對某人的「感激之情」。例如：「我還欠你一杯咖啡。（I owe you a cup of coffee.）」、「我感激你的幫助，我們都欠你一個大大的謝意。（I appreciate your help, and we all owe you a big thank-you.）」

Part 3 簡短對話

Question number 8.

M: Hi, do you think I can learn to play the guitar? 男：嗨，你認為我能學會彈吉他嗎？

W: Sure, anyone can learn if they practice. You just need to believe you're capable of it. 女：當然，只要勤練，任何人都能學會。你只需要相信自己有能力。

M: I'm not sure if I'll be any good though. 男：但我不確定我會不會彈得好。

W: Don't worry. Everyone starts as a beginner. With practice, you'll be playing beautifully. 女：別擔心。每個人都是從初學者開始的。經過練習，你會彈得很棒。

Question. What is NOT one of the suggestions by the woman?
女士建議中，哪一項不是她提出的建議？

A. Seeking help from her teacher A. 向她的老師尋求協助

B. Practicing regularly B. 規律練習

C. Keeping confident C. 保持信心

| 詳解 | 題目問何者不是女子的建議，應從女子的發言中找答案。最後她提到「With practice, you'll be playing beautifully.」這表示她強調了練習的重要性，所以 B 是她提出的建議；女子說「You just need to believe you're capable of it. 」她鼓勵男士相信自己的能力，不要擔心，每個人都是從初學者開始的（ Everyone starts as a beginner.）所以 C 也是她提出的建議；對話中女子沒有提及需要尋求老師的幫助，所以本題正確答案為選項 A。

Question number 9.

M: Hi, do you remember how we met? 男：嗨，你還記得我們是怎麼認識的嗎？

W: Yes, we met each other by accident at a grocery store. 女：是的，我們在一家雜貨店無意間相遇。

M: Oh, right! That was unexpected but it turned out to be a pleasant surprise. 男：對，那真是出乎意料，但結果卻是一個愉快的驚喜。

W: Yeah, you thought I was a thief... but I'm glad it happened. 女：是啊，你當時以為我是小偷…但我很高興那樣的事情發生了。

Question. What is true about the man and the woman?
關於這對男女，何者為真？

A. They met because of a car accident. A. 他們因為一場車禍而相遇。

B. They did not expect to meet with each other. B. 他們沒有預料到彼此會相遇。

C. They are unhappy about how they met. C. 他們對於相遇的方式感到不愉快。

| 詳解 | 本題破題關鍵就在男子一開始問女子，兩人是怎麼認識的，女子回答「we met each

other by accident」，「by accident」是「意外地，果不期然地」，所以正確答案是選項 B。對話中並沒有提到任何有關車禍的事情，選項 A 只是利用相同字彙 accident 刻意造成混淆；雖然女性提到男性當時誤以為她是小偷，但她表示對於相遇感到高興，因此選項 C 當然錯誤。

| 補充 | 「by accident」表示某事是無意間發生的。例如「I knocked over the cup by accident.（我不小心打翻了杯子。）」另一個可用的片語是「by chance」，意思也是偶然地。例如「We bumped into each other by chance on the street.（我們偶然在街上相遇了。）」這兩個片語都用於描述事情發生時沒有預先計劃或意圖的情況。

Question number 10.

M: I have something to tell you.　　男：我有點事想跟你說。

W: Oh? Go ahead.　　女：是嗎？說吧。

M: Well, between you and me, I found David is cheating his wife.　　男：嗯，這是我們之間的祕密喔，我發現大衛對他老婆不忠。

W: Really? That's surprising. I hope it's just a misunderstanding.　　女：真的嗎？那真讓人驚訝。我希望這只是個誤會。

Question. What did the man want to tell the woman? 男子想告訴女子什麼？

A. His secret love for the woman　　A. 他對女子的暗戀

B. A misunderstanding between them　　B. 他們之間的一場誤會

C. A secret about David　　C. 關於大衛的祕密

| 詳解 | 男子說他發現大衛對他老婆不忠（cheating his wife），並且特別強調這是他和女子之間的祕密（between you and me），這明確地說明了男子想告訴女子的是關於大衛的祕密，故本題正確答案是選項 C。男子要告訴女子的一個祕密沒錯，但不是他對女子的暗戀（secret love），所以 A 錯誤；女子希望關於大衛的不忠只是個誤會（misunderstanding），而不是他跟男子之間有什麼誤會。

Question number 11.

W: I had to run to catch the bus because I was late.　　女：我當時得跑去趕公車，因為我遲到了。

M: Did you manage to catch the bus on time?　　男：你有及時趕上公車嗎？

W: Luckily yes, I did.　　女：有，幸好有趕上。

M: You should sit down and rest for a few minutes to catch your breath.　　男：你應該坐下來休息幾分鐘，喘口氣。

Question. How might the woman look now? 女子現在可能看起來如何？

A. Worried and nervous　　A. 既擔心又緊張

B. Out of breath　　B. 喘不過氣來

C. Very comfortable　　C. 非常舒適

| 詳解 | 題目問的是女子現在，也就是在對話的當下，看起來的樣子，從男子最後說「你應該坐下來休息幾分鐘，喘口氣（catch your breath）」可知，女子現在應該是喘不過氣的樣子，所以正確答案是選項 B。

| 補充 | 名詞 breath 是「呼吸」，相同意義的動詞則是 breathe，常見於 out of breath（喘不過氣來）、catch/hold one's breath（屏息，喘息一下）、take a deep breath（深呼吸）、under one's breath（低聲／小聲地說）…等片語中。

Question number 12.

W: It's just down the street, in front of the park. You can't miss it! 女：你就從這條街過去，它就在公園前面。你不會錯過的！

M: Thanks! And could you tell me if they have any books on gardening? 男：謝謝！你知道他們是否有關於園藝的書籍嗎？

W: Sure! They have a great gardening section on the second floor. 女：當然！他們二樓有一個很棒的園藝書區。

M: Great! Thanks for the tip. I'll head there right away. 男：太好了！謝謝你的建議。我會馬上去那裡。

Question. Where could the man be going? 這位男士可能要去哪裡？

A. To a park　A. 去公園

B. To a beautiful garden　B. 去一座美麗的花園

C. To a library　C. 去圖書館

| 詳解 | 題目問男子要去什麼地方，首先可以注意他說過的話。從「... could you tell me if they have any books on...」可知，他要去得地方可能是書局，也可能是書局，也可能是圖書館，所以正確答案是選項 C。雖然對話中也有出現 park，以及和 garden 相關的 gardening，但都只是刻意模糊焦點的錯誤引導，故 A、B 皆不可選。

| 補充 | 在英文裡，有時候多一個 the、少一個 the，意思會完全不一樣，像是「in front of」和「in the front of」。前者是指一物在另一物的前面，而後者則指一物在另一物內部的前部，如 There is a desk in front of the chair.（椅子的前面有張書桌。）There is a desk in the front of the classroom.（教室的前方有一張書桌）。又比方說，「in hospital」是「住院」的意思，也就是「在醫院裡接受醫療」，而「in the hospital」意思是「在醫院裡」，也就是在醫院這棟建築物裡面。

Part 4 短文聽解

Question number 13.

Please look at the following three pictures. Listen to the following talk. Which picture best match the talk?

請看以下三張圖片。聆聽以下談話。哪一張圖最搭配談話內容？

Yesterday when I was riding the U-bike to the MRT station, I saw a motorcyclist hit by a truck on the middle of the road. It drew many people near to watch the accident. Luckily, the motorcyclist fell toward the roadside and just lightly hurt his legs.

昨天我騎著 YouBike 去捷運站時，在路中央看到一位摩托車騎士被一輛卡車撞到。引來許多人圍觀事故。幸運的是，摩托車騎士倒向路邊，只輕傷了腿部。

| 詳解 | 題目問的是談話內容是在敘述哪一張圖，首先，三張圖都有機車騎士，但內容提到這位機車騎士「被一輛卡車撞倒（hit by a truck）」，所以到這裡，第一張圖就可直接排除了；第三張圖雖然也有機車騎士倒在地上，但他是自撞路樹，所以也不是答案。所以正確答案是選項 B。

| 補充 | see 這個動詞在英文文法有所謂「知覺動詞」支撐，其他像是 hear、watch、feel... 等也可以有此類動詞的功能，常見於「S+V+O+OC」的句型，就像是「使役動詞」用法，其後接受詞後，可接原形動詞或分詞作為受詞補語。例如：I heard her cry/crying out loudly at midnight.（我半夜聽見她哭得很大聲。）

Question number 14.

Please look at the following three pictures. Listen to the following sport report. What ball game are they playing?
請看以下三張圖片。聆聽以下體育報導。什麼球賽正在進行？

The game has been in progress for 15 minutes, and things are starting to heat up. Both teams are giving their all, displaying great skill. So far, there have been some close attempts at scoring, but the goalkeepers are doing fantastic jobs protecting their nets from the ball flying in.
比賽進行了 15 分鐘，氣氛正變得越來越熱烈。雙方球隊都全力以赴，並展現了高超的技術。到目前為止,雙方都險些得分，但守門員都表現出色，成功擋住球攻入門網。

| 詳解 | 這是一則體育賽事的報導，前面大半內容都無法確認是在報導哪一張圖的比賽，所以必須再仔細往下聽到後面的部分才行。最後提到，守門員（goalkeeper）都表現出色，成功擋住球攻入門網（net）。其實就算聽不出 goalkeeper，整段唯一最簡單、也是最關鍵的的 net，你必須聽得出來！顯然這是足球場常見的畫面。所以正確答案是選項 B。

Day 16

月　　日

我的完成時間＿＿＿分鐘
標準作答時間 10 分鐘

Part 1 看圖辨義

Questions 1-2

Part 2 問答

Questions 3-7

3. A. I'm not sure if he gets used to smoking.
   B. No, he's quit smoking for two years.
   C. Yes, he did, but he quit last year.

4. A. You probably should, just to make sure he's home.
   B. Yes, I think he'll be fine with a surprise visit.
   C. It depends on how busy you are.

5. A. You can pay me $75 in advance.
   B. Altogether, it will be $120.
   C. Please now pay the final payment of $ 200.

6. A. I know. She's always a lucky girl.
   B. To be frank, I won't envy Betty her good luck.
   C. You're right. Nothing seems to go her way.

7. A. Thanks. I'll keep it in mind.
   B. But you shouldn't try to do everything on your own.
   C. So what can I do to help you?

Part 3 簡短對話

Questions 8-12

8. A. Right. The book you want is placed on the top shelf.
   B. First, walk straight ahead until you reach the crossroad.
   C. Don't drink and drive, or you'll run into trouble.

9. A. Take good care of his company
   B. Take a business trip to Paris
   C. Go on a trip together

10. A. It makes them feel more relaxed.
    B. The break room has more space compared to the old one.
    C. There's a coffee machine in the meeting room.

11. A. Being behind in school work
    B. Having no time to rest
    C. Missing fun activities

12. A. There's mostly no problem with them.
    B. She probably got the worst grade in Math.
    C. She's confident her math grade will improve.

Part 4 短文聽解

Questions 13-14

13.

A

B

C

14.

A

B

C

Day 15 | Day 16 | Day 17 | Day 18 | Day 19 | Day 20 | Day 21

上頁簡答

解答與詳解

1. (A) 2. (B) 3. (C) 4. (A) 5. (B) 6. (C) 7. (A) 8. (B) 9. (C) 10. (A) 11. (A) 12. (C) 13. (A) 14. (B)

Part 1 看圖辨義

For questions number 1-2, please look at the following pictures.

Question number 1.

What is the man? 男子的職業為何？

A. A woodcutter A. 一名伐木工人

B. A wood supplier B. 一名木材供應商

C. A forest hunter C. 一名森林獵人

| 詳解 | 選項 B 明顯是誤導考生，因為圖中有木頭（wood），所以考生可能會選 B，但 supplier 是 supply（供應）的衍生字，表示「批發商」或「供應商」。圖中可以肯定的只是一位伐木工人在工作，無法確定他是供應商，所以正確答案為選項 A。

| 補充 | 「木材」的英文是 wood，「木製的」就是 wooden，例如 a wooden floor（木地板）。中文裡的「木訥，呆板」（形容人不太會說話、口語表達遲鈍），英文也可以用 wooden 來表示。例如：His performances have become wooden and dull.（他的演出變得呆板乏味。）

Question number 2.

What do you use this for? 你用這東西來做什麼？

A. Setting a poem to music A. 為一首詩譜曲

B. Listening to music or talk shows B. 聽音樂或談話節目

C. Watching dramas or movies C. 看戲劇或電影

| 詳解 | 一看到圖片應該就可以推測到此題與單字 listen to、radio 或是 music 有關了。因此務必仔細聽清楚問題中的關鍵單字，選項 A 與 B 都有 music，而選項 C 聽到的是 movies，可以直接剔除。A 的「set... to music」意思是「為…譜曲，幫…寫成歌」，顯然這不是 radio 的功能了，所以正確答案是選項 B。

| 補充 | 與 music 有關的常見慣用語是「face the music」（面對現實；接受批評或懲罰）例如： Just try your best to solve the problem and face the music.（只要盡力解決問題，然勇敢面對就行了；以及「(be) music to one's ears」（佳音，中聽的話）。例如：That's music to my ears. Congratulations on your successful recovery.（真是個好消息！恭喜你康復了！）

Part 2 問答

Question number 3.

He used to smoke, didn't he? 他以前抽菸，是吧？

A. I'm not sure if he gets used to smoking. A. 我不確定他是否習慣抽菸。

B. No, he's quit smoking for two years. B. 沒有，他已經戒菸兩年了。

C. Yes, he did, but he quit last year. C. 是的，他以前抽菸，但去年戒了。

| 詳解 | 題目問的是某人以前是否有抽菸的習慣，選項 A 並沒有回答「他以前是否抽菸」，而是不確定他現在是否習慣抽菸；選項 B 回答他已經戒菸兩年，表示他以前確實有抽菸，所以應以 Yes 開頭來回答，並非用 No，所以錯誤；正確答案是選項 C。這個回答直接確認了「他以前抽菸」這一點，並且補充說明他去年戒菸。

| 補充 | 「used to」是很常見的考試重點，主要是考生們容易對於「used to-V」和「be/get used to + Ving」產生混淆。「used to-V」表示用來表示過去經常做的行為，但現在不再發生了，例如：He used to smoke.（他過去曾抽菸。）另外，「used to-V」不能和「具體的次數（e.g., four times）」或「一段時間（e.g., for two years, for six months）」一起使用，但可以和頻率副詞（e.g., always, usually, seldom）連用。例如：I used to go to Hong Kong. 我曾去過香港。錯誤用法：I used to go to Hong Kong five times.

Question number 4.

Should I call him in advance before visiting him?
我應該在拜訪他之前先打電話給他嗎？

A. You probably should, just to make sure he's home. A. 你應該這麼做，確定他是否在家。

B. Yes, I think he'll be fine with a surprise visit. B. 是的，我覺得他會喜歡驚喜的拜訪。

C. It depends on how busy you are. C. 這要看你有多忙啊。

| 詳解 | 對於「我應該在拜訪他之前先打電話給他嗎？」這個問題的回答，如果是覺得被拜訪者喜歡驚喜的拜訪，那當然就不必先打電話，所以應以 No, ... 開頭來回答，故選項 B 錯誤；只是打個電話應該跟忙不忙沒關係，所以選項 C 的回答不近情理；正確答案是選項 A，因為這個回答直接建議提前打電話，以確保不會白跑一趟。

Question number 5.

How much should I pay you in all? 我總共應該付你多少錢？

A. You can pay me $75 in advance. A. 你可以先付我 75 美元。

B. Altogether, it will be $120. B. 總共是 120 美元。

C. Please now pay the final payment of $ 200. C. 請馬上支付尾款 200 美元。

| 詳解 | 題目問的是總共應該付多少錢，關鍵是「in all」這個副詞片語，它的意思是「總共」，相當於「in total」、「totally」。選項 A 的「in advance（預先）」以及選項 C 的「final payment（尾款）」都是總金額中的一部分，所以都不是答案，故正確答案是選項 B。Altogether 是「總共」的意思。

Question number 6.

Betty has anything but good fortune. 貝蒂就是缺乏好運。

A. I know. She's always a lucky girl. A. 我知道。她一直都是個幸運女孩。

B. To be frank, I won't envy Betty her good luck. B. 坦白說，我不會羨慕貝蒂的好運。

C. You're right. Nothing seems to go her way. C. 你說得對。她似乎什麼事情都不順利。

| 詳解 | 題目說貝蒂總是運氣不好，A 卻回答貝蒂一直都是個幸運女孩，這與對話的意思完全相反，而 B 回答說不會羨慕貝蒂的好運，暗示她運氣好，也是本末倒置，所以正確答案是選項 C，這回答直接呼應了「貝蒂運氣不好」的說法，指出她什麼事情都不順利，完全符合正常的回應。

| 補充 | 「anything/nothing but」中的 but 不是個連接詞，而是個介系詞，相當於「except (for)」，意思是「除…之外」。例如：I want nothing but money.（我只想要錢。→ 除了錢以外我什麼都不要。）又比如：I want anything but money.（我一點都不想要錢。→ 除了錢以外我什麼都可以要。）

Question number 7.

Ask for help when you need it. 當你有需求時，要請求協助。

A. Thanks. I'll keep it in mind. A. 謝謝，我會牢記在心。

B. But you shouldn't try to do everything on your own. B. 但你不應該試圖獨自完成所有事情。

C. So what can I do to help you? C.那麼我可以做些什麼來幫助你呢？

| 詳解 | 題目是善意地建議對方在需要時務必請求協助，選項 B 不針對這樣的建議回答，反而提出另一個建議，不符合對話內容；選項 C 反而說「我可以做些什麼來幫你」，這個回答等於題目那句，是假設對方需要幫助，所以等於沒回答了，故正確答案是選項 A，這個回答表達了感謝並表示會記住建議，符合對話邏輯。

| 補充 | ask 和 for 也可以拆開來，形成「ask + 人 + for help (or anything else)」的句型，例如：I asked my mom for pocket money, but she said no.（我向媽媽要零用錢，但她說不行。）另外「ask for」後面的受詞也可以是「人」，但意思就完全不一樣了。例如：She asked for Ken, but he wasn't here then.（她想和肯見面，但他那時不在那裡。）

Part 3 簡短對話

Question number 8.

M: Excuse me, do you need any help? 男：打擾一下，你需要幫忙嗎？

W: Yes, please. I'm trying to find the library, but I'm not sure which way to go. 女：是的，麻煩了。我在找圖書館，但不知道該走哪條路。

M: Then please pay attention to the directions I'll give you. 男：那請注意我接下來要告訴你的方向。

W: Sure, I will listen carefully. 女：好的，我會仔細聽。

Question. What might the man say next? 男子接下來可能會說什麼？

A. Right. The book you want is placed on the top shelf. A. 沒錯，你要的書就在書架最上層。

B. First, walk straight ahead until you reach the crossroad. B. 首先，直走到十字路口。

C. Don't drink and drive, or you'll run into trouble. C. 不要酒後駕車，不然你會有麻煩。

| 詳解 | 題目問男子接下來可能說什麼話。對話的最後是男子要女子注意聽他說圖書館怎麼走，然後女子說她洗耳恭聽，所以接下來男子當然就開始路線指引的第一句話，而選項 A 的回答顯然是在圖書館內，所以當然錯誤；選項 C 回答「不要酒後駕車，不然…」，與對話的主題完全無關。所以正確答案是選項 B，這句話符合對話的上下文。

| 補充 | notice 和「pay attention to」都是「注意...」的意思，但 notice 是指無意識地注意到身邊的人事物，是沒有預先目的，不在意料之中的，而是指有意識地去「注意」，是有目的性的。例如要提醒對方，旅遊要注意自己的錢財，可以說「Pay attention to your wallet.」不可以說「Notice your wallet. Don't let the thief steal it.」

Question number 9.

M: Hi, Emily. I'm going to take a trip to Paris next month and I was wondering if you could keep me company. 男：嗨，Emily。我下個月要去巴黎旅行，我想知道你是否可以陪我一起去。

W: Sounds great, Mark! I'd love to. 女：馬克，聽起來很棒！我很樂意。

M: We can visit the Eiffel Tower and try some delicious French food. 男：我們可以參觀艾菲爾鐵塔，並嘗試吃些法國美食。

W: I can hardly wait! 女：我等不及了！

Question. What did the man ask the woman to do? 男子要女子去做什麼？

A. Take good care of his company　A. 照顧好他的公司

B. Take a business trip to Paris　B. 去巴黎出差

C. Go on a trip together　C. 一起去旅行

｜詳解｜ 題目問的是男子要女子做什麼事，應將焦點擺在男子說的話。他一開始時問女子，是否願意和他一起去巴黎旅行，而女子回答「I'd love to. 」所以正確答案當然就是選項 C 了。選項 A 刻意以相同字彙 company 來干擾答題，但男子說的「keep me company」是「陪伴我」的意思，與「take good care of his company」的意思是天差地別。選項 B 則多了 business 這個字，完全就錯誤了，business trip 是「出差」的意思。

｜補充｜ company 還會出現在「in good company」這個片語中，表示「（有同樣問題的）大有人在」。例如：If you find it difficult to cope with your family you are in good company.（如果你認為難以處理與家人之間的問題，其實許多人也都有這樣的情況。）

Question number 10.

M: Hi, Emma. How do you think about our new office?　男：嗨，艾瑪，你覺得我們的新辦公室怎麼樣？

W: I think it's much more comfortable compared to the old one. Besides, it has more space and better lighting.　女：我覺得比舊辦公室舒適多了。而且，這裡的空間更大，採光也更好。

M: Agree. And the break room is much better with a coffee machine and snacks.　男：同意。而且休息室也有了很大的改善，還有咖啡機和零食。

Question. What is true about their new office?
關於他們的新辦公室，以下哪項說法是正確的？

A. It makes them feel more relaxed.　A. 它讓他們感覺更放鬆。

B. The break room has more space compared to the old one.　B. 休息室的空間比舊的更大。

C. There's a coffee machine in the meeting room.　C. 會議室有咖啡機。

｜詳解｜ 對話中 Emma 提到新辦公室「比舊辦公室舒適多了」，這表示新辦公室讓他們感覺更放鬆（feel more relaxed），所以本題正確答案就是選項 A。沒有提到休息室（break room）的空間比舊辦公室的休息室大，只說休息室有了很大的改善，並且增加了咖啡機和零食（coffee machine and snacks），所以 B 錯誤。對話中提到咖啡機是在休息室，而不是在會議室，所以 C 錯誤。

Question number 11.

M: How was your day at school? Did you have any fun activities?
男：你今天在學校過得怎麼樣？有什麼有趣的活動嗎？

W: I didn't go to school today, because I caught a bad cold. I'm still not feeling well now.
女：我今天沒去學校，因為我感冒得很嚴重。現在還是覺得不舒服。

M: Oh no, I'm sorry to hear that. Make sure to rest and drink lots of water.
男：哎呀，很遺憾聽到這消息。一定要多休息，多喝水喔。

W: Thanks, John. I hope I'll get better quickly because I don't want to miss more school.
女：謝謝你，約翰。我希望我能快點好起來，因為我不想再錯過更多的課程。

Question. What is the woman worried about? 女子在擔心什麼？

A. Being behind in school work　A. 學業落後

B. Having no time to rest　B. 沒有時間休息

C. Missing fun activities　C. 錯過有趣的活動

| 詳解 | 女子在對話最後說「我希望我能快點好起來，因為我不想再錯過更多的課程（miss more school）。」這裡的 school 是指「學校課業」，表示她擔心因為生病而缺課，導致學業落後，所以正確答案是選項 A。

| 補充 | 英文裡，「進度超前」的簡單說法就是「人 + be + ahead of schedule」，若要表示「比預定時間早了 3 天」可以說「We're three days ahead of time.」，而「進度落後」則是「人 + be behind (in one's work)」，「我們有點落後了。」可以說「We're running a little behind.」

Question number 12.

M: Hi, Sarah. How are your classes going? Do you enjoy them?
男：嗨，莎拉。你的課程進行得怎麼樣？你喜歡上課嗎？

W: They are mostly okay, except that I'm a little concerned about my math grade.
女：大部分都還好，只是我有點擔心我的數學成績。

M: I understand. Just keep practicing and you'll improve.
男：我了解。只要繼續練習，你就會進步。

W: Thanks. I'll try my best.
女：謝謝。我會盡力的。

Question. What is NOT true about Sarah's classes?
關於 Sarah 的課程，哪一項是不正確的？

A. There's mostly no problem with them.　A. 大部分都沒有問題。

B. She probably got the worst grade in Math.　B. 她可能數學考得最差。

C. She's confident her math grade will improve.　C. 她有信心自己的數學成績會進步。

| 詳解 | Sarah 在對話中提到她有點擔心（a little concerned about...）她的數學成績，並沒有表現出對數學成績會有信心的（confident）態度。因此，C 的說法是不正確的，故本題正確答案是選項 C。女子提到「They are mostly okay, except that...」，A 選項的說法是對的；既然大部分課程都 OK，只是有點擔心數學，這意味著她的數學成績應該是最差的，因此 B 選項的說法也是對的。

| 補充 | concern 可以當名詞，也可以當動詞，而這裡的 concerned 就是從動詞用法衍生來的，相當於 worried 的意思。另外，名詞的 concern 表示「關心」或「擔憂」，例如，Her main concern is her math grade.（她主要擔心的是她的數學成績。）

Part 4 短文聽解

Question number 13.

Please look at the following three pictures. Listen to the following announcement. At what place could you hear it?

請看以下三張圖片。聆聽以下宣布。你在什麼地方可能聽到這樣的廣播？

This is the Global Mall information counter, and we're in urgent need of your help! A 5-year-old young boy and his mother got separated. The kid is wearing a white T-shirt and a pair of yellow shorts. If you see him, who, is probably crying loudly, please kindly bring him here. We're on the 1st floor. Many thanks for your help, and enjoy your shopping today.

這裡是環球購物中心的服務台，我們急需您的幫助！一名五歲男孩與他的母親走散了。孩子穿著白色 T 恤和黃色短褲。如果您看到他，可能正在大聲哭泣，請將他帶到我們這裡來。我們在一樓。非常感謝您的幫助，祝您購物愉快。

Ⓐ

B

C

| 詳解 | 首先，題目句一定要聽懂，這是個「問地方（At what place = Where）」的題目，所以即使聽不出 announcement（公開廣播），只要看到這三張不同地方的圖，也知道要問的是錄音內容指的是哪個地方」。接著就要仔細抓關鍵字詞了。聽到「A 5-year-old young boy and his mother got separated.」這句話，就可以直接刪除選項 B 了。聽到最後的「enjoy your shopping today」，也可以把選項 C 剔除，所以正確答案是選項 A。

Question number 14.

Please look at the following three pictures. Listen to the following message. What are the parents probably doing?

請看以下三張圖片。聆聽以下訊息。這對父母可能正在做什麼？

Morning David, your auntie is going to land at the airport around 11:00 a.m. Daddy and I are now on the way to pick her up. Today is Saturday, so there might be a traffic jam on the highway, and we need to go out as early as possible. We'll have lunch in a restaurant, and be back home, along with your auntie, at about 2:00 p.m. See you later. Bye.

早安，大衛，你阿姨大約在上午 11 點會抵達機場。爸爸和我現在正在去接她的路上。今天是星期六，高速公路上可能會塞車，所以我們得盡早出門。我們會在餐廳吃午餐，大約下午 2 點會和你阿姨一起回家。待會兒見，拜拜。

｜詳解｜ 題目問的是這對父母「正在做什麼事」，所以必須注意聽相關播放的內容。第二句提到「Daddy and I are now...，沒錯，很簡單的一個關鍵字：now。只要注意看哪一張圖在呈現的是「on the way to pick her up（正在去接她的路上）」即可，所以正確答案是選項 B。

月　　日

我的完成時間＿＿＿＿分鐘
標準作答時間 10 分鐘

Questions 1-2

Part 2 問答

Questions 3-7

3. A. No wonder he's always behind in his work.
   B. That must help him stay stress-free.
   C. This should be taken as a warning.

4. A. What makes you feel so good?
   B. Count me in! I've been looking forward to it all week.
   C. That makes a good deal! You receive credit card?

5. A. Could you explain a bit more?
   B. What do you think about my figure?
   C. Just wait and see.

6. A. Yes, Joe failed to arrive on time.
   B. I'm sorry to know that you failed to hand in your paper on time.
   C. You really have very good time management skills.

7. A. To put it simply, dreams can come true.
   B. Sure, I'll keep that in mind.
   C. I think it's better you know nothing.

Part 3 簡短對話

Questions 8-12

8. A. Help find back her lost keys
   B. Invite some good friends to have fun
   C. Have the company of the man

9. A. Loss of her money
   B. Not sure about how to deal with things
   C. Running into wild animals

10. A. Help himself to all the food there
    B. Help prepare some snacks for everyone
    C. Being a good guest and avoid being late next time

11. A. Spanish
    B. French
    C. English

12. A. What's so special about it
    B. Where it is located
    C. Whether there's a cafe to relax

Part 4 短文聽解

Questions 13-14

13.

A

B

C

14.

A

B

C

上頁簡答

解答與詳解

1. (B) 2. (C) 3. (B) 4. (B) 5. (C) 6. (C) 7. (C) 8. (C)
9. (B) 10. (A) 11. (A) 12. (A) 13. (B) 14. (C)

Part 1 看圖辨義

For questions number 1-2, please look at the following pictures.

Question number 1.

What is the man doing? 男子正在做什麼？

A. Paying for purchased goods　　A. 支付購買物品的費用

B. Receiving money for purchased goods　　B. 收取購買物品的費用

C. Making bread and cookies　　C. 製做麵包及餅乾

詳解｜圖片中男子是收銀員，女子是顧客，男子正在進行結帳的動作，而女子正從皮包拿出錢來準備結帳，所以正確答案為選項 B。purchased 是過去分詞當形容詞用，表示「已購買的」。

Question number 2.

What is the girl wearing? 女孩身上穿著什麼？

A. A coat and a pair of jeans　　A. 外套與長褲

B. A pair of pants and slippers　　B. 長褲與拖鞋

C. A long-sleeved blouse　　C. 長袖襯衫

詳解｜圖片只有一個人物，沒有背景也沒有其他人或物，就是要你考你穿著的衣物。選項 A 的 coat 是外套，所以錯誤；選項 B 的 slippers 是拖鞋，當然也錯誤。即使聽不出 sleeve（袖子），也聽不出 blouse（女用襯衫），至少 long 一定聽得出來吧，而且要判斷 A、B 錯誤並不困難，因此正確答案是選項 C。

Part 2 問答

Question number 3.

He never goes home without finishing his work. 他沒有做完工作是不會回家的。

A. No wonder he's always behind in his work.　　A. 難怪他總是進度落後。

B. That must help him stay stress-free.　　B. 這一定能幫助他保持無壓力的狀態。

C. This should be taken as a warning.　　C. 這應引以為戒。

| 詳解 | 題目這句表示他很負責任，總是確保完成工作後才離開。因此，工作不會堆積成為壓力源，這樣的習慣有助於讓自己保持無壓力的狀態，所以正確答案是選項 B。「完成工作後才下班」怎麼會進度落後？好的習慣或作為，也不可能有引以為戒的說法，所以 A、C 皆明顯錯誤。

| 補充 | 「N.-free」表示「沒有...的」，用片語來表示的話即「free from + N」。例如：Sugar-free（無糖的）、fat-free（無脂肪的）、guilt-free（無罪惡感的）、gluten-free（無麩質的）、smoke-free（無煙的）、worry-free（無憂的）、noise-free（無噪音的）、pain-free（無痛的）、debt-free（無債務的）、error-free（無錯誤的）

Question number 4.

We feel like going to the concert tonight. 今晚我們想去聽音樂會。

A. What makes you feel so good? A. 你為什麼感覺這麼好呢？

B. Count me in! I've been looking forward to it all week. B. 我也要去！我一整個星期都在期待著。

C. That makes a good deal! You receive credit card? C. 這挺划算的！你們收信用卡嗎？

| 詳解 | 題目這句暗示邀請對方一起聽音樂會，對於這樣的一個提議或建議，一定要將每一個選項的每一個字理解清楚再作答，因為也許看第一句沒問題，但第二句就錯了，務必特別小心。對話中並未提及對方感覺良好，而是表達他們想去聽音樂會，所以選項 A 錯誤；對話中並未提到任何有關支付方式或價格，所以選項 C 的回應毫無相關，所以正確答案是選項 B。「count me in」字面意思是「把我算進去」，也就是「我也要去」的意思，後面繼續說想參加音樂會並且期待已久，完全符合題意。

Question number 5.

I don't quite figure out what you are doing. 我不太明白你在做什麼。

A. Could you explain a bit more? A. 你可以再多做點說明嗎？

B. What do you think about my figure? B. 你覺得我的身材好嗎？

C. Just wait and see. C. 等著瞧吧。

| 詳解 | 題目這句表達自己不理解行為，暗示對方能否解釋或說明一下，所以選項 A 的回答完全不符，因為應該是題目這句的說話者要說的；選項 B 的回答提及了對方的身材，而非對話中的話題，完全與對話無關，所以正確答案是選項 C，它表達不想解釋，但最終對方就會知道，這是一種自然的回應。

| 補充 | figure 當名詞時，指數字、形象、外表。例如：The figure "8" represents infinity.（數字「8」代表無限。）當動詞時，指理解、計算。例如：He couldn't figure out the puzzle.（他無法理解這個謎題。）

Question number 6.

I never fail to finish my paper on time. 我一定會按時完成我的報告。

A. Yes, Joe failed to arrive on time. A. 是的，喬未能準時到達。

B. I'm sorry to know that you failed to hand in your paper on time. B. 很遺憾得知你未能按時交上論文。

C. You really have very good time management skills. C. 你確實擁有很棒的時間管理技巧。

｜詳解｜ 題目這句的說話者表示他「從來不會沒有」（never fail to...）按時完成報告，這是一種「雙重否定，負負得正」的表達，旨在強調「一定會」，所以給予「你具有良好的時間管理能力」的讚美相當合理，所以 正確答案是選項 C。

｜補充｜ 在英文裡，與 time 有關的片語相當多，其中「in time」與「on time」是最容易讓學習者混淆的片語之一。簡單來說，「in time」解作「及時」，「on time」則是「準時」的意思。「in time」主要是形容及時行動或成功爭取到一個時機，又或是能夠在限期之前或機會消失前完成，甚至有種「在千鈞一髮之間掌握了時機」的意味。例如：The police arrived in time to catch the criminals.（警察及時到達捉拿了罪犯。）「on time」則是在一個特定或指定的時間前完成，通常都有日期和時間作為目標，例如準時上班、準時上學、準時交稿…等。例如：The meeting has been scheduled for 2:30pm today. Would you please arrive on time?（今天的會議已定於下午二時三十分舉行。可否請你準時到達參與？）

Question number 7.

Could you tell me the truth in detail? 你能詳細地告訴我實情嗎？

A. To put it simply, dreams can come true. A. 簡單來說，夢想能夠成真。

B. Sure, I'll keep that in mind. B. 當然，我會牢記在心。

C. I think it's better you know nothing. C. 我認為你什麼都不知道比較好。

｜詳解｜ 題目這句是拜託對方詳述事實，而選項 A 提到夢想成真，這與問題無關。選項 B 說會將牢記在心，但沒有提供實情的詳細說明，這與問題不符，故正確答案是選項 C，暗示對方最好不要知道，算是給對方的善意、合理的回應。

｜補充｜ 「in detail（詳細地，仔細地）」是個常見的基礎片語，有時候 in 和 detail 中間還可以擺一個形容詞，例如：He explained the plan in great detail.（他非常仔細地說明這項計畫。）、Let's take an x-ray to look at the area in more detail.（我們來照個 X 光來看看這區塊的更多細節。）

Part 3 簡短對話

Question number 8.

M: Hi, Sarah! How's your day been? 男：嗨，莎拉！你今天過得怎麼樣？

W: Not great, Tom. First, I lost my keys, then my car broke down. It just seems to go from bad to worse. 女：不太好，湯姆。首先，我弄丟了我的鑰匙，然後我的車壞了。一切似乎越來越糟。

M: That sounds rough, Sarah. Is there anything I can do to help? 男：聽起來很不順利，莎拉。有什麼我可以幫忙的嗎？

W: Thanks, Tom. Just having someone to talk to makes it a little better. 女：謝謝，湯姆。有個人可以聊聊天就讓我感覺好了一點。

Question. What does the woman probably want to do?
這位女士可能想要做什麼？

A. Help find back her lost keys　A. 幫忙找回她遺失的鑰匙

B. Invite some good friends to have fun　B. 邀請一些好朋友一起玩樂

C. Have the company of the man　C. 有這位男士的陪伴

|詳解| 題目問女子想要的是什麼，所以必須注意她說的話。女子在告訴男子當日一些不順遂的事情（I lost my keys, then my car broke down）後，男子問她是否需要協助，而女子只說有個人（someone）可以聊聊天就好了，someone 就是「某個人」，而不會是「some good friends」，所以選項 B 錯誤，而對話中女子並未提到需要男子幫她找回鑰匙，所以 A 也錯誤，所以正確答案是選項 C，因為女子最後提到，有個人可以和她聊聊天的話（= 陪伴）就會感覺好一點。

|補充| worse 是 bad 的比較級，所以「from bad to worse」就是「每況愈下」的意思。之所以搭配了 go 這個動詞，可以從「go bad」（變糟，變壞）這個片語來理解就可以了。

Question number 9.

M: Hey, have you ever been camping before? 男：嘿，你以前有露營過嗎？

W: No, never. But I really want to try it. I just hope I won't be at a loss out there in the wilderness! 女：沒有，從來沒有。但我真的想試試看。我只是希望在野外不要不知所措！

M: Don't worry, I'll show you the ropes. Camping is all about enjoying nature and taking it easy. 男：別擔心，我會教你的。露營就是要享受大自然，輕鬆愉快。

Question. What is the woman worried about when going camping?
女子去露營時會擔心什麼？

A. Loss of her money　　A. 花太多錢

B. Not sure about how to deal with things　　B. 不知道如何處理事情

C. Running into wild animals　　C. 遇見野獸

｜詳解｜ 女子表示她擔心在野外不知所措（at a loss），這意味著她擔心自己可能會遇到一些情況不知道該怎麼應對，所以正確答案是選項 B。對話中沒有提到女人擔心花太多錢，所以 A 錯誤；選項 C 刻意以類似字彙的 wild 製造干擾，但她沒有提到擔心遇到野獸，所以 C 也錯誤。

｜補充｜ 「at a loss」這個片語常用於 be 動詞之後，表示「一臉茫然；不知所措」，如果要表示「對於…不知所措」，後面可以接「as to + 名詞」或「to + 動詞詞」，例如：I'm at a loss as to how I can help you.（我不知道該怎　幫你。）

Question number 10.

M: Sorry I'm late. There was a traffic accident on my way here.

W: It's OK. We're just beginning the party. Come in, please.

M: Thanks. Wow! There's so much food here.

W: Just be my guest. There's plenty for everyone!

男：對不起，我遲到了。我來的路上有車禍。

女：沒關係，我們派對才剛開始。請進。

男：謝謝。哇！這裡的食物好多啊。

女：請隨意取用。這裡的食物足夠大家享用的！

Question. What does the woman suggest the man do? 女子建議男子做什麼？

A. Help himself to all the food there　　A. 自己取用那裡的所有食物

B. Help prepare some snacks for everyone　　B. 幫大家準備一些點心

C. Being a good guest and avoid being late next time　　C. 做一個好客人並下次不要遲到

｜詳解｜ 題目問女子建議男子做什麼，我們可以從女子說的最後一句「Just be my guest」可知，她建議男子放輕鬆，可隨意取用派對上的食物，所以正確答案是選項 A，其中「Help himself to...」其實就是在呼應「be my guest」。對話中沒有提到、要他幫忙準備食物，所以 B 錯誤；而選項 C 刻意以「Being a good guest」來與「Just be my guest」造成混淆，但兩者意思完全不同，因此 C 也錯誤。

｜補充｜ 「Be my guest.」是「請自便；別客氣」的意思，本句適用於邀請他人時，表現出的好客之意, 請客人放輕鬆不必拘束。可與「Help yourself!」做替換。句型架構是常見的祈使句型,以原形動詞為首開頭，用以表示祈願、要求。例如：Feel free at home and be my guest.（當自己家，別客氣。）

Question number 11.

M: Do you speak any other languages? 男：你會說任何其他語言嗎？

W: Yes, I speak English and a bit of French. But I feel most at home with Spanish. 女：是的，我會說英語，還會一點法語。但我最擅長的是西班牙語。

M: That's great! Being comfortable with a language makes communication much easier. 男：太棒了！精通一種語言使溝通變得更容易。

Question. What language is the woman good at? 女子最擅長哪一種語言？

A. Spanish A. 西班牙語

B. French B. 法語

C. English C. 英語

| 詳解 | 從三個選項來看就知道題目要你選出某種語言（language），「(be) good at」就是「擅長…」的意思，而對話中女子提到「I feel most at home with Spanish.」，「(be) good at」其實就是「(be) at home with」的意思。所以正確答案是選項 A。

| 補充 | 「at home」是「在家」，可以引申為「無拘無束」、「放鬆」的意思，所以英文裡有「make yourself at home」（當作自己的家，請自便）、「feel at home」（覺得自在）這些說法，後面如果再加個介系詞 with，可用來表示「擅長於…」。

Question number 12.

M: Hi there! Have you ever been to the new park downtown? 男：嗨，妳好！妳有去過市中心的新公園嗎？

W: No. What makes it worth a visit? 女：沒有，那裡有什麼值得去看的呢？

M: It has a beautiful lake and lots of flowers. There's also a small café where you can relax and have a coffee. 男：那裡有一個漂亮的湖泊和很多花。還有一個小咖啡館，你可以在那裡放鬆一下，喝杯咖啡。

W: Then I'll make time to go and see it soon. 女：那我會找時間去看看。

Question. What did the woman ask about the new park? 女子問了關於這座新公園的什麼問題？

A. What's so special about it A. 那裡有什麼特別的

B. Where it is located B. 它位於哪裡

C. Whether there's a cafe to relax C. 那裡是否有咖啡館可以放鬆一下

| 詳解 | 題目問女子問了關於公園的什麼事，所以只要關注女子說過什麼即可。女子第一次發言中表示「What makes it worth a visit?」，worth 是個形容詞，表示「值得的…」，也就是說，她在問這座公園有什麼吸引人的地方，所以正確答案是選項 A。話中女子並沒有問公園的具體位置，因此 B 錯誤；雖然男子在回答時提到咖啡館是該公園特點之一，但這並非女子所問的重點，因此 C 也錯誤。

| 補充 | worth 也可以當名詞，表示「價值」，例如「prove one's worth」是「證明自己的價值」；「... is of great worth.」是「…是很有價值的」。

Part 4 短文聽解

Question number 13.

Please look at the following three pictures. Listen to the following reply. At what place could you hear it?

請看以下三張圖片。聆聽以下回答。你在什麼地方可能聽到這段話？

I happened to see this guy standing on the sidewalk when I was walking out of the Family convenience store this morning. If my memory serves me right, he wore a grey T-shirt and a pair of black shorts. By the way, he was wearing a pair of sunglasses and talking on his cellphone.

今天早上我走出全家便利商店時，碰巧看到這個人站在人行道上。如果我沒記錯的話，他穿著灰色 T 恤和一條黑色短褲。順便提一下，他戴著一副太陽眼鏡，正在講手機。

A　　Ⓑ　　C

| 詳解 | 題目問的是哪一張人物圖是回答（警方）時所描述的男子。前兩句與答題沒有任何關係，答題重點要從「he wore a...」開始：他穿著灰色 T 恤（grey T-shirt）。另外，從三張圖來看，sunglasses 也是關鍵之一。至於黑色短褲（black shorts）和講手機（talking on his cellphone）都與答案無關。掌握以上兩個線索，就可選出正確答案了，所以正確答案是選項 B。圖 A 中男子穿的是襯衫（shirt），圖 C 中男子穿的是汗衫（undershirt）。

| 補充 | 「if my memory serves me right」就是「if I remember correctly」的意思，動詞 serve 後面接「人」時表示「服務（某人）」，「我的記憶給予我正確的服務」，那當然就是「記得沒錯」的意思囉！「if my memory serves me right, ...」有時候也可以簡寫成「If memory serves, ...」。

Question number 14.

Please look at the following three pictures. Listen to the following talk. Who is the speaker's father after work?

請看以下三張圖片。聆聽以下談話。何者是說話者的父親下班後的樣子？

My father is a 50-year-old office worker. He usually wears glasses. He wears a white shirt and a tie to work every weekday. Besides, he always smiles at everyone he meets. When he is back home, he would change into casual wear right away and sit comfortably on the sofa watching TV.

我的父親是一位 50 歲的上班族。他通常帶著眼睛。他都穿白襯衫並打領帶去上班。而且，他總是對遇到的每個人微笑。回到家後，他會立刻換上休閒服，然後舒舒服服地坐在沙發上看電視。

A

B

Ⓒ

| 詳解 | 首先，題目一定要聽到最後一個字，聽清楚題目要問的什麼。錄音中提到「He usually wears glasses.」，所以 A 選項就先刪除了；因為題目問的是「下班後（after work）」的樣子，從「When he is back home, he would change into casual wear right away...」可知，選項 B 錯誤，所以正確答案是選項 C。「casual wear」是「休閒服」的意思，wear 可以當名詞，表示「服裝，穿著」。

Day 18 月 日

我的完成時間＿＿＿分鐘
標準作答時間 10 分鐘

Part 1 看圖辨義

Questions 1-2

Part 2 問答

Questions 3-7

3. A. I didn't expect it either.
   B. Yes, I've known that for long.
   C. Nobody will believe you anymore.

4. A. That's not your suit.
   B. I'm happy to hear that.
   C. Don't you think so?

5. A. Yes, May 10 is an important day.
   B. Of course, our bathroom is very clean.
   C. Sure, it's down the hall to the right.

6. A. Almost every day, even if it's just for a short time.
   B. I'll do the vocabulary exercise later.
   C. I've keep the habit of doing exercise for one year.

7. A. That's right. How about go jogging along the riverside after lunch?
   B. Then, let's not go out and stay home watching movies.
   C. Sound great. Do you bring an umbrella?

Part 3 簡短對話

Questions 8-12

8. A. A barber shop
   B. Man's newest hairstyles
   C. The man's new hairstyle

9. A. In an office
   B. At school
   C. On a train

10. A. clerk and a customer
    B. A boss and an employee
    C. A driver and a passenger

11. A. Join everyone for a birthday party
    B. Make a cake to treat everyone
    C. Meet a friend to catch up

12. A. Waiting for a friend to come
    B. Visiting a night market
    C. Buying movie tickets

Part 4 短文聽解

Questions 13-14

13.

A

B

C

14.

A

B

C

上頁簡答

解答與詳解

1. (C) 2. (B) 3. (A) 4. (B) 5. (C) 6. (A) 7. (B) 8. (C)
9. (B) 10. (C) 11. (A) 12. (C) 13. (A) 14. (B)

Part 1 看圖辨義

For questions number 1-2, please look at the following pictures.

Question number 1.

What is the man doing? 男子正在做什麼？

A. Beating a drum　　A. 打鼓

B. Blowing the flute　　B. 吹笛子

C. Playing the guitar　　C. 彈吉他

| 詳解 | 圖片上我們可以看到一個男人在彈吉他，應馬上聯想到吉他的英文是 guitar，所以只要聽到哪個選項有這個字，答案當然就是它了，正確答案是選項 C。

| 補充 | 「鼓（drum）」、「笛子（flute）」、「吉他（guitar）」…等這些都稱為「樂器（instrument）」。 與這些樂器名稱搭配的動詞，以中文來說可能有「打」、「吹」、「彈」、「演奏」…等不同說法，但英文裡通常可以只用 play 這個動詞就搞定了，所以上述選項中動詞 beat、blow，其實都可以用 play 來取代。但記住，樂器名稱前面要加上冠詞 the。

Question number 2.

Why does the car driver come to this place? 這名汽車駕駛為什麼要來這裡？

A. Buying some tickets　　A. 買車票

B. Get some gasoline　　B. 加油

C. Add oil　　C.（鼓勵人的用語）加油

| 詳解 | 圖片中一輛車來到加油站（gas/gasoline station），聽完三個選項之後，A 選項可以直接排除了（在加油站買「回數票」也已過時了）。本題考的是「到加油站加油」的英文怎麼說。雖然過去的中式英文「add oil」已被列入字典解釋為「加油」，但它的真正意思是用來鼓勵他人所說的「加油」，因此 C 也錯誤。故本題正確答案是是選項 B。

Part 2 問答

Question number 3.

I can't believe you failed the test! 我不敢相信你竟然考不及格！

A. I didn't expect it either. A. 我也沒料到。

B. Yes, I've known that for long. B. 是的，我早就知道了。

C. Nobody will believe you anymore. C. 沒人會再相信你了。

詳解 題目這句是表達對於某事件的驚訝，而回應「我也沒料到」表示同樣對考試不及格感到意外，這與對話中表達的驚訝情緒一致，所以正確答案是選項 A。選項 B 的回應「是的，我早就知道了」這樣的回答會讓人感覺不合邏輯；選項 C 的回應「沒人會再相信你了」與對話中討論的考試結果無直接關聯。

Question number 4.

This suit looks great on you. 這西裝你穿起來很好看。

A. That's not your suit. A. 那不是你的西裝。

B. I'm happy to hear that. B. 我很高興聽到你這麼說。

C. Don't you think so? C. 你不這麼認為嗎？

詳解 當有人讚美你的外表時，表達感謝和愉快是最自然的反應，「我很高興聽到你這麼說」表現了良好的社交禮儀，所以正確答案是選項 B。選項 A 的回應「那不是你的西裝」與對話中的讚美無關，並且引入了一個不相關的話題。選項 C 的回應「你不這麼認為嗎？」是一個反問句，這樣的回應會讓人感到困惑，因為對方已經表達了他們認為這西裝很好看。

Question number 5.

May I use your restroom? 我能用一下你的洗手間嗎？

A. Yes, May 10 is an important day. A. 是的，5 月 10 日是個重要的日子。

B. Of course, our bathroom is very clean. B. 當然，我們洗手間很乾淨。

C. Sure, it's down the hall to the right. C. 當然可以，往這大廳過去後的右手邊。

詳解 「當然可以，往這大廳過去後的右手邊」直接回答了對方的請求，並給出了具體的方向指引，這是一個自然且適當的回應，符合對話的上下文，所以正確答案是選項 C。選項 A 的回應「是的，5 月 10 日是個重要的日子」與對話中的請求完全無關，只是利用相同字彙 may 刻意造成混淆；選項 B 的回應雖然表示同意，但未直接回答對方關於如何找到洗手間的問題。

補充 俗話說「人有三急」，其中之一便是「如廁急」。到了別人家裡，「借一下洗手間」也是很平常的事，不過可別說成「May I borrow your restroom/toilet?」因為 borrow 這個動詞是指「借走」，難不成是想把人家的洗手間搬回家了？

Question number 6.

How often do you do exercise? 你多久會運動一次？

A. Almost every day, even if it's just for a short time.
A. 我幾乎每天都會運動，即使只是短時間的運動。

B. I'll do the vocabulary exercise later.
B. 我等一下會做詞彙練習。

C. I've keep the habit of doing exercise for one year.
C. 我已經保持運動的習慣有一年了。

｜詳解｜ 題目「How often...?」是問「多久一次…」，回應「我幾乎每天都會運動…」是一個自然且具體的回答，說明了運動的頻率，符合對話的上下文，所以正確答案是選項 A。選項 B 刻意以相同字彙 exercise 答題，但這裡的 exercise 並非「運動」的意思，而是「習題」，所以是完全偏離了話題，沒有回答對方的問題。選項 C 雖然提到了運動，但並未直接回答「多久會運動一次」，而是回答持續運動的時間，答非所問。

｜補充｜ 日常生活中有許多事會經常性發生，或變成一種習慣，例如：每週運動 3 天、每月開一次會議、每天倒垃圾…等。像這樣頻率性發生的事情英文可以怎麼表達呢？首先，可以用「數字 + time(s)」，例如：twice a week 一週兩次；可以用「數字 + 時間單位 + 期間」，例如：one hour a day（一天一小時）、four days a month（一個月四天）；可以用「every + 數字 + 複數時間名詞」，例如：every two days（每兩天一次）

Question number 7.

It's rainy and a bit cold today. 今天下雨且有點冷。

A. That's right. How about go jogging along the riverside after lunch?
A. 對，午餐後去河邊慢跑怎麼樣？

B. Then, let's not go out and stay home watching movies.
B. 那麼，我們不出去，在家看電影吧。

C. Sound great. Do you bring an umbrella?
C. 聽起來不錯。你有帶傘嗎？

｜詳解｜ 題目這句說外面下雨且有點冷，所以留在家裡看電影是一個舒適的選擇，可以避免在雨天受涼或淋濕，故正確答案是選項 B。既然題目說外面天氣不好了，當然就不太適合在室外運動，因此這個建議不太合適，選項 A 錯誤。選項 C 的「Sounds great」通常是針對建議給予肯定的回應，但題目這句並非提出建議。

Part 3 簡短對話

Question number 8.

W: You look a bit different today. Got a new haircut?

女：你今天看起來有點不一樣。去理了個新髮型？

M: Right. Last night I went to a barbershop, and they showed me a few newest styles.

男：是的。我昨晚去了男士理髮店，他們給我看了一些最新髮型。

W: You chose the best one. You look more handsome!

女：你選了最棒的髮型。你變得更帥了。

M: Thank you.

男：謝謝。

Question. What are the speakers talking about? 說話者們在談論什麼？

A. A barber shop　　A. 一間理髮店

B. Man's newest hairstyles　　B. 最潮的男士髮型

C. The man's new hairstyle　　C. 男子的最新髮型

| 詳解 | 對話一開始女子就注意到男子的外表變化（look a bit different），並表示對他新髮型（new haircut）的注意，而男子的回答也暗示了他確實有改變了髮型。因此，對話的主題是男子的最新髮型，正確答案是選項 C。雖然男子提到了他去了一間男士理髮店，但這只是對話中提到的一個地點，而不是對話的主題，所以 A 錯誤；雖然有提到一些最新的髮型，但那只是給男子參考的標的，並非對話主題，所以 B 也錯誤。

Question number 9.

W: David, you're late again this morning.

女：大衛，你今天早上又遲到了。

M: I know, I'm really sorry. My alarm didn't go off, so I overslept.

男：我知道，真的很抱歉。我的鬧鐘沒有響，所以我睡過頭了。

W: You should try setting multiple alarms. The next class is about to begin. Please go back to your seat quickly.

女：你應該試著設定多個鬧鐘。下一節課快要開始了。快回去你的座位上。

Question. Where did the conversation take place? 對話發生在哪裡？

A. In an office　　A. 在辦公室

B. At school　　B. 在學校

C. On a train　　C. 在火車上

| 詳解 | 對話中女子提到「下一節課快要開始了（The next class is about to begin.）」這暗示對話不可能在火車上，所以 C 顯然錯誤；如果說對話在學校的「辦公室」，而 David 是個老師，也許選項 A 可以說得通，但後面這句「快回去你的座位上（go back to your seat quickly）」就直接把選項 A 否決掉了，所以 A 也錯誤，故正確答案是選項 B。

| 補充 | 睡覺是 sleep，over 是過頭，兩個字拼在一起的 oversleep 當然是「睡過頭」了，不過，別跟「sleep over」這個片語搞混了。「sleep over」是指在別人家過夜。例如：My mom said I could sleep over in your house on Saturday night.（我媽說我星期六晚上可以在你家過夜。）

Question number 10.

M: Good morning. Where do you need to go today?	男：早安。你今天要去哪裡？
W: I need to go to the airport, please.	女：我要去機場，麻煩了。
M: Sure, it will take about 30 minutes to get there. Is that okay?	男：好的，到那裡大約需要 30 分鐘。可以嗎？
W: Yes, that's fine. Thank you for the ride.	女：可以，謝謝你的載送。

Question. Who are the speakers? 說話者是誰？

A clerk and a customer	A. 店員與顧客
B. A boss and an employee	B. 老闆與員工
C. A driver and a passenger	C. 司機與乘客

| 詳解 | 男子詢問女子要去哪裡並告知所需時間，這是典型的司機載客時會說的話。此外，女士感謝男士的載送（ride），也符合乘客對司機的回應。所以正確答案是選項 C。

| 補充 | ride 當名詞時，表示一個乘坐或行駛的過程。例如：I need a ride to the airport.（我需要有人載我去機場。）另外，ride 可以指在遊樂園中的遊樂設施，如雲霄飛車、旋轉木馬等。例如：The roller coaster was the most thrilling ride at the amusement park.（雲霄飛車是遊樂園裡最刺激的設施。）最後，ride 還可以指一段行駛的路程或旅途。例如：It's a long ride from New York to Los Angeles.（從紐約到洛杉磯的車程很長。）

Question number 11.

W: Hi, John, it's so nice to see you here.	女：嗨，約翰，很高興看到你來了。
M: Hi, Emily! Sorry I'm a bit late. This is for you!	男：嗨，艾蜜莉！抱歉我有點遲到了。這是送給你的！
W: Thank you. Come in, please. We're about to cut the cake.	女：謝謝你。請進。我們正要切蛋糕了。
M: Great! I wouldn't want to miss that.	男：太棒了！這我可不想錯過了。

Question. What is the man going to do? 男子將要做什麼？

A. Join everyone for a birthday party	A. 和大家一起融入生日派對
B. Make a cake to treat everyone	B. 做個蛋糕請大家吃
C. Meet a friend to catch up	C. 和一位朋友見面敘舊

| 詳解 | 本題關鍵在女子說「We're about to cut the cake.」這通常是在生日派對或慶祝活動中會進行的儀式。而男子說「I wouldn't want to miss that.」表示他對這場派對相當期待，所以正確答案是選項 A；因為女子提到「我們正要切蛋糕了」，表示蛋糕已經準備好，不需要再做，故選項 B 錯誤；對話中男子表現出參與派對的期待，而不是單純跟一個朋友敘舊（catch up），故選項 C 錯誤。

| 補充 | miss 當動詞時有多層意義，主要是「錯過」、「避開」、「想念」、「未擊中」這種意思。例如：I missed the bus this morning.（今早我錯過了公車。）、She managed to miss all the traffic by taking a different route.（她走另一條路，成功避開了所有的交通堵塞。）、I really miss my family when I'm away.（我在外時真的很想念我的家人。）、He threw the ball but missed the target.（他投球但未擊中目標。）

Question number 12.

M: Wow! There are a lot of people in line! I doubt we can get tickets for 6:30 p.m.?	男：哇！一堆人在排隊啊！我懷疑我們能否買到晚間 6:30 這場的票。
W: Well, I should have booked the tickets online earlier. What if we fail to get the tickets?	女：唉，我應該早點上網訂票才對。萬一我們買不到票怎麼辦？
M: If so, let's go to the night market nearby to have a big meal.	男：如此的話，我們就去附近的夜市大吃一頓吧。

Question. What are the speakers doing? 說話者們正在做什麼？

A. Waiting for a friend to come	A. 等一個朋友來
B. Visiting a night market	B. 逛夜市
C. Buying movie tickets	C. 買電影票

| 詳解 | 題目問說話者們正在做什麼，而對話中提到排隊（in line）和買票（get tickets），以及擔心是否能買到 6:30 的票，且提到早該上網訂票（should have booked the tickets online earlier），明確表示他們正在排隊買電影票，所以正確答案是選項 C。對話中沒有提到任何關於朋友的內容，所以 A 錯誤；雖然對話最後提到了去夜市，但這只是他們在買不到電影票的情況下的替代計劃，所以 B 也錯誤。

Part 4 短文聽解

Question number 13.

Please look at the following three pictures. Listen to the following announcement. Where would people most likely hear this announcement?

請看以下三張圖片。聆聽以下宣布。人們最有可能在哪裡聽到這則宣布？

May I have your attention, please! The next train to Taipei Station will arrive on Platform 2 in five minutes. Passengers are advised to proceed to the platform quickly. Please have your tickets ready for check by the station staff. Besides, do not stay too close to the platform edge in order to avoid any possible danger. Thank you and enjoy your trip.

請各位注意！開往台北車站的下一班列車將在五分鐘後抵達二號月台。請乘客儘快前往月台，並準備好車票以便站務人員檢查。此外，請不要靠近月台邊緣，以免發生危險。感謝您的搭乘，祝您旅途愉快。

| 詳解 | 看過這三張圖，以及第一句的「May I have your attention, please!」，就知道這是在一個公共場所的廣播內容。接著有許多關鍵字詞的出現，像是「The next train to...」、Platform、「station staff」等，都可以確認看似販售電影票的選項 B 不對。至於要選 A 或 C ，只有一個關鍵，那就是「Please have your tickets ready for check by the station staff.」這句了，因為搭捷運站的票是不需要給站務人員檢查的，所以正確答案是選項 A。

Question number 14.

Please look at the following three pictures. Listen to the following message. Where could Mary be heading?

請看以下三張圖片。聆聽以下訊息。瑪莉可能正要往哪裡去？

Hi George, it's Mary. I was robbed of my purse when I walked on the street near the Royal Hospital one hour ago. I remembered what the robber look like and I'm now going to report this crime. I'm sorry, but I'll be late for our date tonight. I'll keep you updated. Thanks for understanding.

喂，喬治，我是瑪莉。一小時前，在皇家醫院附近的街上，我的錢包被搶了。我看到了搶劫犯的樣子，現在要去報案。對不起，我今晚會晚一些到達約會地點。我會隨時通知你最新情況。謝謝你的理解。

| 詳解 | 題目問的是「瑪莉可能正要往哪裡去？」，而發留言訊息的人是瑪莉。留言訊息提到她的錢包被搶了（I was robbed of my purse）…現在要去報案（report this crime），所以瑪莉現在正要往警察局去，正確答案是選項 B。

| 補充 | 動詞 rob 意指以暴力、威脅或欺騙手段奪取他人財物。例如：The thief tried to rob the bank.（這名竊賊試圖搶劫銀行。）robber 是名詞，指進行搶劫的人，也就是「搶匪，搶劫犯」。例如：The police caught the robber.（警方將搶匪抓到了。）robbery 是名詞，指搶劫這件事，即「搶案」。例如：The store was closed after the robbery.（該商店在這起搶案發生之後即關門了。）

Day 19　月　日

我的完成時間＿＿＿分鐘
標準作答時間 10 分鐘

Questions 1-2

Part 2 問答

Questions 3-7

3. A. I'm really sorry about this.
   B. Thanks! I'm glad you enjoyed it.
   C. Sure, I have voice in this matter.

4. A. No, This is my order, not yours.
   B. I appreciate your help.
   C. Sure, I'll have the chicken salad, please.

5. A. Mr. Lin, the project lead.
   B. Our senior manager is not here.
   C. I finished this report with Ms. Johnson.

6. A. She's sitting on the bed.
   B. She's in good health. Thanks.
   C. She's not home now.

7. A. Too see is to believe.
   B. I'm always guided by feeling, not thought.
   C. Not bad. Have you told him how you feel?

Part 3 簡短對話

Questions 8-12

8. A. At an airport
   B. At an MRT station
   C. In a bank

9. A. wet and foggy
   B. Snowy and windy
   C. Rainy and cold

10. A. 5:30 p.m.
    B. 6:00 p.m.
    C. 7:00 p.m.

11. A. A married couple
    B. A bank teller and a client
    C. A shop clerk and a customer

12. A. On the balcony
    B. In the living room
    C. In the kitchen

Part 4 短文聽解

Questions 13-14

13.

A

B

C

14.

A

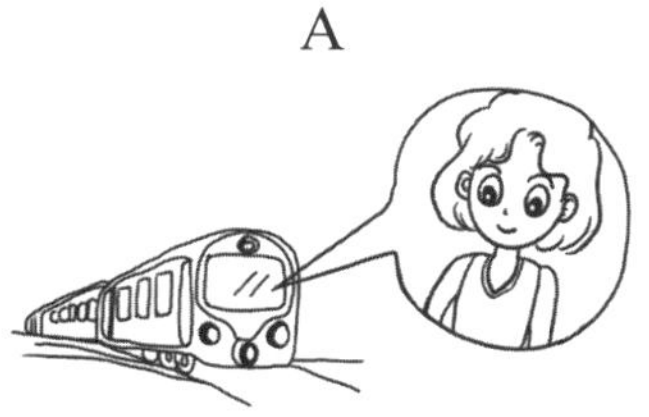

B

C

上頁簡答

解答與詳解

1. (C) 2. (B) 3. (B) 4. (C) 5. (A) 6. (B) 7. (C) 8. (B) 9. (C) 10. (A) 11. (C) 12. (C) 13. (A) 14. (B)

Part 1 看圖辨義

For questions number 1-2, please look at the following pictures.

Question number 1.

What can we know about the man? 我們可以知道關於男子什麼事？

A. He is going to give away this gift. A. 他即將把這禮物送出去。

B. He is not satisfied with his gift. B. 他對他的禮物並不滿意。

C. He is happy to receive this gift. C. 他很開心收到這份禮物。

| 詳解 | 圖片上我們可以看到男子的臉旁有個愛心，以及手上拿著一個生日禮物，這表示他很開心收到這份禮物，所以正確答案是選項 C。

| 補充 | gift 作名詞時指「禮物」或「天賦」，如「She received a gift.」或「He has a gift for music.」。而 gifted 是形容詞，用來形容具有天賦或才能的人，如：She is a gifted artist.。它強調個人在某方面有超常的能力或才華。

Question number 2.

What is the man? 男子是做什麼的？

A. He is a hunter. A. 他是個獵人。

B. He is a magician. B. 他是個魔術師。

C. He is a rabbit handler. C. 他是個訓兔師。

| 詳解 | 圖片中男子抓著一隻從帽子裡出現的兔子，這當然是一種魔術（magic）表演，而魔術師的英文即是 magician，所以正確答案是選項 B。別聽到 rabbit 就以為答案是 C 喔，因為「rabbit handler」是「訓兔師」的意思

| 補充 | 選項 C 的 handler 是從動詞 handle（處理）衍生而來，意思是「訓獸師」，也可以說是「animal handler」。「訓獸師」的另一說法是「animal tamer」，動詞 tame 是「馴化，馴養；制服，使順從」的意思。

Part 2 問答

Question number 3.

Good job! You have a nice voice. 真是棒！你的嗓音不錯。

A. I'm really sorry about this. A. 對於這事我感到抱歉。

B. Thanks! I'm glad you enjoyed it. B. 謝謝。我很高興你能喜歡。

C. Sure, I have voice in this matter. C. 當然，我對這件事有發言權。

｜詳解｜ 對方稱讚你的好嗓音時，以表達感謝及很開心對方能喜歡，這是最合適的回應，所以正確答案是選項 B。當別人稱讚你時，你卻表示歉意，完全不合情理，所以 A 錯誤。選項 C 的 voice 是另外一個意思，也就是「發言權」，也是不相關的回應。

Question number 4.

May I take your order now? 您現在可以點餐了嗎？

A. No, This is my order, not yours. A. 不行，這是我的訂單，不是你的。

B. I appreciate your help. B. 我很感激你的幫忙。

C. Sure, I'll have the chicken salad, please. C. 當然，我要點雞肉沙拉，麻煩了。

｜詳解｜ 服務員在詢問是否可以點餐，A 的回應顯然聽不懂或誤解服務員的問話，且顯得無禮有不合邏輯。B 的回答表達了感謝，但並未回答是否可以點餐，也沒有提供具體的點餐內容，所以錯誤。故正確答案是選項 C，這個回答表示同意並提供了具體的點餐內容，正確回應了服務員的問題。

Question number 5.

Who do you report to? 你的上級主管是誰？

A. Mr. Lin, the project lead. A. 林先生。本專案的領導。

B. Our senior manager is not here. B. 我們的資深經理不在這裡。

C. I finished this report with Ms. Johnson. C. 我和強森女士一起完成這份報告。

｜詳解｜ 首先，一定要知道「report to」是什麼意思！「report to + 人」字面意思是「向…（某人）報告」，引申為「向某人負責，隸屬於某人之下」，所以題目問的是「你的主管是誰？」，A 明確回答了這個問題，指出了具體的人和職位，所以正確答案就是選項 A。B 沒有回答出誰是上級主管，而是提到資深經理不在場，這與問題無關。C 到了某個重要的人物，但並沒有直接回答誰是你的上級主管，答非所問。

｜補充｜ 「report to」指某人向另一人或特定職位匯報工作進度、問題或任務。例如：Employees in the marketing department report to the marketing manager.（市場部的員工向市場經理匯報。）此外，「report to」可以當作是一個及物動詞，改成被動式時，務必將介系詞 to 保留下來。例如：The CEO is reported to by all department heads.（所有部門主管向 CEO 匯報。）

Question number 6.

How is your mother? 你母親還好嗎？

A. She's sitting on the bed.	A. 她正坐在床上。
B. She's in good health. Thanks.	B. 她健康狀況良好。謝謝。
C. She's not home now.	C. 她現在不在家。

｜詳解｜ 本題以疑問詞 how 用來詢問某人的身體或健康狀況。A 只是描述母親的位置（sitting on the bed）而非健康狀況，與問題無關。B 提供了適當的回答，表明母親的健康良好，並表示感謝對方的關心，所以正確答案是選項 B；C 回答母親不在家，這也與問題問及的母親的健康狀況無關。

Question number 7.

I have feelings for this guy. What do you think? 我對這傢伙有感覺。你覺得呢？

A. Too see is to believe.	A. 百聞不如一見。
B. I'm always guided by feeling, not thought.	B. 我總是被感情支配，而非理智。
C. Not bad. Have you told him how you feel?	C. 還不賴。妳告訴他妳的感覺了嗎？

｜詳解｜ 題目這句是對身邊友人表示對某人有愛慕之意，進一步徵詢友人的意見。A 的「百聞不如一見」這句話沒有針對對方的提問回答，不知所云；B 表現出個人的情感取向，但也未回答對方的問題或提供建議；C 的「Not bad.」就直接回答了「What do you think (about this guy)?」這個問題，進而提出「Have you told him how you feel?」這個問題，鼓勵對方表白，所以正確答案是選項 C。

｜補充｜ feeling 及 feel 這兩個名詞意思及用法上有何不同呢？ feeling 指情感、感覺或觸覺，可以用來描述身體或心理上的感受。例如：She had a strange feeling that someone was watching her.（她有一種奇怪的感覺，有人在看她。）feel 當名詞通常指某人或事物給予的單純觸感，或是某人給予周遭的氛圍。例如：She had a happy feel about her after the successful presentation.（在成功的演示之後，她身上有一種快樂的氛圍。）

Part 3 簡短對話

Question number 8.

M: I just found my card doesn't have enough money. I need to add value to it now.	男：我剛發現我的卡上沒有足夠的錢了，我現在需要加值。
W: Let me see... There're three minutes before the next train arrives. I'll wait for you here. Hurry!	女：讓我看看……下一班車還有三分鐘到，我會在這裡等你。快點！
M: OK. I'll be quick.	男：好的，我會快一點。

Question. Where are the speakers? 說話者們在哪裡？

A. At an airport	A. 在機場
B. At an MRT station	B. 在捷運站
C. In a bank	C. 在銀行

| 詳解 | 對話中提到下一班（火）車即將到來（...before the next train arrives），這暗示說話者們在等待鐵軌列車（可能是火車、地鐵、捷運），而不可能是在機場等飛機，更不會是在銀行，正確答案是選項 B。

Question number 9.

M: Jess, bring a coat with you. The weather is going to change tonight.	男：傑絲，帶件外套。今晚天氣會有變化。
W: OK, Daddy, and I should bring an umbrella as well. The weather report also said that the chance of rain will increase later.	女：好的，爸爸，我還應該帶把傘。氣象報告也說晚點降雨機率會增加。
M: Good girl. I'll wait for you at home. Take care.	男：乖孩子。我會在家等你。出門小心。
W: Bye, Dad.	女：再見，爸爸。

Question. What will the weather be like tonight? 今晚的天氣會如何？

A. wet and foggy	A. 潮濕多霧
B. Snowy and windy	B. 下雪且多風
C. Rainy and cold	C. 下雨且寒冷

| 詳解 | 根據對話內容，父親提醒女兒帶外套（bring a coat with you），並且晚點降雨機率會增加（the chance of rain will increase），暗示今晚的天氣會是下雨且寒冷的情況，所以正確答案是選項 C。對話中沒有提到起霧以及下雪的情況，A、B 錯誤。

| 補充 | 日常會話中常聽到用來形容天氣狀況的英文，像是 cold（寒冷的）、hot（炎熱的）、warm - 暖和的、cool - 涼爽的、chilly - 微冷的、mild - 溫和的、freezing - 嚴寒的、boiling - 酷熱的、scorching - 炙熱的、breezy - 有微風的、windy - 多風的、calm - 寧靜的、wet/humid - 潮濕的、dry - 乾燥的、damp - 潮濕的、foggy - 多霧的、misty - 有霧的、hazy - 有霾的、cloudy - 多雲的、partly cloudy - 局部多雲的、stormy - 暴風雨的、showery - 降雨的、snowy - 下雪的

Question number 10.

M: The movie begins at 7:00 p.m. How about we leave at 6:00 p.m.
男：電影七點開始，我們六點出發怎麼樣？

W: It's almost 5:30 p.m. I suggest we go now to have some dinner and go there straight away.
女：現在快五點半了。我建議我們現在就去吃晚餐，然後直接去那裡。

M: That's a good idea.
男：這是個好主意。

W: Then let's go.
女：那我們就走吧。

Question. What time will they leave? 他們會幾點出發？

A. 5:30 p.m. A. 晚間 5:30

B. 6:00 p.m. B. 晚間 6:00

C. 7:00 p.m. C. 晚間 7:00

| 詳解 | 女子建議現在就去吃晚餐（I suggest we go now to have some dinner），並且直接去電影院，而這個建議是在下午 5:30 左右提出的（It's almost 5:30 p.m.），且男子也同意（M: That's a good idea.），所以正確答案是選項 A。

| 補充 | 「How about + Ving」及「How about + 子句」都用來徵求對方的意見或提出建議。例如：How about trying that new restaurant downtown?（試試市中心那家新開的餐廳怎麼樣？）How about we leave early to avoid traffic?（我們早點出發避開交通怎麼樣？）

Question number 11.

M: These goods come to NT$1,150.
男：這些商品共計新台幣 1,150 元。

W: Do you accept any forms of electronic payment?
女：你們接受任何形式的電子支付嗎？

M: Sorry. We don't. We only accept cash or you can pay by credit card.
男：抱歉，我們沒有。我們只收現金或您可以信用卡支付。

W: OK. There you go.
女：好的，這給你的。

Question. Who are the speakers? 說話者們是誰？

A. A married couple A. 一對夫妻

B. A bank teller and a client B. 銀行行員和客人

C. A shop clerk and a customer C. 店員和顧客

| 詳解 | 對話中男子表示應付價格後，女子詢問是否接受電子支付（Do you accept any forms of electronic payment?），在現今智慧型手機的時代，這是商店的顧客常會問的問題，所以正確答案是選項 C。雖然談到價錢，也可能發生在銀行，但銀行行員不會處理商品銷售和價格，也不會回答關於支付方式的問題，故 B 錯誤。

| 補充 | clerk 這個名詞可用來指不同類型的職業或工作人員，其職責可以涵蓋服務顧客、處理文件、處理法律程序或負責票務等。例如：

The clerk helped me find the right size in the store.（店員幫助我在商店找到合適尺寸的商品。）→ 店員，售貨員

She works as a clerk in a law firm.（她在一家律師事務所工作，擔任文書職員。）→ 辦公室職員，文書

The court clerk administered the oath to the witness.（法庭職員向證人宣誓。）→ 法庭職員

The clerk at the train station helped me buy my ticket.（火車站的售票員幫助我買票。）→ 票務員，售票員

Question number 12.

W: Steve, Please pass me the salt and soy sauce.	女：史蒂夫，請把鹽和醬油遞給我。
M: I can't find it, Mom. Where did you put it?	男：媽媽，我找不到。你把它放在哪裡了？
W: I think it's on the shelf next to the microwave stove.	女：我想應該放在微波爐旁邊的架子上。
M: Yes. I got it.	男：好的，我找到了。

Question. Where are the speakers? 說話者們在哪裡？

A. On the balcony	A. 在陽台
B. In the living room	B. 在客廳
C. In the kitchen	C. 在廚房

｜詳解｜ 對話中提到了鹽和醬油（salt and soy sauce），且提到「on the shelf next to the microwave stove」(在微波爐旁邊的架子上)這是廚房常見的物品放置地點。所以正確答案是選項 C。

Part 4 短文聽解

Question number 13.

Please look at the following three pictures. Listen to the following news report. Which picture best describes the news report?

請看以下三張圖片。聆聽以下新聞報導。人們最有可能在哪裡聽到這則報導？

Special report! A man wearing a black full-face veil entered a branch of Future Bank in Wuhua District a few hours ago, then pointing a gun at a bank teller. He forced her to hand over a great amount of money. Finally, he succeeded in running away with about 5 million dollars. The police are now collecting nearby road cameras to search for the suspect.

特別報導！幾小時前，一名戴著黑色全罩式頭巾的男子進入了五華區一家未來銀行分行，並持槍指著一名櫃員。他逼迫她交出大量現金。最後，他成功帶走了約五百萬元逃逸。警方目前正調閱附近的路口監視器尋找嫌疑人。

｜詳解｜ 題目問的是哪一張圖最符合談話內容，所以基本上要大致聽懂其內容在講什麼。第一張圖是「戴頭罩的男子用槍指著兩名銀行行員」，第二張圖是「戴頭罩的男子在戶外用槍指著一名女子」，第三張圖是「兩名警察用槍指著一名戴口罩的男子」，但談話內容一開始說「A man wearing a black full-face veil entered a branch of...（一名戴著黑色全罩式頭巾的男子進入了…）」所以正確答案為選項 A。

Question number 14.

Please look at the following three pictures. Listen to the following message. How will Helen get to meet her client?

請看以下三張圖片。聆聽以下訊息。海倫將搭何種交通工具去見她的客戶？

Hi Mr. Thomas. This is Helen James. I'd like to say sorry that I might be late a bit because I had something unexpected to take care of. I'll be there as soon as possible. By the way, traffic is backed up now on the highway, so I'll take the latest THSR train. See you soon. Bye.

嗨，湯瑪斯先生。我是海倫·詹姆斯。很抱歉，可能會稍微遲到，因為有一件突然要處理的事情。我會盡快趕過去的。對了，高速公路正在塞車，所以我會搭乘最近的一班高鐵。很快就到，再見。

｜詳解｜ 題目問的是「海倫將搭何種交通工具」，只要注意與搭乘交通工具相關內容即可。其中提到「traffic is backed up now on the highway, so I'll take the latest THSR train.（高速公路正在塞車，所以我會搭乘最近的一班高鐵）」，所以正確答案是選項 B。

｜補充｜ 提到「塞車，交通堵塞」，在英文裡主要有幾種說法：最常見的表達就是「traffic jam」，算是個統稱的說法。另外 gridlock 這個字可以用來形容完全停滯或無法移動的情況，而 congestion 的情況不一定是完全停滯，但速度緩慢且密度大。而「Traffic backup」或「The traffic is backed up.」指後方的交通延遲或排隊等待情況。

MEMO

Day 20

月　　日

我的完成時間＿＿＿＿分鐘
標準作答時間 10 分鐘

Part 1 看圖辨義

Questions 1-2

Part 2 問答

Questions 3-7

3. A. It was my boss calling.
   B. My mom is not home now.
   C. The phone is not mine. It's my sister's.

4. A. Their snacks taste not bad.
   B. They set up shop here every weekend.
   C. I often come here twice a week.

5. A. Yes, I've been there before.
   B. No, I've never met him.
   C. Just once, when I was a little kid.

6. A. Great. Thank you very much.
   B. Sure, I'll go move the car over.
   C. I'm not tired. You go first.

7. A. I just worked late to finish a project.
   B. It's up to you. I don't care.
   C. It rained hard last night, didn't it?

Part 3 簡短對話

Questions 8-12

8. A. Carve a stamp
   B. Go window shopping
   C. Copy a key

9. A. In the classroom
   B. In the supermarket
   C. In the office

10. A. Preparing a talk show
    B. Attending a meeting
    C. Working on a sales report

11. A. Taking some cash out
    B. Using an ATM to save some money
    C. Buying concert tickets in line

12. A. A restaurant waiter
    B. A convenience store clerk
    C. A policeman

Part 4 短文聽解

Questions 13-14

13.

A

B

C

14.

A

B

C

Day 15 Day 16 Day 17 Day 18 Day 19 Day 20 Day 21

上頁簡答

解答與詳解

1. (B) 2. (C) 3. (A) 4. (B) 5. (C) 6. (B) 7. (A) 8. (C)
9. (B) 10. (B) 11. (A) 12. (C) 13. (A) 14. (A)

Part 1 看圖辨義

For questions number 1-2, please look at the following pictures.

Question number 1.

How much do you have to pay for a plate of dumplings and two glasses of juice? 你要是點了一盤水餃和兩杯果汁，要付多錢？

A. $300	A. 三百元
B. $400	B. 四百元
C. $500	C. 五百元

| 詳解 | 雖然題目有點長，但抓住關鍵數字英文就可以了！要問的是「1 盤水餃和 2 杯果汁」，需要支付金額是「200 +（100x2)= 400」元，所以正確答案是選項 B。

| 補充 | 不可數名詞（如本題中的 juice）如果真的要數，就要搭配一些特定用詞。例如：a loaf of bread（一條麵包）、a glass of juice（一杯果汁）、two bottles of water（兩瓶水）、a piece of information（一條訊息）、three items of luggage（三件行李）…等。

Question number 2.

What is the man ready to do? 男子準備做什麼？

A. Do magic tricks	A. 變魔術
B. Play music	B. 演奏音樂
C. Take a photo	C. 拍照

| 詳解 | 圖片中男子手裡拿著照相機，旁邊還有一個相機架，如果不是正要拍照，就是剛拍完照的動作，所以正確答案是選項 C。

| 補充 | trick 當名詞時表示「把戲，花招，詭計」，常與 do、perform 等動詞搭配。例如「do the card tricks」表示「玩紙牌戲法」、「a clever trick」表示「巧妙的騙局」

Part 2 問答

Question number 3.

Who were you just talking to on the phone? 你剛跟誰講電話？

A. It was my boss calling. A. 是我老闆打來的。

B. My mom is not home now. B. 我媽媽現在不在家。

C. The phone is not mine. It's my sister's. C. 這電話不是我的。是我妹妹的。

| 詳解 | 題目問你剛跟誰講電話？回答「我媽媽現在不在家」或「這電話不是我的。是我妹妹的。」都沒有直接回答問題，無法作為對問話者的合理回應，所以正確答案是選項A，因為它指出了對話者剛剛接到來自老闆的電話。

Question number 4.

How often does this snack stall come here each week?
這小吃攤每個禮拜會來這裡幾次？

A. Their snacks taste not bad. A. 他們小吃還不錯吃。

B. They set up shop here every weekend. B. 他們每個週末會來這裡擺攤。

C. I often come here twice a week. C.我經常每個禮拜來這裡兩次。

| 詳解 | 「How often」問事情發生的頻率，顯然 A 的回答毫不相關。選項 B、C 都有頻率的字詞（every weekend 以及 twice a week），但題目問小吃攤每個星期來幾次，C 的回答表是說話者自己的行為習慣，而不是描述小吃攤的來訪頻率，也是錯誤的。所以正確答案是選項 B。

Question number 5.

Have you been camping before? 你有去露營過嗎？

A. Yes, I've been there before. A. 是的，我以前去過那裡。

B. No, I've never met him. B. 不，我沒見過他。

C. Just once, when I was a little kid. C. 只去過一次，在我很小的時候。

| 詳解 | 題目問是否有露營的經驗，A 雖然是肯定的回應，但提到的地方與問題問及的露營活動無關，B 雖然是否定的回應，卻回答與某人的見面經驗，與露營活動完全無關，所以正確答案是選項 C，這個回答指出說話者曾在小時候去過露營，直接回應了問題。

Question number 6.

Time's almost up. We should go. 時間差不多了。我們該走了。

A. Great. Thank you very much. A. 好的。非常感謝您。

B. Sure, I'll go move the car over. B. 好的。我先去把車子開過來。

C. I'm not tired. You go first. C. 我不累。你先走。

| 詳解 | 題目這句算是一種建議，但回答非常感謝，並沒有回答對話中該起身離開的建議，所以選項 A 錯誤；B 回答直接回應了前面的建議，表明說話者將去移動車子，符合對話中提到的行動建議，所以正確答案是選項 B；選項 C 的第二句「You go first.」基本上沒有問題，但第一句說不感到疲倦（not tired），與提議者的「Time's almost up.」沒有關聯，所以選項 C 錯誤。

| 補充 | 「時間到！」的英文可以有多種表達方式，除了「Time's up!」之外，你還可以說「Time is over!」、「That's it for time!」、「It's time!」、「The time has come! 等。

Question number 7.

What were you up to last night? 你昨晚在忙些什麼？

A. I just worked late to finish a project. A. 我只是為了完成個專案工作到很晚。

B. It's up to you. I don't care. B. 隨你便。我不在意。

C. It rained hard last night, didn't it? C. 昨晚雨下很大，不是嗎？

| 詳解 | 題目這句當中的「up to」表示「忙於…」，但「up to」其實有很多意思，必須根據前後文意去理解。A 直接回應了問題，說明昨晚忙於工作，所以正確答案是選項 A。B 刻意以相同的「up to」來回答，但它後面受詞是「人」，表示「看某人的意思」，這個回答與問題無關；C 回答提到昨晚的天氣情況，也與「昨晚在幹嗎？」這問題無關。

| 補充 | 「up to」如果與相關動詞形成片語，那麼它的意思就得「拆開來解」了，例如：He filled the glass up to the brim.（他把杯子裝滿到邊緣。）→ up 跟著前面的動詞 fill，「fill up」是「填滿，裝滿」的意思。

Part 3 簡短對話

Question number 8.

W: Do you know where I can get keys made? 女：你知道哪裡可以打鑰匙嗎？

M: I know there's a stamp carving shop that also makes keys. It's inside the shopping mall on Yingzhi Street. 男：我知道有一家刻印章的店也有打鑰匙。它就在英志街的商場裡面。

W: Okay, thank you very much. 女：好的，非常感謝。

M: You're welcome. 男：不客氣。

Question. What is the woman probably going to do? 女子可能會去做什麼？

A. Carve a stamp　A. 刻一個印章

B. Go window shopping　B. 逛街購物

C. Copy a key　C. 複製一把鑰匙

｜詳解｜女子問男子哪裡可以打鑰匙（make keys），而男子回答說有一家印章雕刻店（a stamp carving shop）也提供打鑰匙的服務，這表示女子想找一個地方複製鑰匙（copy a key），所以正確答案是選項 C。雖然男子提到印章雕刻店，但女子問的是打鑰匙，與刻印章無關，，所以 A 錯誤。雖然女子可以在商場內尋找打鑰匙的地方，但她主要目的是找到可以複製鑰匙的地方，所以 B 錯誤。

Question number 9.

M: Do you need a plastic or paper bag?　男：你需要塑膠袋或紙袋嗎？

W: Is it free?　女：是免費的嗎？

M: Two dollars each?　男：1 個兩塊。

W: I'll get one, please.　女：請給我一個。

Question. Where are the speakers? 說話者們在哪裡？

A. In the classroom　A. 在教室裡

B. In the supermarket　B. 在超市

C. In the office　C. 在辦公室裡

｜詳解｜這段對話描述了一位男性員工問一位女性顧客是否需要塑膠袋或紙袋（plastic or paper bag），女性問是否免費（free），男子回答每個兩塊錢（Two dollars each），到這裡答案已經很明顯了，只有在超市或便利商店等購物商店才有可能，所以正確答案是選項 B。

｜補充｜plastic 屬於英檢中級單字，不過即使聽不出來這個字的意思，也能從「need a paper bag」來判斷正確答案。一般來說，「購物袋」是「shopping bag」或「plastic shopping bag」。另外，這個字在醫學上有「整形的」意思，所以「整形手術」就是「plastic surgery」。

Question number 10.

M: Good morning, everybody! I'm sorry I'm late.　男：早，各位。抱歉我來晚了。

W: Hi David, it's OK. We're just about to begin. You're in time to talk now.　女：嗨，大衛，沒關係。我們才正要開始。你現在來得及說話。

M: Thank you, Manager Lee. First, let me show you last month's sales report.　男：謝謝，李經理。首先，我請大家看一下上個月的業績報表。

Question. What are they doing? 他們正在做什麼？

A. Preparing a talk show　　A. 準備一個談話節目

B. Attending a meeting　　B. 參加一場會議

C. Working on a sales report　　C. 進行銷售報表

| 詳解 | 這段對話描述了男子遲到後，女子說他剛好來得及發言（in time to talk），接著男子要先展示業績報表（sales report），根據這樣的情境和內容，可以確定他們正在參加一場會議，所以正確答案是選項 B；對話中並未提到與準備談話節目（talk show）有關的內容，只是刻意重複 talk 這個字意圖造成干擾，所以 A 錯誤；雖然男子提到要展示業績報表，但整段對話更多是關於參加會議的開始階段，所以 C 也錯誤。

Question number 11.

W: Oops! There seems something wrong with the ATM machine!　　女：糟糕！這台 ATM 機器似乎有問題。

M: What's the problem?　　男：什麼問題？

W: It's just not working. I can't get the money for the concert tickets.　　女：它當機了。我沒辦法領錢去買票。

M: Don't worry. Just try another one.　　男：別擔心。試試另一台就好了。

Question. What is the woman doing? 女子正在做什麼？

A. Taking some cash out　　A. 領出一些現金

B. Using an ATM to save some money　　B. 用 ATM 存些錢

C. Buying concert tickets in line　　C. 排隊買演唱會門票

| 詳解 | 對話中女子表示無法從 ATM 機器領錢來買演唱會門票（... something wrong with the ATM machine! ... I can't get the money for the concert tickets.），所以她正在嘗試解決這個問題，所以它正在做「領錢」這件事，正確答案是選項 A。因為正在領錢，領到錢才能去買門票，所以 B、C 錯誤。

| 補充 | 透過 ATM 取款或領錢，正式的英文通常會用到 withdraw 這個動詞，它不僅限於 ATM 取款，也可用於任何取出金錢的情境，包括在銀行櫃檯（bank service counter）或使用網路銀行（online bank）。withdraw 也可以用來表示「撤退，撤離，退出」。例如：I have decided to withdraw from the competition.（我已決定退出賽。）

Question number 12.

M: Hello ma'am, how can I help you today?
男：嗨，夫人，今天我能為您做些什麼？

W: I'm here to report that I lost my wallet somewhere around here.
女：我是來報案的，我在這附近遺失了我的錢包。

M: Can you remember where you last had it or what it looks like?
男：您還記得最後見到它的地方或它的外觀嗎？

W: I think I had it when I left the convenience store earlier. It's brown with a zipper.
女：我想我離開便利商店時還在。它是個帶拉鍊的棕色錢包。

Question. Who could be the man? 男子可能是何人？

A. A restaurant waiter　A. 餐廳服務生

B. A convenience store clerk　B. 便利商店店員

C. A policeman　C. 警察

｜詳解｜ 別一聽到「how can I help you...」就斷定答案是 A 了，本題答題關鍵在女子「I'm here to report that...」的回答，意思是「我是來報案的...」，所以男子應該是派出所裡的警察，正確答案應為選項 C。

｜補充｜ 當你到警察局去報案時，第一句話可以說：
I'd like to report a(n) crime/incident.
I need to file a report.
I'm here to make a report.
I want to report something that happened.
I have something to report to the police.

Part 4 短文聽解

Question number 13.

Please look at the following three pictures. Listen to the following talk. What sport does James enjoy the most?
請看以下三張圖片。聆聽以下談話。詹姆士最喜愛什麼樣的運動？

James feels excited every time he hits the snowy slopes. James started to attend a skiing course when he was young. He enjoys the rush of sliding down the hills and the beautiful views of snow-covered mountains. James even joined a ski club at school to improve his skills. His dream is to visit famous ski resorts around the world someday.
詹姆士每次踏上雪白的斜坡都感到興奮。他從小開始參加滑雪課程。他喜歡急速滑下山坡帶來的衝擊感，以及雪山美景。詹姆士甚至加入了學校的滑雪社來提升自己的技巧。他的夢想是有一天能夠造訪世界各地著名的滑雪度假村。

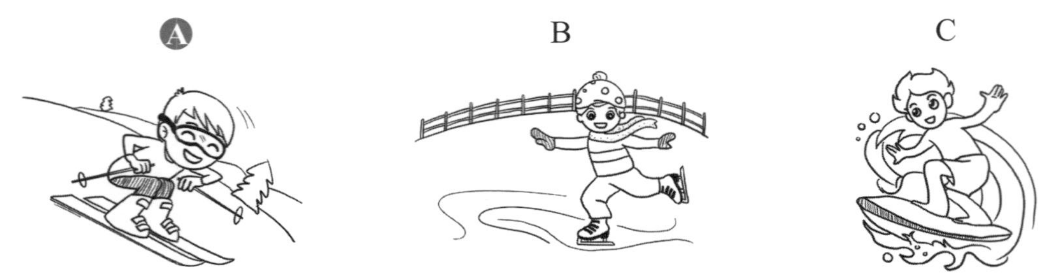

| 詳解 | 三張圖片呈現的是三種不同的運動：滑雪（skiing）、溜冰（ice-skating）、衝浪（surfing）。所以在聽錄音播放時，要注意與這三種運動有關的關鍵字詞。第一句提到「 He enjoys the rush of sliding down the hills... joined a ski club...」（他喜歡急速滑下山坡…加入了滑雪社…），所以正確答案為選項 A。

Question number 14.

Please look at the following three pictures. Listen to the following message. In which restaurant will they have dinner?

請看以下三張圖片。聆聽以下訊息。他們將在哪一間餐廳吃晚餐？

Hi, Mr. Hsu. This is Caren Lai from Yuantai Trade Co. I'm about to board the plane in 5 minutes, and I will land at the Taoyuan International Airport at around 5:00 p.m. I had earlier sent you the address of the restaurant where we'll meet and have dinner together. It is located across from a convenience store. See you later.

徐先生，您好。我是源泰貿易公司的賴凱倫。我大約 5 分鐘後要登機了，大約 5 點左右會抵達桃園國際機場。我先前已將我們晚上碰面並一起吃飯的餐廳地址發給您了，就在一家便利商店對面。稍後見。

| 詳解 | 題目問的是他們將在哪一間餐廳共進晚餐，答題關鍵只有在倒數第二句：It is located across from a convenience store.（它就在一家便利商店對面），其中「across from...」是「在…對面」的意思，所以正確答案是選項 A。

| 補充 | 「在…對面」除了「across from...」之外，也可以用 opposite 來表示，注意這時候的 opposite 是介系詞。例如：The post office is opposite the bank.（郵局在銀行對面。）

Day 21

月　　日

我的完成時間＿＿＿＿分鐘
標準作答時間 10 分鐘

Part 1 看圖辨義

Questions 1-2

Part 2 問答

Questions 3-7

3. A. Yes, that was indeed an accident.
   B. No, we just met and had a cup of coffee!
   C. Yes, but I don't know much about him.

4. A. George and Mary tried very hard to win it.
   B. Health is the best prize in life.
   C. It's a tie.

5. A. I'm afraid visitors aren't allowed in on weekends.
   B. How are they doing?
   C. Of course, come in please!

6. A. Sure. Please wait a moment.
   B. How would you like your steak?
   C. You're welcome. It's nothing.

7. A. Autumn is my favorite season.
   B. My name is Teddy.
   C. Actually, I have many.

Part 3 簡短對話

Questions 8-12

8. A. The woman's new dress
   B. The woman's birthday
   C. A UNIQLO shop

9. A. In a movie theater
   B. In a music concert
   C. In the living room

10. A. Fix up their new home
    B. Move to a new house
    C. Change the lighting of their house

11. A. Riding motorcycles
    B. Travelling by bike
    C. Having dinner in a great restaurant

12. A. Worried
    B. Nervous
    C. Confident

Part 4 短文聽解

Questions 13-14

13.

A

B

C

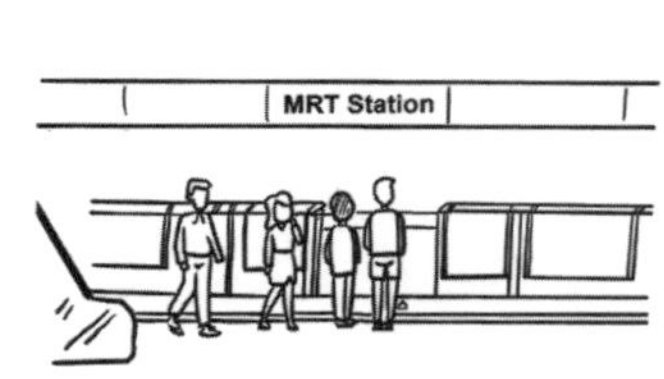

14.

A

B

C

上頁簡答

解答與詳解

1. (C) 2. (B) 3. (C) 4. (C) 5. (B) 6. (A) 7. (C) 8. (A)
9. (C) 10. (B) 11. (B) 12. (C) 13. (C) 14. (C)

Part 1 看圖辨義

For questions number 1-2, please look at the following pictures.

Question number 1.

Where is the boy? 男孩在哪裡？

A. In a library　　A. 在圖書館

B. In the museum　　A. 在博物館

C. At the zoo　　A. 在動物園

|詳解| 圖片中男孩背著背包，看著前方兩隻大象在活動，再對照選項中聽到的三個地點 library、museum、zoo，可確定正確答案是選項 C。

Question number 2.

What is she ready to do? 她正準備做什麼？

A. Apply paint to the floor　　A. 將地板刷油漆

B. Paint the wall　　B. 將牆壁刷油漆

C. Paint a picture　　C. 畫一張油畫

|詳解| 從圖片中女子的穿著，手拿著刷子及一桶油漆，並坐在階梯上，我們可以知道她正要進行刷油漆的工作。不過三個選項都有 paint 這個字，那就必須仔細聽清楚前後相關字詞。選項 A 的「apply paint to...」其實就是 paint 當及物動詞的意思，表示「將…刷上油漆」，但聽到後面的受詞 floor（地板）就可以斷定是錯誤答案了；選項 C 的 paint 是「繪畫」的意思，「paint a picture」就是「畫一張油畫」。答案為選項 B。

Part 2 問答

Question number 3.

Do you know the man we met by accident last night?
你認識昨晚我們碰巧遇到的那個男人嗎？

A. Yes, that was indeed an accident.　　A. 是的，那確實只是一場意外。

B. No, we just met and had a cup of coffee!　　B. 不，我們只是見個面，喝杯咖啡而已！

C. Yes, but I don't know much about him.　　C. 是的，但我對他不太了解。

| 詳解 | 題目問對方是不是認識昨晚遇到的某人，其中「by accident」是「碰巧地，意外地」的意思，而選項 A 刻意重複 accident 干擾答題，但「那確實只是一場意外」並沒有針對問題在回答，所以錯誤；選項 B 的回答完全與問的問題無關，故 B 也錯誤；選項 C 表示有認識但不太了解，是合乎常理的回答，所以正確答案是選項 C。

| 補充 | 要表達某件事「偶然或無意間、碰巧」發生時，也可以用「by chance」、accidentally。例如：By chance, I found the book I was looking for in a second-hand bookstore.（我碰巧在一家二手書店找到了我正在尋找的那本書。）、I accidentally bumped into my old friend at the supermarket.（我無意間在超市裡碰到了我的老朋友。）

Question number 4.

Who won the first prize? 誰贏得了頭獎？

A. George and Mary tried very hard to win it. A. 喬治和瑪麗非常努力要拿下它。

B. Health is the best prize in life. B. 健康是生命中最當的財富。

C. It's a tie. C. 和局收場。

| 詳解 | 題目問誰贏了，但別一看到人名開頭就認定是答案了。A 選項描述的是他們努力的程度，而不是回答頭獎的獲得者，所以錯誤；B 選項「健康是生命中最大的財富。」則與問題無關，只是刻意重複 prize 來引誘答題；所以正確答案是 C，tie 在比賽、競賽當中，有「和局，不分勝負」的意思，也就是沒有人獨贏頭獎，這是合情合理的回答，所以正確答案是選項 C。

Question number 5.

I visited my parents-in-law last weekend. 我上週末去拜訪了我岳父母。

A. I'm afraid visitors aren't allowed in on weekends. A. 恐怕週末時訪客禁止進入。

B. How are they doing? B. 他們好嗎？

C. Of course, come in please! C. 當然，請進！

| 詳解 | 題目這句是告知對方一件過去的事情（我上週末去拜訪了我岳父母。），A 選項卻說訪客在週末不被允許進入，顯然與告知事件無關，只是刻意以 visitors 混淆答題；B 選項詢問對方長輩近況，是正常合理的回應，所以正確答案是選項；C 選項是邀請訪客進入的回應，但在對話中的上下文並未顯示對方有需要進入的需求，所以錯誤。

| 補充 | 「名詞（人物）- in-law」的複合名詞很多，其中 in-law 是代表姻親關係。例如：parents-in-law（岳父母，妻子或丈夫的父母）、brother-in-law（姊夫，嫂夫，夫妻的兄弟）、sister-in-law（妹夫，弟妹，夫妻的姐妹）、son-in-law（女婿，女兒的丈夫）、daughter-in-law（媳婦，兒子的妻子）、father-in-law（公公，婆爺，妻子或丈夫的父親）、mother-in-law（婆婆，岳母，妻子或丈夫的母親）、brother-in-law (= husband's brother)（夫的兄弟）、sister-in-law (= husband's sister)（夫的姐妹）、niece-in-law（侄女或外甥女，通常指非直系親屬但通過結婚而有聯繫的女性）

Question number 6.

May I have some more milk, please? 麻煩可以再給我一些牛奶嗎？

A. Sure. Please wait a moment. A. 請稍等一下。

B. How would you like your steak? B. 你的牛排要幾分熟？

C. You're welcome. It's nothing. C. 不客氣。這沒什麼。

| 詳解 | 題目這句是提出一項需求，也許是對服務人員或到別人家作客的情境。A 的回表示同意，並請對方稍待片刻，是合理正常的回應，所以正確答案是選項 A；B 反問「你的牛排要幾分熟？」完全是雞同鴨講，所以錯誤；雖然「不客氣。這沒什麼。」是一個常見的禮貌回應，但它通常用來回答對方的感謝或道歉，而不是用來回應請求，所以 C 也錯。

| 補充 | 「May I...?」是日常生活中常用來表示一種禮貌請求或徵求許可的句型，同時顯示出問話者尊重對方的意願。如果在句尾加個逗點（,）以及 please，可以更加展現禮貌性的語氣。例如：May I borrow your pen, please?（我可以借用你的筆嗎？）、May I have a moment of your time?（我可以佔用你一點時間嗎？）

Question number 7.

Who's your favorite singer? 你最愛的歌手是誰？

A. Autumn is my favorite season. A. 秋天是我最愛的季節。

B. My name is Teddy. B. 我的名字是泰迪。

C. Actually, I have many. C. 其實，我有很多（最愛的歌手）。

| 詳解 | 題目是 who 開頭的問句，一般設想回答要有人名，不過還是要聽完整句之後才能做判斷。A 的回答完全是雞同鴨講，只是刻意以相同字 favorite 來混淆答題；B 雖然提到了名字 Teddy，但也是毫不相關的回答，所以正確答案是選項 C，「其實，我有很多（最愛的歌手）。」表明說話者有很多喜愛的歌手，符合對話情境。

Part 3 簡短對話

Question number 8.

M: What a nice dress! 男：很好看的一件洋裝！

W: Thanks. I bought it at a UNIQLO shop in the nearby shopping mall. 女：謝謝。我在附近購物商場的 UNIQLO 店買的。

M: Is it a birthday gift you got for yourself? 男：它是你自己買給自己的生日禮物嗎？

W: You can say that again. 女：你答對了。

Question. What are the speakers talking about? 說話者們在談論什麼？

A. The woman's new dress A. 女子的新衣服

B. The woman's birthday B. 女子的生日

C. A UNIQLO shop C. 一家 UNIQLO 商店

| 詳解 | 對話中男子讚美女子的洋裝，而女子則回答洋裝是她自己買給自己的生日禮物，表示說話者們正在討論女子新買的衣服，所以正確答案是選項 A。雖然也有提到女子的生日，以及這件衣服在一家 UNIQLO 商店買的，但這些都不是對話討論的重點，所以 B、C 皆不可選。

| 詳解 | 「疑問詞」開頭的感嘆句經常可用來表達「…真可愛啊！」、「天氣真好！」、「…真是好吃！」來特別強調情緒，像是「What a lovely day!（今天真美好啊！）」、「What a surprise!（太驚訝了！）」、「How adorable (the baby is)!（這寶寶真可愛呢！）」，要注意的是，雖然是以疑問詞為句首，但主詞、動詞的位置是依照「肯定句／直述句」的語序。

Question number 9.

M: Can you change a channel? This program is so boring. 男：你可以換個頻道嗎？這節目好無聊。

W: OK. Let's see what's on other channels now… You want to watch a talent show? 女：好的。我們來看看其他頻道有什麼…你要看才藝表演的嗎？

M: I prefer to watch singers sing and dance. 男：我比較喜歡看歌手又唱又跳的。

Question. Where are probably the speakers? 說話者們可能在哪裡？

A. In a movie theater A. 在電影院裡

B. In a music concert B. 在音樂會中

C. In the living room C. 在家裡客廳

| 詳解 | 對話一開始就提到「切換頻道（change a channel）」，且兩人還討論到看什麼節目，這表示他們可以自由選擇要看的節目（I prefer to watch...），自然是在家裡才有可能了，所以正確答案是選項 C。

| 補充 | 看到誰／節目在電視上，介系詞要用 on，「What's on TV?」就是「有什麼電視節目？」或是「電視在播什麼？」。如果用「in the TV」，就會變成是在 TV 這部機器裡面了！當然，「on the TV」也是一樣的概念，就是指「在電視機上面」。例如：I love to watch animal channels on TV.（我喜歡看電視上的動物頻道。）、Just press the ON/OFF button on the TV.（看下電視機上的開機／關機按鈕就好了。）

Question number 10.

M: I think this is the best place we've looked for these days.
男：我想這是我最近尋找的最棒的地方了。

W: I agree. The lighting is good and it has three rooms. Besides, it is not far away from the MRT station.
女：我同意。這裡採光佳且擁有三房。此外，距離捷運站也不遠。

M: OK. I've made up my mind. We can move in next month.
男：好的。我決定了。我們下個月就可以搬進來了。

Question. What are they going to do? 他們即將做什麼？

A. Fix up their new home　A. 修繕他們的新家

B. Move to a new house　B. 搬新家

C. Change the lighting of their house　C. 改變他們家裡的燈光照明

｜詳解｜題目問說話者們將要做的事，所以要注意與未來時態或時間有關的動作。其中提到「We can move in next month.」，所以正確答案是選項 B。對話中沒有提到他們計劃進行任何修繕或整修，他們只是討論他們最近找到的房子的好處，因此選項 A 是錯誤的。雖然對話中提到新房子的採光好，但沒有提及改變燈光照明的事，因此 C 也是錯誤的。

Question number 11.

W: Can we take a rest now? My feet are really sore.
女：我們可以休息一下嗎？ 我的腳好痠。

M: Ten kilometers isn't very far! Come on! Let's ride another five kilometers.
男：十公里沒有很遠啊！來吧！我們再騎個五公里。

W: OK. But I'll have a good dinner later.
女：好吧。但是我晚餐要吃一頓好的。

Question. What are they doing? 他們正在做什麼？

A. Riding motorcycles　A. 騎摩托車

B. Travelling by bike　B. 騎腳踏車旅行

C. Having dinner in a great restaurant　C. 在一家很棒的餐廳吃晚餐

｜詳解｜本題關鍵字句在一開始女子說的「My feet are really sore.」以及男子回答說「Let's ride another five kilometers.」。雖然 ride 可以用來騎摩托車也可以用來騎腳踏車，以及騎摩托車騎久了雖然也會累，但不會是腳酸的問題，更不可能是在餐廳用餐，最有可能當然是騎腳踏車了，所以正確答案是選項 B。

Question number 12.

M: Jessica, the match is about to begin. How are you feeling now?	男：潔西卡，比賽要開始了。你現在感覺如何？
W: I'm well-prepared. I've kept practicing for a long time.	女：我都準備好了。我已經持續練習很久了。
M: Good for you.	男：你真棒。

Question. How is the woman feeling now? 女子現在感覺如何？

A. Worried	A. 擔憂的
B. Nervous	B. 緊張的
C. Confident	C. 有自信的

| 詳解 | 對話中女性表示「I'm well-prepared. I've kept practicing for a long time.（我都準備好了。我已經持續練習很久了。）」這顯示她感到有信心準備好比賽，所以正確答案應為選項 C。

| 補充 | 除了 worried、nervous、confident 之外，以下形容詞都可以用來形容一個人當下的心情或感受詞：excited（興奮的）、relaxed（放鬆的）、content（滿足的）、enthusiastic（躍躍欲試的）、anxious（焦慮的）、calm（冷靜的）、frustrated（沮喪的）、hopeful（充滿希望的）、bored（無聊的）、grateful（感激的）、irritated（惱怒的）、pleased（高興的）、amused（娛樂的）、overwhelmed（崩潰的）、indifferent（漠不關心的）、surprised（驚訝的）、resigned（認命的）、optimistic（樂觀的）。

Part 4 短文聽解

Question number 13.

Please look at the following three pictures. Listen to the following broadcast. Where could you most likely hear it?

請看以下三張圖片。聆聽以下廣播。你最有可能在哪裡聽到這則廣播？

Good afternoon, ladies and gentlemen. This is where we share important updates and news. Remember to stand clear of the doors when they're closing. Safety first! We have a clean-up in progress at platform two, so please be aware of this. If you need help, our staff in red vests are here to help. Enjoy your ride and have a great day ahead!

各位女士先生，午安。這裡是我們分享重要更新和消息的地方。當門要關閉時，請記得遠離門口。安全第一！我們正在二號月台進行清潔，請多加留意。如果需要幫助，穿紅色背心的工作人員會在這裡提供協助。祝您乘車愉快，並祝您今天有個美好的一天！

｜詳解｜ 三張圖片呈現的是三個不同的地方，而題目問說談話內容可以在哪個地方聽到。圖 A 是遊覽車內，圖 B 是百貨商場內，圖 C 則是捷運站內，所以在聽錄音播放時，只要抓到 platform 這個最關鍵的字詞即可。它出現在「We have a clean-up in progress at platform two, so please be aware of this.」所以正確答案是選項 C。

Question number 14.

Please look at the following three pictures. Listen to the following message. Which picture best matches what you hear?

請看以下三張圖片。聆聽以下訊息。哪一張圖最符合你聽到的內容？

Mom, Dad, and little Timmy are sitting on the sofa and watching TV together. They talk about their day and share stories. Mom tells about her work at the office, Dad talks about his day fixing cars, and Timmy shares his adventures at school. They laugh and enjoy being together as a family. The TV show brings them closer, and they look forward to more evenings like this.

媽媽、爸爸和提米坐在沙發上一起看電視。他們聊天，分享彼此的一天。媽媽談論她在辦公室的工作，爸爸談論他修車的一天，而提米分享他在學校的冒險故事。他們笑著，享受著作為一個家庭在一起的時光。這個電視節目使他們更加親近，他們期待著像這樣的更多美好的夜晚。

｜詳解｜ 三張圖都與家庭活動有關，圖 A 是家人一起用餐，圖 B 可以看成是家人們在家裡唱歌同樂，圖 C 是一起看電視。而本題破題關鍵就是第一句「Mom, Dad, and little Timmy are sitting on the sofa and watching TV...（媽媽、爸爸和提米坐在沙發上一起看電視）」，所以正確答案是選項 C。

Day 22

月　　日

我的完成時間＿＿＿＿分鐘
標準作答時間 10 分鐘

Day_22.mp3

Part 1 看圖辨義

Questions 1-2

Part 2 問答

Questions 3-7

3. A. Sounds not bad.
   B. How much does your bicycle cost?
   C. I often go biking on weekends.

4. A. Nothing. Just be brave!
   B. No, thanks. I'm already full.
   C. The chocolate is really delicious.

5. A. I don't think so.
   B. That's a good deal.
   C. It's not looking too good.

6. A. Just take your time. No rush.
   B. I can't wait for it.
   C. No doubt. I'll be coming soon.

7. A. It's four thirty.
   B. Sure. What's the problem?
   C. Three times a week.

Part 3 簡短對話

Questions 8-12

8. A. Their school life
   B. A new library
   C. How to make use of time after classes

9. A. A brother and a sister
   B. A manager and one of his parents
   C. A boss and an employee

10. A. Try a popular online game
    B. Find out more online games
    C. Enjoy more free time

11. A. She will go to complain with her neighbors.
    B. She will make louder noises to fight with them.
    C. She can't do anything to avoid it.

12. A. She has difficulty paying attention to classes.
    B. She doesn't have enough time to study.
    C. She is always too shy to ask questions.

Part 4 短文聽解

Questions 13-14

13.

A

B

C

14.

A

B

C

上頁簡答

解答與詳解

1. (B) 2. (C) 3. (A) 4. (C) 5. (C) 6. (B) 7. (B) 8. (B) 9. (C) 10. (A) 11. (A) 12. (A) 13. (C) 14. (B)

Part 1 看圖辨義

For questions number 1-2, please look at the following pictures.

Question number 1.

Where are the shoes? 鞋子在哪裡？

A. In front of the sofa　　A. 在沙發前面

B. Behind the sofa　　B. 在沙發後面

C. Under the sofa　　C. 在沙發下面

| 詳解 | 本題考的是用來表示「位置」的介系詞，A 的「in front of」表示「在…前面」，B 的 behind 表示「在…後面」，C 的 Under 表示「在…前面」，從圖片中的位置關係來看，正確答案是選項 B。

Question number 2.

Where are these people? 這些人在哪裡？

A. In a library　　A. 在圖書館

B. In a restaurant　　B. 在餐廳

C. In the hospital　　C. 在醫院

| 詳解 | 圖片中左邊是醫生，中間是病人，右邊是護士，從這三人的關係，以及動作（醫生為病患看診）去判斷，這個地方是醫院或診所，所以正確答案是選項 C。

Part 2 問答

Question number 3.

The rain has stopped. Let's go biking now 雨停了。我們出去騎腳踏車吧。

A. Sounds not bad.　　A. 聽起來還不錯。

B. How much does your bicycle cost?　　B. 你的腳踏車要多少錢？

C. I often go biking on weekends.　　C. 我經常在週末時去騎腳踏車。

| 詳解 | 題目這句主要目的是提出一個去騎腳踏車的建議，回應說「聽起來還不錯。」表達了對騎腳踏車這個提議的積極態度，也正確回應了這個建議，所以正確答案是選項 A。

因為對方提出了一個活動建議（出去騎腳踏車），而不是在談論腳踏車的價格，所以 B 錯誤。C 的回答雖然是關於騎腳踏車的話題，但並沒有正確回應這個建議。

| 補充 | sound 當不及物動詞時，有「不及物」及「不完全不及物（= 連綴動詞）」兩種用法，前者是「響起」的意思，有進行式，而後者是「聽起來」的意思。例如：The thunder sounded loudly, scaring the dog.（雷聲響得很大，把狗嚇壞了。）、It sounds like a good idea.（聽起來像是個好主意。）、She sounded as if she were the boss.（她說話彷彿她是老闆。）

Question number 4.

Your mouth looks horrible! What have you been eating?
你的嘴看起來好恐怖！你剛吃了什麼？

A. Nothing. Just be brave! A. 沒事。勇敢一點就好了。

B. No, thanks. I'm already full. B. 不用了，謝謝。我已經飽了。

C. The chocolate is really delicious. C. 這巧克力真是美味。

| 詳解 | 題目問對方剛剛吃了什麼，A 回答「沒事。勇敢一點就好了。」並不適合對話的情境；B 回答「不用了，謝謝。我已經飽了。」這個回答也與對話的問題無關；C 是針對題目的直接回應，解釋了嘴巴沾滿巧克力的恐怖樣子，所以正確答案是選項 C。

Question number 5.

How's everything going? 一切都還好嗎？

A. I don't think so. A. 我不這麼認為。

B. That's a good deal. B. 就這麼說定了。

C. It's not looking too good. C. 情況不太樂觀。

| 詳解 | 題目問一切是否正常或順利進行，並不是針對某事件詢問意見，所以 A 錯誤；B 這個回答與對話的問題無關，因為它是在回應某個交易或協議是否滿。所以正確答案是選項 C，因為這個回答直接回應了對話中的問題，表明目前的情況或者進展並不理想。

Question number 6.

Summer vacation is coming soon. 暑假快到了。

A. Just take your time. No rush. A. 慢慢來就好。不急。

B. I can't wait for it. B. 我等不急了。

C. No doubt. I'll be coming soon. C. 那當然。我很快就過來了。

| 詳解 | 題目這句提到即將到來的暑假，而不是要對方放鬆或慢慢來，所以 A 錯誤；「I can't wait for it.」這個回答直接回應了暑假即將到來這句話，表達了期待的心情，所以正確答案是選項 B。C 的回答與對話的內容無關，因為它是在回應自己即將到達某地，而不是即將到來的暑假。

Question number 7.

Excuse me. Do you have time? 不好意思。你有空嗎？

A. It's four thirty. A. 現在四點半。

B. Sure. What's the problem? B. 當然。有什麼事嗎？

C. Three times a week. C. 一個星期三次。

｜詳解｜題目是禮貌地詢問對方是否有時間（可以幫個忙或談談化之類的），而不是詢問現在幾點。本題其實就是考你知不知道「have time（有時間）」與「have the time（知道現在的時間）」之區別。A 的回答與對話的內容無關；B 的回答直接回應了對方的詢問，表明自己有時間並詢問對方需要什麼幫助或解決什麼問題，所以正確答案是選項 B；C 在回答問題「你多久做某事一次」，而不是回應對是否有時間的詢問，所以錯誤。

Part 3 簡短對話

Question number 8.

M: Hi! Did you see the new library they built across the street from our school?
男：嗨！你看見我們學校對面新建的圖書館了嗎？

W: Yes, I noticed it yesterday. It looks modern and spacious.
女：是的，我昨天注意到了。它看起來現代化而且寬敞。

M: I heard they have a great collection of books and study rooms inside.
男：我聽說裡面有豐富的書籍收藏和研究室。

W: That's awesome! I'll check it out after classes today.
女：太棒了！今天下課後我會去看看。

Question. What are the speakers talking about? 說話者們在談論什麼？

A. Their school life A. 他們的學校生活

B. A new library B. 新的圖書館

C. How to make use of time after classes C. 如何利用課後的時間

｜詳解｜整個對話都是關於他們討論學校對面新建的圖書館，包括位置（across the street from our school）、外觀（It looks modern and spacious.）和內部設施（have a great collection of books and study rooms inside），所以正確答案是選項 B。雖然對話中提到了學校，但重點在於討論新建的圖書館，所以 A 錯誤；雖然最後一句提到女子計劃在下課後去圖書館，但這並非整篇對話的重點，所以 C 錯誤。

｜補充｜study」當名詞時，指的是學習或研究某一主題或學科的活動或過程，如「I have to do my studies before the exam.」（我必須在考試前用功唸書。）作為動詞時，study 表示認真地閱讀、研究或學習某一主題或學科，如「She studies biology at university.」（她在大學時念生物學。）。動詞形式也可以表示專注地思考或考慮某事物，例如，He studied the problem carefully before making a decision.（他在做出決定之前仔細地研究了問題）。

Question number 9.

M: Hey, how's everything at home with your family?
男：嘿，妳家裡的一切都還好嗎？

W: Well, we're managing, but my brother got into some trouble at school, and now my parents are trying to solve problems.
女：嗯，我們還在處理，但我弟弟在學校惹了點麻煩，現在我父母正努力解決問題。

M: Oh no, I hope they work things out soon. Let me know if there's anything I can do to help.
男：哎呀，希望他們能盡快解決。如果有什麼我可以幫忙的，隨時告訴我。

Question. Who might be the speakers? 說話者們可能是誰？

A. A brother and a sister
A. 一對兄妹

B. A manager and one of his parents
B.一名經理及他的父母之一

C. A boss and an employee
C. 一位老闆與一名員工

｜詳解｜ 從男子開頭第一句話「how's everything at home with your family? 」（妳家裡的一切都還好嗎？）可知，對話中男女之間的關係並非家人，所以正確答案是選項 C。

｜補充｜ trouble 當名詞時，常與其他字詞形成慣用語。例如 make trouble（製造麻煩或引發問題）、get into trouble（惹上麻煩）、take the trouble to-V（不辭勞苦地去做某事）、be in trouble（陷入困境）、have troouble with（遇到…的麻煩）。另外，所謂的 trouble-maker 這個複合名詞，就來自「make trouble」這個片語。例如：He's a known troublemaker in the neighborhood.（他是這個社區裡有名的麻煩製造者。）、 Stop making trouble for your sister.（不要再給你妹妹惹麻煩了。）

Question number 10.

M: Hey, have you been enjoying your free time lately?
男：嘿，最近有好好享受空閒時間嗎？

W: Not really, I've been feeling bored of the same old routine. I want to try something new.
女：其實沒有，我一直很厭倦一成不變。我想要嘗試一些新的事物。

M: How about trying out that newest online game everyone's talking about? It might be a fun change from your usual activities.
男：要不要試試大家都在談論的那款新的線上遊戲？這或許會是一個有趣的改變，脫離你平常的活動。

W: That's a good idea! I'll look into it and give it a try this weekend.
女：這個主意不錯！我會查查看，這個週末試試。

Question. What is the woman going to do? 女子將要做什麼？

A. Try a popular online game A. 嘗試一款流行的線上遊戲

B. Find out more online games B. 尋找更多線上遊戲

C. Enjoy more free time C. 享受更多的空閒時間

｜詳解｜ 題目問女子將要去做何事，可以從女子說的「I want to try something new.」開始找答案，接著男子問「How about trying out that newest online game everyone's talking about?」而女子回答「That's a good idea!」表示她樂意去試試看，這裡的「online game everyone's talking about」就是「popular online game」的意思，所以正確答案是選項A。

Question number 11.

M: Good morning! Did you sleep well? 男：早安！你睡得如何？

W: Not really. I had to put up with noisy neighbors last night. 女：其實不太好。昨晚我得忍受吵鬧的鄰居。

M: That's tough. Maybe you should talk to them about it. 男：那真是夠難受的。也許你應該跟他們談談。

W: Yeah, I'll try to. 女：是啊，我會試試看的。

Question. What will the woman do to solve her problem?
女子將如何解決她的問題？

A. She will go to complain with her neighbors. A. 她會去跟她的鄰居抱怨。

B. She will make louder noises to fight with them. B. 她會發出更大聲的噪音來對抗他們。

C. She can't do anything to avoid it. C. 她無法做任何事情來避免這個問題。

｜詳解｜ 女子最後表示她會試著跟鄰居溝通解決噪音問題（Yeah, I'll try to.），這是因為男士建議她這樣做（Maybe you should talk to them about it.）。所以正確答案是選項A。B選項「她會發出更大聲的噪音來對抗他們」是不正確的，因為這不是解決問題的方式。C 選項「她無法做任何事情來避免這個問題」也不正確，因為她已經表明她會試著去解決問題，即使這需要一些努力。

Question number 12.

M: Hey, how did your exams go? 男：嘿，考試考得怎麼樣？

W: Oh, not too good. I studied hard, but I wish I had more time to prepare. 女：哎，不太好。我努力準備了，但我希望能有更多時間準備。

M: In fact, you just need to stay quiet for a while and focus on studying. 男：其實，你只需要冷靜一下，專心上課就好了。

W: You really get me. Thanks for your suggestions. 女：你真了解我。謝謝你的建議。

Question. What is the problem with the woman? 女子的問題是什麼？

A. She has difficulty paying attention to classes. A. 她上課無法專心。

B. She doesn't have enough time to study. B. 她沒有足夠的時間來準備。

C. She is always too shy to ask questions. C. 她總是過於害羞不敢提出問題。

| 詳解 | 本題問的是女子本身的問題在哪，雖然女子一開始說「I wish I had more time to prepare.」，似乎說出了她自己的問題，但從男子說「In fact, you just need to stay quiet for a while and focus on studying.」以及女子回應的「You really get me.」可知，女子真正的問題是過動、無法專心的問題，所以正確答案是選項 A。

| 補充 | 動詞 stay 的本意是「留下」，可以單獨使用，比如：Stay.（不要走/留下）。stay 還可以強調保持一個特定的狀態，後面要接形容詞，例如：stay young/awake/positive（保持年輕 / 清醒 / 積極的心態）。另外，keep 也有「保持某種狀態」 的意思，但它強調的是，透過主動做一件事來維持不變，而 stay 強調原本已經處於一種狀態。比如說，如果有人在公共場合大聲喧嘩，那麼我們可以說「Could you keep quiet, please?（你能安靜點嗎？）這時候就不適合用 stay 了。而如果對方原本就處於安靜的狀態，我們提醒對方繼續保持安靜，就可以說「Could you stay quiet, please?」

Part 4 短文聽解

Question number 13.

Please look at the following three pictures. Listen to the following sports report. Which picture best matches the report?

請看以下三張圖片。聆聽以體育播報。哪一張圖最能搭配這則播報？

We're now entering the final exciting stages of the match. Players of both teams are trying their best to get the ball. What? Jordan from the Red team pushed Gordon from the Blue. Billy was hit on the waist. It looks like he is going to fall on the ground.

我們現在正要進入這場比賽的最後刺激階段。兩隊球員都在努力爭搶球。什麼？紅隊的喬丹推了藍隊的戈登一把。戈登的腰部被撞了一下。看起來他要跌倒在地上了。

| 詳解 | 三張圖片呈現的是籃球場上的不同動作與樣態。而題目問播報內容是在說哪一張圖。本題重點就在「Jordan from the Red team pushed Gordon from the Blue. Billy was hit on

the waist.」（紅隊的喬丹推了藍隊的戈登一把。戈登的腰部被撞了一下）這兩句，只有圖 C 有推撞的樣子，所以正確答案是選項 C。

Question number 14.

Please look at the following three pictures. Listen to the following introduction. What will the customer probably have for the first dish?

請看以下三張圖片。聆聽以下介紹。這位顧客的第一道餐可能是哪一個？

Good evening, sir. Here's our menu. Our Italian noodle sets have been popular especially for tourists. They're cooked with fresh tomatoes and basil for a delicious flavor. For the first dish, you have three choices: fresh chicken salad, Italian ham, and creamed corn soup to go with your Italian noodles. So, would you like to choose one or later?

先生，晚安。這是我們的菜單。我們的義大利麵套餐一直很受歡迎，尤其是觀光客。它們用新鮮的番茄和羅勒烹製，味道美味。至於第一道菜，您可以選擇新鮮雞肉沙拉、義大利火腿或玉米濃湯來搭配您的義大利麵。那麼，您想要選擇哪一道或者稍後再選呢？

| 詳解 | 本題第一個關鍵字詞是「first dish」，所以重點就在「For the first dish, you have three choices: fresh chicken salad, Italian ham, and creamed corn soup...」這句，第一道菜有三種選擇：雞肉沙拉、義大利火腿或玉米濃湯，而三張圖片分別是圖 A 的麵食，圖 B 的沙拉餐，圖 C 的水餃，所以正確答案是選項 B。

我的完成時間______分鐘
標準作答時間 10 分鐘

Part 1 看圖辨義

Questions 1-2

Part 2 問答

Questions 3-7

3. A. You're welcome. Just go back home now.
   B. Be brave, and don't look back.
   C. I'm glad I could support you.

4. A. Good idea. It'll help us relax and clean up.
   B. Sure. We had better work out every day.
   C. Taking a bath every day is a good habit.

5. A. Thank you. I will.
   B. I can't help laughing.
   C. Need you go so soon?

6. A. So far so good.
   B. Sure. I've been an adult.
   C. I understand.

7. A. She wanted to discuss our weekend plans.
   B. I lost my keys again.
   C. She had no call to do that.

Part 3 簡短對話

Questions 8-12

8. A. Family
   B. Friendship
   C. Trust

9. A. Doctor and nurse
   B. Prince and princess
   C. Host and guest

10. A. At 1:15 p.m.
    B. At 1:30 p.m.
    C. At 1:45 p.m.

11. A. It's raining hard.
    B. It's quite sunny.
    C. It's windy and cool.

12. A. Breakfast
    B. Lunch
    C. Snacks

Part 4 短文聽解

Questions 13-14

13.

A

B

C

14.

A

B

C

上頁簡答

解答與詳解

1. (A) 2. (B) 3. (C) 4. (A) 5. (A) 6. (C) 7. (B) 8. (B) 9. (B) 10. (C) 11. (B) 12. (B) 13. (B) 14. (B)

Part 1 看圖辨義

For questions number 1-2, please look at the following pictures.

Question number 1.

What is the man going to do? 男子將要做什麼？

A. Go to sleep A. 去睡覺

B. Have breakfast B. 吃早餐

C. Enjoy a sun bath C. 享受日光浴

| 詳解 | 從圖片中窗外景色可知，現在是晚上，且床上的男子準備要睡覺了，所以正確答案是選項 A。從 B 的 breakfast 以及 C 的「sun bath」都可以知道是錯誤的選項。

Question number 2.

What is the weather report likely to say? 天氣報導可能說什麼？

A. It's raining cats and dogs. A. 現在正下著大雨。

B. The strong typhoon is around the corner. B. 強颱即將來到。

C. Pay attention to outdoor heat. C. 注意戶外高溫。

| 詳解 | 圖片中可看見颳起強風，但還沒有下雨，也沒有太陽，所以選項 A 和 C 都不對，正確答案是選項 B。

| 補充 | 「around the corner」從字面上翻譯，是指某人、事、物就在轉角處，也就是表達地理位置上的「在附近」；此外，也能用在表達時間點上的「即將到來」，通常可以在前面加上 just 或 right，強調「就快要到了」。例如：My birthday is right around the corner, so I'm planning the party.（我的生日就快到了，所以我正籌備著生日派對。）

Part 2 問答

Question number 3.

Thank you. You always back me up. 謝謝你。你總是支持我。

A. I'm up here. A. 我就在上面這邊。

B. Be brave, and don't look back. B. 要勇敢，不要回頭。

C. I'm glad I could support you. C. 我很高興我能支持你。

|詳解| 題目中的「back... up」是「支持」的意思。A 這句刻意重覆「up」，但顯然與題目這句不相關，所以錯誤；B 表達了鼓勵和支持，但與原句的感謝不相關，因此也不適合作為回應，所以正確答案是選項 C，直接回應了這個感謝，表明對能夠支持（support）對方感到高興和滿足。

|補充| back 這個字大家都知道有「背部，後面」等意思，但是與它有關片語或慣用語不勝枚舉，例如「back down」有認錯或者是放棄、打退堂鼓的意思；而「back off」可以表達要求對方不要再指手畫腳、一直插手介入，也可以表示退後的意思，通常是用來威嚇他人向後退，或是指因為驚嚇而後退。

Question number 4.

After exercising, we had better take a bath. 運動後，我們最好洗個澡。

A. Good idea. It'll help us relax and clean up. A. 好主意。這會幫助我們放鬆並且清潔身體。

B. Sure. We had better work out every day. B. 當然。我們最好每天運動。

C. Taking a bath every day is a good habit. C. 每天洗澡是一個好習慣。

|詳解| 題目這句提到運動後最好洗澡的建議，A 直接回應認同這是一個好主意，並且解釋了洗澡的好處，所以正確答案是選項 A。B 的回答雖然也是一個好建議，但並沒有直接回應運動後洗澡的建議，因此與原句不相關；「每天洗澡是一個好習慣」雖然也是正確的陳述，但它與運動後洗澡的建議無關。

Question number 5.

Please tell me if you need help. 若你需要幫忙，請讓我知道。

A. Thank you. I will. A. 謝謝。我會的。

B. I can't help laughing. B. 我忍不住笑了出來。

C. Need you go so soon? C. 你需要這麼早走嗎 ？

|詳解| 題目這句是提出一個善意的請求，而 A 表達會在需要幫忙的時候告訴對方，以及準備告知需要幫助的意願，所以正確答案是選項 A。B、C 的回答皆與對話內容無關，並且不符合用來回應對方的提議。

|補充| need 當助動詞時，可表示必要性或義務，例如：She need not apologize for being late.（她不需要為遲到道歉。）need 的否定形式是 needn't。例如：You needn't go if you don't want to.（如果你不想去的話，你不必去。）在疑問句中，need 作助動詞通常用來表達建議、勸告或詢問的意思。例如：Need I say more?（我還需要再說什麼嗎？）

Question number 6.

You had better do your homework by yourself. 你最好是自己做作業。

A. So far so good. A. 目前為止還好。

B. Sure. I've been an adult. B. 當然。我已經是個成年人了。

C. I understand. C. 我了解。

| 詳解 | 題目這句也算是提出一項建議，而 A 的回答（目前為止還好）與對話內容無關，不是正確回應；B 的回答中，adult 是「成年人」，而「能否自己完成作業」跟是不是成年人無關，所以也錯誤；正確答案是選項 C，因為它表達出理解對方的提議用心，是最貼近對話的正確回答。

Question number 7.

Why did your mom call you down? 你母親為什麼罵你？

A. She wanted to discuss our weekend plans. A. 她想要討論我們的周末計畫。

B. I lost my keys again. B. 我又把鑰匙給弄丟了。

C. She had no call to do that. C. 她沒必要那樣做。

| 詳解 | 題目這句中的動詞片語「call (someone) down」是「責罵（某人）」的意思，所以針對「你母親為什麼罵你？」這個問題，A 的回答顯然錯誤，因為只是想討論什麼事情的話，不會用責備的方式；「把鑰匙給弄丟了」確實可能是會被責備的原因，所以正確答案是選項 B；C 這句當中的 call 是個名詞，等同於 need 當名詞的意思，「她沒必要那樣做」並沒有直接回答「你母親為什麼罵你？」，所以也錯誤。

| 補充 | 如果要用 call 表示「打電話給某人」，可以用「call someone」或「call someone up」或「make a (phone) call to someone」。

Part 3 簡短對話

Question number 8.

M: Our relationship was as close as ever it had been. 男：我們的關係如同以往一樣親密。

W: I feel the same way. You're like family to me, and I value it more than anything. 女：我也同感。你對我來說就像家人一樣，我比任何事情都珍惜這份情誼。

M: It's comforting to know we can always count on each other, no matter what. 男：知道無論如何我們都可以互相依靠這件事，讓人感到安心。

Question. What are the speakers talking about? 說話者們在談論什麼？

A. Family A. 家庭

B. Friendship B. 友誼

C. Trust C. 信任

Day 22 Day 23 Day 24 Day 25 Day 26 Day 27 Day 28

| 詳解 | 他們提到彼此「像家人一樣」（You're like family to me...），這意味他們實際上不是家人的關係，所以 A 錯誤；對話中兩人談到的重點是親近關係（as close as ever）、可以互相依靠（count on each other），這並非完全來自信任，也不是談話的重點，故 C 也錯誤。所以正確答案是選項 B，因為對話談到了彼此的關係親密和依靠，表達了他們的友誼之深厚。

Question number 9.

M: I feel so lucky to have you in my life. You bring so much happiness into my world.	男：我覺得自己很幸運有你在我的生命裡。你為我的世界帶來了很多快樂。
W: That means a lot to me. I cherish every moment we spend together.	女：這對我來說意義重大。我珍惜我們一起度過的每一刻。
M: I promise to always be there for you, through good times and bad.	男：我答應無論好壞，我都會一直在你身邊。
W: Thank you for everything.	女：謝謝你的一切。

Question. Who are probably the speakers? 說話者們可能是誰？

A. Doctor and nurse	A. 醫生與護士
B. Prince and princess	B. 王子與公主
C. Host and guest	C. 主人與賓客

| 詳解 | 對話中的男女展示了一段親密關係，彼此之間有深厚的感情和互動，包括「I feel so lucky to have you in my life.」、「I cherish every moment we spend together.」等，這與醫生和護士之間的專業關係不符，且主人和賓客之間的對話通常不會表達出如此深情和承諾，所以 A、C 都不對，故正確答案是選項 B，這符合王子和公主之間常見的浪漫對話模式。

Question number 10.

M: The next subway will arrive at 1:30 p.m. Should we leave here at 1:15 p.m.?	男：下一班地鐵會在下午 1 點 30 分到達。我們要不要在下午 1 點 15 分離開這裡？
W: OK, but I want to buy a cup of Starbucks coffee. How about we get the later train?	女：好的，不過我想買杯星巴克的咖啡。我們等下一班列車好嗎？
M: Sure. Then I'll go get one, too. Let's go.	男：好的。那我也去買一杯。我們走吧。

Question. What time will they probably get on the subway train?
他們可能會在幾點搭上地鐵？

A. At 1:15 p.m.	A. 在下午 1 點 15 分
B. At 1:30 p.m.	B. 在下午 1 點 30 分
C. At 1:45 p.m.	C. 在下午 1 點 45 分

| 詳解 | 對話中提到女士想買咖啡，因此他們決定等待下一班較晚的列車（How about we get the later train? / Sure.），而最快可以搭上列車的時間是 1:30 p.m.，所以他們最後上車的時間一定會比 1:30 p.m. 這個時間更晚，所以正確答案是選項 C。

Question number 11.

W: It's so bright out there! Luckily, I have an umbrella and a pair of sunglasses.
女：外面太陽好大！幸好我有一把傘和太陽眼鏡。

M: I forgot to bring mine, and now I feel my skin on my head is burning.
男：我忘了帶，現在感覺頭皮都被曬傷了。

W: The weather report says it will rain later in the afternoon. You can relax.
女：氣象報告說下午晚些時候會下雨。你可以放心。

Question. How is the weather this morning? 今天早上的天氣怎麼樣？

A. It's raining hard. A. 下大雨了。

B. It's quite sunny. B. 相當晴朗。

C. It's windy and cool. C. 風很大且涼爽。

| 詳解 | 首先要注意題目問的是今天早上（this morning）的天氣狀況，女子後來說「The weather report says it will rain later in the afternoon.」，所以男女兩人當下談話是在早上，可以從一開始女子說的「It's so bright out there! Luckily, I have an umbrella and a pair of sunglasses.」推知，早上天氣相當晴朗，故正確答案是選項 B。

Question number 12.

M: I heard the Italian noodles here are very delicious.
男：我聽說這裡的義大利麵非常好吃。

W: Probably true! I feel hungry from the look of these meal photos.
女：可能是喔！看到這些餐點照片，我肚子都餓了。

M: Besides, its desserts are good.
男：另外，它的甜點也很棒。

W: Then, let's go inside and have a full meal right away.
女：那麼我們馬上進去飽餐一頓吧。

Question. What are the speakers mainly talking about?
說話者們主要在談論什麼？

A. Breakfast A. 早餐

B. Lunch B. 午餐

C. Snacks C. 點心

| 詳解 | 本題考的是對於食物與餐點的認知，對話一開始就提到美味的義大利麵（Italian noodles），後來又看到美味的甜點（dessert），雖然可以說是 snack（點心）的一

種，但並非整個對話談論的重點，所以 C 必然錯誤；而就義大利麵是要當早餐或中餐來說，肯定是中餐會比較合理些，所以正確答案是選項 B。

| 補充 | 除了「have a full meal」之外，「「飽餐一頓，大吃一頓」」還可以說「have a hearty meal」、「enjoy a feast」、「eat heartily」、「dig in」、「feast on delicious food」等。

Part 4 短文聽解

Question number 13.

Please look at the following three pictures. Listen to the following report. Which picture best describes the report?

請看以下三張圖片。聆聽以下報導。哪一張圖最能說明這則報導？

This weekend, the long-waited Plum Blossom Zoo, not far away from the Water Park, is going to open. It has many animals like lions, giraffes, and monkeys. There are also fun rides and a playground for kids. Visitors can enjoy snacks and drinks at the zoo's cafes. It's a great place for families to spend time together and learn about animals.

這個週末，期待已久的梅花動物園即將在離「水公園」不遠處開幕。園內有許多動物，如獅子、長頸鹿和猴子。還有許多有趣的遊樂設施和兒童遊樂場。遊客可以在動物園裡的咖啡廳享用小吃和飲料。這是一個很棒的地方，家庭可以一起來觀度時光，並學習有關動物的知識。

A　　　　B　　　　C

| 詳解 | 三張圖片呈現的是不同地方的家庭戶外活動，而題目問的是報導內容是在說哪一張圖。雖然可以從一開始的「the long-waited Plum Blossom Zoo（期待已久的梅花動物園）」這句話掌握答案了，不過畢竟「Plum Blossom」不容易聽得出來，且後面又提到「Water Park（水公園）」、「playground for kids（兒童遊樂場）」，難免會讓考生一時之間無從選擇。其實只要再仔細聽取「It has many animals like lions, giraffes, and monkeys.（有許多動物，如獅子、長頸鹿和猴子。）」這句話，大概就能靜下心來選出正確答案 B 了。

Question number 14.

Please look at the following three pictures. Listen to the following news report. Which picture best describes the report?

請看以下三張圖片。聆聽以下新聞報導。哪一張圖最能夠說明這則報導？

Local news. This early morning there was a car accident taking place at the intersection of 2nd North Rd. and 1st East Rd. A little boy was hit by a car when he was walking across the road. It is reported that the car driver was looking at his cellphone and failed to find that the traffic light had turned red. The boy was sent to hospital earlier and is in the midst of emergency care now.

本地新聞。今天清晨在北二路和東一路的交叉口發生了一起車禍。一名小男孩在穿越馬路時被一輛車撞到。據報導，該名駕駛正在滑手機，沒有注意到紅燈已經亮起。小男孩已經被送往醫院並正在接受急救治療。

A

B

C

| 詳解 | 從這三張交通事故的圖來看，可以抓住兩個重點：一、小男孩是走路還是騎腳踏車；二、汽車駕駛有無使用手機。我們可以從報導中聽到「A little boy was hit by a car when he was walking across the road.」所以選項 C 可以直接刪除，接著再注意到「It is reported that the car driver was looking at his cellphone...」，所以再把雙手握方向盤的選項 A 剔除，答案就是選項 B 了。

Day 24

月　　日

我的完成時間________分鐘
標準作答時間 10 分鐘

Part 1 看圖辨義

Questions 1-2

Part 2 問答

Questions 3-7

3. A. Sure. I like this dress.
   B. Thanks! It's comfortable too.
   C. I already have enough suits.

4. A. Thanks. You're very kind.
   B. Sorry, but I forget to bring my card.
   C. What will you need it for?

5. A. Micky is not home.
   B. Room service.
   C. Yes, how can I help you?

6. A. A table of four, please.
   B. Maybe we should consider a smaller one.
   C. Just keep some space between us.

7. A. When would be a good time for you?
   B. No matter how the weather is, I'll go.
   C. Do you care how people talked?

Part 3 簡短對話

Questions 8-12

8. A. Study harder but not stay up late
   B. Learn to stay calm
   C. Seek advice from her teachers

9. A. The story of the film is confusing.
   B. Its special effects are amazing.
   C. Its actions are perfect.

10. A. Jogging
    B. Yoga
    C. Jogging and yoga

11. A. Going to the gym every day
    B. Running for two hours every day
    C. Going jogging every morning

12. A. Sometimes
    B. Every weekend
    C. Once a week

Part 4 短文聽解

Questions 13-14

13.

A

B

C

14.

A

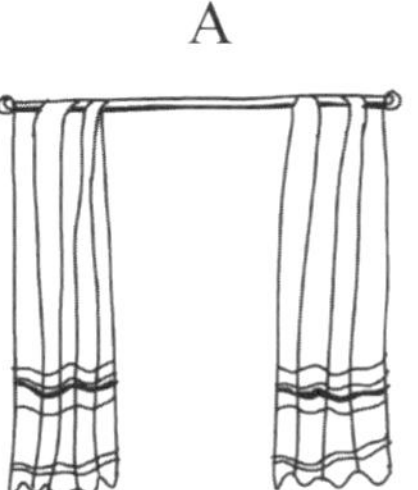

B

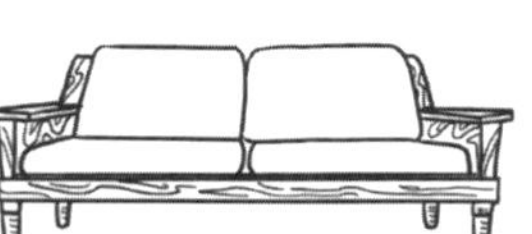

C

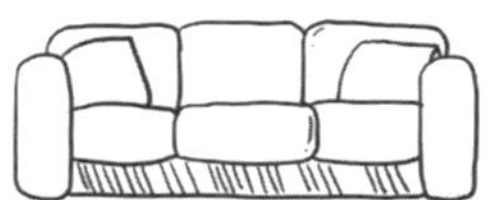

上頁簡答

解答與詳解

1. (B) 2. (A) 3. (B) 4. (C) 5. (B) 6. (B) 7. (A) 8. (C) 9. (B) 10. (C) 11. (B) 12. (A) 13. (C) 14. (B)

Part 1 看圖辨義

For questions number 1-2, please look at the following pictures.

Question number 1.

What is the woman who's standing? 站著的女人是做什麼的？

A. An office clerk	A. 辦公室職員
B. A hair-cutter	B. 理髮師
C. A shop keeper	C. 商店老闆

| 詳解 | 圖片中坐著的（seated）男子是去理髮的客人（guest），站在他身後（at the back of）的自然是理髮師了。英文裡的「理髮師」有多種講法，包括 barber、hairdresser、hair-cutter 等，所以正確答案是選項 B。

| 補充 | 雖然 haircutter 也可以指稱「理髮師」，但它的原意其實就是「剪髮者」，可以指專門從事剪髮的人，其的工作主要集中在剪髮本身，不涉及其他的髮型設計或化妝等服務，而 hairdresser 通常指的是一位專業從事髮型設計和造型的人，他們不僅僅是剪髮，還包括染髮、燙髮、造型等服務。至於 barber，則是指專門從事男性髮型修剪、理髮和修面的人。與 hairdresser" 和 haircutter 不同的是，barber 專門處理男性髮型和鬍子修剪，通常他們會提供剃鬍、修整鬍子、修剪髮型等服務。

Question number 2.

Who is sitting in the middle? 坐在中間的這位是誰？

A. Tony

B. Joan

C. Andy

| 詳解 | 題目問「坐在中間的是誰」，所以關鍵字就是 middle，正確答案是選項 A。

| 補充 | 本題（這張圖）也可能問你「Who's sitting next to...?」（坐在…旁的是誰？）、「Who's sitting at the right/left of...?」（坐在…的右／左手邊的是誰？）、「Where are the boys?（這些男孩在哪裡？→ 圖書館 library）

Part 2 問答

Question number 3.

That hat really suits you. 那頂帽子真的很適合你。

A. Sure. I like this dress. A. 當然。我喜歡這件洋裝。

B. Thanks! It's comfortable too. B. 謝謝！而且它也很舒服。

C. I already have enough suits. C. 我已經有足夠多的西裝了。

| 詳解 | 題目這句「那頂帽子真的很適合你。」除了是讚美，也是一種建議，但 A 回答喜歡這件洋裝，顯然牛頭不對馬尾，是不知所云的回應，所以不對；B 的回答，除了表示感謝，也表達個人的認同，是正確合理的回應；C 的回答則刻意以相同字彙 suit 干擾，原本說的是帽子，卻回應西裝，是不合道理的回應。

| 補充 | 這裡的 suit 是及物動詞，表示「適合…（某人）」的意思，也可以用它的衍生字 suitable 來表達，用於「be suitable for」這個片語中。類似用法還有 fit（使合身）這個動詞，也可用「be fit for」來表示。例如：The paints fit me well. I'll take it.（這褲子非常合我的身。我就要這件了。）

Question number 4.

Dad, I want to borrow your car for tomorrow. 爸，我明天想借你的車。

A. Thanks. You're very kind. A. 謝謝。你人真好。

B. Sorry, but I forget to bring my card. B. 抱歉，我忘了帶名片。

C. What will you need it for? C. 你要做什麼用？

| 詳解 | 兒子向爸爸借車，爸爸的反應是問「你要做什麼用？」這是一個合理的反應，因為爸爸想知道兒子需要車子做什麼事情，這樣他可以更好地評估是否可以借車，以及有什麼需要特別注意的事情。因此，正確答案是選項 C。A 的回答雖然是客套話，但在這個情境下，與借車的請求並無直接關聯；B 回答顯然是不相關的，因為忘了帶名片與借車無關。

Question number 5.

May I ask who's there? 請問是哪位？

A. Micky is not home. A. 米奇不在家。

B. Room service. B. 客房服務。

C. Yes, how can I help you? C. 是的，我可以幫你什麼忙？

| 詳解 | 題目這句可能是在家裡時有人在外按門鈴，或者在飯店房間內，客房服務人員來提供服務，因此「Room service」是經常會聽到的回應，所以正確答案是選項 B。如果是在家，有人來按鈴，你卻直接說「某某人不在家」，顯然是不適當的回應。A 的回答通常是提供服務的人在說的話，顯然是錯誤的回應。

| 補充 | 這裡的「May I ask who's there?」也可以說「Who's that?」、「Who is it?」、「Who's at the door?」、「Who's knocking?」、「Who's ring the bell?」等。

Question number 6.

The table took up too much space. 這張桌子太佔空間了。

A. A table of four, please. A. 麻煩給我們四人用的桌子。

B. Maybe we should consider a smaller one. B. 或許我們應該考慮一個小一點的。

C. Just keep some space between us. C. 只需在我們之間保留一些空間即可。

| 詳解 | 題目這句指出桌子佔用了太多空間，因此回答應該是建議考慮使用一個較小的桌子來節省空間，所以正確答案是選項 B。A 的回答刻意以相同字彙 table 來表達「麻煩給我們四人用的桌子」，與對話情境不符；C 的回應可能是在建議使用桌子時保持彼此一些安全的空間，也對話情境不符。

Question number 7.

We have to talk this matter over. 我們得好好討論一下這問題。

A. When would be a good time for you? A. 你何時有空呢？

B. No matter how the weather is, I'll go. B. 不論天氣如何，我都會去。

C. Do you care how people talked? C. 你在乎人家怎麼談論嗎？

| 詳解 | 題目句表達出需要討論的意圖，所以回答提出可以討論問題的時間安排，以便進行溝通，符合對話的語境和需要，所以正確答案是選項 A。選項 B 討論天氣和是否去的決定，與「討論這個問題」毫不相干。選項 C 談到是否在乎人們如何談論，與討論具體問題或事項也不相關。

| 補充 | 「talk... over」意思是「仔細討論…」，常用於分析或評估一個主題或決策，以便做出明智的選擇或取得共識，相當於「discuss thoroughly」、「Go over」。例如：Let's discuss this proposal thoroughly to understand all its implications.（讓我們徹底討論這個提案，以了解它所有的影響。）

Part 3 簡短對話

Question number 8.

M: Hey, Sarah! How's school going for you this semester? 男：嘿，莎拉！這學期的學校生活怎麼樣？

W: To tell the truth, I've felt a bit torn up about it and sometimes helpless. 女：老實說，我有些感到心煩意亂，有時感到無助。

M: Oh no, that sounds tough. Have you talked to your teachers about it? 男：哦不，聽起來很棘手。你有跟老師們談過嗎？

Question. What does the man suggest the woman do? 男子建議女子做什麼？

A. Study harder but not stay up late　　A. 更努力用功，但不要熬夜

B. Learn to stay calm　　B. 學會保持鎮定

C. Seek advice from her teachers　　C. 向她的老師尋求建議

| 詳解 | 男子在對話中提出了問題後，建議女子去找她的老師尋求建議（Have you talked to your teachers about it?），這是對女子在學校生活中遇到困難的實際建議，所以正確答案是選項 C。對話中男子沒有提及女子應該更努力學習或不要熬夜，也未建議她學會保持鎮定，所以 A、B 均錯誤。

Question number 9.

M: Hey, Sarah! Have you seen the new movie that came out last week?　　男：嘿，莎拉！你看了上週上映的新電影嗎？

W: Hi! Yes, I watched it yesterday; it's really amazing, though I couldn't always tell the robots and humans apart.　　女：嗨！是的，我昨天看了。雖然真的很棒，但有時我分不清楚機器人和人類。

M: Yeah, that can be confusing sometimes.　　男：是啊，有時候確實會有點混淆。

Question. What does the woman think about the movie?
女子對這部電影有什麼看法？

A. The story of the film is confusing.　　A. 電影情節令人困惑。

B. Its special effects are amazing.　　B. 特效非常驚人。

C. Its actions are perfect.　　C. 動作非常完美。

| 詳解 | 女子提到電影很棒，不過她提到分不清楚誰是機器人、誰是人類，意即電影的 AI 特效，這是她對電影的正面評價和觀感，所以正確答案是選項 B。A 選項刻意提到對話中出的 confusing，但其實就是指「分不清楚誰是機器人、誰是人類」的特效，並非電影的故事情節，所以錯誤。另外，也沒有提到對電影的動作場面有任何評論，故 C 選項也錯誤。

Question number 10.

M: Good morning, Sarah! Did you go for your morning jog today?　　男：早安，莎拉！你今天早上去跑步了嗎？

W: Morning! Not today, I'm taking a break from jogging for the time being. I'm trying out yoga instead, to see if I like it better.　　女：早安！今天沒有，我暫時不跑步了。我改練瑜伽，看看我會不會更喜歡它。

M: That sounds like a good idea. How are you finding yoga so far?　　男：聽起來是個好主意。你目前覺得瑜伽練得怎麼樣？

Question. What could be the woman's morning exercise in the future?
女子未來的晨間運動可能是什麼？

A. Jogging　　A. 跑步

B. Yoga　　B. 瑜伽

C. Jogging and yoga　　C. 跑步和瑜伽

｜詳解｜本題關鍵句在女子說的「I'm taking a break from jogging for the time being.」其中「for the time being」就是「暫時地」的意思，這意味她並沒有放棄跑步，只是想嘗試別的（瑜珈）看看，所以未來的晨間運動兩者都有可能，故正確答案是選項 C。

Question number 11.

M: Hey Susan, I've noticed you've been hitting the gym a lot lately.

男：嘿，蘇珊，我注意到你最近常去健身房。

W: Oh, hi! Yeah, I've started running for 2 hours on end every day.

女：哦，嗨！是啊，我已經開始每天連續跑步兩小時了。

M: Wow, how do you manage to keep it up?

男：哇，你是怎麼堅持下去的？

W: It's difficult, but I feel so much better afterward. I think I'm finally getting into a routine with it.

女：這有點難，但跑完後感覺好多了。我想我最後一定可以養成這個習慣。

Question. What habit does the woman try hard to keep?
女子努力想要養成什麼習慣？

A. Going to the gym every day　　A. 每天去健身房

B. Running for two hours every day　　B. 每天跑步兩小時

C. Going jogging every morning　　C. 每天早上去慢跑

｜詳解｜女子提到她已開始每天連續跑步兩小時（running for 2 hours on end every day），並且覺得堅持下去有點困難，卻也在事後感覺良好，並希望最終能夠養成這個習慣（finally getting into a routine with it），所以正確答案是選項 B。「on end」是「連續吧」的意思。選項 A 刻意重複 gym（健身房）這個字誤導答題，雖然現實中，每天上健身房也是一種挑戰，但不是這篇對話強調的重點。

Question number 12.

M: Hey Emily, I heard you'll visit your grandpa and grandma this weekend.
男：嘿，艾蜜莉，我聽說你這個週末要去看你的爺爺奶奶了。

W: Yes, I try to visit them every now and then. They always enjoy seeing me and telling stories from the past.
女：是的，我會盡量每隔一段時間去看他們。他們總是喜歡見到我，並且喜歡講過去的故事。

M: That's nice of you. How are they doing these days?
男：你真是太好了。他們最近怎麼樣？

W: They're doing well, thanks.
女：他們還好，謝謝。

Question. How often does Emily visit her grandparents?
艾蜜莉多久去看她的祖父母一次？

A. Sometimes A. 有時候

B. Every weekend B. 每個週末

C. Once a week C. 每週一次

詳解 本題考的是「every now and then」這個副詞片語，它也是「頻率副詞」的一種，相當於 sometimes、at times、not always 等，所以正確答案是選項 A。選項 B 刻意提到 weekend，試圖呼應第一句「I heard you'll visit your grandpa and grandma this weekend.」，但重點還是在下一句的「I try to visit them every now and then.」，至於 C 的「Once a week」對話中並未提及。

Part 4 短文聽解

Question number 13.

Please look at the following three pictures. Listen to the following announcement. On which means of transportation can you hear it?
請看以下三張圖片。聆聽以下宣布。你可能在哪一種交通工具上聽到這則廣播？

Ladies and gentlemen, we apologize for the delay. Due to track maintenance ahead, our train will be slowing down briefly. Please remain seated and ensure all belongings are safely stowed. We appreciate your understanding and patience.
各位乘客，很抱歉讓大家久等了。因為前方有軌道維修作業，列車將會稍作減速。請各位保持坐姿，並確保所有物品妥善放置。非常感謝您們的理解與耐心。

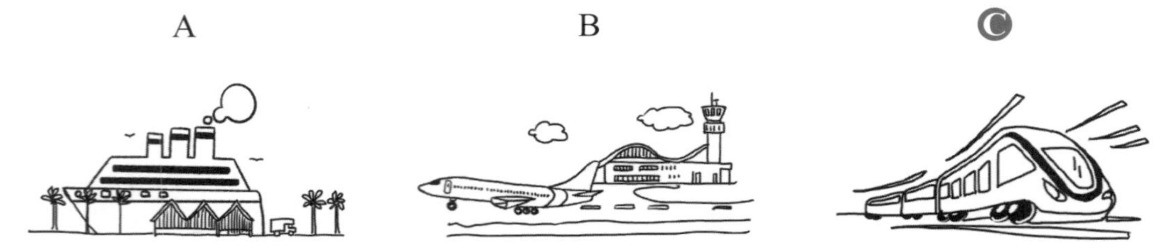

｜詳解｜ 三張圖片呈現的是不同的大型客運交通工具，A 是郵輪、B 是客機，C 是高鐵或高速列車。本題關鍵字詞就在第二句：Due to track maintenance ahead, our train will be slowing down briefly.（因為前方有軌道維修作業，列車將會稍作減速。）其中只要抓到 track 或 train 這兩個字之一，大概就知道答案了，故正確答案是選項 C。

Question number 14.

Please look at the following three pictures. Listen to the following talk. What is a gift for the speaker?

請看以下三張圖片。聆聽以下談話。哪一個是給說話者的禮物？

Next month I'll be moving into a new apartment which is located downtown. My daddy promised that he will buy me a two-seater sofa, so I want to look for curtains of certain style to be a good match with that sofa. My best friend Selina suggested I go to a nearby shop where I can select from a variety of curtain items available.

下個月我將搬進一間位於市中心的新公寓。我爸爸答應要買給我一張兩人座沙發，所以我想找些特定風格的窗簾來搭配這張沙發。我的好朋友 Selina 建議我去附近一家店裡挑選各式各樣的窗簾商品。

｜詳解｜ 題目問的是，那一件傢俱是給說話者的禮物，所以我們注意有出現「禮物」或是「買給誰什麼東西」的句子。其中提到：My daddy promised that he will buy me a two-seater sofa...（我爸爸答應要買給我一張兩人座沙發），其中「two-seater sofa」是「兩人座沙發」，也就是給說話者的禮物，所以正確答案是選項 B。

Day 25

月　　日

我的完成時間_______分鐘
標準作答時間 10 分鐘

Part 1 看圖辨義

Questions 1-2

Part 2 問答

Questions 3-7

3. A. This ring costs NT$ 20,000.
   B. Sorry, I've run out of my cash.
   C. I made lots of money last year.

4. A. I think it depends.
   B. To see is to believe.
   C. That's so kind of you to say so.

5. A. I'm second to none in singing.
   B. OK, take your time.
   C. I'll hold a party next weekend.

6. A. Me too. I like rope jumping.
   B. Let's try to swim the river.
   C. Wait a minute. You should warm up first.

7. A. No, I haven't been served yet.
   B. Yes, check out, please.
   C. No, wait a moment.

Part 3 簡短對話

Questions 8-12

8. A. She's a beginner driver.
   B. The road conditions might not be good.
   C. She might not know about some warning signs.

9. A. Sweep the floor in the kitchen
   B. Do the dishes
   C. Clean up the dining table

10. A. To a breakfast shop
    B. To her kid's school
    C. To the MRT station

11. A. In the post office
    B. At the bus stop
    C. On the street

12. A. Sharing something interesting with her
    B. Wash his hand after coming back home
    C. Keep something secret

Part 4 短文聽解

Questions 13-14

13.

A

B

C

14.

A

B

C

解答與詳解

上頁簡答 1. (B) 2. (B) 3. (B) 4. (A) 5. (B) 6. (C) 7. (A) 8. (A) 9. (C) 10. (B) 11. (C) 12. (C) 13. (B) 14. (C)

Part 1 看圖辨義

For questions number 1-2, please look at the following pictures.

Question number 1.

What is the cat on the right doing 右邊這隻貓在做什麼？

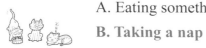

A. Eating something　A. 吃東西

B. Taking a nap　B. 小睡一下

C. Looking at something　C. 盯著某物看

詳解　本題考你聽不聽得出簡單的位置副詞，「左邊」是 left，「中間」是 middle，「右邊」是 right。題目問「on the right」的這隻貓在做什麼，雖然沒聽到有 sleep / sleeping 的選項，但 eating、looking 都是很簡單、很容易聽出的單字，用刪除法也可以得知正確答案是選項 B。nap 就是 short sleep 的意思。

Question number 2.

Who is the smallest? 最小的是誰？

A. Butch

B. Fluffy

C. Rex

詳解　圖片中有三隻狗，和前一題一樣，這類題型可能考你位置關係，也可能考舉止動作或體型大小。只要抓到題目關鍵字 smallest 就可以選出正確答案是選項 B 了。

Part 2 問答

Question number 3.

How much do you have on hand? 你手頭上有多少錢？

A. This ring costs NT$ 20,000.　A. 這枚戒指要二萬台幣。

B. Sorry, I've run out of my cash.　B. 抱歉，我現金用完了。

C. I made lots of money last year.　C. 我去年賺了很多錢。

| 詳解 | 題目這句問對方手頭上有多少錢，A 卻回答戒指的價格，答非所問；B 回答說現金用完了，這表示他手頭上沒有現金，是合理且符合情境的回答，所以正確答案是選項 B；C 回答去年賺了很多錢，但這與問及對方手頭上有多少錢的問題無關。

| 補充 | 除了「on hand」之外，相信「in hand」以及「at hand」也讓許多學習者感到霧煞煞，它們在意思與用法上有何不同呢？「at hand」是「在手邊，在附近，隨時可取用」的意思，例如：When I write, I always have a dictionary at hand（我在寫作時，我手邊總有一本字典）。「on hand」有「在手上，尚待處理，在場」的意思，例如：It is always advisable to have some cash on hand.（手頭上有些現金總是好的。）「in hand」也有「在手上」的意思，但他比較偏向於「餘下的，在控制下，正在處理中的」。例如：I am keeping the situation in hand.（情況在我控制之中。）

Question number 4.

Do you believe people are kind at heart? 你認為人性本善嗎？

A. I think it depends. A. 我覺得這要看情況而定。

B. To see is to believe. B. 眼見為憑。

C. That's so kind of you to say so. C. 你這麼說真是太好了。

| 詳解 | 題目這句是詢問對某項議題的看法，這是一個主觀性很強、見仁見智的問題，因此「這要看情況而定」是符合邏輯的回答，所以正確答案是選項 A；認不認為人性本善，跟是不是有親眼看見什麼，顯然無關，故 B 錯誤；C 的回答是用來回應對方的讚美或感謝，但與詢問意見的問題無關。

Question number 5.

Please hold on a second. 請稍等一下。

A. I'm second to none in singing. A. 我在唱歌方面毫不遜色。

B. OK, take your time. B. 沒關係，慢慢來。

C. I'll hold a party next weekend. C. 我下個週末要舉辦派對。

| 詳解 | 題目這句常在電話英語中聽到，或是生活、職場對話中也會用到。A 回答自己在唱歌方面很厲害，與對話中要求稍等的內容無關，只是刻意用相同字彙 second 產生混淆；B 回應說「沒關係，慢慢來」，表示願意等待，符合對話的情境和語境，所以正確答案是選項 B。C 提到下個週末要舉辦派對，也與對話情境無關。

| 補充 | 除了「Hold on a second」之外，表示「請稍等一下。」的英文說法還有：「Just a minute/second/moment, please.」、「Hang on a minute/second/moment.」、「old tight for a minute/second/moment.」、「Give me a minute/second/moment.」、「Hold your horses for a minute/second/moment.」

Question number 6.

I can't wait to jump into the swimming pool. 我迫不及待要跳進游泳池了。

A. Me too. I like rope jumping. A. 我也是。我喜歡跳繩。

B. Let's try to swim the river. B. 我們試著游過那條河吧。

C. Wait a minute. You should warm up first. C. 等一下，你應該先熱身一下。

| 詳解 | 「開始游泳前要先熱身」，相信很多人都有這樣的正確觀念，否則會有抽筋等危險，所以正確答案是選項 C，「warm up」是「熱身，暖身」的意思。A 回答「Me too」只是個誘餌，讓你誤以為可能是正確答案，後面的「我喜歡跳繩」顯然與題目句無關；題目表達的是對於跳入泳池游泳的期待，C 卻回答游過那條河，也是搭不起來。

Question number 7.

Have you been waited on, Miss? 小姐，有人已經為您服務了嗎？

A. No, I haven't been served yet. A. 沒有，還沒有人服務過。

B. Yes, check out, please. B. 是的，請結帳。

C. No, wait a moment. C. 沒有，請稍等一下。

| 詳解 | 「Have you been waited on, Miss?」是詢問是否已經有人為您提供過服務過了。這裡的「wait on＋人」相當於「serve＋人」，常用於餐廳服務英語中，因此，回答 A「沒有，還沒有人服務過。」直接回應了對方的問題，表達了還未獲得服務的情況，所以正確答案是選項 A。B 的回答是在已經用完餐，準備離開時說的話，所以不符；C 的「請稍等一下」應該是在確認客人的狀況之後，去做因應的處理，所以應該是服務生要說的話才對，所以也錯誤。

| 補充 | 「wait on sb.」看起還好像是「讓某人等待」，但其實是是「為某人服務」或「接待某人」，通常指的是提供服務或幫助，例如：The waiter waited on us attentively throughout the meal.（服務生在整頓餐點期間非常細心地為我們服務。）

Part 3 簡短對話

Question number 8.

M: Hey, Sarah, are you ready for our road trip tomorrow? 男：嘿，莎拉，你準備好明天的公路之旅了嗎？

W: Yeah, I'm excited because this is the first time I hit the road! 女：是啊，我很興奮，因為這是我第一次上路！

M: Don't worry. I'll be seated beside you and give you any necessary warnings. 男：別擔心，我會坐在你旁邊，給你任何必要的警告。

W: That sounds good. I'll be very careful. 女：聽起來不錯。我會非常小心的。

Question. Why is the woman worried? 女子為何感到擔憂？

A. She's a beginner driver. A. 她是新手駕駛。

B. The road conditions might not be good. B. 路況可能不好。

C. She might not know about some warning signs. C. 她可能不知道一些警告標誌。

| 詳解 | 對話中提到這是她第一次上路（the first time I hit the road），因此她可能因為新手駕駛缺乏經驗而感到不安，所以正確答案是選項 A。「路況可能不好。」以及「不了解警告標誌。」雖然可能都是潛在的擔憂，但對話中並未提到女子對這些事情的擔憂，所以 B、C 皆錯誤。

Question number 9.

M: Hey, Sandy, have you finished cleaning the kitchen yet? 男：嘿，仙蒂，你把廚房打掃完了嗎？

W: Almost done! I just need to put the dishes away and wipe the dining table. 女：快完成了！我只需要把碗盤收起來，擦一下餐桌。

M: Great job! I'll sweep and mop the floor in the living room while you finish up. 男：做得好！我會在你忙完之後打掃客廳及拖地。

W: Thanks! That would be a big help. 女：謝謝！那會是很大的幫助。

Question. What does the woman do to help housework?
女子在幫忙家務時做了什麼？

A. Sweep the floor in the kitchen A. 打掃廚房地板

B. Do the dishes B. 洗碗

C. Clean up the dining table C. 清潔餐桌

| 詳解 | 題目問女子在幫忙家務時做了什麼，所以應注意女子的發言。她說「I just need to put the dishes away and wipe the dining table.（我只需要把碗盤收起來，擦一下餐桌。）」所以提到「打掃地板」的 A 可以率先剔除，女子提到的「put the dishes away」意思是「將盤子收整好」，而 B 選項刻意提到 dishes，但「do the dishes」是「洗碗」，所以錯誤；故正確答案是選項 C；wipe 是「擦拭」的意思，意思與「clean up」差不多。

Question number 10.

M: Hey, Lisa, are you going out for breakfast now? 男：嘿，麗莎，你現在要出去吃早餐嗎？

W: Actually, I need to drop my kid off at school first before that. 女：其實，我得先把孩子送到學校，然後再去吃早餐了。

M: OK. Take your time. We can meet later. 男：好的。慢慢來。我們稍後見。

W: Thanks! It won't take long. Let's meet in half an hour at the MRT station. 女：謝謝！不會花很久的時間。我們半小時後在捷運站見面。

Question. Where is the woman ready to go? 女子準備去哪？

A. To a breakfast shop　A. 去早餐店

B. To her kid's school　B. 去她孩子的學校

C. To the MRT station　C. 去捷運站

| 詳解 | 女子提到她必須先送孩子去學校（I need to drop my kid off at school first），然後再去吃早餐。因此，她當下正要去的地方是孩子的學校，所以正確答案是選項 B。雖然對話中提到外出吃早餐（going out for breakfast），以及半小時後在捷運站和男子碰面（Let's meet in half an hour at the MRT station.），但都是之後要去做的事。

Question number 11.

M: Excuse me. Do you know where the nearest bus stop is?
男：請問一下，您知道最近的公車站在哪裡嗎？

W: Well, keep walking straight until you reach the post office, and then turn left. It's just down the road on your right.
女：嗯，一直往前走，直到你到達郵局，然後左轉。公車站就在你右手邊。

M: Thank you so much! How long does it take to get there?
男：非常感謝！走到那裡要多久呢？

W: It should only take you about ten minutes on foot.
女：步行大概只需要十分鐘左右。

Question. Where could be the speakers? 說話者可能在哪裡？

A. In the post office　A. 在郵局裡

B. At the bus stop　B. 在公車站

C. On the street　C. 在街上

| 詳解 | 對話中女子指示男子一直往前走到郵局，然後左轉（keep walking straight until you reach the post office, and then turn left），公車站就在右手邊的路邊，這表示說話者在大街上，不可能在建築物（郵局）內，當然也不可能在公車站旁，所以 A、B 顯然錯誤，正確答案是選項 C。

Question number 12.

M: Hello Jane, I'm coming home soon! It's been a long day at work.
男：哈囉，珍，我快到家了！今天工作真是辛苦。

W: Remember to cover your hand when entering the door lock password.
女：記得在輸入門鎖密碼時遮住你的手。

M: Thanks for the reminder.
男：謝謝提醒。

W: How was your day? Did anything interesting happen at work?
女：你今天過得如何？工作中有什麼有趣的事情嗎？

Question. What did the woman remind the man to do? 女子提醒男子做什麼？

A. Sharing something interesting with her　　A. 跟她分享一些有趣的事情

B. Wash his hand after coming back home　　B. 回家後洗手

C. Keep something secret　　C. 保守某個祕密

｜詳解｜ 題目問女子提醒男子做什麼，所以應注意女子的發言，她跟男子說「Remember to cover your hand when entering the door lock password.」（記得在輸入門鎖密碼時，遮住你的手），然後男子回答說「Thanks for the reminder.」 其中 reminder 是 remind 的名詞，表示「提醒（的事情或物）」，所以正確答案是選項 C。「keep... secret」就是「保守…的祕密」。選項 A 刻意要呼應對話最後提到的「Did anything interesting happen at work? 」，但並非對於男子的提醒事件，也沒有提到要她回到家後去洗手，故 B 也錯誤。

｜補充｜ 「It's been a long day.」常用來表示「經過了漫長（辛苦）的一天」，也許是在工作或是學校上課，如果把 day 換成 week，也有類似意義，例如：I've had a really long week, so I just want to sleep this weekend.（我經歷了很漫長的一週，所以這週末只想睡覺。）但要是把 day 換成 time，意思又完全不同了。你可以對一位好久不見的朋友說「It's been a long time!」，表示是「久違了。」

Part 4 短文聽解

Question number 13.

Please look at the following three pictures. Listen to the following talk. What is Vivian going to do next Saturday?

請看以下三張圖片。聆聽以下談話。薇薇安下週六將要做什麼？

Vivian will be busy next week. First of all, she has full courses on the first three weekdays, and has to attend after-school Chinese classes on Monday, Wednesday and Friday nights. Before Sunday, when there'll be a surprise party at a friend's place, she'll have some time to help prepare for it. So she can't help putting off a date with her boyfriend scheduled on Saturday.

下週薇薇安會很忙碌。首先，她在前三個工作日有滿滿的課程，並且週一、週三和週五晚上還要去上課後中文班。在週日舉行的一場驚奇派對之前，她將有些時間可幫忙準備。因此，她不得不推掉原定週六和男朋友的約會。

A

B

C

｜詳解｜題目問 Vivian 下週六會做什麼，所以應特別注意這個時間點提到的活動，從「So she can't help putting off a date with her boyfriend scheduled on Saturday.」可知，她下週六不會和男友去約會，所以圖 C 就可以先排除了。圖 A 看起來是正在進行派對的活動，而圖 B 是派對的準備工作，我們再從「Before Sunday, when there'll be a surprise party at a friend's place...」（在週日舉行的一場驚奇派對之前，她將有些時間可幫忙準備⋯）可得知，派對舉行的時間就是週日，所以 A 就不是答案了，故正確答案是選項 B。

Question number 14.

Please look at the following three pictures. Listen to the following message. What is the speaker going to do tonight?
請看以下三張圖片。聆聽以下訊息。說話者今天晚上將要做什麼？

Hello, Jack. It's me. My stomach is feeling upset now and I need to take a leave of absence and leave work early. I believe it's wiser to go see a doctor. Sorry, I need to call off our movie date for tonight. If I feel better tomorrow morning, let's have breakfast together. By the way, go to bed early tonight. Don't stay up late. See you.
嗨，傑克。是我。我現在肚子感覺不舒服，需要請假並提早下班。我想還是去看醫生比較保險。抱歉，我得取消今晚我們的電影約會。如果明天早上感覺好些，我們一起吃早餐吧。順便說一下，今晚早點睡。不要熬夜。再見。

A

B

Ⓒ

｜詳解｜題目問說話者今天晚上將要做什麼，所以應特別注意「今天晚上」這個時間點提到的活動。從「Sorry, I need to call off our movie date for tonight.」可知，今天晚上不會去看電影，所以圖 A 就可以先排除了。而前面一句「I believe it's wiser to go see a doctor.」提到不去看電影的原因是去看醫生比較保險，所以正確答案是選項 C。雖然也有提到圖 B 的「一起用餐」，但從「If I feel better tomorrow morning, let's have breakfast together.」可知，也許是「明天早上」才有可能。

Day 26

月　　日

我的完成時間______分鐘
標準作答時間 10 分鐘

Questions 1-2

Part 2 問答

Questions 3-7

3. A. Why not?
   B. No, are you free now?
   C. Yes, swimming is bad for me.

4. A. I won the first prize.
   B. I've caught a bad cold.
   C. Bingo! You're so smart.

5. A. I don't think they are that matched.
   B. Yes, I'll go with them.
   C. The blouse is more expensive, right?

6. A. I've been to Japan several times.
   B. I have no idea.
   C. I have been busy with work.

7. A. With the help of my father
   B. I find it in a big city.
   C. Not too bad.

Part 3 簡短對話

Questions 8-12

8. A. She might have more than one bowl.
   B. She isn't confident the man will make it.
   C. She wants to offer help to the man.

9. A. Drinks
   B. Fruit
   C. Bread

10. A. Tonight
    B. Tomorrow night
    C. Next Saturday

11. A. By the table
    B. At the balcony
    C. In bed

12. A. To a department store
    B. To a wire and cable shop
    C. To the store where TVs are fixed

Part 4 短文聽解

Questions 13-14

13.

A

B

C

14.

A

B

C

上頁簡答

解答與詳解

1. (B) 2. (C) 3. (A) 4. (B) 5. (A) 6. (C) 7. (C) 8. (A)
9. (B) 10. (C) 11. (C) 12. (C) 13. (C) 14. (A)

Part 1 看圖辨義

For questions number 1-2, please look at the following pictures.

Question number 1.

What is the woman doing? 女子正在做什麼？

A. She's cooking.	A. 她正在煮菜。
B. She's cutting vegetables.	B. 她正在切菜。
C. She's eating dinner.	C. 她正在吃晚餐。

｜詳解｜圖片中女子手拿著一把菜刀在切菜，也許是正要煮菜，但可別認為選項 A 是對的（除非題目問的是「What is the woman ready to do?」）。cooking 是「煮飯，煮菜」，選項 B 的 vegetables 是「蔬菜」、選項 C 的 eating dinner 是「吃晚餐」，所以正確答案是選項 B。

Question number 2.

What animal is behind the dog? 在狗後面的是什麼動物？

A. A cat	A. 貓
B. A sheep	B. 綿羊
C. A duck	C. 鴨子

｜詳解｜看到圖片中有好幾隻動物，腦海中應隨即浮現用來表達位置關係的介系詞，比方說「在前面（in front of）」、「在後面（behind）」、「在右邊（at the right of）」、「在左邊（at left right of）」、「在旁邊（beside / next to）」…等。在狗的後方是一隻鴨子，所以正確答案是選項 C。

Part 2 問答

Question number 3.

Let's go swimming, shall we? 我們一起去游泳，如何？

A. Why not?	A. 為何不？
B. No, are you free now?	B. 不，你現在有空嗎？
C. Yes, swimming is bad for me.	C. 是的，游泳對我來說不太好。

| 詳解 | 題目這句是提出建議或邀約，回答「Why not?（為何不？）」就等於同意一起去，沒有反對的意思，所以正確答案是選項 A；B 的回答是詢問對方是否有空，並不是對「一起去游泳」這個建議的直接回應；C 先回答 Yes 但卻說自己不適合去游泳，前後矛盾，故不可選。

| 補充 | 「Why not？」有好幾種用法，其中一個是用來表達「贊成」、「沒有特別需要拒絕的理由」的意思。事實上，這樣的回答通常會給人一種積極，甚至「無所謂」、「都可以啦」的感覺，比起只回答「Yes.」，更容易給人留下積極向前的印象。另外，它也經常會跟 Sure 一起使用，例如：A: Let's go drinking tonight! There is a nice bar near-by. B: Sure, why not?（A：今晚來去喝酒吧！附近有一間很棒的酒吧喔！ B：當然好，這有什麼問題？）

Question number 4.

You look pale. What's the matter? 你看起來臉色蒼白。怎麼了？

A. I won the first prize. A. 我贏得首獎了。

B. I've caught a bad cold. B. 我得了重感冒。

C. Bingo! You're so smart. C. 賓果！（你答對了！）你真聰明。

| 詳解 | 題目這句的 pale 是「蒼白的」，「look pale」有「病懨懨」的意思，而「What's the matter?」是用來詢問原因。「贏得首獎」應該是相當開心，不會看起來生病的樣子，故 A 錯誤；caught 是 catch 的過去式，「catch a bad cold」確實可能是「look pale」的原因，所以正確答案是選項 B；C 的回答是一種誇讚，不過不是用來說明生病的原因。

Question number 5.

Does this blouse go with my skirt? 這件襯衫和我的裙子相襯嗎？

A. I don't think they are that matched. A. 我不覺它們很搭。

B. Yes, I'll go with them. B. 是的，我會和他們一起去。

C. The blouse is more expensive, right? C. 這襯衫比較貴，是吧？

| 詳解 | 題目句當中的「go with」是「與…搭配」的意思，也就是指選項 A 中的動詞 match，所以直接回答「I don't think they are that matched.」等同於不認同襯衫和我的裙子很搭，符合對話情境，正確答案是選項 A。選項 B 則刻意重複「go with」，但意思完全與題目句的「go with」不同；C 的回答反問襯衫是不是比較貴，不合語意邏輯。

| 補充 | 除了「與…搭配」之外，「go with」（與…搭配／協調／和諧）可以用在許多種情境。例如：This wine goes particularly well with seafood.（這種酒配海鮮最合適。）、This vase goes very well with the flowers you bought me.（這花瓶和你買給我的花非常搭配。）

Question number 6.

Where have you been recently? 你最近到哪裡去了？

A. I've been to Japan several times. A. 我去過日本數次了。

B. I have no idea. B. 我不知道。

C. I have been busy with work. C. 我最近工作很忙。

｜詳解｜題目這句雖然是 where 開頭的問句，但通常出題都會有陷阱，比方說，問你最近這陣子去哪了（怎麼都沒消息），A 回答「我去過日本數次」，雖然有提到日本這個地方，但不合對話情境，因為答非所問；B 顯然也不是正常、一般人的回答，所以正確答案是選項 C，雖然沒有提到去了什麼地方，但其實「Where have you been recently?」這句話也可以用來問「最近都在忙什麼？」。

Question number 7.

How do you find your new job? 你覺得你的新工作如何？

A. With the help of my father A. 有我爸爸的幫忙

B. I find it in a big city. B. 我在大城市裡找到。

C. Not too bad. C. 還不差。

｜詳解｜本題關鍵在於 find 這個動詞的另一個意思。除了「找到」之外，find 還有接近 feel 或 think 的意思，而「How do you find your new job?」並不是「你怎麼找到你的新工作？」，而是「你覺得你的新工作如何？」有了這一層的認知之後，就可以確認正確答案是選項 C 了。

｜補充｜那如果要表示「你怎麼找到你的新工作」呢？可以用 land、get、secure 等動詞，也就是「How do you land your new job?」又比方說，如果你剛辭了工作，正在找下一個工作，你卻告訴朋友「I am finding a new job.」這可搞笑了！因為 find 是「找到」，不是「正在找」，這時候要用「look for」才對，或者可以說「I'm trying to find a new job.」

Part 3 簡短對話

Question number 8.

M: Hey, I'm thinking of making spaghetti tonight. 男：嘿，我今晚打算做義大利麵。

W: So you'll use that recipe we found online last time? 女：所以你會用上次我們在網路上找到的那個食譜嗎？

M: That's right. I believe I can make it. 男：沒錯。我相信我能做出來。

W: I think I'll have a second helping if it turns out as good as the online photos! 女：如果你可以做得像網路上的照片那樣好，我想我會吃兩份。

Question. What does the woman mean? 女子的意思是什麼？

A. She might have more than one bowl. A. 她可能不只吃一碗。

B. She isn't confident the man will make it. B. 她沒有信心男子能成功做出來。

C. She wants to offer help to the man. C. 她想給男子提供協助。

詳解 對話中女子的第二次發言提到「I think I'll have a second helping if it turns out as good as the online photos!」表示如果男子做出像網路上食譜的照片那樣，她會吃兩份，這裡的 helping 不是「幫忙」，而是餐點的一份，所以正確答案是選項 A。對話中女子並沒有表達對男子能否成功做出來的懷疑，且與沒有提到要提供協助，而是表達她對男子做菜表現的期待，所以 B、C 均不可選。

Question number 9.

W: What's in the picnic basket? 女：野餐籃裡有什麼？

M: Apples, bananas and oranges. 男：有蘋果、香蕉、和柳橙。

W: Great! They are to my taste. 女：太好了！都是我愛吃的。

M: I also packed some sandwiches and a bottle of lemonade in this bag. 男：我還準備了兩個三明治和一瓶檸檬水在這袋子裡。

Question. What's in the basket? 籃子裡有什麼？

A. Drinks A. 飲料

B. Fruit B. 水果

C. Bread C. 麵包

詳解 題目問籃子（basket）裡有什麼，可以從對話一開始女子說的「What's in the picnic basket?」以及男子回答「Apples, bananas and oranges」來看，這些東西都是水果類，所以正確答案是選項 B。雖然最後還提到了「sandwiches and a bottle of lemonade」，但不是在 basket 裡，而是 bag 裡的東西，因此 A、C 不可選。

Question number 10.

W: Let's go to the movies tonight, shall we? 女：我們今晚一起去看電影，好嗎？

M: I'm sorry but I must work overtime tonight. 男：我很抱歉我今晚必須加班。

W: Well, some other time, O.K.? 女：好吧，下次好嗎？

M: Sounds good. Let's plan it for next weekend instead. 男：聽起來不錯。我們就定下週末吧。

Question. When will they probably go to the movies? 他們可能何時去看電影？

A. Tonight A. 今晚

B. Tomorrow night B. 明晚

C. Next Saturday C. 下週六

|詳解| 對話中提到「今晚去看電影」的是女子說的「Let's go to the movies tonight, will you?」這句，不過男子回答說「I'm sorry but...」，顯然 A 是不可選了；接著女子提議改天再去，而男子也同意（Sounds good.）並提出下週末（next weekend）去，所以 B 當然也不是答案，所以正確答案是選項 C。

Question number 11.

W: It's time to get up!	女：該起床了！
M: Come on! It's still early.	男：拜託！現在還早。
W: No, it's eight o'clock now.	女：不，現在已經 8 點了。
M: Can we sleep a little longer? I'm really tired today.	男：我們可以睡久一點嗎？我今天真的好累。

Question. Where are the speakers? 說話者們在哪裡？

A. By the table	A. 在桌子旁
B. At the balcony	B. 在陽台
C. In bed	C. 在床上

|詳解| 對話中提到女子提醒男子該起床了（It's time to get up!），男子回應說現在還早，然後女子指出已經八點了，最後男子請求可以再睡一會兒（Can we sleep a little longer?），這些情境都暗示他們在床上的對話，所以正確答案是選項 C。

|補充| in bed 其實就是指「蓋棉被躺在床上」的狀態。例如：In winter, I like to stay in bed to keep warm.（冬天時我喜歡窩在被窩裡保暖。）不過「on the bed」是單純指「在床上」的位置，例如：Cody sat on the bed and took off his socks.（Cody 坐在床上並脫襪子。）

Question number 12.

W: Did you check if the cable TV is correctly linked?	女：你有沒有確認一下有線電視是否正確連接？
M: Sure, but I still can't see anything.	男：有啊，但我還是什麼都看不到。
W: Is the TV broken?	女：是電視壞了嗎？
M: I'm not sure. Maybe we should have it repaired.	男：我不確定，也許我們應該把它送修。

Question. Where will they probably go? 他們可能會去哪裡？

A. To a department store	A. 去百貨公司
B. To a wire and cable shop	B. 去電線電纜賣場
C. To the store where TVs are fixed	C.去修理電視的店

| 詳解 | 對話中男子提到「I'm not sure. Maybe we should have it repaired.」表示他不確定電視是否壞了，並建議將其送修。這裡用了「使役動詞＋O.＋P.P.」的被動用法，所以「have it repaired」就是將電視送修，正確答案是選項 C。百貨公司通常不修理電視或提供電視修理服務，所以 A 錯誤。B 則刻意重複 cable（電纜線）這個字，因為不確定是什麼問題，所以當然也不可能將電視送去電纜賣場修理。

| 補充 | 「使役動詞＋O.＋原形 V / P.P.」是五大句型中的「S＋V＋O＋OC」，其中代表主動行為的「原形 V」以及被動行為的「過去分詞（P.P.）」都叫作「受詞補語」，另外知覺動詞中的 see、watch、hear、feel 等，也適用於此句型。例如：He made me clean my room.（他要我打掃房間。）、I saw him leave the building.（我看到他離開了大樓。）

Part 4 短文聽解

Question number 13.

Please look at the following three pictures. Listen to the following announcement. Where could be the speaker?
請看以下三張圖片。聆聽以下宣布。說話者可能在哪裡？

Alright everyone, here's our first stop. Please line up here with your carry-on bags or luggage. We'll explore the beautiful gardens here and learn about their history. Remember to stay together so you won't get lost. After our visit, we'll have some time for photos before heading to the next exciting spot. Enjoy your time here!
大家好，這裡就是我們第一個停靠點了。請大家帶著隨身包包或行李，在這裡先排好隊。我們將探索這裡美麗的花園，並了解它們的歷史。請記得一起行動，以免走失。參觀結束後，我們會有一些時間拍照，然後前往下一個令人興奮的景點。祝大家在這裡玩得愉快！

A

B

Ⓒ

| 詳解 | 三張圖看起來都與觀光、導遊、遊覽車等有關，而題目問說話的人什麼地方。從第二句「Please line up here with your carry-on bags or luggage.（請大家帶著隨身包包或行李，在這裡先排好隊。）」就可以知道，這位導遊（說話者）絕不可能在遊覽車裡面，所以 B 可以直接排除掉。接下來她又說「We'll explore the beautiful gardens here...」，但圖 A 中的導遊後方可以看到動物園，所以也不會是在這個地方，因此我們以刪除法即可得到正確答案是選項 C。

Question number 14.

Please look at the following three pictures. Listen to the following recorded message. Which button do you press if you'd like to ask help from someone?

請看以下三張圖片。聆聽以下錄音訊息。如果你要找人尋求協助，應按哪個按鍵?

Welcome to City Bank Customer Service! For English service, please press 1. For assistance with lost or stolen cards, please press 2. For inquiries about loans and mortgages, please press 4. For information on our banking products and services, please press 5. For all other questions, please remain on the line for a real person available. Thanks for your patience.

城市銀行客服中心您好！如需英文服務，請按 1。若有遺失或被盜卡片需求，請按 2。如欲查詢貸款或抵押貸款，請按 4。如需了解我們的銀行產品與服務，請按 5。如有其他疑問，請稍待線上真人客服接聽。感謝您的耐心等候。

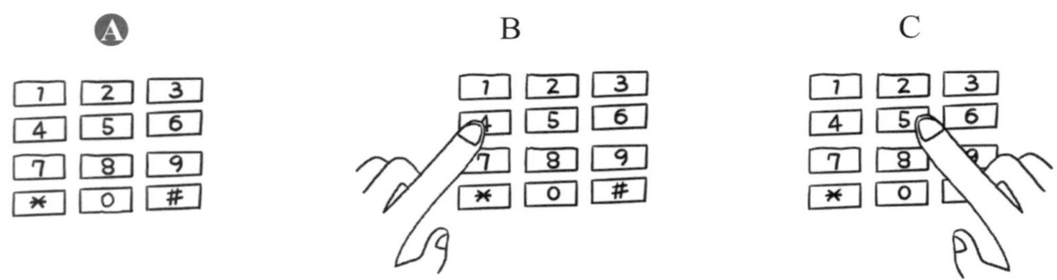

|詳解| 三張圖明顯告訴你，這題考的就是「要按哪個按鍵」，所以題目一定要先聽清楚，題目問句中的 press 是「按下」的意思，「ask help from someone」是「請求某人協助」，而這裡的 someone 其實就是「接聽電話的真人」，而不是電話中預錄的語音。破題關鍵字詞是「a real person」，就在倒數第二句的「 For all other questions, please remain on the line to a real person available. 」，這裡「remain on the line」就是不按任何按鍵，等待電話自動接通，所以選手指頭沒有放在任何按鍵上的圖，正確答案是選項 A。

MEMO

Day 27

月　　日

我的完成時間______分鐘
標準作答時間 10 分鐘

Part 1 看圖辨義

Questions 1-2

Part 2 問答

Questions 3-7

3. A. Wait. You need to sweep it first.
   B. Yes, be my guest, please.
   C. No, the mop is over there.

4. A. History
   B. Tomorrow's exam
   C. Yes, math problems.

5. A. No, thanks.
   B. I don't like coffee.
   C. Yes, I don't have any problems.

6. A. She even laughs in her dreams.
   B. I don't care about her crying.
   C. It must be your funny looks.

7. A. Both 110 or 119 are OK.
   B. I don't know the policeman's phone number.
   C. The XL size suits me well.

Part 3 簡短對話

Questions 8-12

8. A. He can't afford the best sneakers.
   B. The shoe shop doesn't have the best sneakers he wants to buy.
   C. He had enough money to buy any sneakers.

9. A. Library visitors
   B. Classmates
   C. Online game players

10. A. He left during the rush hours.
    B. He was busy with his work earlier.
    C. He met somebody on the way.

11. A. He suggests taking a trip to Seattle.
    B. He thinks Montreal is better than Seattle.
    C. He likes to go fishing by the lake and mountain climbing.

12. A. She hates going to Hawaii.
    B. She wants to go to California again.
    C. She might want to visit Hawaii.

Part 4 短文聽解

Questions 13-14

13.

A

B

C

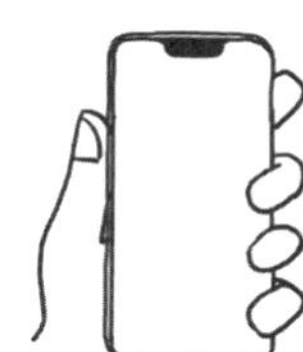

14.

A

B

C

上頁簡答

解答與詳解

1. (B) 2. (C) 3. (A) 4. (B) 5. (A) 6. (C) 7. (A) 8. (C) 9. (B) 10. (A) 11. (B) 12. (C) 13. (C) 14. (B)

Part 1 看圖辨義

For questions number 1-2, please look at the following pictures.

Question number 1.

What is the lady probably doing? 女子可能在做什麼？

A. Using her notebook computer　A. 使用她的筆電

B. Surfing the Internet　B. 上網

C. Playing games on her cellphone　C. 玩手機遊戲

| 詳解 | 圖片中女子坐在一部桌上型電腦（desktop computer）前打電腦，也可能正在上網查資料，或玩遊戲等，但其使用的絕不會是筆電（notebook computer）或手機（cellphone），所以正確答案是選項 B。

| 補充 | notebook 一字其實只是「筆記本」的意思，雖然有人會以為它也有「筆電」的意思，而平常老外也聽得懂是因為有當下情境的輔助，可以直接猜對，同時也不會去指正對方的錯誤，所以漸漸大家都以為 notebook 可以用來指稱筆記型電腦了。事實上，英文裡有個字就是在指「筆電」，就是 laptop 或是 laptop computer。lap 這個字單獨用時是指人坐下來時大腿形成的平面，筆記型電腦因為常被人放在腿上使用，因此叫 laptop。

Question number 2.

What are these people doing? 這些人在做什麼？

A. Loading the furniture onto the truck　A. 將傢俱載上貨車

B. Looking for some pieces of furniture　B. 尋找幾件傢俱

C. Unloading the furniture　C. 將傢俱卸下

| 詳解 | 這張圖片的關鍵處是左方搬椅子的男子往「離開車子的方向」走，所以絕對不會是要把傢俱載上（load）貨車，而是在卸貨（unload），而圖片也看不出他們在尋找傢俱的樣子，所以正確答案是選項 C。

Part 2 問答

Question number 3.

Let me mop the floor. 我來拖地吧。

A. Wait. You need to sweep it first. A. 等等。你應該先掃地。

B. Yes, be my guest, please. B. 是的，請不要客氣。

C. No, the mop is over there. C. 不，拖把在那裡。

| 詳解 | mop 雖然是很簡單的單字，但單獨一個字可能不容易聽得出來，如果是「mop the floor」，應該就會簡單些了！對話的情境是一個人想要拖地，但在他開始之前，另一個人提醒他應該先掃地，因此，正確的答案是選項 A。B 這句話是同意對方去拖地，但卻說不用客氣，在這個情境中並不合適；C 這句話是認為對方不用拖地，卻又指出拖把的位置，前後矛盾。

Question number 4.

What are you studying for? 你為什麼在讀書？

A. History A. 歷史。

B. Tomorrow's exam B. 明天的考試。

C. Yes, math problems. C. 是的，數學問題。

| 詳解 | 因為題目問的是正在讀書的目的（studying for），不是問在讀什麼或讀哪一科，所以 A 錯誤，而題目是 wh- 開頭的問句，不是 Yes/No 的問題，所以 C 也錯誤，故正確答案是選項 B，原句應為「I'm studying for tomorrow's exam.」。

Question number 5.

Would you like another cup of coffee? 你要再來一杯咖啡嗎？

A. No, thanks. A. 不用了，謝謝。

B. I don't like coffee. B. 我不喜歡咖啡。

C. Yes, I don't have any problems. C. 是的，我沒有任何問題了。

| 詳解 | 題目問對方是否想要再來一杯咖啡 ，A 的回答是禮貌地拒絕再來一杯咖啡的方式，表示不需要了，但同時感謝對方的提議，所以正確答案就是選項 A。B 表達的是對咖啡本身不喜歡，但如果不喜歡咖啡，又怎會喝了第一杯呢？所以 B 錯誤；C 的回答也與是否要再來一杯咖啡的問題無關。

| 補充 | another 也可以當「代名詞」，表示「另一個」或「再一個」。例如：I can't answer this Question.　Please show me another.（我無法回答這問題。請再問別的問題。）、The little boy drank a glass of wine and asked for another.（這小男孩喝了一杯酒後，要求再來一杯。）

Question number 6.

What is she laughing at? 她在笑什麼？

A. She even laughs in her dreams. A. 她連作夢都會笑。

B. I don't care about her crying. B. 我並不在乎她在哭。

C. It must be your funny looks. C. 一定是你那好笑的表情。

｜詳解｜ 題目中的「laugh at」就是「對著…笑」，也就是在問「她笑的原因是什麼？」。A 回答她在夢中都會笑，並沒有針對「笑什麼」回答，不符對話的情境；B 卻說不在意她哭，不知所云，所以錯誤。所以正確答案是選項 C，「funny looks」正好作為「laugh at」的受詞。

｜補充｜ 與「笑」有關的動詞，像是 laugh、smile... 等，均可搭配介系詞 at，形成一個「及物動詞片語」。例如：He smiled at her when she entered the room.（當她進入房間時，他對她微笑了一下。）、The children chuckled at the funny cartoon.（孩子們對這部有趣的卡通片輕笑不止。）、He grinned at the camera for the photo.（他對著相機咧嘴一笑，拍了張照片。）

Question number 7.

What number should I dial to call the police by cellphone?
我手機該打幾號來報警？

A. Both 110 or 119 are OK. A. 撥 110 或 119 都可以。

B. I don't know the policeman's phone number. B. 我不知道那個警察的手機號碼。

C. The XL size suits me well. C. 這件 XL 尺寸的相當適合我。

｜詳解｜ 題目問的是如何用手機報警，在台灣，可以撥打 110 或 119 兩個號碼，所以正確答案就是選項 A。問的是報警專線，B 卻回答某位警員的手機號碼，顯然不符情境；C 這句話是在談論衣服尺寸，與報警電話號碼無關。

｜補充｜ dial 也常當名詞用，通常指的是電話或其他設備上的撥號盤或撥號器。例如：The old phone had a rotary dial instead of buttons.（那部老式電話是使用轉盤撥號器，而不是按鈕。）、I found the correct number on the dial of the safe.（我在保險箱的撥號盤上找到了正確的號碼。）

Part 3 簡短對話

Question number 8.

W: May I help you, sir? 女：先生，有什麼需要嗎？

M: Yes, please. I want to buy a pair of sneakers. 男：是的，麻煩了，我想買一雙運動鞋。

W: O.K. Around how much are you looking to spend? 女：好的。您大概預算多少呢？

M: Price is no object. Just show me the best. 男：價格不是問題。只要給我看最好的。

Question. What does the man mean? 男子的意思為何？

A. He can't afford the best sneakers. A. 他無法負擔最好的運動鞋。

B. The shoe shop doesn't have the best sneakers he wants to buy. B. 這家店並沒有他想要買的最好的運動鞋。

C. He had enough money to buy any sneakers. C. 他有足夠的錢可以買任何運動鞋。）

｜詳解｜ 既然題目問的是「男子的意思」，以及從三個選項內容來看，我們可以直接從他第二次發言的「Price is no object.」來判斷，object 在這裡是「目標」的意思，「價格不是目標」的字面意思，就是「價格不是問題」，所以這名男子有足夠的錢可以買任何運動鞋，正確答案是選項 C。

｜補充｜ 去購物時，如果覺得自己口袋麥克麥克，想一展出手闊綽的英姿時，常常會用到「價格不是問題」這句話，而除了「Price is no object.」，還可以這麼說：

Money is no object.
Budget is not a concern.
I can afford it regardless of cost.
I'm not worried about the price.
Cost is not an issue.
I'm willing to pay any price.
I have unlimited funds.

Question number 9.

W: Let's go to the library for tomorrow's exam. 女：我們去圖書館準備明天的考試吧。

M: Oh, no. I can't. Mom asked me to stay at home. 男：哎呀，不行。媽媽叫我留在家裡。

W: How about we study together online instead? 女：那我們改在線上一起唸書吧？

M: That sounds like a good idea. 男：聽起來是個好主意。

Question. Who could be the speakers? 說話者可能是誰？

A. Library visitors A. 圖書館的訪客

B. Classmates B. 同班同學

C. Online game players C. 線上遊戲玩家

｜詳解｜ 「明天的考試（tomorrow's exam）」和「在圖書館準備（go to the library）」均暗示這兩個人是準備考試的同學，而不是圖書館的訪客或線上遊戲玩家，所以正確答案是選項 B。選項 A 提到對話中的 library，選項 C 提到對話中的 online，都只是干擾答題的效果。

Question number 10.

W: How come you are so late? 女：為什麼你這麼晚到？

M: The traffic is rather busy at this time almost every day. 男：幾乎每天在這個時間交通都比較擁擠。

W: In that case, you should leave home early! 女：既然如此，你就應該提早出門啊！

Question. Why did the man come late? 為什麼男子晚到？

A. He left during the rush hours.
B. He was busy with his work earlier.
C. He met somebody on the way.

A. 他在尖峰時刻出門。
B. 他早先前有工作要忙。
C. 他在路上遇到別人。

| 詳解 | 對話中男子提到交通在這個時間通常很擁擠（The traffic is rather busy at this time almost every day.），顯示他在交通高峰時段出門造成了遲到，所以正確答案是選項 A。對話中有 busy 這個字，但並不是指他因為工作忙碌而遲到，也沒有提到他因為在路上遇到別人，所以 B、C 皆錯誤。

Question number 11.

W: I plan to go for a trip.
M: Cool! Where do you want to go?
W: Maybe Seattle is my first choice.
M: How about Montreal? I've been there. There is a lake to the east and a mountain to the west.

女：我計畫要去旅行。
男：酷！你想要去哪？
女：也許西雅圖是我的第一選擇。
男：蒙特羅呢？我去過那。它的東邊有湖，西邊有山。

Question. What does the man mean? 男子的意思為何？

A. He suggests taking a trip to Seattle.
B. He thinks Montreal is better than Seattle.
C. He likes to go fishing by the lake and mountain climbing.

A. 他建議去西雅圖旅行。
B. 他覺得蒙特羅比西雅圖好。
C. 他喜歡去湖邊釣魚及爬山。

| 詳解 | 對話中女子先提到想去西雅圖旅行（Maybe Seattle is my first choice. ），而男子問她覺得蒙特羅如何（How about Montreal?），並表示他有去過，也大略介紹了一下，這顯示他覺得蒙特羅比西雅圖好，所以 A 錯誤，而正確答案是選項 B。雖然他提到蒙特羅有湖和山，但這不意味著他喜歡去湖邊釣魚及爬山，所以 C 錯誤。

Question number 12.

M: Hey, how was your vacation?
W: It was terrible. I went to California and it rained all week.
M: Oh! What a pity! You know, Jenny and I are planning to spend our vacation in Hawaii this summer. Why not join us?
W: Tell me the exact date, so I can check my schedule.

男：嘿，你的假期如何？
女：糟透了！我去了加州，結果下了一整個禮拜的雨。
男：喔！真可惜！你知道嗎？我和珍妮今年暑假計劃要去夏威夷。你要不要加入呢？
女：告訴我確切日期，我確認一下我的行程表。

Question. What does the woman probably mean? 女子可能是什麼意思？

A. She hates going to Hawaii. A. 她討厭去夏威夷。

B. She wants to go to California again. B. 她想要再去加州一次。

C. She might want to visit Hawaii. C. 她可能會想去夏威夷看看。

| 詳解 | 女子在對話的最後，詢問確切日期，顯示她對去夏威夷旅行有興趣或可能性（Tell me the exact date, so I can check my schedule.），這表示她可能會想去夏威夷看看，所以正確答案是選項 C。另外，她沒有提到她討厭夏威夷或任何負面情緒，並提到她在加州的經歷是糟糕的，所以不太可能想再去一次，故 A、B 皆錯誤。

Part 4 短文聽解

Question number 13.

Please look at the following three pictures. Listen to the following message. What is a gift sent by uncle David?

請看以下三張圖片。聆聽以下訊息。大衛叔叔送了什麼禮物？

Hi, Uncle David. It's Jane! I got your gift and it's really awesome. Now I can easily text, call or LINE my friends wherever I am. Remember how I said my old phone didn't work well? For the past week, I had relied on our home phone and a "big cellphone," the tablet, which was not easy when I went out. Your gift has made everything much easier.

嗨，大衛叔叔。我是珍。我拿到你的禮物了，那真的太棒了。現在我無論在哪裡都能輕鬆地發短訊、打電話或是用 LINE 聯繫我朋友們了。還記得我曾說過舊手機壞掉了嗎？過去一星期以來我只能依賴家裡的電話和一台笨重的「大手機」— 平板電腦，出門時很不方便。您的禮物讓我生活方便許多。

A

B

C

| 詳解 | 看完三張圖片，腦海中應立即浮現這三種設備的英文名稱：wireless phone、tab / pad / tablet PC、smartphone / cellphone。接著仔細聽題目要問的是哪一個是大衛叔叔送的禮物。首先，先抓到出現 gift 的位置：I got your gift and it's really awesome. Now I can easily text, call or LINE my friends wherever I am.，這裡可以確定 A 必然錯誤，因為家用電話無法發短訊或用 LINE 聯繫朋友。接著是智慧型手機與平板電腦的選擇了。訊息中提到「a "big cellphone," the tablet, which was not easy when I went out」，顯然

David 是不喜歡使用平板的，否則也不會在一開始時說 uncle 送的禮物非常 awesome 了，故正確答案是選項 C。

Question number 14.

Please look at the following three pictures. Listen to the following phone talk. Which package should Joseph have received?
請看以下三張圖片。聆聽以下電話談話。約瑟夫本來應該收到的衣服是哪一套？

Hello, my name is Joseph, and I'm making this phone call to complain that I received the wrong package. I ordered a black coat and white pants, but I got a white coat and black pants instead. It's not what I expected, and I need the correct items as soon as possible. Can you please check what went wrong with my order? I have the order number ready if you need it. Thank you for helping me solve this issue quickly.
您好，我名叫約瑟夫，而我打這通電話是要投訴我收到了錯誤的包裹。我訂購了一件黑色外套和白色褲子，但我收到的卻是一件白色外套和黑色褲子。這不是我期望的，我希望能盡快收到正確的商品。您可以幫忙查看一下我的訂單出了什麼問題嗎？我已準備好訂單號碼。謝謝您幫助我迅速解決這個問題。

| 詳解 | 本題最關鍵的地方不是在談話內容，而是在題目的問句，確切來說，是題目問句的動詞時態：過去完成式。「should have received」表示「當時／原本應該收到」，其實也就是 Joseph 當初訂的是什麼，那就是本題的答案了。電話談話中提到「I ordered a black coat and white pants（一件黑色外套和白色褲子）, but I got...」，到這裡答案就出來了，got 後面講什麼也不重要了，故本題正確答案是選項 B。

MEMO

月　　日

我的完成時間______分鐘
標準作答時間 20 分鐘

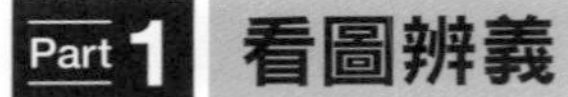

Questions 1-5

1.

2.

3.

4.

5.

Part 2 問答

Questions 6-15

6. A. No, just a little.
   B. I'm afraid not.
   C. Yes, I like Japanese food.

7. A. Say it again!
   B. Who knows?
   C. Come on!

8. A. I'll be right over.
   B. Sorry, I can't come over right now.
   C. I'm not feeling well, so I need to see a doctor.

9. A. Yes, it's my own.
   B. No, it doesn't work any longer.
   C. No, I don't need to work with the computer.

10. A. Yes, my house quaked rather hard.
    B. No, it shocked me very much.
    C. Yes, I didn't feel at all.

11. A. That's a black tie party.
    B. Don't worry. You are pretty beautiful.
    C. You can say that again.

12. A. How come? I'm ready to go.
    B. What time is it?
    C. I'm right behind you!

13. A. So, what's the problem?
    B. That's what I like to hear!
    C. I look forward to your support.

14. A. You will be able to finish the book.
    B. You should go home to rest.
    C. You can clean the house.

15. A. Nice to meet you.
    B. It's up to you.
    C. As usual. And you?

Part 3 簡短對話

Questions 16-25

16. A. The woman likes to wear gloves.
    B. She has beautiful eyes.
    C. The dress suits her very well.

17. A. The man's nephew
    B. The man's niece
    C. The man's cousin

18. A. To a restaurant
    B. To the gym
    C. To the dentist's

19. A. At a bakery
    B. At a convenience store
    C. At a flower shop

20. A. He is a firefighter.
    B. He is a policeman.
    C. He is a manager.

21. A. In a library
    B. In a restaurant
    C. In a hotel

22. A. Make many foreign friends
    B. Surfing the Internet to learning new things
    C. Practicing everyday

23. A. The man was the tallest in his school.
    B. They were classmates.
    C. The man was a baseball player.

24. A. She thinks *Alien: Romulus* is not worth seeing.
    B. She wants to see a movie with outstanding lighting and sound.
    C. She is interested in the sci-fi movie.

25. A. There's only one left in this shop.
    B. There're a few colors of it to choose from.
    C. The woman thinks it is too short for her.

Part 4 短文聽解

Question 26-30

26.

A

B

C

27.

A

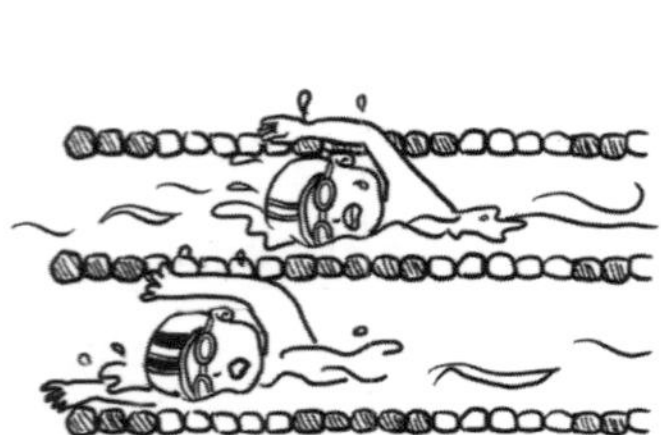

B

C

28.

A

B

C

29.

A

B

C

30.

A

B

C

上頁簡答

解答與詳解

1. (B) 2. (A) 3. (C) 4. (B) 5. (C) 6. (B) 7. (A) 8. (C) 9. (B)
10. (A) 11. (A) 12. (C) 13. (B) 14. (B) 15. (C) 16. (C)
17. (B) 18. (C) 19. (A) 20. (B) 21. (C) 22. (C) 23. (B)
24. (A) 25. (A) 26. (A) 27. (C) 28. (B) 29. (A) 30. (B)

Part 1 看圖辨義

For questions number 1-5, please look at the following pictures.

Question number 1.

What is the woman doing? 女子在做什麼？

A. She's making up a test. A. 她正在補考。

B. She's putting on makeup. B. 她正在化妝。

C. She's brushing her teeth. C. 她正在刷牙。

| 詳解 | 本題考你知不知道「make up」以及 makeup 的意思。前者是動詞，表示「彌補，組成，佔…（多少百分比）」，後者當名詞，表示「妝（容）」，常搭配 put on 表示「化妝」。圖片中女子 裡拿著一支口紅擺在嘴唇上，顯然是在化妝的動作，所以正確答案是選項 B。

Question number 2.

What is true about the picture? 關於這張圖，何者為真？

A. The toothpaste is cheaper than the shampoo. A. 牙膏比洗髮精便宜。

B. The toothbrush is the most expensive item. B. 牙刷是最貴的。

C. The towel is more expensive than the toothpaste. C. 毛巾比牙膏貴。

| 詳解 | 「何者為真」的問題只能一個個選項來看，牙膏是 $115，而洗髮精（shampoo）是 $150，所以正確答案就是選項 A。牙刷是 $85，沒有比牙膏和洗髮精貴，所以 B 錯誤；毛巾是 $55，牙膏是 $115，所以 C 也錯誤。

| 補充 | 最高級的寫法是「the＋形容詞最高級」，因為 expensive 音節多於三個，所以不寫成「形容詞原級＋est」，而改寫成「most＋形容詞原級」。與此用法相同的最高級形容詞，例如「最困難的：difficult → the most difficult」、「最美麗的：beautiful → the most beautiful」…等等。加 -est 的形容詞最高級的，例如「最快的：fast → fastest」、「最懶的：lazy → laziest（去 y 加 iest）」。大部分的形容詞都是這樣的規則變化，不規則話的，像是「好的：good → better（比較級）→ the best（最高級）」、「壞的：bad → worse（比較級）→ the worst（最高級）」。

Question number 3.

What's the weather like on Wednesday? 星期三的天氣如何？

A. It's a raining day. A. 是個下雨天。

B. It's a sunny day. B. 是個晴朗的日子。

C. It's a cloudy day. C. 是個多雲的天氣。

| 詳解 | 看了圖片應該可以先設想到題目要問天氣狀況，腦海裡可以先準備好 rainy、sunny、cloudy 這些單字。題目問星期三的天氣，所以正確答案是選項 C。

| 補充 | 聊到天氣時，如果沒有要那麼精確形容起霧（foggy）、多雲（cloudy）等狀態，只是要講溫度上的變化，我們可以用基本的 cold（冷）、cool（涼）、hot（熱），來形容氣溫帶給人的感受。除了基本的這三個單字，還可以學一下「超冷」的 freezing，比 freezing 不冷一點，程度和 cold 差不多的，也可以說 chilly。如果想要表達比 hot 還要更熱的程度，可別只會說「so hot」，還可以用 scorching hot、burning hot 來表達「熱到快燒起來」啦！

Question number 4.

What is the boy ready to eat? 男孩準備吃什麼？

A. A sandwich, a glass of milk, and an apple A. 一個三明治、一杯牛奶和一顆蘋果

B. A sandwich, a glass of juice, and a banana B. 一個三明治、一杯果汁和一根香蕉

C. A hamburger, a glass of juice, and a banana C. 一個漢堡、一杯果汁和一根香蕉

| 詳解 | 圖片中桌上放著三主種食物：牛奶、三明治、香蕉，英文分別是 milk / juice、sandwich、banana。既然題目要問的是準備吃什麼，那麼這三個單字就缺一不可了，所以正確答案是選項 B。

Question number 5.

What will the woman probably do next? 女子下一步可能要做什麼？

A. Cry for help A. 哭喊救命

B. Go swimming B. 去游泳

C. Have her hair dried off C. 把頭髮弄乾

| 詳解 | 圖片中女子剛洗完澡從浴室出來，頭上還包著毛巾，所以從三個選項來看，她接下來最有可能做的就是把頭髮吹乾，所以正確答案是選項 C。

Part 2 問答

Question number 6.

Do you speak Japanese? 你會說日語嗎？

A. No, just a little. A. 不，只會一點點。

B. I'm afraid not. B. 恐怕是不行。

C. Yes, I like Japanese food. C. 是的，我喜歡日式料理。

| 詳解 | 題目是個 Yes/No 的問句，不過這樣的題目在考試中往往正確答案不一定是 Yes 或 No 開頭的就可能是正確答案，還是要仔細聽清楚每一個字才行。A 的「just a little（只會一點點）」是一種「肯定」的回答，應以 Yes 開頭才對；「I'm afraid not.」是一種禮貌表達不會說日語的方式，所以正確答案是選項 B。C 是答非所問，只是刻意以 Japanese 這個字造成干擾。

| 補充 | 「拒絕」的英文除了 Sorry、「No, thank you.」外，你還可以用「I'm afraid (that...)」，語氣上比較正式且委婉，例如：I'm afraid that I can't go to dinner with you this Friday.（我恐怕這星期五不能去跟妳吃晚餐。）不過，如果把 afraid 和 not 位置對調，變成「I'm not afraid.（我並不害怕。）」那又是另一回事了。

Question number 7.

Rome wasn't built in a day, was it? 羅馬不是一天造成的，對不對？

A. Say it again! A. 說得好！

B. Who knows? B. 誰知道？

C. Come on! C. 拜託！

| 詳解 | 題目是個帶有附加問句（..., was it?）的句型，意義上是徵詢意見，認不認同的問題，同時也是一個 Yes/No 問句，不過因為三個選項都不是以 Yes 或 No 開頭，所以應一個個選項來分析。首先，「Say it again!」是個慣用語，相當於「You can say that again.」常用來表示認同，所以正確答案就是選項 A。因為「羅馬不是一天造成的」是一句諺語，是理所當然的事，就像太陽從東邊出來一樣，所以「Who knows?」的回答是違反常理的；「Come on!」是一種用於鼓勵或敦促對方做某事的表達，顯然與題目的問句不搭。

Question number 8.

When are you coming over? 你什麼時候要過來？

A. I'll be right over. A. 我馬上就結束。

B. Sorry, I can't come over right now. B. 抱歉，我現在不能過來。

C. I'm not feeling well, so I need to see a doctor. C. 我感覺不舒服，所以我得去看醫生。

| 詳解 | 本題關鍵在「come over」這個片語的意義。「come over」看似簡單，大家都知道是

「過來這裡」，但要注意的是，它用來表達「請對方過來你這裡」。首先，A 回答說「I'll be right over.」，這是「我馬上就好了。」的意思，但並未回答何時要過來，所以錯誤；B 是站在被問者的角度，所以不應該說 come over，應該是 go over，去到另外那一邊，也就是問的人的地方。 C 說「not feeling too well」感覺不太好，所以他需要「see a doctor」，也就是說他用說明的方式告訴問者他不會過去了，所以正確答案是選項 C。

Question number 9.

Does the old computer work? 這台老舊的電腦還能用嗎？

A. Yes, it's my own. A. 是的，是我自己的。

B. No, it doesn't work any longer. B. 不，它再也不能用了。

C. No, I don't need to work with the computer. C. 不，我不需要用這電腦來工作。

｜詳解｜本題關鍵在於考生是否理解「work 當動詞且主詞是『事物』時」的意思，此時的 work 意思是「有作用，正常運作」。題目問「這台老舊的電腦還能用嗎？」A、C 答非所問，B 說這台電腦再也不能用（doesn't work any longer）了，正確回答了問題，所以正確答案是選項 B。

｜補充｜not any longer＝no longer（再也不）。「no longer」第一個常見位置的可能性，就是放在 be 動詞、助動詞的後面。例如：I'm no longer interested.（我不再感興趣了。）、They will no longer be enemies.（他們不會再是敵人了）。no longer 另一個位置，是在一般動詞的前面。比方說：They no longer work for us.（他們不再是我們的員工了。）

Question number 10.

There was an earthquake last night, wasn't there? 昨天晚上有地震，對不對？

A. Yes, my house quaked rather hard. A. 是的，我家搖得相當厲害。

B. No, it shocked me very much. B. 不，那讓我非常驚訝。

C. Yes, I didn't feel at all. C. 是的，我完全沒有感覺到。

｜詳解｜附加問句的表現只是詢問「對不對？」的口氣，所以題目這句等同於「Was there an earthquake last night？」B、C 的回答皆前後矛盾，只有 A 的回答前後一致，所以正確答案是選項 A。

｜詳解｜附加問句的寫法：將代替主詞的代名詞和動詞倒裝，而這動詞必須和主要句子裡動詞的肯定否定相反。像是此句裡的附加問句是「was it? 」代替主詞的代名詞 it 放在動詞後方。而附加問句裡的動詞 was 和主要子句裡的動詞 wasn't 相反。靈活運用到其他的句子上，像是「They are....」， 後面的附加問句就要寫成「aren't they?」

Question number 11.

Does this party have a dress code? 這個舞會有沒有服裝上的規定？

A. That's a black tie party. A. 這是要著正式服裝的晚宴。

B. Don't worry. You are pretty beautiful. B. 別擔心，你很漂亮。

C. You can say that again. C. 你說得沒錯。

| 詳解 | 題目問的是這個舞會有沒有服裝上的規定（code），A 直接回答了問題，說明這是一個要穿正式服裝的晚宴。tie 是領帶，「black tie」為黑色領帶，引伸為正式服裝。B 回答「別擔心，你很漂亮」與是否有服裝規定無關；C 的意思是「你說得沒錯」，也沒有針對問題在回答。

| 詳解 | 名詞 code 在英文裡有很多種意思，最常見的是「密碼，編碼，代碼」。例如：In the program, Code Tenderloin students learn the basics of coding.（在該計劃中，Code Tenderloin 的學生學習基礎的程式編碼。）、The problem is that a missing bar or hyphen in the computer code.（問題出自：電腦代碼中缺少了一個連字符。）

Question number 12.

Come on! Let's go together. 來吧！我們一起去。

A. How come? I'm ready to go. A. 怎麼了？我已經準備好要出發了。

B. What time is it? B. 現在幾點？

C. I'm right behind you! C. 我隨後就到。

| 詳解 | 題目這句催促要一起去，A 回答前後矛盾，因為既然我已經準備好要出發了，又怎麼會反問「怎麼了？」；B 回答「現在幾點？」與對方的邀請無關，也沒有表達同意或不同意的意思，所以也錯誤。C 的回答意味著馬上跟過去，也表達了同意的意思，所以正確答案是選項 C。

Question number 13.

I can do it. No problem. 我可以做這件事。沒問題。

A. So, what's the problem? A. 那麼，問題在哪？

B. That's what I like to hear! B. 這就是我想聽到的。

C. I look forward to your support. C. 我期待你的支持。

| 詳解 | 題目這句表達了能夠完成任務並且沒有問題，A 卻反問「問題在哪？」，顯然是不正常、不知所云的回應；B 表示對這個訊息感到滿意和支持，是正確合理的回應，所以正確答案是選項 B；既然對方已經表示可以做，沒問題了，C 卻說我期待你的支持，顯然不合理，沒聽懂對方說的話，所以錯誤。

Question number 14.

I wasn't feeling well this afternoon. 我下午身體不太舒服。

A. You will be able to finish the book. A. 你可以看完這本書。

B. You should go home to rest. B. 你應該回家休息。

C. You can clean the house. C. 你可以清理屋子。

| 詳解 | 既然對方說自己下午時身體不太舒服，A 回答「你可以看完這本書」，以及 C 回答「你可以清理屋子」都是沒有顧慮對方的感受，也沒有解決對方的問題，都是不正常的回應，故 A、C 皆錯，正確答案是選項 B，建議他應該回家休息，這是對身體不適的適當回應和建議。

| 補充 | well 通常是當副詞用，而一般來說，感官動詞（look、sound、feel、taste...）後面接形容詞作為主詞補語，那為什麼會有「feel well」的用法呢？因為這種用法屬於慣用表達，雖然有時可能與一般的感官動詞後接形容詞的搭配規則不同，但在描述健康或身體狀態時是常見且被接受的用法。例如：She hasn't been feeling well lately.（她最近身體狀況不太好。）

Question number 15.

Hey Kevin! What's up? 嘿，凱文，最近好嗎?

A. Nice to meet you. A. 很高興見到您。

B. It's up to you. B. 隨便你。

C. As usual. And you? C. 一如往常。你呢？

| 詳解 | 對話中的一方問候另一方最近如何，A 的回答不適合用於這種已經認識的情況，並且沒有回應到問候的內容；B 的回答聽起來是不禮貌的，且與問候問句的內容毫不相干。C 的回答是一種常見的回應方式，表達自己情況如常並禮貌地詢問對方，所以正確答案是選項 C。

| 詳解 | 對於問候的話「你好嗎？」通常可以怎麼回答呢？以下是一些常聽到的話：
Pretty good（很好）、Could not be better.（不會再更好了。＝好得不得了；棒極了。）、Great.（很棒）、So far so good.（目前一切不錯。）、OK.（還行。）、Not bad.（還可以。）、As usual.（和平常沒兩樣。）、Nothing special.（沒有什麼特別的。）、Not feeling so good.（我覺得不太。）、Terrible.（糟透了。）

Part 3 簡短對話

Question number 16.

W: How do I look in my new dress? 女：我穿這件新洋裝看起來如何？

M: It fits you like a glove and matches your eyes perfectly. You look wonderful. 男：它非常合妳的身而且完美地搭襯妳的眼睛。妳看起來美極了。

W: Thank you! I'm glad you think so. 女：謝謝。很高興你這麼認為。

M: You're welcome! 男：不客氣。

Question. What does the man mean? 男子的意思是什麼？

A. The woman likes to wear gloves. A. 女子喜歡戴手套。

B. She has beautiful eyes. B. 她有一雙漂亮的眼睛。

C. The dress suits her very well. C. 這洋裝很適合她。

| 詳解 | 題目問男子所言意思為何，所以應關注他的發言部分。對話中男子讚美女子的新洋裝非常合身並且搭配她的眼睛（It fits you like a glove and matches your eyes perfectly.），女子對此表示感謝，所以正確答案是選項 C。男子的回答並沒有提到女子喜歡戴手套，而是在形容洋裝合身像手套一樣，所以 A 錯誤。男子的回答雖然提到洋裝搭配了女子的眼睛，但並沒有單獨讚美她的眼睛，所以 B 也錯誤。

| 補充 | 當作名詞時，suit 意指一套衣服或服裝，例如：He wore a sharp suit to the job interview.（他穿了一套整潔的西裝去面試。）當作動詞時，suit 意指「適合，合適」。例如：The job perfectly suits her skills and interests.（這份工作完全適合她的技能和興趣。）

Question number 17.

W: What a cute little girl! Whose is she? 女：好可愛的小女孩喔！她是誰的？

M: My eldest sister's. 男：我大姊的。

W: She looks just like her mother, doesn't she? 女：她看起來像他媽媽，是吧？

M: Yes, she's got her mother's eyes and smile. 男：是啊。她有著她媽媽的眼睛和微笑。

Question. Who is the little girl? 這小女孩是誰？

A. The man's nephew A. 男子的外甥

B. The man's niece B. 男子的外甥女

C. The man's cousin C. 男子的表妹

| 詳解 | 對話中男子說這個小女孩是他大姊的（My eldest sister's.），由於大姊是男子的姐姐，因此這個小女孩是男子的外甥女，正確答案是選項 B。nephew 是指男子的姐姐或兄弟的兒子，而不是女兒，所以 A 錯誤。cousin 可以指堂、表兄弟姐妹，但是對話中已經提到了是他大姊的小孩，所以 C 錯誤。

Question number 18.

M: You look bad. What's wrong with you? 男：你看起來真糟。發生什麼事了嗎？

W: I have a toothache. 女：我牙痛。

M: Why don't you have it treated? 男：為什麼你不去做治療？

Question. Where does the man think the woman should go?
男子認為女子應該去哪裡？

A. To a restaurant A. 去餐廳

B. To the gym B. 去健身房

C. To the dentist's C. 去牙醫診所

| 詳解 | 對話中女子說「I have a toothache.」，而男子問女子為什麼不去做治療（Why don't you have it treated?），這裡考的是 toothache 和 dentist 之間的連結關係，所以正確答案是選項 C。去餐廳或去健身房（gym）都無法解決牙痛的問題，所以 A、B 均錯誤。

| 補充 | 「N's」形式表示一個地方或場所的用法在英文中比較常見，除了「the dentist's」（牙醫診所）之外，還有一些常見的例子，例如：The doctor's（醫生的診所或辦公室。The barber's（理髮店）、The butcher's（肉店）、The baker's（麵包店）、The florist's（花店）、The stationer's（文具店）、The greengrocer's（蔬菜水果店）

Question number 19.

W: May I help you, sir? 女：先生，需要幫忙嗎？

M: Yes, please. I want to buy a birthday cake. 男：是的，麻煩你。我想要買一個生日蛋糕。

W: OK. What size do you want? 女：好的。您要什麼尺寸的？

M: The smallest, please. 男：麻煩您，最小的就可以了。

Question. Where does the dialogue happen? 這個對話是發生在哪裡？

A. At a bakery A. 在麵包店

B. At a convenience store B. 在便利商店

C. At a flower shop C. 在花店

| 詳解 | 對話中提到男子要買生日蛋糕（I want to buy a birthday cake.），女子問他要什麼尺寸的蛋糕（What size do you want?），顯示這個對話發生在麵包店或蛋糕店，因為這是一個常見販售蛋糕的地方，所以正確答案是選項 A。

Question number 20.

M: Excuse me. Miss, may I see your driver's license?
男：對不起，小姐，我可以看一下你的駕照嗎？

W: Why? Anything wrong?
女：為什麼？有什麼不對嗎？

M: You just ran through the red light.
男：你剛闖紅燈。

W: Sorry, I think I didn't notice that.
女：對不起，我想我沒有注意到。

Question. Who could the man be? 男子可能是誰？

A. He is a firefighter.　A. 他是消防員。

B. He is a policeman.　B. 他是警察。

C. He is a manager.　C. 他是經理。

| 詳解 | 對話中男子要求看女子的駕照（Miss, may I see your driver's license?），並指出她剛剛闖紅燈（ran through the red light），這顯示男子可能是一名警察，因為選項中只有警察有權執行交通違規的執法，故正確答案是選項 B。

| 補充 | 除了「闖紅燈」（run through the red light）之外，其他常見的交通違規（break a traffic rule）還有：speeding（超速）、running a stop sign（無視停車標誌）、illegal U-turn（非法迴轉）、driving without a seatbelt（未繫安全帶）、reckless driving（駕駛過失）、failure to yield（不讓路）、driving under the influence （DUI）（酒駕）、using a mobile phone while driving （distracted driving）（開車時使用手機）、failure to signal（未打方向燈）、illegal parking（違停）

Question number 21.

M: Welcome! How can I help you?
男：歡迎光臨，需要什麼幫忙？

W: I'd like to check in. I've made a booking.
女：我想要登記入住。我有訂房。

M: Could I have your name, please?
男：請問你的名字是？

W: Catherine Chen.
女：凱瑟琳・陳。

Question. Where does this conversation take place? 這段對話在哪發生？

A. In a library　A. 在圖書館

B. In a restaurant　B. 在餐廳

C. In a hotel　C. 在旅館

| 詳解 | 對話中女子提到她想要登記入住並且有訂房（I'd like to check in. I've made a booking.），其中 booking 就是「預訂」的意思，不過餐廳的場合不會需要「check in」，更別說是圖書館了，所以應該是在飯店，正確答案是選項 C。

| 補充 | 抵達飯店，在辦理入住（check in）時，通常會用到「I booked a＋房型＋for 一段時間.」這個句型。例如：I booked a standard room for two nights.（我訂了一間標準房間要住兩晚。）如果旅館住宿費有包含早餐的話，想問早餐什麼時間可以享用你可以這

樣說：Excuse me, what time is breakfast?（不好意思，早餐是幾點？）而在辦理退房你可以說：Could you please call a cab for us?（能不能請你幫我們叫一輛計程車呢？）當你需要飯店人員告訴你哪條路線最快，你可利用「What is the quickest way to get to＋目的地?」這個句型。

Question number 22.

M: Lisa, how did you learn so many languages?	男：麗莎，你是如何學這麼多種語言的？
W: I am open to accept the new things, especially foreign cultures.	女：我接受新的事物，尤其是外國的文化。
M: The how can you have a good command of them?	男：那麼你為什麼可以駕馭多種語言？
W: The secret is to use it as often as you can.	女：祕訣就是，盡可能經常使用。

Question. What is the woman's suggestion to learn languages?
那女人對於語言的學習是怎麼建議的？

A. Make many foreign friends	A. 結交許多外國朋友
B. Surfing the Internet to learning new things	B. 上網學習新的事物
C. Practicing everyday	C. 每天練習

| 詳解 | 對話中女子提到學習語言的祕訣是盡可能經常使用（The secret is to use it as often as you can.），這意味著每天都要練習使用語言才能掌握它們，所以正確答案是選項C。雖然結交外國朋友可以幫助語言學習，以及上網學習新事物雖然有助於知識的擴展，但對話並未提到這些，所以A、B均錯誤。

| 補充 | command 有兩種詞性。當名詞時，語意為命令、指令，除了指一個明確和具體的指示或指令，還可以表示掌握或控制某技能的能力，常見片語為「have a good command of...」，例如：He has a good command of the English language.（他精通英語。）又例如：She was in command of the entire operation.（她指揮整個行動。）

Question number 23.

W: Oh, John, look at you. You were the shortest student in my class. What makes you so tall?	女：哇！約翰，看看你，你以前是班上最矮的學生。是什麼讓你長這麼高呢？
M: Exercising. I play basketball in my school.	男：運動。我在學校是打籃球的。
W: What a surprise!	女：真令人驚奇！
M: It really helped me grow taller and improve my game skills too!	男：打籃球確實讓我長得更高且也增進了我的球技。

Question. What is true about the speakers? 關於說話者，何者為真？

A. The man was the tallest in his school.	A. 男子曾是學校最高的。
B. They were classmates.	B. 他們曾是同班同學。
C. The man was a baseball player.	C. 男子曾是棒球員。

| 詳解 | 對話開頭女子提到約翰以前是她班上最矮的學生（You were the shortest student in my class.），顯示他們曾是同班同學，所以正確答案是選項 B。雖然男子提到他在學校是打籃球的（play basketball in my school.）且女子也說他現在長得很高，但這不能意味他是全校最高的，所以 A、C 均錯誤。

| 補充 | 「以 What 或是 How 為首的感嘆句」句型為「What a＋（形容詞）＋＋名詞」、「How＋形容詞＋（名詞＋be 動詞）」。例：What a genius!＝How genius!（真是天才！）、What an interesting game!＝How interesting the game is!（真是有趣的遊戲！）

Question number 24.

W: Did you see the movie *Alien: Romulus*?
女：你有沒有看過《異形：羅穆路斯》？

M: No, but I know that one. The lighting and sound are outstanding.
男：沒，但是我知道那部電影。它有絕佳的燈光與音響效果

W: Ricky asked me to see it but I am afraid it's a boring movie.
女：Ricky 問我要不要一起去看，但是我怕這是一部無聊的電影。

Question. What does the woman probably mean? 這女人可能意味什麼？

A. She thinks *Alien: Romulus* is not worth seeing.
A. 她覺得《異形：羅穆路斯》不值得看。

B. She wants to see a movie with outstanding lighting and sound.
B. 她想要看燈光與音響效果絕佳的電影。

C. She is interested in the sci-fi movie.
C. 她對科幻電影感興趣。

| 詳解 | 對話中女子表示她擔心《異形：羅穆路斯》是一部無聊的電影（I am afraid it's a boring movie.），這暗示她認為這部電影不值得去看，所以正確答案是選項 A。雖然對話中確實提到了這部電影有絕佳的燈光與音響效果（The lighting and sound are outstanding.），且那確實是一部科幻片，但女子擔心可能是一部無聊的電影，所以 B、C 錯誤。

Question number 25.

W: This pair of pants are too long. Could you shorten it for me?
女：這褲子太長了，你可以幫我修短一點嗎？

M: No problem.
男：沒問題。

W: By the way, do you have another color?
女：對了，你們還有其它顏色的嗎？

M: I'm afraid not. This is the last one. Would you like to take it?
男：恐怕是沒了。這是最後一件。你要嗎？

Question. What is true about this pair of pants? 關於這條長褲，何者為真？

A. There's only one left in this shop.
A. 在這家店只有這一件。

B. There're a few colors of it to choose from.
B. 它有幾種顏色可供挑選。

C. The woman thinks it is too short for her.
C. 女子認為對她來說太短了。

| 詳解 | 對話中女子問是否還有其它顏色（do you have another color?），而男子表示這是最後一件（I'm afraid not. This is the last one.），這意味這家店裡只剩下這一件長褲了，所以正確答案是選項 A。另外，既然男子表示這是最後一件，所以當然也沒有更多顏色可挑選，所以 B 錯誤。女子一開始問男子可否幫她把褲子修短一點，這表示她覺得褲子太長了，所以 C 明顯錯誤。

| 補充 | 台語和英文也有通喔！不過在英文裡，「take it」可不只「拿去」這麼簡單喔！比方說，「Take it from me.」可不是「從我這兒拿去吧」，而是「聽我的準沒錯。」例如：Take it from me — he'll be a hotshot before he's 30.（聽我的準沒錯 — 他三十歲之前就會大紅大紫。）又比方說，「Take it as it comes.」麼意思呢？其實它是「順其自然吧。」在面對很愛討價還價的客人，有些老闆不耐煩時會說「Take it or leave it.」就是「要就要，不要就拉倒。」、「要不要隨便你。」

Part 4 短文聽解

Question number 26.

Please look at the following three pictures. Listen to the following introduction. Which item do guests have to pay for?
請看以下三張圖片。聆聽以下介紹。客人需要自費的是哪個項目？

Welcome to V-Hotel, and let me introduce our facilities to you. You can enjoy Wi-Fi, breakfast, and gym access free. But if you want to use the swimming pool or order room service, you need to pay extra. If you have any questions or need assistance during your stay, feel free to ask. We hope you have a pleasant time with us.
歡迎來到「V 酒店」，我跟您介紹一下我們的飯店設施。您可以免費使用 Wi-Fi、享用早餐和使用健身房。但如果您想使用游泳池或叫客房服務，則需額外支付費用。如果您在住宿期間有任何問題或需要幫助，請隨時告訴我們。希望您在我們這裡度過愉快的時光。

| 詳解 | 從三張圖片可以猜到是三種不同的娛樂設施，而題目問會員需要自費（pay for）的是哪個，短文中的關鍵句是「But if you want to use the swimming pool or order room service, you need to pay extra.（但如果您想使用游泳池或叫客房服務，則需額外支付費用。）」所以正確答案是選項 A。

| 補充 | facility 指的是「設施，設備」，多以複數形式出現。例如：The school offers excellent facilities including labs and sports fields.（這所學校提供優秀的設施，包括實驗室和運

動場。）那麼單數的 facility 會用在什麼情況呢？它可以用來指「（產品或服務等的）功能」或是「（個人的）能力，技能」。例如：He has great facility in singing.（他很有唱歌的才能。）

Question number 27.

Please look at the following three pictures. Listen to the following talk. What does the speaker usually do on Saturday mornings?

請看以下三張圖片。聆聽以下談話。說話者通常在週六早上做什麼？

I love morning exercise, and I'll take a shower every time after that. Then I'll feel in very good spirits. I usually do 50 push-ups right after getting up before I eat breakfast every day. On Saturday afternoons, I spend one to two hours swimming. I'm good at freestyle. I believe that exercising regularly is the best way to maintain good health.

我喜歡晨間運動，每次運動後都會淋浴，然後會感到精神特別好。通常我每天早上一起床就會先做 50 個伏地挺身，然後再吃早餐。週六下午，我會花一到兩個小時游泳，我擅長自由式。我認為定期運動是保持健康的最佳方法。

A　　B　　Ⓒ

｜詳解｜ 三張圖片看來都是運動項目，可以現在腦海裏準備好 swimming、table tennis（桌球）以及 do push-ups（伏地挺身）等詞彙。接著題目中的關鍵字詞「on Sunday mornings」要掌握到。首先，談話提到，每天早上一起床就會先做 50 個伏地挺身（I usually do 50 push-ups right after getting up before I eat breakfast every day.）至此，答案就已經出來了，正確答案是選項 C。至於同樣出現 Saturday 的句子（On Saturday afternoons, I spend one to two hours swimming.）只是個煙霧彈，是週六下午，所以 A 錯誤。

Question number 28.

Please look at the following three pictures. Listen to the following message. Where will the speaker go after playing basketball?

請看以下三張圖片。聆聽以下訊息。說話者在打完籃球後會去哪裡？

Hi Susan. Hope you're having a good day! I'm going to play basketball with friends this afternoon. After that, I can ride my motorbike to pick you up in front of the library where you were studying this morning. Then let's go try some delicious food for dinner at the famous food stand nearby afterward. See you soon!

嗨，蘇珊。希望你今天過得愉快！今天下午我要和朋友們去打籃球。之後，我可以騎摩托車到你今早去念書的圖書館門口接你。然後我們去附近一攤很有名的美味小吃攤吃晚餐。再見！

| 詳解 | 題目問的是打完籃球後會去哪裡，我們可以從錄音訊息中的「I'm going to play basketball with friends this afternoon.」提到說話者下午和朋友們去打籃球。接著又說「After that, I can ride my motorbike to pick you up in front of the library where you were studying...」表示在打完籃球之後，他會騎摩托車到蘇珊去念書的圖書館接她，所以正確答案是選項 B。

Question number 29.

Please look at the following three pictures. Listen to the following short story. Which picture best describes the story?

請看以下三張圖片。聆聽以下簡短故事。哪一張圖最能夠描述此故事內容？

Last Sunday, I went picnicking with some good friends. The weather was cool even though it was cloudy and a bit windy. We had a happy chat about our favorite movies, funny stories, and future plans. Everyone prepared delicious food and drinks like sandwiches, fruit salad, and lemonade. It was a relaxing day surrounded by nature, and we all had a great time together.

上個星期天，我和一些好朋友去野餐了。天氣雖然多雲且有點風，但很涼爽。我們開心地聊著我們喜歡的電影、有趣的故事，還有未來的計劃。每個人都準備了美味的食物和飲料，像是三明治、水果沙拉和檸檬汽水。這是一個被大自然包圍的放鬆日子，我們都度過了美好的時光。

| 詳解 | 題目問的是哪一張圖最能夠描述此故事內容，三張圖中只有一張在室內用餐，其餘兩張都是戶外野餐活動，從第一句「Last Sunday, I went picnicking with some good friends.」可知，室內用餐的圖 C 可以直接排除掉，接著再從「The weather was cool even though it was cloudy and a bit windy.」可知當天的天氣是多雲且有點風，但很涼爽，顯然大熱天的圖 B 也不是正確答案，所以正確答案是選項 A。

| 補充 | 野餐（go picnicking）時會用到的詞彙包括野餐墊（picnic blanket）、野餐籃（picnic basket）、食物和飲料（food and drinks）、烤肉（barbecue）、水果（fruit）、沙拉（salad）、曬太陽（sunbathing）、享受自然（enjoying nature）、戶外活動（outdoor activities）、園地或公園（park）…等。

Question number 30.

Please look at the following three pictures. Listen to the following short talk. Which country does Andy love best?

請看以下三張圖片。聆聽以下簡短談話。安迪最喜愛的國家是哪一國？

My name is Andy. I travel abroad very often. The country I visit most often is Japan, but I've never climbed Mt. Fuji. I hope I can reach the top of it one day! If you ask me which country is my favorite, I'll say France, because the night view in Paris is unforgettable to me. By the way, I'll meet my old friends in the States next month, so maybe I can share something interesting with you then.

我叫安迪。我經常出國旅行。我最常去的國家是日本，但我從未爬過富士山。希望有一天我能登頂！如果你問我最喜歡哪個國家，我會說法國，因為巴黎的夜景讓我難以忘懷。對了，下個月我會去美國和老朋友見面，或許到時候我可以和你們分享一些有趣的事情。

| 詳解 | 圖 A 是美國的自由女神像，圖 B 是法國的巴黎鐵塔，圖 C 是日本的富士山，所以這三張圖代表的是三個國家。題目問安迪最喜愛的國家，從「If you ask me which country is my favorite, I'll say France...（如果你問我最喜歡哪個國家，我會說法國）」這句話可清楚斷定，正確答案是選項 B。

| 補充 | abroad 與 aboard 是兩個經常被搞混的字彙。abroad 是副詞，指在「在國外，到國外」。例如：She studied abroad in France last year.（她去年在法國留學。）aboard 是介系詞，指在（船、飛機、火車等）交通工具上。例如：We are aboard the cruise ship heading to the Caribbean.（我們正在郵輪上前往加勒比海。）

聽力測驗答對題數與分數對照表

答對題數	分數	答對題數	分數	答對題數	分數
30	120	20	80	10	40
29	116	19	76	9	36
28	112	18	72	8	32
27	108	17	68	7	28
26	104	16	64	6	24
25	100	15	60	5	20
24	96	14	56	4	16
23	92	13	52	3	12
22	88	12	48	2	8
21	84	11	44	1	4

閱讀測驗答對題數與分數對照表

答對題數	分數	答對題數	分數	答對題數	分數
30	120	20	80	10	40
29	116	19	76	9	36
28	112	18	72	8	32
27	108	17	68	7	28
26	104	16	64	6	24
25	100	15	60	5	20
24	96	14	56	4	16
23	92	13	52	3	12
22	88	12	48	2	8
21	84	11	44	1	4

台灣廣廈國際出版集團
Taiwan Mansion International Group

國家圖書館出版品預行編目（CIP）資料

GEPT全民英檢初級聽力測驗初試1次過／國際語言中心委員會 著
; -- 初版 -- 新北市 :
國際學村, 2024.07
面； 公分
978-986-454-367-0 (平裝)
1. CST: 英語. 2. CST: 檢定

805.1892 113007714

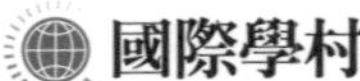

GEPT全民英檢初級聽力測驗初試1次過

每日刷題10分鐘，1天2頁，一個月後高分過關！

作　　者／國際語言中心委員會
編輯中心編輯長／伍峻宏・**編輯**／許加慶
封面設計／陳沛涓・**內頁排版**／菩薩蠻數位文化有限公司
製版・印刷・裝訂／皇甫・秉成

行企研發中心總監／陳冠蒨
媒體公關組／陳柔彣
綜合業務組／何欣穎
線上學習中心總監／陳冠蒨
產品企製組／顏佑婷
企製開發組／江季珊、張哲剛

發 行 人／江媛珍
法律顧問／第一國際法律事務所 余淑杏律師・北辰著作權事務所 蕭雄淋律師
出　　版／國際學村
發　　行／台灣廣廈有聲圖書有限公司
地址：新北市235中和區中山路二段359巷7號2樓
電話：（886）2-2225-5777・傳真：（886）2-2225-8052

代理印務・全球總經銷／知遠文化事業有限公司
地址：新北市222深坑區北深路三段155巷25號5樓
電話：（886）2-2664-8800・傳真：（886）2-2664-8801
郵政劃撥／劃撥帳號：18836722
劃撥戶名：知遠文化事業有限公司（※單次購書金額未達1000元，請另付70元郵資。）
讀者服務信箱／cs@booknews.com.tw

■出版日期：2024年07月
ISBN：978-986-454-367-0